COMMEMORATIVE EDITION:
Two Books Under One Cover

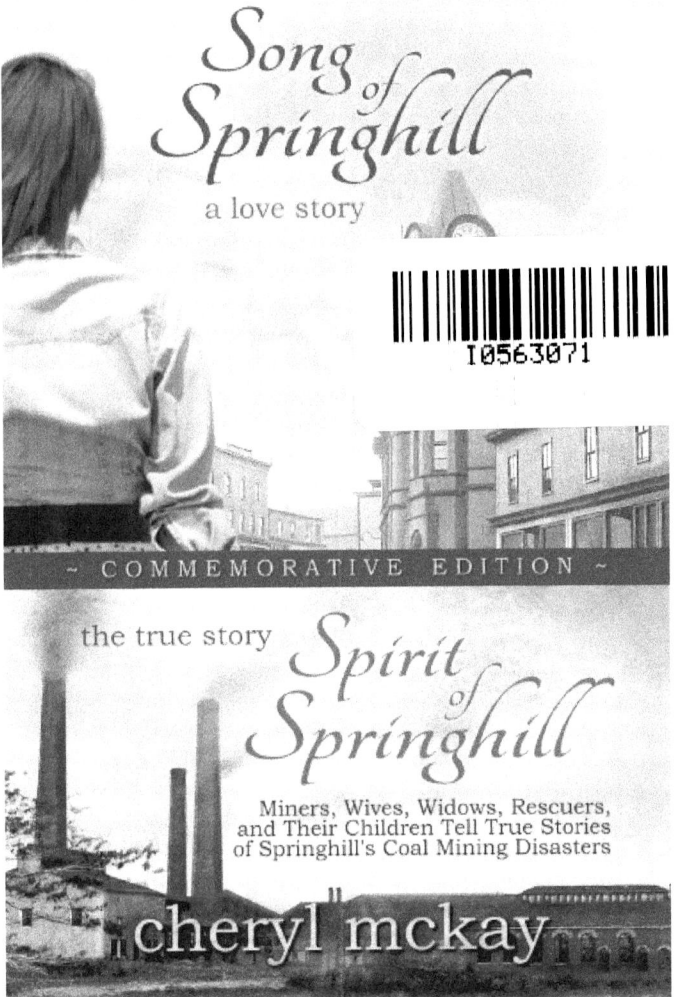

an inspirational romance novel based on historical events

Song of Springhill

a love story

I0563071

~ COMMEMORATIVE EDITION ~

the true story *Spirit of Springhill*

Miners, Wives, Widows, Rescuers,
and Their Children Tell True Stories
of Springhill's Coal Mining Disasters

cheryl mckay

Dedication:
For "Dado"
My grandfather who survived the 1958 Bump in
the Springhill, Nova Scotia coal mines.
He was the inspiration for this story.

Book One:

Song *of* Springhill

a love story

an inspirational romance based on historical events

By
Cheryl McKay

By Cheryl McKay

Greetings from the Flipside a novel (with Rene Gutteridge)
Never the Bride a novel (with Rene Gutteridge)
Finally the Bride: Finding Hope While Waiting
25 Dates with God (series)
Finally Fearless: How Overcoming Anxiety Helped Me Find True Love
Extraordinary (co-writer, film)
Indivisible (co-writer, film)
The Ultimate Gift (screenplay)
The Ultimate Life (screen story by)
Gigi: God's Little Princess DVD (screenplay)
Wild & Wacky, Totally True Bible Stories Series (with Frank Peretti)

SONG OF SPRINGHILL: A LOVE STORY

Springhill Main Street cover photo supplied by and used by permission of the Springhill Heritage Museum.

Girl with suitcase photo licensed from monamakela.com – Fotolia.com

Kissing couple photo by Lisa Crates, lisacrates.us

Cars and keyboard photos and artwork, and Cover Design by Christopher Price (Roads & Rivers Media)

Special thanks to Valerie Ruddick MacDonald (and her late mother, Norma June Ruddick) for permission to create a character inspired by Maurice Ruddick, *The Singing Miner*.

Special thanks to Tom McKay and Joyce Harroun for permission to share the story of Charles Hugh McKay.

This novel is based on the screenplay by the same author. To inquire about the screenplay rights, contact: Cheryl@purplepenworks.com.

Published in the United States of America

Commemorative Edition

ISBN-13: 978-1-946344-04-5

ISBN-10: 1-946344-04-4

For those who dare
to believe
miracles still happen

TABLE OF CONTENTS

Song of Springhill

The following story is a work of fiction, inspired by actual events. Think of this novel like the film *Titanic*, where an actual disaster is used as the backdrop for a fictional love story. Unless otherwise noted in the copyrights segment, the characters in this novel are creations of the author and not based on actual Springhill residents. Authentic details have been painted into the setting, character dialogue, circumstances, and are used by permission of those who allowed the author to interview them during her research. The rest of the information used is available in the public domain.

The author created this book's fictional, family-owned company to closely explore the story's fictional characters. This book's fictionally-named company and owners are not based on any actual entity or any of its associates. Similarities to any actual entity or its associates are entirely coincidental and beyond the intent of the author and publisher.

Great care has been taken to honor the town, its people, and the time period. Occasionally, creative liberties are taken with the setting for the sake of the story. The true-life backstory of this novel includes three actual disasters that occurred in the town of Springhill:

The 1956 Explosion
The 1957 Main Street Fire
The 1958 Bump

Enjoy your journey back to the fifties through
Song of Springhill.

chapter 1

October 30, 1956

Hannah peeked out of the guestroom. Rhythmic snores droned from the master bedroom, like they were in stereo sync. They wouldn't wake for hours. Maybe even noon. But today, she wouldn't be here at noon. Adrenaline surged through her thin frame. Her legs trembled.

This had to work. This was not time for one of her miscalculations or poor judgment calls. She'd been accused of that a lot lately. Whether it was true or not.

She clutched two suitcases, then took one last look around her room.

So much she was leaving behind. Clothing, shoes, cheap jewelry. Most of it chosen for her anyway. She had packed what mattered; she was sure of it. One last glance at the closet. There was that garment bag. A knowing settled over her, as warm as the midday sun. She would never wear what was inside that bag. It was not coming with her.

Memories flooded as she ducked into the shadowed hallway. She held her breath. Too long, she'd endured the bitter here. Wave upon wave, it had pounded her shores, overwhelming the sweet. Now, with each creak of the floorboards beneath her feet, her spirits lifted.

As she neared the front door, she couldn't bring herself to look into the living room. The shiny, black grand piano she'd dusted every single day before she'd played for the past three years would stay behind. She'd find a way to buy one of her own someday; she was sure of that. Even if she had to find twenty extra music students to pay for it.

Outside, the gravel crunched beneath her feet. At the car door, the key shook in her hand. It clattered against every part of the metal except the hole. She used her other hand to steady it, till it finally went in.

Gently, she put the suitcases into the backseat, the same two she'd used since she was a teenager. All she'd keep of her life's belongings fit inside a pair of cubes. But she had what she needed, including the journal.

His journal.

The only treasure she had of his, tucked inside the pocket of one of the suitcases. All of it, in her daddy's handwriting. She'd read it so many times that she had most of his entries — his prayers — memorized.

A thud resounded. Hannah whipped around toward the cottage. Had someone heard her? She didn't spot anyone, and the front door remained closed.

It was time to test her 1947 blue Studebaker Champion to see if she still had enough champ left in her to make the trip. The Champ was hardly new when Hannah bought her. Winters and salt laden roads had eaten away parts of the frame since, yet she had a hum to her — some may call it a rattle — that soothed Hannah like the lullaby her mama used to sing. It was familiar and always there. But not a sound she wanted lighting up the neighborhood when trying to escape unnoticed. The Champ was her first big possession, paid for with what little money she'd managed to tuck away from those music lessons she'd given.

Those kiddos were the only people she'd miss from this city. The way Eli cheered when he finally got the C sharp minor chord right on the guitar. Or the way Joy beamed when her right hand could play a different rhythm than her left on the piano. Now, that was a special talent. Not everyone had it. Hannah knew well how to blaze across the keys in different rhythms; it came so naturally to her. But the same did not characterize her life; it always seemed out of sync, especially with her desires.

An ache knotted Hannah's throat. She couldn't say goodbye to those kids. She'd had to keep far too many secrets these days. Telling them about this—planning for this exact moment—she couldn't do it.

Headlights turned the street corner, startling her. She ducked down behind the car in the driveway, hoping whichever neighbor was coming home at this hour didn't see her. The vehicle passed with a whir. She waited a couple more seconds, released her breath, then slid onto the driver's seat.

She steeled herself against tossing up a prayer as she pulled the door closed. No, it wasn't needed; this was up to her alone. She could do this. And she wasn't sure anyone would listen anyway. She had prayed enough for intervention in the past.

That her mother wouldn't die, for starters.

But it would be fine. All she had to do now was push on that gas and fix her eyes on her destination.

Her neck throbbed. As she glanced in the rearview, the purple bruises were still visible. Why didn't she grab her collared sweater? Well, maybe because she hated that dark pink and white garment. It made her look like a wrapped up piece of ribbon candy.

And this would be the last time someone would leave a mark.

Hannah turned the key in the ignition. The Champ sparked to life. Just like that engine, she had the power within her to run, the power to not be a victim any longer. How had she forgotten that for the past three years? It was all a blur. But with the Champ's racket, it was time to get out of here. She pressed on the gas, knowing she'd never see that little yellow cottage again. An unfamiliar feeling, the corners of her mouth turned up.

Her stomach fluttered; she'd waited her entire life. Now, it was time to return to the place her father used to call *home* until twenty-seven years ago.

Until his death, a smattering of hours before her birth.

A place called *Springhill*.

October 31, 1956

HANNAH STRETCHED OUT HER FINGERS. They hurt, throbbed from her grip on the steering wheel. She had to calm down. Gripping herself tightly wasn't necessary anymore, right?

How many miles had she driven by herself before this trip? Ten, maybe fifteen at a time. Her odometer had logged over one thousand since yesterday morning. She'd stopped only for fuel or a quick bite, and to sleep in Quebec. The silver-haired motel attendant there didn't appear to notice that she'd lied about her name. Not when he handed over keys to her room, or when she dropped them back off this morning before she left. "Have a safe one out there," he'd said, as he slid the keys back onto the nail below Room 21.

Safe. Something she hadn't known in a long time, but fully intended to find.

The sun glared off her back windshield. Within a few hours, it would settle in for the night.

Energy surged through her as she read:

WELCOME TO SPRINGHILL. Population 7,802.

The brown wooden sign tilted slightly to the left. Yet it looked as sturdy as the hills she'd passed on her way into this idyllic town.

And she did feel welcome. Even as a stranger. Maybe a small town was just what she needed. A place with roots, with personal history. Would she like living where most people knew one another by name? And probably their quirks, habits, let alone their secrets? It wasn't a place to remain anonymous. But maybe people here had your back.

Maybe Springhillers—as her mama used to call them— would care if something felt or seemed off. Maybe they actually looked each other in the eyes instead of turning the other way. How could she feel like a stranger and at-home, all at once?

She snaked the Champ through a few side streets off Junction Road. Slowing to a crawl, she surveyed a few homes—all different styles and colors. And small. Very small. Cozy was a nicer way to look at it, especially since they seemed so inviting. So different from where she grew up.

If only her mother had moved them back here. Or even stayed here from day one. Maybe life would have been different. Her mother would still be alive.

As she surveyed the neighborhoods, she felt like a new

homeowner, taking a stroll through a brand new house, eyeing fixtures, moldings, and windowpanes. Not that she really knew what that felt like. Having a place of her own lived only in her imagination. Her dreams.

The Champ turned up Main Street, a hilly road that was home to businesses on both sides: gift shops, bakeries, a grocery store, a church. A newspaper office, a furniture store, a café, a hardware store, a pharmacy, a diner. Well, they sure had what they needed here.

Just about every store was personalized with a name, whether a surname or first. No doubt, the people of this town ran Springhill's Main Street. A rounded clock tower on the post office showed it was almost two-thirty.

On the sidewalk, two old men sat on a white bench with black lettering on it. They laughed heartily at some private joke. When the old fella with the overalls and straight metallic looking hair leaned forward, doubled over, she made out the phrase behind him: "Liars Bench."

"What on earth?" A chuckle escaped her lips. What kinds of lies were they telling each other? Was one pretending to be a hero? Was the other spinning tall tales of his royal British roots? With a bench like that in town, she might fit right in.

Though she preferred to think of her lies as protection.

When the two old guys looked over at her, one signaled his salute. She returned the gesture, then continued the Champ's crawl up Main Street by All Saints Church. There was a place she knew from Mama. A little girl played hopscotch out front. Oh, to be as safe as that little girl seemed.

It was time to focus. She had to find *her*. In a town this size, someone must know if Aunt Abigail still lived here. Or

"Abby" as her mother used to call her. Hannah's heart would rest better when she tracked her down. What if she wasn't alive anymore? What if she didn't want her here? There wasn't any reason she wouldn't, was there?

Regardless, Hannah would never retrace her steps to where she'd been. No matter what happened here, going back to Toronto was not an option.

Did her aunt look anything like Daddy? Maybe she'd see for herself. Today, perhaps. Her stomach fluttered again.

At the top of Main Street, on her right, rested a building that had plenty of lights. The sign out front blinked: Hector's Pool Hall. The P in pool was dimmer, barely hanging on like the last of a candle's wick. Hopefully, someone in there could help her.

♫ ♫ ♫

The eleven ball ripped into the corner pocket with a clunk. Josh Winslow blew on the end of his cue stick. Blue talc puffed into the air. Josh had no intention of losing this round to his comrade, Moosey. No, he couldn't, or Moosey would be an insufferable braggart all night underground, like a vulture circling its fallen prey.

When Josh first coined the name Moosey, it had nothing to do with the giant taxidermied head mounted over Moosey's fireplace. A hunted down trophy of Moosey's grandfather. No. The moniker had everything to do with Moosey's rotund frame getting caught between the coalface and a stone pack. This was during Moosey's first night on Josh's team, 4500 feet below the earth's surface. Moosey may not have appreciated the comedy with a side of pain at the time, but Josh and his buddies sure did. They still laughed about it. Thankfully, Moosey had a healthy sense of humor to go with his appetite.

Josh sunk his number nine as Hector delivered chips and vinegar to the pool table. "Smack it up, now, Josh. Don't got much time left."

"Thanks, Hector."

When Hector opened this pool hall, it was his way of finding a new path in life, outside "the deeps," those dark, musty shafts carved deep into the earth's surface. Hector was a one-man show. Couldn't afford any employees. Josh liked to give him business whenever he could. Well, that, and he liked to beat Moosey at Eight Ball or Snooker.

Moosey grabbed a fist full of Josh's fatty delight. "Hector, you need to teach my Rosalie how to crisp up chips like this. Mmm, mmm."

Josh wondered how — on a miner's salary — Rosalie could keep Moosey fed.

"Don't you two gotta get to the mines?" Hector asked.

Josh looked at the clock: two-thirty. Hector was right. When the rake operators brought miners up from the prior shift, there'd better be a new crop to head down and keep that production going. Three o'clock, on the dot.

Mine productivity controlled this town's survival. More than once Josh had to wait underground while the rake operators sent up coal cars with the black stuff, instead of letting their aching bodies warm the rail cars. Moving coal took priority. But was the company paying them for their time waiting? Not a chance. Well, at least he had a job and could put food on his table.

Even if it was a table for one.

Josh sunk his last striped ball. He aimed for that black eight when the front door chimed someone's arrival.

A female. An attractive one at that. Seeing an unfamiliar woman around here was momentous. Even *Springhill Record* newsworthy.

"So and so's Great Uncle Marv visited this weekend." Yes, they did report that stuff. Sometimes, Springhill was a slow news town. Slow news days were good because it meant there were no problems in the mines.

Maybe this chestnut-haired beauty was unattached. A man could hope, right?

Too many months, years even, had passed since he'd been willing to request a date. Much to the chagrin of Mary Lou Lipnicki, who relentlessly dropped the most obvious hints.

Hector waved. "Good aft'noon, young lady."

Moosey's elbow met Josh's ribs. "Classy chassis, eh?"

Josh tossed his pool stick on the table and strolled over, calm, collected and—

"Ow!" Where did that table come from?

After glancing Josh's way, Classy Chassis spoke to Hector: "Good afternoon, Sir. I'm looking for a woman named Abigail Wright. Do you happen to know if she still lives in Springhill?"

Josh stepped in before Hector could answer. "Abigail Percy is her name now. She and her family live across the way from me. At Five Maple Street. Her husband, Ray, he's one of my best friends."

"Wonderful!" Relief swam in her deep brown eyes. Her olive skin was so clear, so untouched by the harsh sun.

"Where is Maple?"

"Who would be askin'?" Josh ignored Moosey's snort.

"Hannah Wright. I'm Abigail's niece."

Hector asked, "Are you Melvin's daughter?"

Josh swallowed. He hadn't heard that name in a long time.

She looked at Hector. "You knew my father?"

"Well, color me overjoyed." Hector reached over the counter to gather her into an enthused embrace. Josh noticed her upper torso tense. Hector kept on hugging. At least she was polite about it.

"Everybody knew Mel. 'Specially us fixtures who've been here for more decades than we can high enough count. I'm Hector."

"Nice to meet you, Hector." Hannah smiled. It may have been small, perhaps even reserved, but it lit up her whole face.

Josh jabbed a thumb over his shoulder toward his friend. "That big guy over there...he's Moosey. And I am Joshua Theodore Winslow the sixth. Don't tell anyone..." He leaned in a bit closer, catching her scent. A fragrant lotion. Feminine, but not overpowering. "There's only a fifth and a fourth Joshua Theodore. Three, two, and one...they were made up. And unless I settle down soon, there won't be a seventh."

Moosey chortled.

Was he coming on too strong? Josh didn't care. It never hurt to let a seemingly kind and attractive young woman know he was available. He took her hand in a gentle shake. If she were Melvin's daughter, she was in her late twenties, five years younger than he was. As he lingered, she removed her hand from his. This woman wasn't going to make it easy.

He searched for a sparkle in her eyes but sensed something else. Fear, maybe? One who protects herself with walls. Thankfully, breaking down barriers didn't scare him. After all, he was a miner adept with a pick. He considered this woman a welcome challenge.

Moosey gave his shoulder a nudge. "Come on, Winnie. Pit time."

Winnie. Not exactly a strong name to impress a lady. But silly names underground signaled acceptance as part of a team. She'd learn that soon enough if she were going to stick around. His insides warmed at the thought.

"Hannah, I can escort you to Abigail's on my way to the mines."

"That won't be necessary. If you could just give me directions?"

He swung his arm the direction of the doorway. "Head down Junction Road. Turn right on Maple. You can't miss it. It's where Oreo, the Dalmatian, sits."

♫ ♫ ♫

As Hannah drove down the road, she wondered why that man looked at her the way he did. Josh was his name. She was a stranger to him, right? At his age, had he not found a suitable wife? He was pleasing to the eyes, certainly, with his chiseled nose and strong jaw line. But he was glancing the wrong direction. She may be here to seek connection, but *that* was not the kind she was looking for.

As Hannah spotted the street sign for Maple, there he was. Oreo, the Dalmatian, right on the corner. Josh was right. The dog's abdomen rose and fell rhythmically with each pant. If only life were that simple for humans. This was a predictable place in many ways.

And for Hannah, predictable—like the classics she'd played on the ivory keys for the past decade—was just what she needed.

chapter 2

Hannah pulled the Champ up to a home, its front door sporting a five and an acorn wreath with autumn-colored ribbons. The Percys' place. Was she finally about to meet her father's family? *Her family?*

Five Maple Street was a modest dwelling, like most homes she'd passed. This one, hunter green. An A-frame roof. Leaves had fallen from the trees and littered the yard. Its wide, open front and side yard were a plus, especially for kids. That Joshua Theodore fellow did say "family." She wondered how many kids they had. Maybe she could teach them how to play music, if they didn't already know.

Lights in various windows signaled life. Hannah swallowed, trying to squelch the bile that threatened to rise up.

She got out of her car, leaving her two suitcases inside. Best not to presume anything. Or look like she was. As she approached the front door, she shivered, not sure if it was nerves or the late-October chill.

Finally, she knocked.

She couldn't make out words but heard voices. It

sounded like festive chatter. Maybe kids sparring? Not in that bad way. Not like where she'd come from.

The door swung open. A breathless woman stood there, a little boy clinging to her left leg as if he made her drag him across the whole living room to reach the door.

"Can I help y—" but the woman stopped, her eyes blinked. "Hannah?"

Her aunt recognized her? Without ever having met her? A big smile spread across Abigail's beautiful face.

All Hannah had to do was nod before her aunt flung open the screen door, with Clingy Boy still attached. She took Hannah into a hearty embrace. People in this town sure liked to hug.

"Well, aren't you the spittin' image of my brother?"

"Aunt Abigail?"

Abigail released her embrace, but held Hannah's shoulders tightly. A good tight. "It's really you, Hannah?"

"Yes." Tears stung as she nodded at the aunt she had never met before, well, other than maybe the week she was born. She had often dreamed about this moment. "I know I should have called first, Aunt Abby. I didn't know your last name."

"You never have to call first, Honey. You don't even have to knock. This is Springhill. You come right on in." With the little boy attached to her ankle, Abigail maneuvered away from the door, motioning for her to step inside. Footsteps barreled somewhere nearby.

Hannah eased through the doorway. "I was hoping I could, I mean, would it be possible for me to stay here for a while? With you?"

"Of course. We have a guest cabin in back that comes in your size." Happy tears spilled from Abigail's eyes. "I can't believe you're here."

Dishes rattled in the room next to them, as a chase ensued. "Don't worry," Abigail said. "That wasn't a bump in the mines. No. That's just a couple of my earthquake-causing kiddos."

A girl cried out, "Lucas, get back here."

Hannah looked behind her, spotting an entryway to a dining room. Before she could step out of the way, a boy ran past her, almost knocking her into Abigail.

"Kids!"

The hot-to-trot girl whirred by next. As the boy tried to make his exodus through the other doorway—which looked like it went to the kitchen—the girl grabbed his arm and swung him around. "Lucas, I'm gonna kill you!"

He laughed, escaped her grip and headed into the adjoining living room, using the coffee table as a barrier between them. They looked to be young teenagers.

Lucas taunted with smooching noises. "Garrett loves Liesel."

"Does not, Cootie Nest." The girl reached over the table, punched his arm.

Hannah chuckled.

"Kids, knock it off," Abigail said. "Come meet your cousin."

The girl lunged toward her brother, forcing him back onto the couch.

That didn't quiet him. "Liesel loves Garrett."

The girl pinned him down. She sure could hold her own. Maybe she could teach Hannah a few offensive moves. "Drop dead twice, Lucas."

Abigail bent down to detach the toddler from her ankle and picked him up. "You have any children,

Hannah?"

"No."

"Would you like a few?"

She smiled, wondering if her aunt ever got any peace. Yet, an undeniable delightfulness permeated the dwelling.

Liesel yelled, "If you so much as breathe those words again—"

When Lucas's smooching sounds continued, they were met with a mouthful of pillow.

A younger girl skipped into the room from the kitchen. "Why are we kissing?"

"Lindy, say hello to Hannah, my niece."

"Hi, Hannah, Mom's niece. I'm Lindy. Her favorite." The girl's smile showed off a missing front tooth. "I'm eight and two quarters." The young girl looked just like her mother. Abigail and Lindy both sported dark hair and eyes.

A muffled sound squeaked out from under the couch pillow. "I'm Lucas."

Abigail said, "Lucas and Liesel are twins, but they weren't born likeminded. This is Lenny." Abigail bounced the light brown haired little boy in her arms.

"You have four children?"

Her aunt paused then said, "For now."

Four wasn't enough?

Liesel hopped off her brother and bounded over to Hannah. "Hi, Hannah. I'm Liesel. And no, I was not kissing Garrett."

Hannah laughed. "Well, you know, I was wondering."

The confident teen winked at Hannah. "That doesn't mean I didn't want to." Liesel was a stunning young woman. Long, wavy blonde hair. Clear blue eyes. She looked nothing like her mom or little sister. Her aunt would be in trouble, if this Garrett boy took notice of this blossoming beauty.

Lucas shared Liesel's lighter features. A handsome boy, his hair longer on top than the sides, like many singers these days. It flopped over his eyes after being pillowed. When he got a little older, he'd probably also have to fend off the young ladies...those he wasn't interested in, anyway.

Liesel said, "I'm so glad you're here, Hannah. We need more strong women in this household."

She didn't know if she could live up to the strong moniker, but Hannah had only been here a few moments and already sealed a connection. Why was it this place felt safe so soon? She sensed she was going to like it.

THE FACT HER UNCLE, Ray Percy, worked underground both fascinated and scared Hannah. When he came home from work, his dark blond hair was damp, from an apparent shower at the mines. Yet, coal dust still caked under his nails. Was this what her father looked like when he came home after his mining shifts? She'd have to ask Uncle Ray more questions about what it was like beneath the ground's surface.

"Da-da," Lenny said, as his father hugged him at the door. She wasn't sure why, but a lump lodged in her throat as she watched the little boy with his daddy.

"It's so great to meet you, Hannah. My wife, she's wanted to find you for a long time. And here you are."

Hannah's mom had always promised one day they'd go to Springhill. But she knew, deep down, her mom didn't want to face this little town that took away the love of her life. Too many memories. Since her mama died when she was fifteen, she had no control after that. She couldn't travel to Springhill by herself.

Until now, when she grabbed control and the Champ's wheel. What took her so long?

"Make yourself at home," Ray said, as he climbed the stairs, vowing his nap would be short.

Abigail insisted Hannah relax after her trip, instead of helping with dinner. She was glad to see they at least had an upright Heintzman piano in their living room. She sat down on the bench and tested the keys.

Lindy roped Lucas into a game of Chinese Checkers on the living room floor behind her. Liesel couldn't be bothered with "kid's play" and sat on the bench beside Hannah. The teen watched her hands flow across the keys.

Hannah toyed with a melody. Some may call it haunting, foreboding, but she liked its mix of minor and dissonant chords. There was something about getting lost in the melodies. Especially when she didn't have to worry about who was coming up behind her.

"That tune…it's so sad," Liesel said. "You make that up?"

Hannah nodded. Why was Liesel staring at her neck? She adjusted her clothing, hoping her blouse collar was high enough. Should have grabbed that ribbon-candy sweater.

As she started her melody again, Liesel hummed a perfect harmony in a lilting soprano. So, musical talent runs in this family.

It was one of those moments that felt so right, like when a loved one comes home safely from a long trip and offers a warm embrace. It lulled Hannah toward believing nothing bad could happen here.

Only she knew all too well that wasn't true. This place was not safe from danger. It may not be the same perils she stared in the face in Toronto. Yet hazards lurked, deep below the surface, in unpredictable and life-threatening ways.

♫ ♫ ♫

Liesel slurped her stew. Of course, she knew this wouldn't capture the right attention, but Lindy kept hogging their houseguest. Would she just stop bombarding Hannah with frivolous questions already? Liesel felt a slice of justice that Hannah didn't answer most of them. Instead, she redirected, distracted Lindy from her non-answers. Clever.

Lindy didn't notice, since flapping her lips was the eight–year-old's favorite form of exercise. Liesel knew diversion techniques well. Especially if she'd ever come home from school after a bad report card day or didn't want to answer one of her mother's relentless interrogations. It's not like she was a bad seed or anything, right? She just wanted her space, the right to withhold her thoughts. She could exchange secrets with Hannah, though.

Maybe Hannah would even be willing to talk about those bruises on her neck. Liesel wasn't a little girl anymore. She was fourteen; she could handle it.

Considering nothing thrilling ever happened in this town, Hannah's visit brought excitement. Thank God, she was much closer in age than Mom—who sometimes felt so ancient. Mom understood absolutely nothing about being a teenager in the fifties. Times were changing faster than Mom's adamant "no" to her request to trade in her one-piece bathing suit for a two-piece with a little skirt. She'd seen one in a magazine. Plus, her friend from needlepoint class, Claire, got one.

Her mom couldn't even support her listening to that fresh guy on the music scene. Elvis. Mom was afraid his music would incite defiance. What was so rebellious about the words to *Love Me Tender* or *Hound Dog*? Elvis was a complete dreamboat. Why couldn't Mom see that? Hannah had to be different. Surely, since she was into music, she'd be a fan of this new rock-n-roll stuff.

Listening to it made her feel grown up. For some reason, Mom still thought of her as an adolescent. Lucas was the same age—actually two minutes and fourteen seconds younger—and yet he'd get special treatment. Privileges, as if he were more responsible. His idea of responsibility was letting six mice out of their cages in science class, then admitting it. She slurped another bite.

"Liesel." All it took was that look from her mother to correct her manners. Okay, so, stew slurping wasn't her most mature plan of attack.

Lindy prattled on, sharing with Hannah useless historical data about their lives. Though, Hannah didn't appear to mind.

Dad rescued Hannah with a question of his own. "So, what made you come visit us now?"

"I wanted to come long ago. I had to save up the money to make the trip."

"Hannah, you could have contacted us," her mom said. "We would have helped you."

And that, she believed. Her mother has always been

about assisting family — blood relatives or not — even when they couldn't afford it.

"How far away is Toronto?" The young interrogator was at it again.

"About 1000 miles."

"Whoa! That must have taken a thousand hours to drive," Lindy said.

"It doesn't take one hour per mile, Lindy," her dad said. "You should figure out the math, if she averages 50 miles per hour." There goes Dad, turning this into an object lesson of a mathematical variety. He loved numbers. Each day when he came home, he tried to guess how many coal boxes they'd filled for that shift or how much the final tally weighed for the day. He had a vested interest; the miners' pay depended on it.

"It took two days." Hannah was patient; she'd give her that. "I stopped in Quebec on the way. My mother and I used to go there when I was younger, always in time for the Winter Carnival. We loved to watch the competitors build ice sculptures."

"I want to go sometime." Lindy's inquisition continued. "How did you save the money? And what did the trip cost? Are you staying for a while or going back?"

"Lindy, one question at a time," Mom said.

"It's okay," Hannah said. "I saved up by teaching kids to play musical instruments. The piano and guitar, mostly."

"Ooh. Do you know how to play the ukulele? I want to learn."

"Sorry, Lindy. That isn't in my repertoire."

"So, Hannah," her dad said. "When I was getting off shift today, I ran into Hector on Main Street. He said you met my best friend, Josh, at the pool hall?"

"Yes. Josh told me how to find your wife."

Hmm...Josh. Liesel wondered if Hannah might be the match they'd been waiting for. It made no sense to her whatsoever, why—on God's green and fruitful earth—a guy like Josh was still available. More than once, Liesel had wished she were ten years older to snag him for herself. But thankfully, she had another dreamboat that had recently captured her eye—and not just Elvis.

Someone in-the-flesh and her age: Garrett.

Her dad's stare yanked her out of daydreaming. "What's this I heard about Liesel getting kissed today?"

So Dad had Garrett on the brain too. Liesel buried her rapidly heating up cheeks in her hands. Not the scoop she wanted leaked to her father.

"I feel like all the juicy stuff happens when I'm underground," Dad said.

"Lucas spreads rumors of the false variety," said Liesel.

Lucas laughed so hard that she was about to kick his chair under the table. He'd never see it coming. But her mother—who had eyes everywhere, including under tables—slapped a firm hand on her knee. How did Mom always forecast her moves so well?

Dad took his last bite of stew. "Anyone want to make a skating rink tonight? Gonna freeze out there."

"Me."

"Me."

"Me," Liesel added to the affirmative chorus of her siblings.

Hannah asked, "So, you aren't going out dressed up for Halloween tonight?"

"Oh, no," Lindy said. "Mom says All Hallow's Eve is

the devil's holiday. Instead, we get a big festival at church tomorrow night for All Saints' Day."

Her sister was actually giddy about this? Ugh! Eight-year-olds. "They make us dress up like our favorite Bible characters and bob for apples." Liesel rolled her eyes. "You should come." Why should she be the only one forced to attend that sleepfest?

"Don't listen to Liesel. It's nifty." Lindy beamed at Hannah. "We get candy. Cherry Blossoms, Coffee Crisp, Chuckles, Necco Wafers, Fizzies, Charleston Chew, and my personal favorite, the Nik-L-Wip Wax Candy."

Lucas said, "She doesn't sleep for days from her sugar overdose."

"One day, I'm going to own a candy store on Main Street. Sweet Lindy's Penny Candy. Everything will cost one penny."

"Lindy has an uncanny ability to state the obvious," Liesel said. Enough focusing on little sis. "Dad! You are coming tomorrow morning, right? To my recital?" She caught his quick glance toward her mother. "You forgot?"

"No, no. I need to confirm with Josh that he can switch shifts with me tomorrow."

She didn't care he was covering up. All that mattered was that he said he'd come. And Dad's word...it was golden. The one solid she could depend on was that her dad would always be there for her. Liesel said, "Good. 'Cause I want you to hear me sing up there. It's the first time Mrs. Collins has given me a solo."

"Of course, Baby. Wouldn't miss it."

She caught her mother's displeased look. "If you ask me, rock-n-roll has no place in your school. It's not—"

"Mom, please. You'll love the show. And Hannah, you

need to come too." While there were times Liesel wished for serious space between her and the family, this was not one of them. She couldn't wait for them to see her on that stage, in all her glory.

♫ ♫ ♫

November 1, 1956
It was Thursday, All Saints' Day, the start of a new month. A perfect day for Hannah's new life to begin, even if saint was the last name she'd give herself.

The original, carefully set out plans she'd had for this weekend would never happen. She didn't even think twice when she deposited her calendar in the rubbish beside her rollaway cot. She had no need for it anymore.

Time to forget what was behind and look toward what was ahead. Wasn't that one of Mama's favorite sayings?

She opened the drawer to the cherry oak dresser. For now, it was hers. Despite how small it was, her clothes fit. She needed to earn money so she could buy more. As she pulled out her favorite cream sweater with the little pastel flowers, she caught a glimpse of herself in the round mirror attached to the dresser.

Soon, those lines under her eyes would disappear. She bundled up with her jacket and scarf. As she opened the door to her guesthouse, the crisp air slapped her in the face. This place felt cooler than Toronto, perhaps because it was close to the Atlantic Ocean, sandwiched between the Gulf of St. Lawrence and Bay of Fundy. The winds felt stronger too.

The whole yard beside the driveway before her was a slushy, yet even layer of liquid. Ray used a hose last night to cover it in water. Once it froze, it would be the Percys' makeshift skating rink. What a wonderful way to take advantage of the already chilling temperatures. They had the perfect yard for it too. Flat surface, not many trees in the way. She might just borrow a pair of skates herself, once it froze over. The last time she'd been on a rink was with her mother in Quebec, that final time they went to the Winter Carnival. She'd just turned fifteen.

Her mama's church had taken up a collection to send them. After making the drive from Toronto—which sometimes was the best part of the trip—Mama would tell stories about Daddy, stories she swore she'd not told another soul. Like the time he unofficially proposed. Not the proposal everyone else heard about on the cliffs of Heather's Beach in time for the sunset. That happened once he'd bought her that precious ring for forty dollars. But the first time. High School hallway—roaring twenties, Jazz Age, Grade 9—after he'd spotted Freddie Lester honing in on his territory, which he'd realized wasn't officially his yet and he'd better make it so. Days later, she had a promise ring. She didn't mind that its metal was so soft it wouldn't keep its shape. Mama and Daddy shared a love that, back then, while skating with her mother, Hannah believed she'd find one day. She was sure of it.

How had she been so deceived?

After the trek up the highway, she and her mother would head to the Carnival. They'd felt tiny, standing below the artists with their chisels and their determination, carving bigger-than-life-sized ice castles—ones they'd dream of sleeping in, minus the cold. The festival was a pre-Lent tradition, where people enjoyed unique delicacies. Beaver tail pastries topped with cinnamon and sugar. Maple taffy. When they didn't fill up on sweets, they'd gorge on meat pies with a side of chips and vinegar. They never liked how they felt after they ate—nighttime groans were common in their little motel—but it sure was a treat on the way down. They'd eat while watching the canoes race across the St. Lawrence River, swift and elegant, like her mama was. Hannah always wanted to try it, but Mama reminded her it was a man's competition.

That last time they'd skated, Mama took a spill and ended up with a bruise the size of a grapefruit on her thigh. They'd laughed, despite her pain. They never ate a grapefruit again without remembering—and chuckling.

As her mother sat splayed on the ice, she looked up at Hannah. "This is what it's about, Hannah."

"What, Mama? Landing on your tailbone?" She giggled. When she had reached down to help, Mama guided her down to the cold ice.

"Making memories. With you." Mama reached out, touching her face.

Normally, she hated when Mama did that, but for some reason she didn't shrink back that day. "Mom, we're in public."

"If we could afford a camera, I would capture you right here. I wish you could see how beautiful you are, Hannah."

"You have to say that. You're my mother."

"No, that's not it. There's something in your eyes, Hannah. A life inside them. A hope. Never lose that."

Hannah had no idea that would be their last vacation. Ever.

As she rounded the side of Aunt Abigail's home, she was grateful her mother wasn't there to discover that light had all but disappeared.

Just as she arrived at the front door to the main house, Ray and Abigail stepped out. Abigail toted Lenny, but she almost tripped on a loose board. "Ray, my Dear, is it tomorrow yet?"

Ray arched a guilty brow. "I know. I'll fix it, Dear."

"Sure you will."

"Tomorrow."

Hannah saw the affection in Abigail's smile. No doubt she'd heard that phrase before. She wondered if her mother had heard Daddy say "tomorrow" about something that didn't come for them.

"Ready to go?" Abigail asked Hannah.

"Yes."

"I was expecting you to come inside for breakfast."

"So was I. Honestly, I haven't slept that late in a long time." Or felt that much peace. "I'll be okay."

"We better get going, so we're not late. Liesel is the fourth act on stage."

They set off to walk to school. The loose gravel crunched beneath their feet. Just like in Toronto. Except here she had no need to look over her shoulder.

"So, Josh didn't mind working for you today?" Hannah's breath wafted into the cool air.

"Well, Josh said he didn't mind when he got home after eleven last night. I'll bet he second-guessed that choice as he rode down the rake at seven this morning."

"Well, I'm sure Liesel appreciates this."

"I'd do the same for him…if he had something he wanted to do, like go on an evening date, perhaps." Ray cut his eyes toward Hannah, mischievousness swimming in them. It made her insides leap. Excitement? Fear? She wasn't sure. She did not want to have *that* conversation.

"What's it like down there?" Hannah had only heard a little of what the mining life was like, from stories her mother used to tell about her father.

"It's dark. Sometimes hot, stuffy. All we can see is what our lamps light up. But the smells? Whew! I could tell you who was nearby in the dark, just takin' a whiff."

"Really?" That didn't sound like a perk.

"But you know what? You're surrounded by friends. We laugh, we tell stories, not all of them true. We sing, make up songs about the mines. It's like spending all day with the best friends you could ever hope for. Every last one of them would back you up if you needed it. Lay down their lives, even."

Abigail cleared her throat. "Best friends?"

"Well, all of my best friends except one." He put his arm around his wife, pecked her cheek, while they continued to walk.

That didn't sound anything like how her mother described the mines. Mama always thought of mining as something to fear, at least as the outsider hoping her husband would come home each day. She feared every trek down could be his last.

And one day…it was. One blustery afternoon in 1929.

Hannah's birthday.

But Ray didn't make it sound like a mode of survival. He made it sound magical. Desired, even.

"You're not afraid?"

"No. I'm not afraid."

Somehow, she believed him.

THE SCHOOL'S AUDITORIUM filled to capacity with students, parents, siblings. The choir sang the first two numbers together. The third piece was an a cappella harmony sung by three Mulatto sisters. She didn't recognize the song, but the lyrics were about their father, a miner. She suspected they penned it themselves. Their voices had a perfect blend, boisterous volume and strength.

Then came the Percys' little star, Liesel. Hannah's head bopped to the beat as the blonde beauty pranced around the stage, commanding a special presence. Liesel sang a rendition of Teresa Brewer's popular smash, *Music, Music, Music*. The teen was mesmerizing, her blue eyes sparkling in the stage lights. Her long, wavy curls bounced as she stepped to the beat. Such personality and life she had. As she sang for all to put a nickel in the jukebox, the audience clapped and swayed back and forth. They couldn't help it; her enthusiasm was infectious.

Abigail tapped her toe, despite her rock-n-roll protests. Hannah could grow used to a place that celebrated music. And the students who played instruments...how did kids, from a town this size, gain so much talent?

Lucas sat with his friends, a few rows away from them. He feigned disinterest, but he couldn't stop glancing at his twin.

After hamming it up for the audience, Liesel sang to her classmates on the choir risers behind her. When her eyes landed on a particular boy, her face turned bright crimson. It probably had to do with the lyrics at that moment, something about kissing him. Hannah wondered if this boy were the other half of the "Liesel loves Garrett" mantra.

As Liesel hit that final note, a full octave above middle

C, the school auditorium exploded in well-deserved applause.

After a few more lively numbers, the whole choir started *Goodnight, Irene*. Laughter spread throughout the audience. Just as Hannah wondered if she were observing an inside joke, Abigail whispered, "Every musical group in town—and there are many—now ends all sets with this song."

Hannah looked forward to finding out more of this town's inside jokes.

In the foyer after the show, Hannah watched other proud parents dote on their talented kids. When Liesel emerged from the auditorium and spotted her family, she darted over and hugged her dad first.

"Thank you so much for coming, Dad. It means a lot. My friends up there...Joyce, Janet, Mae. Their dad's couldn't come today."

"I am exactly where I want to be, Liesel."

"You were wonderful," Abigail beamed as she bounced a fussy Lenny.

Liesel kissed her little brother's forehead. "I'm glad Lenny didn't add to the soundtrack. Daddy, will the ice freeze by this weekend?"

"I'm lacing up my skates."

"Hannah, we can find you a pair. And for my next school recital, we should get you to play." She leaned in, snapped her fingers twice and through gritted teeth said, "Good ole Teach missed my pivotal cues."

Abigail said, "I think maybe Hannah should play in church sometime."

Hannah just smiled. No need to get into her thoughts about playing in church. She didn't want to offend them or do anything to criticize their faith. This was a faith her mother and father shared, though Hannah was never sure why. Life — or whoever was responsible up there — certainly never gave her mother what she desired. Having faith didn't change anything. He didn't show up when people needed him most.

HANNAH FOUND HERSELF STANDING outside All Saints' Church on the corner of Junction and Main. After Liesel's show, she'd told her aunt and uncle she wanted to do a little exploring. Why not get a sense of this place while she could stroll along and enjoy her relative anonymity? Plus, she could drum up ideas of what she could do to earn money.

Knowing he would take Josh's afternoon shift, she felt tempted to ask Uncle Ray if she could tag along for a few hours. She ached to see what her dad saw down there. But she knew better. She was certain they would never let a woman underground.

Instead, standing on Main Street, she beheld All Saints. Its white paneling made the place look so pure. They kept it clean, its lawn manicured, even though the green had started its transformation to autumn brown. Angled frames stood above the windows. The tallest tower to the church's side held its main entrance. She'd always liked those rounded, archway style double doors. But she didn't know if she could step foot over that threshold, let alone ask for a job as the pianist. No. It wouldn't be here. She'd find something else. Whoever sat on that bench needed to believe in the lyrics of hymns.

He Leadeth Me.

Come Thou Almighty King.

Old Rugged Cross.

Her mama used to hum them all; she'd learned them in this very place. Knowing her parents stepped inside those walls was the only draw to going inside one Sunday.

A banner rested between two fence posts. It announced tonight's All Saints' Festival for the whole family. This place would fill with carefree, Christian holiday celebrants. Liesel may not want to admit it, but Hannah suspected she'd enjoy it anyway.

Hannah strolled up the rest of Main Street to get a closer look at the delightful collection of locally owned stores. She studied the family names: Martin's Groceteria. Lipnicki's Five & Dime. McKay's Drugstore. Logan's Bakery. Nancy's Trinkets. Harroun's Clothing Store & Accessories. Avalon's Dance Club & Diner. She pictured Sweet Lindy's Penny Candy; yes, that would fit right in.

A red, white, and blue striped barber pole spun outside Westbury's Main Street Barber Shop, next to the Springhill Record newspaper. What news happened around here to keep ink to the presses? Perhaps the reporters had to write about stories from nearby cities. This place had such a different feel from Toronto. Almost protected. Like nothing could go wrong here.

She arrived at the empty Liar's Bench and couldn't help herself. She took a moment to sit on the bench, try it on for size. Perhaps generations of tall tales were told here. She wondered if her father had ever sat here with a buddy. What stories would he have told? Oh, how she wished for a recording.

As she rose from the bench, she saw the tall smokestacks below, at the bottom of Main Street. Steam floated out of them. The mine grounds hummed, in full operation.

Should she dare walk to the site and take a look around? Fear and curiosity battled each other, making her want to stay away and summoning her to explore at the same time.

She walked the final stretch of Main Street to the Cumberland Coal archway.

Curiosity won out.

chapter 3

Josh Winslow rode up the rake from the No. 4 mine's 5,500 foot level, where Ray Percy's team worked by day and his own team worked by night. He fought several yawns as the rake bumped endlessly and its wheels squeaked. He felt giddy to have the rest of the night off. But not for sleep. The idea of running into Ray's niece, Hannah, gave him a new energy. He had to take advantage of his rare night off.

The rake slowed to a stop at the surface, its tracks protruding from the mouth of the No. 4 mine. Josh squinted at the first rays of sunshine he'd seen in eight hours. He looked forward to getting into the Wash House so he could get rid of the black grime that covered his hands and face. He'd brought his favorite dungarees for a change of clothes today, in case he ran into her.

Hannah. He liked her name.

And her eyes.

All he had to do was wheel down his clothing bucket from the ceiling—unless one of his prankster comrades had stolen them—and get on with his day.

He grabbed his empty lunch box and stepped off the

rake. He spotted his regular team, waiting to ride down to their level.

Ray Percy shook Josh's coal-dusted hand. "Thanks for swappin' shifts with me today, Josh."

"No problem. I'm sure Liesel loved having you there. I think I'll pop over to your house and cast an eye on that niece of yours."

"Hannah's been here, what? A day?"

"One fine day," Josh interrupted with a smile.

"And like lickety, you know about her."

"Percy, we're talkin' Springhill. A beauty like Hannah tows in..."

Moosey bumped Josh's shoulder on purpose. His weight could knock him over if he tried. "We don't have to stare at your ugly face tonight, Winnie?"

"I'll be here tomorrow, Moosey. Uglier than ever."

The rake operator hollered for the men to hurry up.

"Ray, watch my boys down there tonight."

Ray nodded. "You can count on it." Ray's jaw clenched.

"Somethin' up, Ray? You look stressed."

"Abigail told me this morning. We have another on the way."

"Wow. Number five for Five Maple." Josh squeezed his buddy's arm. "No frettin', Percy. Singin' Isaak has eleven kids. He makes it on a miner's salary. I don't know how, but he does."

Ray slowly nodded, gave him a half smile as he got on the rake. Josh watched his comrades ride down into the dark tunnel.

Josh wondered what it must be like to have eleven kids of your own. Or even five. To look into the face of a child and see that familiar crooked nose, or the color of their mama's eyes reflecting back. He'd always wanted a big family of his own. But for some reason, it had eluded him. Had he been too picky so far? The old ladies at church possessed suggestions, but none of them ever made his heart skip a beat. Or even speed up a little. None. He wanted to find that one that made him feel like home when he embraced her. The one who looked at him like he was home for her.

Once he cleaned up, Josh decided not to walk to Maple by the steep trek of Main Street. Normally, he loved the social time with all the folks in town. Today, he didn't want to risk landing in the usual seven or eight conversations with locals. Especially Mary Lou Lipnicki. Sure was a challenge to extract himself from conversations with her. If he bee-lined it for home, maybe he'd spot Ray's houseguest hanging around. He decided to walk up Queen Street, pass by Junction Road, and head to Maple by way of Wolsley Street.

As he turned the corner onto Wolsley, he saw the Percy twins, Liesel and Lucas, doing a favorite pastime from when he was their age: racing tires. Lucas expertly used his steel rim to guide his tire to go faster and faster, yet not fall over. Liesel tried to keep up and laughed as hers tumbled over.

Josh waved at the kids as he arrived at the corner of Maple. "Hey Liesel, is Hannah at your house right now?"

"Hmm…and why would you like to know?" She sauntered over.

Why was it that lass could see through anything? Because she always had romance on her mind, perhaps. "Well, is she?" he asked.

"I don't think so. Haven't seen her since she came to my recital this morning. But I'm hoping to talk her into going to All Saints' Festival tonight so I don't have to suffer alone in my boredom. If you wanna happen to show up and run into her…"

So subtle, that blonde one. Josh asked, "Who are you dressing up as this year?"

"Mary Magdalene, of course."

Oh boy, Ray would have his hands full with this one. Josh hoped the next child would be a son, for Ray's sanity.

Josh headed toward his house across from theirs, Eight Maple. Tonight, after the festival, he would ask Hannah if she'd like to share a milkshake at the diner.

♫   ♫   ♫

Hannah had spent the last hour or so, wandering around the mine grounds, snaking between buildings and smoke stacks. It appeared two different mines were in operation. They both had openings where train cars and tracks protruded. Silver metal and black buildings were erected above the mine on wood that looked like stilts, with various ramps or walkways coming out of those.

Other buildings peppered the property. She peeked through windows, figuring out what functions each building served. When she looked in one white building, all she could see from the high windows were lots of buckets raised to the ceiling with clothes and other personal items dangling out.

When she walked around to the front, seeing the sign

labeled "Wash House," she thought she had seen Josh coming out. She backed up and ducked behind the building. She wasn't ready to be social yet and she was sure—being a woman—she'd stick out on the mine grounds. She didn't plan her scout strategically. The place flooded with men changing shifts, including Uncle Ray. If he hadn't been surrounded by other men, including the man she recognized from the pool hall, Moosey, she might have said hello. At least she'd see Uncle Ray at home tomorrow. Maybe he'd answer more questions about what it was like underground.

Once the place cleared, she walked around the rest of the property. Did her father walk on these same spots? Which bucket did he use? Was he working in the mine labeled No. 2 or No. 4? Hmm. Maybe she could sneak into one.

She could grab a pulley, lower a bucket and use someone else's clothes, right? No, the man operating the train car would see right through her. This was men's territory.

She ducked away from a building that looked like an office. No sense running into any officials.

That's when she stumbled on it: a structure labeled Lamp Cabin. From her mother's stories, she knew her father would visit this building right before he would go underground to drop off his numbered check tag. In exchange, he'd get a lamp with the same number. That way, if anything bad happened underground, management would know which miners were underground by numbers on the board. The miners would pick up this check tag at the end of their shifts when they returned their lamps.

Hannah fingered the smooth metal in her pocket. She

pulled it out, gazing at his brass check tag. She'd held onto it since she was a child, and almost never left home without it, unless her clothing had no pockets. She'd always called it her good luck charm, even though she didn't believe in luck, let alone the *good* kind.

#712.

This same check tag hung on that board the night her father died. The mine company gave it to her mother after they confirmed his death.

"Not often we see a woman out here. Can I help you, ma'am?" Oops. The Lamp Cabin worker had spotted her.

Hannah hesitated. Was she ready to step inside? She'd come so far. She willed herself to put one foot in front of the other.

"Hello there, Sir. My name is Hannah Wright. My father used to be a miner here. I wanted to—" her voice caught in her throat. What was she doing? Trying to get to know her father through objects? Places? Strangers?

"Say no more, Hannah. I understand."

His warm smile encouraged her to move inside. She strolled over to the check tag board that showed the numbers of those currently underground. Which one was Ray's or which nail had #712 hung from the night her father didn't surface?

The man said, "He was number 712."

Hannah whipped his direction. He remembered that detail?

"I always recall the ones that never got picked up." He extended his hand. "My name is Don Fritz. I started working 'bout the same time as your dad. We went to school together. Right here at Springhill High."

Hannah had never been anywhere that people knew

her father. Yet here, no matter who she ran into, they knew him. That wasn't a coincidence. People invested in their neighbors, co-workers. Their memories were long too.

She swallowed. "Which mine did he work in? The number two or four?"

"Two. Four wasn't open then. We opened that one up about twenty-five years ago. Most miners, if given a choice, would choose that one instead of two. They feel like it's safer."

Safer. If only that mine had opened two years earlier, maybe her father would have lived. At least the four was where her uncle was working today. He would be safer.

"What can you tell me about my dad?" she asked.

Just then, a piercing whine erupted. It sounded like a train going fast on a set of tracks. Was that normal? She'd never been here to recognize its sounds. She couldn't make sense of it. Mr. Fritz rushed to the window.

Was something wrong?

Suddenly, a loud boom erupted, then what could be described as a strong gust of wind.

The floor beneath her feet shook.

"Get down!"

Hannah followed his lead and slammed down to the floor that trembled beneath her, as sounds popped and crackled. Mr. Fritz got up to peek out his window.

"Well, I'll be." He lifted his eyes. "Sweet Jesus."

"What's going on?"

Still looking up, Fritz said, "Please be down there with every last one of 'em."

Hannah slowly worked her way to her feet and over to the doorway. Her entire body went from warm to cold in seconds. They were just a mere acre away from the fresh blast. Smoke billowed far above the mine she had seen labeled No. 4 minutes before.

That one that was supposedly safer.

The one that held Ray in its clutches.

Now, its opening—if that's even what it was anymore—didn't look remotely like it did a few minutes ago. Was it completely blown away? Before, it had some sort of hole where the train cars came up on the tracks. But now? Shambles.

Two bodies lie motionless near the opening. Weren't they just standing outside, working with the crew? Another man tried to stand, flailing his arms. His limbs were on fire. His anguished hollers echoed across the entire mine yard.

"What just happened?" She gulped for air, in and out.

Mr. Fritz dashed out from behind the counter on his way to the door. "I think the mine exploded."

♫ ♫ ♫

Josh had just sat down for his after-work snack—which for him was more like a pre-dinner meal. Eggs and cheese on leftover, homemade bread.

The loud blast interrupted him, mid-bite. It even rattled the timbers of his home. He dropped his sandwich and ran out of his house.

He looked toward the mines below. Hovered above was a large black, mushroom cloud of smoke. What on earth? A hundred and fifty, or two hundred feet above the mines, maybe?

Fast footsteps crunched behind him. Lucas and Liesel

bounded down Maple, his direction.

"What's going on down there, Josh?" Liesel yelled.

"I have no idea."

Abigail rushed out the front door, balancing Lenny, with Lindy behind them. "Josh! Did something happen at the mines?"

"I'll go see," Josh said. "I'll report back. Stay here with the kids."

"Huh-uh. I'm going." Liesel and Lucas said, in unison, in one of their rare twin moments.

"We're all going," Abigail said.

"You aren't supposed to be under stress, Abigail." Josh tried to throw an unspoken hint with his eyes that Ray had confided their news. Another Percy baby was on the way. He didn't know if the kids had been told yet.

"We'll stay back, out of the way. But we're going." She would not relent. Josh led the way down Maple. He heard Abigail muttering a prayer under her breath.

They joined swarms of others, young and old, racing out of their homes. Lights were left on. Doors flung open. Homes abandoned with only one thought in mind:

Find out what happened at that mine.

He wasn't the only one. Every Springhiller knew someone underground. Josh picked up his pace. He had to get there to check on Ray. He had five kids to raise; Josh didn't.

Why couldn't he have been underground instead?

Ambulances raced by. Josh covered his ears to shield the sirens, but kept on moving.

They'd always had to live with the risks involved in the mining industry. It ran like an undercurrent, like blood through veins. They all knew it was there but never saw it…until it hemorrhaged.

It never stopped the miners from showing up for work. Some days, they could get lulled into believing "the big one" was a risk of the past. After all, this town hadn't had a catastrophic disaster since February 21, 1891. Long before any of their times.

Although, that did not mean the smaller ones didn't count. Since 1937, there had only been one year no one died. Yes, just one, 1947, a welcomed reprieve. Every other year, accidents claimed lives.

Josh would never forget the one day just over twenty-seven years ago, one of those smaller accidents claimed five men. These incidents were harsh reminders the danger wasn't gone. But today, this felt different.

This was big. Would it be 1891 all over again, when 125 men perished in an explosion?

Josh was a few strides ahead of the Percys, as they raced under the Cumberland Coal archway. Except Liesel. She was right on his heels.

Was there any chance his team was still alive? He should be down there with them right now. He could have helped. Ray would still be above ground where he belonged, with his family.

At least he could help now, even go underground on a search team to find them all. He wouldn't give up, not until every last one of them was found.

As he climbed the hill beyond the archway, his chest felt like it would split open. He couldn't spare a second to catch his breath. If he knew anything about being underground in an explosion, it was likely his comrades were having a lot harder time breathing than he was right now. Liesel bumped into him as he arrived a few yards from the pithead. He turned around to face her. "Stay here, Liesel. I'll find out what's going on."

"I want to help."

"I promise. I'll do everything in my power to find your father." He put his hands on her shoulders, gave them a firm squeeze. "Stay here. I mean it! I will take care of this."

As he turned to view the site, it drew what little air he had left. It was like he'd been sucker-punched. Charred bodies littered the bankhead's mouth. Those workers...who were they? He was sure he knew them. Sure he'd just seen them face-to-face during that moment when all that was on his mind was finding Hannah. But which man was which? He couldn't even tell.

Firemen tried to douse the blaze with their hoses near the opening. How was it, just a bit ago, the rake was here to drop them off at the end of a shift?

Policemen fought to push onlookers back. Josh beelined for the pithead. Dread took up residence in his gut.

Josh recognized the guard from church. He did not try to stop him. "Go on."

Rescue workers led a man out of the mine, bleeding from his forehead, burns on his face. Clothes with holes in them. Singed. Josh tried to figure out who he was. Again, his mind couldn't make sense of the image. But this was his shift; he knew just about everyone underground.

Emergency workers rushed to the miner's aid.

The man shoved them away. "My son. Has anyone seen Matthew?"

Josh knew that voice. Caleb MacQuarrie. The shock must have dulled Caleb's obvious pain because no man would normally be able to walk around with those burns, let alone think straight. Caleb and Matthew were one of many father-son teams who worked down here together. Something Josh thought he would have done with his father.

His father died before he was old enough to work underground. He was only five years old at the time. But as soon as he was seventeen, he went straight into the deeps. He had to take care of his mother, right? She hated every day he went to work. She didn't want to lose her son too. Thankfully, she never had to face that through the time of her death a few years ago. He was sure she was enjoying her own heavenly reunion with his dad.

Caleb's wife had died around the same time, a few years back. An undetected, tiny hole in her heart left a giant one in Caleb's. Josh could still picture the church that day of the funeral. White trilliums everywhere. Her favorite flower. And now, Matthew was all Caleb had left for relatives in this town. Caleb yelled to someone behind Josh. "Did Matthew turn in his check tag yet?"

Josh turned around to see Fritz standing at the barricade line. "No one has come up yet. Just you."

"I need another lamp." Caleb swung the broken lamp as he walked toward Fritz, paying no attention to his burns, his own blood.

"Sir!" An emergency worker tried to guide Caleb in the opposite direction of the Lamp Cabin. "Please let us help you." The worker pointed to a station being set up with nurses.

Caleb kept walking and held out his broken lamp. "Fritz, can I have a new one?"

Josh raced over to Caleb. "Caleb, get medical attention. Let me go look for Matthew. I know what level he would have been on."

"No, he's my son. Fritz, I need that lamp."

Fritz took the broken lamp and headed off with Caleb. Who could blame him? If that were his son underground, Josh would do the same.

Josh followed them to get his own lamp; he couldn't very well help without it.

Once he jogged back to the bankhead, he saw his boss, Cal Weston, about to head underground. Cal was never afraid to get his hands dirty or put himself in personal danger when his men were stuck underground. He'd been at this job for twenty some years, but was still young enough to dive in there with the rest of them. And for that, Josh respected him.

Cal was about to descend. He stopped and turned to Josh. "What are you doing?"

"Let me go with you, Cal."

"No. Josh, you are not a trained draegerman. You go in there barefaced, and you'll die. No question. Who will that help?"

"Moosey. Jonesy. Quinn. Ray Percy."

"The gas will kill you. I need you out here. Help the men we bring out."

"Cal, please."

"When we get a fresh air base set up, you can go in then. Not before."

Cal headed into the mines. It would be a while before the fans were running. Only those like Cal, in draeger gear, had the best chance of surviving rescue attempts. The gasses could get bad down there after a disaster. They could kill quicker than a cave-in. At least Cal had the mask.

Moments later, Matthew's father Caleb entered the jaws of the mine's former mouth. He cared less about rules, about not having draegerman apparatus. Nobody tried to stop him, despite his third-degree burns and cuts.

Why couldn't he do more? It was his fault his best friend — Abigail's husband, Liesel's beloved father — was stuck underground.

He glanced out across the crowd, landing on Abigail, whose eyes met his. Hannah walked up from behind Abigail and joined her. This had to be so foreign to her. She'd barely been in town two days. He'd hardly spent a day outside their tight knit community, and even he would never get used to this. The volatility. How often lives hung in the balance.

From the distance, he could see the strain on Abigail's face. The fear. Ray shouldn't have even been down there; Josh should have. And there was no way to know if Ray were alive or dead.

♫ ♫ ♫

"Come out, Daddy. Come out. Come out, Daddy." If Liesel said it enough, maybe he would hear her. He would come walking out of that mine. She'd tell him he could never go back. She'd do whatever she had to do. So would Lucas, now that they were almost fifteen years old. They would figure out another way to make money. If only he could live.

"Daddy, you can do it." Daddy understood her more than Mom. So much more. He got that she was changing, that she was growing up. She needed to spread her wings a little bit. Even in this, she'd take responsibility. She'd deliver newspapers for the *Halifax Chronicle-Herald* every day or the *Springhill Record*'s weekly paper on Thursdays before school. Lucas could get a job delivering milk for Springhill Dairy. Something.

They could even open Lindy's store a decade early if that would help. Yes, they would come up with a family business on Main Street to run together. Anything to get Daddy out of that mine.

She couldn't look at her mother. She knew she was praying beside her. That's what she always did when she got nervous about something, which was often. Her mom was a competent worrier. For the first time, she understood a little of what her mother felt almost every day. Before now, it was never much of a reality to her. She'd heard the stories. In fourth grade, this boy in her class, Brooks, lost his father. But it hadn't hit this close to home before.

And Daddy…he always came home.

"Why did he have to switch?"

Liesel heard the words escape her mother's mouth from behind her. She tried to make sense of them, tried to hear them differently, but no. She heard them right. Even if it sounded like her mother was talking through a tunnel.

The words haunted her, echoed twice, then three times: *"Why did he have to switch?"*

Tears blurred her vision, as she looked up at her mom, her cousin standing beside her.

Her mom looked over, their eyes meeting for the first time since the unspeakable.

"I'm sorry, Liesel. I didn't mean…" Her mom couldn't even finish the words. Liesel knew why.

Mom blamed her.

Liesel stared at her and then decided. This was up to

her. She sprung up and broke into a sprint, shoving aside anyone in her path. She headed for the barricades. Didn't matter what they thought. She was going down there.

"Liesel, don't!" Mom yelled.

She heard other footsteps behind her, but she didn't dare stop to look. It was her fault her dad was underground; she'd be the one to get him out. Or she'd die trying. She didn't care.

She hurtled a police barrier as an officer tried to catch hold of her arm. She gave him the slip.

If she could make it to the opening, she could get lost in the dark. She'd go off in a different direction than the search party, cover areas no one thought to look. She would find him, no matter—

A searing pain shot through her left shoulder as a tight grip enclosed her arm, sending her full-force backwards. The policeman.

A second officer grabbed her from the other side.

"Let me go. Let me go! My father's down there. Let me go." The two officers turned her around and carried her by the arms back toward the barricade. No amount of flailing deterred them. They wouldn't let up.

One officer said, "Girl, you can't go."

"But I have to save him."

The man tightened his grip. "You can't do anything down there. A mine is no place for a lady. It's dangerous."

"You think I care? If my father dies, I don't want to live anyway."

They deposited her on the other side of the barricade.

She didn't care how many people around her glared like she was crazy. They didn't understand; they didn't know this was her fault.

"Come on, Liesel." She heard Hannah's quiet voice in the crowd. She felt her gentle touch on her shoulder. Hannah took her hand, but didn't lead her back to where they were before. Where her mother was. Her brothers, her sister. She couldn't face them. Ever.

Not if her father never came home.

chapter 4

A stocky man carrying a camera on top of a bulky tripod bumped into Hannah. When the operator tried to capture Liesel's distraught face, Hannah put her hand in front of the lens. She didn't care if this were a live broadcast. Her cousin's pain was not for the world to exploit.

The camera operator shifted his equipment to the bankhead activity, while a reporter spoke into an attached microphone. "The company states there's little hope anyone trapped below is alive. There's a chance of another explosion if they don't reduce the air supply below by sealing off the mine, temporarily."

Why were people in the crowd forced to listen to that dismal reality? This was not what Liesel needed to hear right now. It could send her over the ledge she already stood on.

"If they reduce the air supply," the reporter continued, "that lowers the odds of survival even more. They won't be able to breathe underground."

Liesel turned back to eye the reporter.

"No, no. Keep going, Liesel." Hannah directed the girl

forward, away from the men, away from their hopeless words.

His voice droned on. "The rescuers are in as much danger as the trapped men. But they forge ahead, hoping to find survivors."

The rescuers. Hannah had seen Josh at the opening of the mine, trying to help.

Hannah let go of Liesel's hand as they arrived on the hillside, a bit away from the crowd, but still close enough to the mine opening to monitor what was going on. Liesel turned back around, to watch the pithead. She knelt on the cold, damp ground. She wouldn't take her eyes off that opening.

At least the kid didn't shove Hannah away. It gave her something to do, even though it felt like nothing.

Was this what it was like the day her mother sat out here? The day her dad was trapped with those other men? Four or five of them. She even went into labor with Hannah, standing on this hill, the moment they told Mama her beloved would not be returning. Her mama used to say the Lord knew she needed a blessing to focus on during her loss. Hannah had a hard time swallowing that logic. A mother and father should experience the child they made together, not with one mourning the other's loss. Why did life seem so messed up?

Hannah swiped a hot tear with the back of her hand. This wasn't the time to focus on herself; this time was for Liesel. She had to be strong for the kid.

Hannah knelt down beside her and waited. For what, she didn't know yet. But she didn't want to force the fourteen-year-old to talk about this tragedy that no words could touch.

There had to have been over one hundred people below them, standing there in the cold, waiting. Despite the many hours that passed, the crowd did not thin. It grew. Relief groups set up nurses' stations, comfort stations, booths with free food and snacks.

Some rescuers suited up in what looked like the most uncomfortable, heavy gear ever designed. Large metal boxes were harnessed on their backs while many tubes connected to various parts of their one-piece jumpsuits on the front. How could they even move in those things? But she guessed breathing was more important, with all the warnings about poisonous gasses down there. What if Uncle Ray and his friends didn't have those? She hadn't seen regular miners wearing them. How could they breathe?

Hannah caught Abigail waving up at her. She pointed to the kids, then motioned toward home. Hannah waved her onward, an unspoken surety that she'd stay right by Liesel's side. Abigail balanced Lenny in her arms as she headed away from them, with Lucas and Lindy following.

Wasn't it a smattering of hours ago Hannah thought about how precious and innocent the Percy children's lives were? All they had to worry about was getting too bored at the All Saints' Day Festival. That should have been going on right now. Hannah was sure no one was in church unless they were holding a prayer vigil. There would be no one around to celebrate this day. How many more lost souls would be honored here soon in the form of funerals?

Hannah saw the man Josh was talking to—when the man first went underground—come out of the shattered opening. He bolstered a man who had trouble walking. He didn't look like he was a rescued miner, rather, another man who went down to help in the rescue operation. These men...they didn't seem to think twice about risking their lives to save someone else.

Josh and several other workers waiting at the mine's opening helped him. A few others followed, again, all rescuers, not miners. Were the reporters right? Should the mine be sealed off? Were they overcome by the gas? If they shut the opening, it would almost certainly seal the fate of the men.

She heard the man say to Josh, "We got down as far as the 3,200. We didn't find anyone else...alive or dead. We hope they found a way to go deeper into the mine to escape the gas. But through that level, the gas is thick. I can't keep these men down there."

Another man emerged and collapsed beside him, gasping for fresh air.

If the rescuers couldn't keep searching this way, how could they find the trapped miners?

Josh said, "If you didn't find bodies down the slope then some of them must have gone below. They're waiting for us, Cal. I'm going to suit up."

"Josh, no!"

"I mean it, Cal. Those are my men!" She watched Josh charge for the Lamp Cabin, no doubt in search of one of those custom outfits the other rescuers were wearing to try to keep the gas out of their lungs. Though what good were they, if everyone still collapsed?

Would Josh even make it out alive? Her heart raced, watching him head for the Lamp Cabin. Was this a good idea? She wrestled. She wanted her uncle back, but would Josh die trying to save him? Was Ray even still alive? Would Josh die in vain?

A faint hum started nearby in the crowd below. She looked around, across the wives, children, other concerned family members, until her eyes landed on a handsome looking, dark-skinned man. He stood out because he was the only dark-skinned man there. The lilt of his voice was pleasant, like a songbird. It transcended the ugliness around them, turning the volume down on the chaos.

As his hums continued, she recognized the tune:

Amazing Grace.

One of her mother's favorites, especially on bad days, for whatever reason.

The children around him—who were spitting images of him—joined his humming in harmony. She recognized two of them from Liesel's show. He must be the miner dad they sang about. The rising song penetrated the buzz of the crowd, as others joined in with them. Perhaps they all hoped for "amazing grace" to step into this town and rescue its own.

But Hannah didn't see any grace around. All she saw was danger and death and risk of more losses. She wondered if grace even existed.

For Josh's sake, she hoped so. He emerged from the Lamp Cabin in that special uniform. Nothing was going to stop him from going down, she was sure. She only hoped it wasn't too late and that he would come back up.

Alive, and with Ray Percy.

♫ ♫ ♫

Josh couldn't hear anything except the sound of his own breath...in and out. In and out. His heartbeat thudded in his ears. He needed it to calm so he could hear, just in case one of his comrades tried to signal him. A sign of life. One tap on a pipe. One kick of a boot. One cry.

When the indicator on the surface showed air being used from a compressed air line, they knew it was possible some men were still breathing underground...still awaiting rescue.

There was no way he could stay above ground one minute longer. Yet now that he was down here, he heard nothing but the deafening sound of silence. He was sure if Moosey were still alive, he'd hear him any moment, asking for a burger with a side of vinegar chips. He had to be getting hungry down here. Josh would buy him a burger every day for the rest of his life, if he could find him. No, not buy. Make. Yeah. He'd cook for Moosey and his wife, Rosalie.

How did this slope get so torn up? It didn't look anything like the path he was used to. Straight, steep pathways. Levels intersecting. Where were they? And where was the trolley and its tracks? Cal said that's what started all this. The rake, a disengaged car sending almost the entire trolley back down into the mine. No wonder it exploded. It was full of coal.

Did his team work far enough away from the rail to avoid the crash? The flames? The poisonous gas that was sure to have followed?

Even with his breathing apparatus, he found getting a good breath to be harder than loosening virgin coal. Forty-five pounds on his back, from the oxygen tank, didn't help either. The walking spaces were narrow. If he found any miners, could he lead them outside? Why did this have to feel so impossible?

In all likelihood, the men were dead.

That's what Adam Sawyer had told the crowd. He had to be covering, in case the worst were true. As the mine's owner, Adam wouldn't raise false hopes. But Josh couldn't accept that. No, he had to keep pressing forward. The compressed air readings proved that. There had to be a way. With about a hundred men still missing, he couldn't stop.

IT HAD TO BE DONE, but Josh still hated it.

Cal's men filled the No. 4 opening with blocks, sealing the holes with cement. People in the crowd whimpered, even protested. He couldn't bear to look at them. He knew the dangers. The meter readings below told them the mine was about to explode again. If anyone survived and it did explode, they'd for sure be killed in the second blast. So would the rescuers. Maybe even some onlookers. But how could he sit here and watch them entomb the men?

Just a few hours, Cal had promised. Then they could unseal it. Just enough to snuff out the fires. The air was feeding it, yet Josh knew all too well that same air was their lifeline below.

His legs felt rubbery as he started the walk toward Maple. Not sleeping for a couple days had caught up to him. As he arrived outside of his home, he looked across the street at the Percy home. He wouldn't go check on them. Not until solid news surfaced.

One way or the other.

Sleep escaped Hannah. She reclined on the cot, staring at the guest cabin ceiling. What would have happened if she'd shown up in Springhill a couple days later? No matter how hard this was, she was glad to be here. Abigail had told her—over a cup of tea in the wee hours of the night—it was as though Hannah was prompted to come. She would agree, if she believed in that sort of thing. But she didn't. This timing was no coincidence. She was running. Running to avoid one disaster only to land squarely in the middle of another.

Yet this was a different mess. They needed her here. They even loved her a little. Plus, they were fighting *for* life, not against it.

She had been so caught up in the effects of the explosion, she almost forgot what Saturday was supposed to be. The thought didn't even flit across her mind until evening. She expected to feel something. Sad. Empty. Regretful. Yet she didn't. She was exactly where she belonged.

She stopped her mind from going over the reactions that were sure to have exploded when they realized she wasn't coming back.

The past few days felt like they stood still, as everyone waited for news. Each hour that passed meant fading hope the outcome would change for anyone who hadn't surfaced.

Sunday would dawn soon. What was Uncle Ray doing? Was he even still alive? Was he down there hoping for that moment when a rescue team would arrive and carry them to safety? There had been no news of him or Moosey, or anyone else on Josh's team as far as Hannah knew. Every time she went, Hannah would see Josh, but he never came to talk to anyone in the Percy family. Was he avoiding them, or was he just focused on helping? She wondered if he ever went home. He looked like he hadn't slept since this whole tragedy began. She'd heard enough talk at the mines to know he was risking his life every moment he chose to go down.

When Hannah drifted off to sleep, the sun was already starting to peek out of its slumber. It seemed like a moment later when she woke up to a knock. She opened the door, still wearing her pajamas.

Liesel stood there. "It's time for us to take our shift. Lucas said they unsealed the mine."

Hannah quickly dressed and met Liesel out by the road. When they arrived at the mines, instead of going to their usual post behind the barricade, Liesel headed straight for the Lamp Cabin.

When they stepped inside, Hannah knew what she was doing: checking the board.

Liesel traced her fingers down the round, brass check tags. She shook her head.

Ray's number was still there. Of course she knew it would be, but she had to check. Liesel touched the soft metal that her father held days earlier, then she headed out the door.

Hannah followed. Instead of going to the mine opening, the girl headed for a bench outside the Lamp Cabin.

"I wish they would let us go down and look," Liesel said, as she sat down.

"Me too, Liesel."

"What if he needs water or food or…he could be hurt, trapped somewhere, waiting for us to find him."

"I hope he is waiting. And if he is, they'll get to him. Josh will find him."

Liesel continued to watch off in the distance, seeming to wrestle with something, before she finally spoke again.

"Hannah, do you believe in heaven?"

This was not the time to shatter the young woman's hopes, to plant seeds of doubt. "I want to."

"But you don't."

"Liesel, I—" Hannah knew she had to choose her words carefully. "My mother and father did. I guess I hope there is a heaven, and that my parents are enjoying their happily ever after. It's just, when you're stuck down here, and you watch all that goes on around us, it's hard to imagine that something else is out there. Someone who watches us suffer this way." The hollow words only made her feel colder. She kicked herself. Why couldn't she keep her opinions quiet?

"Well, I believe in miracles. And it's our turn to get one."

Hannah smiled at Liesel, admired the girl's strength. She wanted to believe her, to share her faith, to find some honest way of encouraging her. "I do know, no matter what happens, you will be okay. Your family will survive."

"Our family."

Hannah liked the sound of that. It had been so long since she'd felt like part of one.

It seemed like every reporter from all over the world had focused in on this little town called Springhill, sharing the stories of hardship and the miracle when someone would come out alive. Hannah had to avoid the sharp eyes of their cameras. The last thing she needed was to end up plastered in some newspaper article or TV broadcast that could run in Toronto.

Whoever they found was brought to the surface, dead or alive. Each time a new face emerged, anticipation rose: was it him?

As night began to fall, Hannah said, "Liesel, we should head home." They'd already been there all day while the rest of the Percy clan attended a prayer vigil at All Saints.

As they got up, Hannah saw another rescuer resurface, yanking off his gasmask. Josh. Something in his face told her the news wasn't good. Liesel didn't notice, so Hannah encouraged her away from the mine yard, glad the girl didn't look back.

ON MONDAY MORNING, a neighbor came over to stay with the Percy children so Hannah could go with Abigail to Legion Hall. It wasn't a good sign to be summoned there. Abigail did not tell the children why they were leaving, as she bundled up in her woolen coat.

Sleet slapped their faces as they walked toward Main Street.

As they arrived at the sidewalk outside the cement building, Hannah could see through the window. Cot after cot was set up inside. This was not a makeshift hospital to treat the wounded. No. These cots cradled those whose lives ended abruptly.

They stepped inside.

A nurse looked over and headed their way, a look of recognition on her face. Her sympathetic eyes, her curved downward mouth spoke volumes. Did this mean the identification was positive?

With her hand, the nurse escorted Abigail to the

correct cot.

Abigail lifted the sheet, revealing the body beneath. She broke down in a rack of sobs that seemed like they would never stop. Hannah froze in place. She willed one foot to step forward, then another. What else could she do, but stand behind Aunt Abby in support?

Abigail whispered over Ray's lifeless body. "You're never going to know this one, Ray. You'll never know him. Or her." Abigail massaged her abdomen. "We didn't pick a name yet. We always do that together."

She's pregnant? A chill crawled down the back of Hannah's spine. Another unborn child who would never know his or her father because of these mines. Plus she'd never really know her uncle, the one she'd just barely met.

Men in St. John's Ambulance Brigade uniforms came in the front door with another casualty on a stretcher. How many would there be before this was over?

Hannah glanced around the room, seeing similar moments playing out for other families. They were here to identify loved ones too.

Then, her eyes landed on Josh. She didn't realize he was here. He looked catatonic, next to a lifeless body. Distinct. Large. No doubt, Moosey. Josh didn't look away from the cot. It was as if no one else were around him, no one except his fallen friend.

Abigail asked the nurse, "Do they know what happened?"

"Details have been sketchy, but it sounds like after those train cars dislodged, it caused a spark down there. One pithead worker said a guy trapped below, around the 5,500 level, talked to the office by phone. He and others couldn't get by the rubble that had become the mine. As far as I know, they haven't found those men yet. But your Ray…he was near the tracks that got the worst of it."

Hannah wondered, how could they allow this to happen to the men? Their own people? Why did life have to be like this in a town that felt like it should be so safe, innocent even? She'd only been here a handful of days and, already, it pierced her to watch such tragedy strike these beloved people. She would never understand why any man would choose to go underground, to put his life at risk. Was it worth the price these families would pay if they traded in their lives? Those left behind would say no. That's what her mother would have said.

How could they do this to people they loved? Couldn't they find another way to provide? She could have grown up with a father here. Her life would not have turned out like it did. And Liesel…she would have her father back, as would so many other fatherless children.

Oh, Liesel. How would they tell her? Hannah tried to swallow the lump. It wouldn't budge.

Through the window, Hannah saw a flurry of commotion. People coming out of stores, running down the street toward the mines. Something was up.

Even Josh looked up from Moosey's body.

Nurses, volunteers, and family members headed for the door. Hannah and Abigail stepped out of Legion Hall.

A swarm of Springhillers raced toward the mines.

Liesel almost bowled them over, breathless, life in her eyes. A wide grin on her face.

"What's going on?" Abigail asked.

"Come on!" Liesel didn't wait, expected them to follow. They followed slower than the teen wanted. She looked back but kept walking. "Mom, you're not going to believe this. They just found a group of men. Alive. As many as fifty. They're bringing them up now. Daddy's gotta be with them! Let's go." As Liesel turned to walk toward the mines, Abigail caught up to her.

"Liesel, baby, no."

"Mother! This is the miracle we were waiting for. Come on." She smiled again and turned back toward the mine yard when Abigail grabbed her arm, stopping her daughter from pressing forward. Defiance crept up on Liesel's face. "What?"

As tears spilled, Abigail shook her head.

"Mom?"

"It's not our miracle, Liesel. It's someone else's."

"What do you mean?"

Abigail stood there wordlessly.

Liesel looked back toward Legion Hall. She charged over to the glass window. Its unobstructed view an advertisement for all the death on the other side. She scanned body after body lying on that sea of cots. Hannah watched as it sunk in: for them, this was over. They had their answer.

"No, No. You saw him?"

Abigail nodded.

With an anguished cry, the teenager ran away from them, the opposite direction of the mine. She dodged many others who raced to find out if they had good news awaiting them at the bottom of that hill.

"Liesel!" Abigail yelled.

But there was no point in calling after her. She wouldn't look back.

And Hannah couldn't blame her.

chapter 5

Liesel stared at the frozen ground of Hillside Cemetery. She should not be here. None of them should. Her family, some of their friends, all in a cluster. They gathered around the future resting place of her dad.

On a normal day, she would have been at school, bored out of her mind. Mrs. O'Brien would be droning on about converting fractions into percentages about now. But today, life wasn't normal.

A better day would have been Dad sneaking them out of school. "Playing hooky," he called it. They could have gone to Prince Edward Island, even though the ferry trips seriously stretched their family's budget. But this?

She looked up at the trees. Anything to not look at Reverend Bacon or her mother's face. Her sister's. The sun shone through the bare birch and elms, their green leaves long changed and fallen. Her mom had really wanted to hold the service at the cemetery, even though the ground was too frozen to bury her father.

Her mittens were no match for the wind.

Everywhere else in town, the light dusting of snow

from a couple days ago looked like slushy dirt. But not here. Not on the hillside. It was far enough away from the mines to leave the pristine flakes untouched.

Except on those plots where family members had already held services.

The last time she'd been here at Hillside Cemetery was to play hide-and-seek with her brother and his friends. It was a warm summer night. Sunset held off till far into the evening. They got away with it three nights in a row until the caretaker caught them. He didn't turn them in, but he made them promise not to come back. They were ruining his grassy landscape. They'd kept their word. Their games resumed in the woods off North Street.

She would have preferred to have never come back here. Certainly not for this.

She glanced at another plot. A funeral was ending. It was for yet another family member who decided to die, long before he should have. Well, decided was not the right word. These men didn't get a choice. How was that determined anyway? Who got to live, who died?

"A miracle of God," they called it, when the men were found alive.

Fifty of them.

Even though she didn't go to the mine to watch that rescue of those fifty men, she'd heard all about it for days. And it was, no doubt, sensational. How they'd made themselves a cave, trying to block off gasses. How they'd used the pipes to breathe. How they panicked when they saw the cement in the water as a sign the company had sealed off the mine opening above. How they banned together, helped one another, in hopes those above hadn't stopped looking for them. Fifty men. Couldn't her father have been fifty-one? Would that have been so hard?

How did those fifty get picked to live when the others, almost forty of them, got marked for death?

Reverend Bacon had already done two of these services today. One was for Matthew. He never came up either. Not alive anyway. Liesel remembered seeing Matthew's father, Caleb, go in and out of the mines, blood dripping down his arm. Burns on his face.

"Liesel, lace your skate."

While Reverend Bacon prattled on, using some Bible verse or purportedly inspiring quote he yanked out for funerals, all Liesel could hear was her father's voice. It was almost like he was still there.

She may not have told her dad how much she loved being with him on that rink. That wasn't the cool thing to do. Secretly, some of her favorite memories were playing with her dad.

"You're it." He'd tag her and skate off before she could even finish tying her laces. He was a big kid sometimes; he loved to win.

Why didn't he win this battle?

Her eyes glanced over the surnames on the stones.

Percy. Wright.

This whole plot was reserved for their family. Even she, one day, would be snoozing below the earth she stood on. That was a creepy thought.

Hannah's father was here. What it must be like to see her birthday splayed as another person's death date. There had been a space for her mother beside him, but she never moved in. Hannah must have had her buried in Toronto.

She could hear her sister, Lindy, sniffling. She was always so emotional. She cried when *Betty Crocker Cooking*

School of the Air radio show was canceled two years ago, even though not once did she have the right ingredients to accurately cook a meal. She cried when Daddy got her a cookbook to make up for it. Lindy cried when she found out Betty Crocker was as fake as Betty Boop. General Mills had made her up.

When her mother joined Lindy's sniffling, Liesel refused to look back at them or cry or pay any attention to the pastor's words. She didn't want to join them. What difference did it make now? Could words or tears honestly change anything?

She knew Josh was behind her. If anyone knew how she felt...it was him. He hadn't said a word to her since all this happened. She couldn't blame him. What was there to say? *"I'm sorry I lived instead."* This wasn't his fault, no. He shouldn't shoulder that burden.

Guilt taunted. How much longer could she live with herself, knowing she was completely to blame?

♫ ♫ ♫

Hannah's aunt maneuvered the packed aisles of Martin's Groceteria with a small shopping cart. Hannah carried Lenny so Abigail could keep her hands free. The little boy had gotten used to her. She hadn't spent much time with toddlers, but she was warming up to him too.

Abigail took a can of green beans off the shelf. "I can't believe Lucas has to go to the police station after school. Since when does he get into vandalism?"

From behind the counter, Martin spoke up. "Can't say

that I blame him. I know we like our welcome sign, but he's right. We did lose thirty-nine men of our population. He was just'a makin' it more accurate."

"Tell that to the Sheriff, Martin."

"Will do. He is my son-in-law."

"Don't be fixin' this for him. Lucas can pay the consequences with community service." Abigail went down another aisle, pulled boxes of pasta and soup cans from the shelves and placed them in her cart. Hannah noted the prices here. She guessed they were higher than the city because of the added cost to truck everything in.

Two pounds of hamburger .55 cents. Sausage .49 cents a pound. Pot Roast .32 cents. One hundred pounds of flour, $6.49. How could Abigail afford to feed her family with these prices? No wonder she avoided most of the meats.

"They take my husband and give me a hundred and ten dollars a month. They call it compensation, as if that's enough. Ray brought in sixty every week."

Sixty a week. That's the value of risking your life?

"Aunt Abby, I'll find work. Some kind."

They brought the cart to the checkout counter. When Martin finished adding up the order, Abigail looked at the total. She checked the contents of her billfold.

"Martin, I'm sorry. Could you take back one bag of rice and one of those pastas?"

"You keep what'cha need for them kids. I can float'cha."

Tears brimmed Abigail's appreciative eyes.

AFTER THEY UNLOADED GROCERIES, Hannah ventured back to Main Street. She had to find a job. But what was a woman to do when the main industry in town was coal mining? It was too bad she couldn't take Lindy up on her offer to hire her at Sweet Lindy's Penny Candy. Lindy promised not to eat all the profits if they could open the store a decade early. But Hannah knew she had to do something long before the eight-year-old was mature enough to pull off her enterprising venture. Plus, they had no start up money to try to something new.

Hannah visited Lucas and Liesel's high school, hoping to find a place to teach music. But the music teacher had been there for over thirty years. She had no retirement plans, no need for an assistant.

After Hector turned her down, since he couldn't afford any employee except himself, she headed for the Five & Dime. Maybe that would be a fun place to work. But then she met Miss Mary Lou Lipnicki. She was about Hannah's age, blonde bobbed hair, and spoke with a high-pitched, almost whiny voice. For some reason, she seemed to feign politeness. That was a first for this town, where everyone had been pleasant and friendly. Did Mary Lou have something against Hannah already?

Mary Lou filled a jar with one-cent lollipops. "You got smog in that there noggin'? Nobody 'round Main Street can hire outside family. And you are not a Lipnicki."

Obviously, that door was closed to her too.

After a long day of searching, Hannah stirred rice at the stove. Abigail steamed vegetables.

Lucas set the table. "Mom, please. It's the best solution for us to get enough money to live on."

"No, Lucas."

They'd been going round and round, since Hannah joined them.

The walkie-talkie sitting on the kitchen table boosted Lindy's voice, though fuzzy. "Is the baby gonna pop out a boy? Over."

Her question went ignored as Lucas continued his protest. "I want to work in the mines."

"Nobody *wants* to work in the mines, Lucas. They only do it because they have to," Abigail said.

"And I have to. We need it."

"They won't let you. You are not seventeen, thanks to my good Lord." Abigail put her hand over the stove, feeling for warmth. "Lucas, please gather more coal for the stove."

"We could tell them I'm old enough."

"You know how I feel about lying."

Lindy's voice screeched over the radio again. "I'm placing my order for a sister. S-I-S-T-E-R. Got it?"

Abigail picked up the walkie-talkie. "Lindy, come help set the table while your brother goes outside to get the coal. And if you keep making noise with this...whatever it is, I'm going to make you return it to Josh."

Someone rapped at the front door. Lucas put his hand on the back porch screen door. "You said yourself it's the only job in town that pays enough for our family."

Was there no other way to save this family? To keep them in their home? Keep them fed? Not to mention the new little one on the way.

Lindy entered with a casserole.

"Who was at the door, Lindy?" Abigail asked.

"Josh is here, Mom. He made us dinner. Finally. A vacation from rice and green stuff."

Josh entered behind Lindy and removed his hat. He hadn't been inside this house since the disaster.

"Josh, I want you to teach me how to make casseroles," Lindy said.

Abigail nodded to the casserole dish and looked at Josh. "Thank you, Josh."

"And desserts," Lindy added.

Hannah glanced at Josh. Would she have the chance to get to know him soon?

Closer.

Maybe not in the way he had hinted. He wouldn't even know it was happening.

She had an idea of how to save this family. As far as she knew, this was the only way to do it.

AS SHE WAS GETTING READY for bed, Hannah rubbed cream on her neck. The bruises had faded. Seemed like a lifetime ago, when she'd left that little yellow cottage in her rearview.

As she put the cream bottle back, her engagement ring clattered out of the cosmetic pouch. She stuffed it back inside. It was bound to be worth something, wasn't it? Yes. She could sell it. But not here. Maybe in Amherst. People in Springhill would gossip about the new girl selling an engagement ring. It hardly looked like an heirloom, so anyone would suspect it was new when she got it.

She had inherited her mother's wedding and engagement rings upon her mother's death, ones Mama faithfully wore and never removed, even though Daddy was gone. Hannah intended to use them when her turn at love came. And yet, for some reason, she hid them. Couldn't bring herself to use them.

Shouldn't that have told her something before she

accepted this new, shiny one? She knew her mother wouldn't have approved of him and didn't want to equate their love — or whatever it could be called — to the genuine love her parents held for each other.

Inside her cosmetic pouch was a tiny box that held those two precious rings of Mama's. It was tempting to put them on, just to hold her mother closer. But she had always vowed she wouldn't wear them until the man she'd marry would place them on her finger. She knew of the strong possibility that she'd never get married. Still, she resisted the urge to try them on and tucked them back into the tiny box.

Hannah curled up with the tattered journal. She never got tired of reading her daddy's words. Her finger traced across a page. *Lord, my heart aches to be a father. We've tried for so long to bring a new life into this world. I pray you bless me with a little girl.*

Daddy considered her a blessing before Mama was even pregnant. A lump formed in her throat. How much she wished she could have known a man who loved a daughter he didn't even have yet, one who would write journal entries of prayers about her. They were petitions to the Lord, whom her daddy believed could change their plight. The entries were so plentiful, years worth, dating back five years before her daddy died, and before her mama finally conceived. This was obviously something they had desired for a long time before it came to pass. He'd even given her a name:

Hannah Melody.

Hannah, for the woman in the Bible who had trouble conceiving until God blessed her with a baby. And Melody, partly after himself, Melvin, and because he knew she would bring music into his life.

How painful it must have been to her mother, to experience the joy of her daddy's answered prayers without him. What kind of God does that to people? Gives them what they ask for when they can no longer be here to enjoy the blessing? And what kind of God leaves a fifteen-year-old girl an orphan? And why didn't he rescue her when...

No, she couldn't blame him for that one.

She'd made bad choices. She couldn't blame him for not showing up the handful of times she'd asked. She got herself into that mess. But her parents? They loved him, served him, believed him. And look where it got them.

Buried in the earth.

Anger swelled inside her.

Chip. Chip. Chip. What was that odd noise, coming from outside?

She got up and peeked out her window. A person stood on their lawn, lit up by a street lamp.

She put on her coat and stepped outside. The cold, night air slapped her in the face.

The house was dark, everyone likely asleep. She spotted Josh in the front yard with a long, sharp garden tool, banging on the now frozen ice rink that Ray made. It hadn't been used yet. Not even once, as if it were a sled abandoned at the top of an inviting, snowy hill no one dared to enjoy.

"Josh, what are you doing?"

He didn't look at her, just kept chipping away at the ice. "Ray always liked a smooth rink. The bumps make Lindy fall."

"It's late, Josh. This will keep."

When he didn't stop chipping, Hannah fought within herself. Should she touch him? Should she try to comfort? Let him know he can stop blaming himself? It's something he should already know, but maybe he needed to hear it. She gently touched his arm. He froze, not looking at her. Was this a bad idea? She didn't pull away.

After a long, uncomfortable silence, he spoke. "Does she...does Abigail wonder why I'm here? Every time she sees me, she must."

"No, she doesn't. Nobody here thinks like that, Josh."

"I should have saved him."

"You tried. We all know it."

"What if I had been there?"

"You'd be dead." She kept her hand steady on his arm. It felt strong and muscular. Yet he'd chosen to be vulnerable with her, instead of putting up a front. She'd never been this close to a man who was willing to do that.

The porch light came on. Hannah quickly released his arm as they both turned to the door.

Abigail stepped out, a robe over her nightclothes, hugging her sides to stave off the cold.

"Josh, it's okay to go home. We're okay."

"Abby, I'm sorry. If I hadn't…" He stopped, as if he couldn't continue to speak.

Abigail stepped down off the front steps, carefully, the same board still broken because "tomorrow" didn't come for Ray. She walked over to Josh, across the ice, even though she only had on slippers. She maintained an affectionate grip on his shoulders. "You did Ray a favor, Josh, because he asked you to. Because that's the kind of friend you were. This was not your fault."

Abigail took Josh in the warm embrace he'd probably

needed since this whole tragedy stuck. Tears streamed down his face.

Hannah spotted Liesel watching them out her window. Did she hear what her mother said?

Hannah slipped away and headed inside the main house. She ascended the stairs and found herself outside Liesel and Lindy's room. She knocked lightly. There was no point to waking Lindy too.

She was met with only silence. Liesel wouldn't come to the door.

"WOULD YOU MIND?"

"Not at all, Aunt Abby." Hannah knew it took a lot for her aunt to ask her to help pack Ray's clothes. Hannah couldn't imagine the pain of taking a husband's belongings and putting them in a box labeled "Salvation Army." Did her mother go through this same ritual with her dad's clothes?

With every item that went in the box, she wondered if Abigail remembered the last time he wore it. What jokes he'd told. What he was doing. How he'd smiled. The way Abigail brought them to her nose his scent must have still been there.

Hannah promised to take the box to the donation place, so Abigail wouldn't have to. But instead, she carried them to the guest cabin. If her plan had any chance of working, she'd need them.

Hannah took out her father's journal and turned to a blank, yellowed page. She wrote inside:

I always wondered why my father made the choice he did to work in the mines. Until the day I found myself backed into the same corner, in a town with one industry: coal. Every day, beneath the surface, will be a battle to survive. I have no choice but to join them.

She fingered Ray's old jeans, t-shirts, belts. Thankfully, he had several of those. She opened a bag, labeled Lipnicki's, pulled out a little disguise. A mustache, bushy eyebrows, a man's wig, left over from their Halloween collection. An Ace bandage.

She wrapped the Ace bandage around her breasts to flatten them. Thankfully, her small frame did not make that too difficult. She breathed in and out, eyeing herself in the mirror, as she went through the metamorphosis.

Could she pull this off?

chapter 6

Bryce Sawyer hated the mines. Always. For as long as he could remember. He hadn't missed them at all in the past four years since he left this town behind, coughing on his dust. For him, Springhill should have been named after winter, as cold as its people were toward him. He hadn't done anything to them. It was all on their consciences. No way was this his fault.

His guitar and backpack strained his shoulder and neck muscles as he walked down Main Street, toward the Cumberland Coal entrance. He hoped none of the shop owners would notice him; he was in no mood for idle chitchat. Perhaps they wouldn't recognize him anyway. Not like they were expecting his return.

As he neared the archway, that same souring he always felt there settled into the pit of his stomach. He didn't want to step foot on this property, but there was no point going by the house. His father wouldn't be there.

His father never came home after a disaster. As the mine owner, he worked around the clock, in the same clothes, from the office. No doubt, he even slept on that unsightly orange couch, the one his mother booted out of their home more than a decade ago. That atrocity would be his father's bed until every last sliver of paperwork got filed, every "T" crossed, "I" dotted. He had his priorities.

As he walked across the grounds, he hoped there wouldn't be too many miners coming and going. Deliberately, he'd timed his arrival not to coincide with a shift transition. Well, if they'd even gone back to work yet. He didn't know. But if they had, he was sure the timing would be the same. Nothing ever changed here. Unless you count the number of men working for his father. That was often in flux.

That's why everyone hated them.

The last thing he needed were miners mouthing off about what a disappointment he'd been. Or how much people hated his family because they owned the mines that kept taking lives of the men in this town. He'd gotten enough of that growing up in schools around here.

When he stepped inside the Cumberland office, his father was involved in a conversation with Cal Weston, his long-time mine manager. They didn't even notice him waiting.

The room was scorching. The radiator—which hadn't lost its obnoxious ping—worked too well in this tiny box, poor excuse for an executive's office. Sweat broke out under his clothing.

He swallowed hard. His father looked more stressed than usual. Unhealthy, even. He'd aged a lot in the past four years since he'd seen him. His hair more silver, the lines on his face more defined. His brow, no doubt, was permanently creased from all the anxiety. But what could he expect, after a tragedy struck the workers of this company? His dad always did have a conscience, no matter how many people died serving him. This town both hated and depended on this industry.

And there it was. That hideous, orange couch. A bunched up sheet and pillow rested on the end. A few more holes exposed the shabby craftsmanship. If his mother were still alive, she'd have it burned, even if it weren't in her parlor anymore. Not that she ever came down here to see Dad anyway. She always said the mining grounds were no place for a woman. If Dad wanted to see her, he'd have to show up for dinner; she wasn't bringing it to him. Wasn't worth the walk across Lisgar Street. Thoughts of his spirited mother accented that hole inside him, left by the only one that ever liked him, not just loved him.

Was his father fighting physical pain? Something about the way he massaged his shoulder didn't look good.

Cal asked, "Are you sure you're okay, Adam?"

"I'm fine."

"Maybe you should head home. You ain't lookin' so hot."

"But I need to finish these reports."

"The Union can wait one more day."

They had no idea who just walked in the door, or they would have paid attention. Workers and engineers came and went, often to check the clipboards on the wall beside him. Logging progress, coal tonnage, gas levels, accidents, safety inspections. They must have assumed he was one of them.

But he'd never be one of them. Ever.

He may have broken a lot of promises in the past, but that was one vow he planned to keep.

When he realized his father and Cal weren't talking, he

looked over from the clipboards to find them staring at him. Did his dad not have anything to say to him? His long lost son?

Cal finally spoke. "Hello, Bryce. Welcome back."

"Cal." Bryce nodded at him. Despite everything, he always liked Cal. He was the one good choice his father made. That, and pursuing his livewire mother. He looked back at his father. "When the prodigal son returned home, his father gave him a party."

"The prodigal son's father was happy to see him."

Bryce smirked. Some things never changed.

"Well." Cal cleared his throat. "I'm going with Mr. Rush on his gas inspection. We hope to let the men go back to work tomorrow, Mr. Sawyer." Who could blame the mine manager for not wanting to witness this not-so-happy reunion?

His dad nodded as Cal headed out, then winced in pain.

"So, I hear you've had an eventful time, Dad."

His father sized up Bryce's luggage. "What's the matter? Can't live off your guitar anymore?"

Bryce was not about to give his father the satisfaction of telling him all the ways his time away from Springhill had been a failure. "So, how many men, Dad?"

"We saved eighty-eight."

"And how many did you lose? Fifty-five? Sixty?"

"Thirty-nine." His father blew out a breath. Already, it seemed he was losing patience with him.

As if saved by the door, a man walked in. Mustache. Unkempt hair. Scrawny fellow. Not someone Bryce had met before, and for that, he was grateful.

His dad asked, "What can I do you for, Sir?"

The guy cleared his throat then shifted back and forth. "I'm here to apply for a job, Sir."

"We just closed a whole mine shaft. We still need to figure out if we have room for the displaced men."

"Please, sir. I, I need the work." The poor guy looked petrified, eyes darting about the room.

"What's your name?"

That was Dad. If someone else needed attention, his father gave it to him. Who cares that he hasn't seen his own son in four years? Let's have a "getting to know Mr. Scrawny party" instead.

"My name's Mel. Mel Wright."

"Any relation to Melvin Wright?"

The man hesitated, then finally said, "He was my second cousin."

"Melvin worked for me decades ago. Before you were born, I assume? Try back here in a few months. We'll see if we can find a place for ya."

The man waited a few moments, then shuffled out. Bryce almost felt bad for the fellow. He knew what it was like to need money, only to confront slammed doors.

Bryce noticed his father turn toward the back wall and hold onto the corner of his desk. Something had to be wrong. He was breathing so heavily.

"Dad, are you okay?"

His father's face went white as he grabbed his left arm and fell over.

BRYCE WALKED DOWN THE STERILE, cream-colored halls of All Saints' Hospital. He headed back toward his father's room with a cup of coffee, trying not to look into the other patient rooms. But that would be like not looking at a derailed train while passing by. It was hard to miss the families surrounding their men with gauze-wrapped limbs. No doubt those burned in the explosion. One had a leg held up in a sling. Their families seemed happy by their bedsides. The alternative was gathering around headstones.

He saw one little girl, five, maybe six years old bring a drawing to her father. He received her with open arms, despite two wrapped elbows. A smile stretched across his face. So that's what it was like. A doting dad.

Bryce walked to the last room in the hall, and stepped into his father's room, balancing the fresh coffee. He was tempted to get an orange blanket, just so his dad would feel more at home in this colorless environment. "Don't tell Nurse Grumpy I got this for you."

His dad took the cup appreciatively. Bryce had left the room for more than coffee. He needed the space after what he'd asked his father. A question he was sure the old tycoon never expected.

His father finally spoke. "So, you think you should take my place at the mines."

"It's what you've always wanted, right?"

His father's nostrils flared in and out as he took deep breaths. "Not like this."

"I've been around mines my whole life."

"Around. Not in. You are hardly qualified to run my company."

"And you are? In this shape?"

"You don't give a rip about those mines or the people in them. You need money because—"

"This is not about money, Dad. You ordering another heart attack?" A passion that surprised even him rose.

When he left Springhill, he didn't care if he never saw his father again. Then he'd heard about the disaster. The idea of his father, alone, going up against the town and its opinions drove him nuts. Why, he wasn't sure. But here he was, fighting to stay with him. And not just with him, but to help manage the place. Not go underground, of course, but to be in charge.

"If I didn't know any better," the tycoon even grinned a little bit, "I would think you actually cared about what happens to your old man."

♫ ♫ ♫

It was the first time Josh had been called to the mines since all rescue attempts had come to a grinding halt. They were told to bring work clothes, in case they were assigned to a new shift after the meeting.

He couldn't get the thought of the deceased men out of his head. How did they know for sure the rest of them were dead when they sealed that mine the second time? And not just for those few hours. It was still sealed. They told him and everyone else no one could possibly be alive. It had been over a week since the last man was rescued. He hated the idea they were buried underground, and not in the proper way.

But Josh cared about the rescuers too. They had already risked so much. Another blow up would have wiped out so many more. More men than those who were trapped and likely not alive. It wasn't worth the risk after that point. But sealing the mines meant some of their friends were underground, rotting. It was hard to get closure without a body.

Those who still considered themselves employees of Cumberland Coal, whether they liked it or not, filed into the Lamp Cabin, including those who'd survived the explosion and were well enough to leave the hospital.

As Josh stepped into the back, he spotted him:

Bryce Sawyer.

What on earth was Bryce doing here?

Josh enjoyed the company of most people. Yet, Bryce was about his least favorite person; he had been for a long time.

Cal Weston rallied the men to begin their meeting. "Adam Sawyer is at All Saints, recovering. We're not sure when he will return."

Josh heard Isaak, next to him, as he uttered a prayer for Adam. He always respected Isaak's deep faith, his willingness to go straight to prayer, on the spot. Isaak didn't get into that "I'll pray for you later" stuff. He got right down to business with "The Man Upstairs."

Bryce stepped forward next to Cal, straightening his back as if he were trying to look taller. "Until my father returns, I am taking over."

Was he kidding? Josh scanned the other perplexed faces in the room; he was not alone.

A fellow miner, Hicks, shot his hand up but didn't wait to be called on. "Boy? Y'ever been in a mine? I don't think so." Josh always liked Hicks, even though he'd never been on a team with him. In his forties, Hicks had worked here for a couple of decades.

Bryce ignored Hicks. Didn't even look his direction. "We will not reopen the number four. There's too much damage. So, for those who worked there, we're moving you to the two where the other miners have been."

A young man shouted out, "I got transferred to the four 'cause two ain't safe." Josh knew of him as "Lazy Haze," an affectionate nickname given to him underground by his team. He was a laborer, not a full-fledged miner. He couldn't be more than twenty-two.

"You need work. At least my company is providing a solution."

Another miner, Eddie Plummer, known as Plum, bit into a cracker before speaking up with his mouth full. "Didn't take long to become *your* company, Bryce. Boy, you ain't got nothing to do with this company. We kept it goin'."

Another miner Josh didn't recognize spoke up, his forehead creasing with beads of sweat. "When can we go into the four to recover the rest of the bodies?"

Cal said, "Not for a while."

"We need to bury our comrades!"

"It's not safe yet. We are not risking anyone else's life."

"Except when you need coal. Then you'll send us down."

Others voiced similar sentiments:

"They deserve a proper burial."

"We ain't working till they get it."

One by one, miners walked out. Five, six of them maybe. But then it stopped. The rest of them stood there, not sure of what to do. Too many of them had families to feed. While it was tempting, Josh wouldn't know what to do if he walked out. Mining was his life, not just his lifeline.

"Anyone else care to join them?" Bryce looked many of them in the eye, straight on, as if to challenge them. It made

Josh want to spit, to walk on out principle. How could Cal and especially, Adam Sawyer, let this happen?

No one made a move.

"There's plenty of work. I'm sure you guys would like to receive a paycheck again. We need you to start right away. We have production to make up for. Cal will give you shift times and team information."

For the first time, Bryce glanced Josh's way, stared at him. Cal called out teams and shift times. It all sounded like a jumble. A mix of familiar and unfamiliar names.

As soon as the ridiculous meeting ended, Josh traipsed outside. He breathed in the air, knowing he was appointed to head down now, on the first shift back. The idea of going down with all new people, even if he knew some of them, made his mind wander over those he'd lost. It wouldn't be the same. Did he have to start all over again? Form new bonds? It reminded him of what it was like after a break-up with a young lady, knowing he'd need to have those same "getting-to-know-you" conversations with someone new.

In the mine yard, Cal Weston jogged over to him. "Josh, wait up."

Josh stopped. "I can't believe we gotta put up with Bryce playin' at mining, Cal."

"That's why I need you down there, Josh. Your father was one of the best overmans I ever had. That's why I assigned you to run the new team at the 13,000 level."

Lazy Haze and Hicks passed by, heading for the Wash House to suit up. Lazy Haze's whole body trembled as he said, "I can't do it. Can't go down again. I hate the number two."

Hicks guided the younger man. "It'll be fine, Lazy Haze. I's with ya."

"And Bryce will agree to this promotion? For me?"

"He knows. And he agreed, without the pay boost."

"Figures."

Josh's jaw tensed as he saw Bryce heading their way. Mark Steinberg, the head of the Miner's Union was with him. He'd always liked Mark. No-nonsense, a bit of a hard-nose, but always looking out for the miners.

Bryce put his hands on his hips and looked Josh in the eye. "Winslow, don't you have a lamp to pick up?"

Josh glared at Bryce, then shook Mark's hand. "About time the Union stepped in. Glad you're here, Mark."

"I'm here to do an inspection. I'd love to meet with you after you have a chance to go down. Cal tells me you'll be leading a team?"

Josh glanced at Bryce. "That's right. We need people who actually know how this place is run."

Josh recalled the many times Bryce swore he'd never play a role in the operations of this place. Even taunted Josh for doing so himself. "So Bryce, whatever happened to, 'I'll never sink as low as you, Winslow?'"

Bryce took a step forward, leaving his face inches from Josh's. "Signing your paycheck, Winslow, hardly as low."

Josh stared Bryce down before heading off for the Wash House alone. As much as he believed in this place and this town, he wasn't sure this would be worth it. Trying to help keep a company afloat for someone so undeserving?

He had to remember…this wasn't just about Bryce or himself. This was about Springhill and its people. They needed to come back from this disaster, for everyone's sakes.

♫ ♫ ♫

When Hannah first arrived under the arches of
Cumberland Coal, she noticed a large group of miners in a
meeting. After it broke up and the miners dispersed, some
heading into the number two mine, Hannah walked over to
the office front door, disguised as Mel. Hopefully, no one
would recognize Ray Percy's shirt. She tried to pick out as
many plain shirts as he had, and donated away the ones
with memorable patterns.

She couldn't fail again. Abigail and her kids were
depending on this. Her aunt, of course, would never
approve; she had to keep this idea a secret.

She cleared her throat, stepped inside the office, and
folded her hands so they wouldn't shake. The same man
who was with the owner the last time now sat at the main
desk, buried in a mountain of paperwork. He looked to be
close to her age. Feathered, sandy brown hair. He reminded
her of a boy she went to high school with, one she had to
coach herself to not fall for. The type whose love stories
never turned out well for the girl.

His green eyes looked up at her. "You again."

"Yes. I know what the owner said."

"You need a translator?"

So, he wasn't going to make this easy. But she thought
she saw empathy that first time she visited. He went back
to looking at paperwork.

She did her best to lower the register of her voice.
"Listen to me. Please." She swallowed twice, then
approached his desk in three large strides. A passion rose
up in her. "My family lost people in that explosion. The
compensation from here won't put scraps on the table.

Have you ever needed a job so bad, but no one would give you a chance?" She knew she had his attention. She didn't have her feminine side for appeal. But whatever she was doing as "Mel" was putting a crack in his armor. "I mean no disrespect, Sir. What's your name?"

"Bryce. My father owns this place, but now I'm running the show. You got papers?"

"Papers?" *What did that mean?*

"Can't mine without papers. But you can work as a laborer. They carry coal and build stone packs."

"Really? Does this mean..."

Bryce smiled at her. She wasn't sure what was behind his implicit yes. Something she couldn't explain flashed across his green eyes. Almost like he was being mischievous. "I have a guy down there who loves working with newbies. I'll put you with Josh Winslow's team. Weekdays, three to eleven."

Why did he appear to enjoy the idea of sending her to Josh's team? She was elated *and* sunk. Could she pull this off? Would Josh see through her disguise? It was a chance she'd have to take. If he figured her out, he may even understand a little.

Bryce got up from the desk and walked her over to a bulletin board that had a diagram on the wall labeled *No. 2 Layout.* It showed the downward slope and the working levels that intersected it. Bryce pointed to the 13,000 foot level, two levels above the mine's lowest point.

"Winslow's team is on this level."

"Wow. That looks, ah, far down." Hannah swallowed, as her voice rose too much. She cleared her throat.

"About two miles. Welcome to the deepest coal mine in North America."

After Bryce handed her a stack of paperwork to fill out as a new employee, she found herself writing her name as H. MEL WRIGHT and checking the box that said male.

He sent her to the Wash House to get boots, a miner's coat and gloves. Fritz, in the Lamp Cabin, assigned the mine's newest employee a check number: #364.

She placed her tag on the board and took a charged up lamp that had the same number engraved. She was grateful Fritz didn't ask questions, given that she had spoken to him not long ago about her father. With Bryce there, Fritz didn't seem too talkative. In fact, his friendliness drained out of him, the way black and white photos unsaturated the colors of real life.

Bryce walked her over to the train car. His forehead glistened with beads of sweat, as they got closer.

"A full day comes to about ten dollars. But I'm only paying you for half today." He breathed heavier too. What was wrong with him? Wasn't she the one going underground?

Bryce spoke to the operator who worked the trolley at the mouth of the mine. "Take Mr. Wright down to Winslow's level, 13,000."

The operator rolled his eyes, like he had no patience for Bryce. Did no one like this guy? "This rake don't go down that far. He'll have to catch the other."

So that's what it was called: a rake. Wasn't it the rake of coal cars that dislodged and caused the explosion?

"Fine. Take him as far as you go." Bryce headed the other way, unbuttoning the top of his shirt, even though the temperature outside was chilly. Having experienced enough anxiety in her life, she could recognize the symptoms. What was he so afraid of?

"Get in," the rake operator said.

She climbed onto a seat. The rake lurched forward as it began its trek down into "the deeps" of the number two mine. That's what Mama said Daddy called this place. The clack of the wheels loudly bumped. She flipped on her lamp, offering a bit more illumination.

With each lurch forward, she questioned her wisdom. It took an eternity to travel down to the stop. It was so dark on both sides. Work lights offered little visibility on the way down. The air quality changed too, like it was getting thin. Was it getting harder to breathe? How would exerting so much physical energy affect her ability to breathe down here? How had her father stood it? And Josh? Or Ray? How would she?

She fingered her father's check tag, still safely stowed in her pocket. If he could do it, so could she. She took out the solid, shiny piece of brass and opened her hand. She used her lamp to see its number: #712.

"I know you're new here, guy," the rake operator said, "but you're supposed to drop that check tag off at the Lamp Cabin when you come down. Not sure how Fritz missed that one, when he gave you that lamp."

"Oh, okay. He did tell me. I forgot." Didn't want Fritz getting in trouble on her behalf. Nor did she want to explain this wasn't her check tag. She shoved it back into her pocket.

The rake screeched as it stopped. It was time to hop out and catch the other rake that went deeper into the mine.

"Head down thataway." He swung his arm toward the darkest cave she'd ever seen.

If she hadn't made so many mistakes in her life, she'd wonder if this were the biggest one of all.

chapter 7

Josh arrived at his new level. Familiar faces had been assigned to his team: Isaak, Plum, Hicks, and Lazy Haze. Lazy sat against the wall of coal instead of working. He hoped that name didn't mean they'd have to carry his weight for him. He may be just a laborer — not a miner picking coal — but that didn't mean his job wasn't important to everyone's safety. If people like Lazy Haze didn't keep up with the stone packs — move them or build new ones as they advanced on the coalface — the roof could cave in on them. They'd had enough losses around here lately.

"Come on, Lazy. Get to work on those stone packs." Josh smiled. "Don't want the roof kissin' Isaak's bald spot."

Isaak shot him a grin. At least he brought his good humor to work with him today. As always. "If you had eleven kids, you'd lose some of that hair too, Josh."

Josh had been blessed with good genes and a full head of hair. But he'd give up every last strand for a house full of kids. At this rate, would he even have one or two? His dream of having a flock was so out of reach, as the one desire he'd always wanted most seemed so elusive to him:

A wife to love. Cherish. Honor. Protect. Raise children with him.

Everyone from his school days — except him — had progressed in this way. Most accused him of being too picky when he'd try to date. But he knew. The right person was out there for him. He just hadn't found her yet.

Why did his thoughts suddenly flit to Hannah? Maybe because he *had* found that person and she wouldn't say yes to a date yet. He wouldn't know for sure until she'd give him a chance and let him get to know her. Let him see the real her, so he could figure out if her arms around him brought comfort like his mother's handmade blanket. He could still picture Mom on the couch, knitting the various shades of blue together.

Lazy Haze bumbled over to his stone pack and threw a rock in the middle.

Isaak's smooth, calming voice spoke. "Hang in there, Haze. We're all fine."

"For the here and now."

Hicks muttered to Josh and Isaak, "He hasn't been the same since the explosion. I should'a been caught with him, but I got me a flu that day. Best flu I ever had."

Josh whipped around to eye Lazy Haze. "You were trapped?" No wonder. He should lighten up on the kid.

"For over three days."

"How 'bout you, Josh?" Hicks asked. "Was you workin' that day?"

"Day shift."

"Now, ain't that stinkin' lucky."

Luck had nothing to do with it. He doubted the Percys felt that was lucky. All he felt like doing was picking coal. And hard. He grabbed a pick and started banging at the coalface.

Plum said, "Why's any of us workin'? I can't see doin' nothin' for this company till they let us empty the four."

Isaak picked at the black wall beside Josh. "We don't like it either. But it's time we move forward. As a team. As a town. This is our survival, and those people out there...they are depending on us."

"Move forward? Tell that to my brother whose son ain't been buried." Plum spit on the floor.

Isaak put down his pick and rested a comforting hand on Plum's shoulder. Plum opened a chocolate bar and took more than a mouthful.

Josh couldn't remember seeing Plum when he wasn't munching on something. In a way, he reminded him of Moosey, without the consequential weight gain. Boy, he sure did miss his old pal. "We all lost people, Plum. I know this isn't the team we're used to. But we can do this."

Isaak nodded. "Josh is right. Let's hold it together."

Out of the darkness came another lamp. Its light bounced across the walls as a man stepped into view. "I'm looking for Josh Winslow's team. I'm here to build rock stacks."

Everyone else turned to look at the stranger too. He looked young. Definitely on the small side.

Lazy Haze chuckled. "Rock stacks? That's a good'un. Anyone here smell a newbie?"

Josh stepped forward and shook the man's hand. "Stone packs." His hand sure was small. Did he even have any muscles built up for this line of work? "I'm the overman, Josh Winslow. Name?"

"Mel."

Plum grunted as he licked the last of the chocolate

from his lips and grabbed his coal pick. "Always stuck with the newbies."

Hicks pointed back toward Plum. "That's grouchy over there. We call him Plum. And I'm Hicks. We were all newbies at one time."

"I'm Al Hazen, the other rock stacker." Lazy Haze cracked himself up. Nice to see him lighten up. Perhaps working with the newbie would be a good distraction for him. A fart slipped out of Haze.

"Lazy Haze!" Hicks covered his downwind nose.

Isaak stepped forward, also offering a handshake. "I'm Isaak Revere. You need any help, just sing out, 'kay?"

AFTER A FEW HOURS, the team gelled, getting into a groove. Lazy Haze showed Newbie how to crisscross timbers when building a pack. Then, he shared about his time underground in the explosion. "From Thursday to Monday mornin'. Fifty of us was sittin' in a cave, waitin' for thems to come get us. Torture, it was."

Newbie asked, "And you still came back down?"

"Yep. I was frettin' every day, even before that happened. Us laborers, we make less than them boys picking coal, but the risk...it's all the same."

Suddenly, they heard a loud thud. The newbie was on his butt, with timber over his shoulder. Apparently, this one needs to build up some muscle power.

The newbie tried to laugh it off. "Sorry. Balance."

Isaak stepped in, offered Mel a hand. "Don't you be worrying down here, Mel. Disasters like that, they don't happen very often. And if we ever get a bump, best place to be is next to a pack. Right where you're working."

"A bump...that's like an underground earthquake, right?"

Lazy Haze said, "Better known in town as the widow-maker. And number two...she's the widowest makingest."

"Stop scaring the boy, Haze," Isaak said. "Ya been in Springhill long, Mel?"

"Couple weeks."

"You favor an old buddy of mine. Melvin Wright. Any relation?"

"He's a distant cousin."

Huh. With another relative in town, maybe Hannah would stick around.

At the shift's end, the team took the slow, two-mile ride back up to the mouth of the mine. Bone tired, no one had much energy. Except Isaak, who always had enough left in him to sing or hum a song on the skyward jaunt. Josh had ridden back up from the deeps with him before, even if they hadn't been on the same team. He was grateful to have him now.

The six of them schlepped toward the Lamp Cabin to drop off their lamps and pull their check tags off the board.

As they headed for the Wash House, Josh noticed the newbie hurting more than the rest. Josh remembered those days, when first exercising muscles he didn't know existed. "It'll get easier, Mel."

Right when they opened the Wash House door to shower with the other miners, the newbie whirled the other way.

Lazy yelled out, "Hey, Mellie. Where ya goin'?"

But Newbie disappeared.

♫ ♫ ♫

Hannah was sure, if her face hadn't been covered in black coal dust, everyone on her team would have seen her cheeks as red as a Christmas bow.

Not expecting to get a job on the spot, she hadn't quite thought through how all of this was going to work. But walking into a Wash House with naked men expecting her to shower with them...she certainly wouldn't get away with that.

She broke into a fit of giggles on her brisk walk back to the guest cabin. What a predicament. She knew she had to sneak into her haven before Josh showered and came home across the street. She couldn't risk him seeing Mel coming and going. But how would she navigate a distant cousin working in town who hadn't come to meet Abigail? She had to use her real name to get paid. H. Mel Wright. No other cover story would have worked.

Oh, well. She didn't have time to solve all the intricacies of her plan. What she needed was a hot shower and food, then a bed.

Since she didn't realize Bryce was going to send her underground, she hadn't packed lunch. Her team generously shared, but the physical labor made her ravenous.

Hannah stepped into the steaming shower and watched the black go down the drain. It took a while. With her aching muscles, she didn't mind.

She put on her nightclothes and wrapped herself in a plush, light pink robe that Abigail left for her, along with other clothes. She must have noticed Hannah didn't have much.

She put on her loafers and headed for the Percys' back door. Abigail always left it unlocked.

Inside, Liesel was at the stove, warming up soup. What was she doing up so late? The scent of its vegetables, broth, chicken, and fresh herbs wafted through the kitchen.

"Hi, Liesel."

"Would you like soup?"

"Yes, if you don't mind."

"I didn't feel like eating earlier. Mom wondered where you were."

"I'm sorry." Hannah had forgotten, in her impromptu trip two miles below the earth's surface, that she should have let Abigail know she wasn't coming home. But there was no time. She could hardly make a phone call in front of Bryce, using her own voice.

"Been out looking for a job." At least that wasn't a lie. Hannah joined Liesel at the table over a warm bowl of goodness. She watched the blue-eyed beauty sip some soup and added crackers to her own.

"Liesel, how are you?"

Liesel kept her eyes on her food for a few beats. It was clear Hannah wasn't asking the obligatory question, expecting an empty answer. Liesel filled her mouth. Buying time, perhaps? "Mom's been wondering what brought you to town. Specifically now. I didn't tell her about..." The fourteen-year-old motioned toward Hannah's neck.

So, she did see the bruises.

The girl continued. "If there's one tip I can give you about my mother...she doesn't deal well with lies. She's maddeningly good at seeing through them. Take my word for it. Not that I make a habit of lying all the time. But if there's ever something you'd rather not talk about, you're better off telling her that instead of making something up."

Hannah was sunk. It wasn't even her past she was trying to hide so much as her immediate present. Telling Abigail meant she'd risk her job, the one this family needed her to have. Hannah had so much practice at lying in Toronto. Maybe she'd be more adept than Liesel thought.

"Now, why are we talking about me, Liesel? I asked how you are doing."

The teenager paused, then sported a coy smile. "I'd rather not talk about it."

SUN WARMED HANNAH'S EYELIDS. She had no desire to open them. She'd stay here a little while longer, not that she could move anyway. Footsteps bounded outside the guest cabin. After a short knock, the door opened before she could even say, "Come in."

Abigail stepped inside the doorway. "I was gettin' worried, when you never came in for breakfast. You always sleep this late?"

Hannah sat up, trying to clear the fog, but her muscles ached so badly she could hardly sit up. All this, after a half-day's work?

"Is that my brother's journal?" Abigail pointed to the journal on the nightstand.

"Yes. My mother had it."

"I gave that to your dad for his birthday one year. Mom told me to. Said he was struggling in his faith and needed to write down his prayers so he could record the good Lord's answers once they came. I was probably just five or six at the time, so I had no idea what I was giving him. Did he use it that way?"

"He did." Should Hannah point out the way the good Lord answered was hardly the way her father would have wanted? "What time is it?" Hannah asked.

"Two-thirty."

Oh, no. Hannah flew out of bed, adrenaline surging. The muscle pain didn't matter. She had to be underground in thirty minutes, and she was nowhere near dressed in her disguise.

"Hannah, I've been wanting to ask you —"

"I am so sorry to cut you off. Thank you for waking me up. I'll have money for you soon. I have a new job and need to get ready, right away. Do you mind?"

Hannah shoved her stuff in a bag, trying to shield Abigail from pieces of her disguise, ones that included Ray's old clothing. What should she do? She couldn't change here in daylight. She should take her car, park at the corner of another street so Abigail thinks she left and went to work somewhere else.

"It's not about money. Hannah, why did you move here so suddenly?"

"I promise, Aunt Abby. We will talk. I started tutoring music students. Some in Amherst. I have a session in half an hour."

Abigail relented. Hannah dashed out with her bag. Once again, she had to leave home without packing a lunch.

Hannah parked her car outside Springhill Motel on Fir Street. She ducked in the backseat to change into Ray's clothing and put on her mustache, eyebrows, and wig. When she saw a group of miners heading her direction, she crouched down in the seat. Once they passed, she inched back up.

Hannah rushed the rest of the way to Cumberland Coal Mines. Ray's boots were way too big for her. It took three pairs of socks to stop her feet from riding up the boots. She'd have to buy a new pair as soon as she could.

As she stepped through the arches, she felt ready for another day of tough work. Well, ready may be a strong word. But an excitement existed in her at the idea of seeing her team again.

When she arrived at the mine opening, she took a spot on the rake, ready to begin the two-mile trek below the earth's surface.

HANNAH AND LAZY HAZE threw large stones into the middle of the pack they were building. They'd already put in a couple of hours.

Hicks yelled, "Hey, Newbie."

She asked Lazy Haze, "I guess that's me?"

"Well, it ain't me, ya jar head."

"Missing my shovel." Hicks hiccupped. "Would'ya go down the next level, see if ya can find one with my last name, Jones, on it? Someone 'borried' it."

Hannah nodded to Hicks, wondering how to get to the next level. Plus, she thought Hicks was his last name. Oh, well. She wanted to get along with them. Might as well do what they'd asked. She heard a chuckle as she walked the direction he pointed.

Hannah moved her head from side to side, looking at the sloped walkway by the dim light. Her lamp lit up a few feet before her. It was steep, burning the muscles in her legs. Black coalfaces surrounded her on both sides. She walked about one hundred or so yards before she arrived at another working level.

The team was joking, laughing it up. Not paying any attention to their visitor.

Leaning against the coalface was a shovel. She bent down. It took a few swivels of her head to get the light to shine in the right place. And there it was: Jones inscribed on the handle. Hmm. That wasn't so hard.

She picked up the shovel and started to walk away.

A man yelled, "Hey, Nosebleed! What'choo doin' with my idiot stick?"

The group of miners stopped their conversation and focused on her. Well, who they thought was a him. She swallowed. "Mr. Jones told me to get his shovel."

At first, it was silent. Then, laughter roared. All of them, at her. She had no idea why.

"You hear that folks? Jones. Jones told him."

What in the world was so funny? Then, the rest of the miners grabbed their shovels from the coalface, showing her every single shovel was labeled Jones. Ah. The brand name.

She smiled back, nodded, trying to be a good sport.

"You must be a newbie," the rightful owner of the shovel said. "Only newbies fall for that one."

She put the shovel back in place, nodded at the men, and retreated up the slope.

When she returned to her team, empty-handed, everyone looked at her and smiled. Then they started clapping. Slowly at first, then full-blown applause.

She was sure her face was crimson as she smiled back, taking a manly bow.

Hicks said, "Welcome to the team, Rocky. Isaak done that trick on me."

"And me," said Plum.

The men smacked Hannah's shoulders, much harder than they would if they knew she were a woman.

Josh rested his arm around her. "All part of the initiation, Rocky."

And now, she had a name. She was part of the team.

Lazy Haze cracked up and emitted a loud fart.

"Ugh. Haze." Hicks covered his nostrils. "We got enough deadly gas down here."

"Sorry. I gets'a nervous."

Their joke at Hannah's expense worked. For the first time in her life, she felt like she was part of something. A whole other kind of family. She knew they'd never welcome her into this club if they knew who she really was. But today, they didn't know.

She was beginning to understand what drew her father down here to this work. These men. Even though the risk was, that one of these days, she may not return home.

chapter 8

Chip. Chip. Chip.

All she wanted to do was sleep when she heard that familiar sound. She peeked out the curtain. Last time, Josh was doing that out of desperation to serve this family. This time, he'd chip, then peek over her direction at the guest cabin. Was he trying to draw her out? He got louder.

Chip. Chip. Chip.

Good grief. He was going to wake everyone, if she didn't get out there. She threw on her coat and shoes and went outside.

She hobbled over to him. She couldn't move any faster because her muscles hurt so badly. Obviously, if she weren't careful, she would give herself away. "What are you doing, W—"

Oops. She almost called him Winnie. "Josh?" It was so cold she could see her breath.

"Chores," he said, his cheek dimpling.

How did he even have the energy for this, after their hard day at work? He had yet another pick in his hand. She smiled at the irony: he had no idea they'd just spent the day together.

"People on this side of Maple go to bed at night," she said.

"I figured you'd come out eventually so I could ask you."

"Ask me what?"

"If you've heard of my famous tour of Springhill's thirty-eight streets."

"If that's your not-so-subtle request for an outing, I don't date miners."

"That's swell. They frown upon dating minors in these parts."

She rolled her eyes at his corny joke.

He said, "Not dating miners limits you to Hector at the pool hall and Mr. Yeardly...he runs the furniture store. You might want to buy him a new hearing aid for your first date, if being heard is important to you."

Yes, it was. Josh seemed like a kind enough man. But she was hardly ready to consider going out on a date, despite his persistence.

And his dimples.

"I'm sorry, Josh. I can't."

"Can't? Or won't?"

"You decide. Thank you for helping the Percys with the skating rink."

"Have they used it, you know, since?"

"No, I don't think so, anyway. I suspect they're still avoiding it."

"Well, I'm going to make sure it's ready, as soon as they are."

"I've got an idea. How about you come back in the morning when they're not sleeping?" She flashed a smile his direction before turning around to head back toward the guest cabin.

"I'll consider that an invitation. Thank you. That's most pleasant and unexpected." He was not going to give up so easily on her. But from what she'd seen of him so far underground, she wasn't surprised. Loyalty, persistence, and hard work defined Joshua Theodore Winslow, the Sixth.

SATURDAY MORNING BROUGHT a welcome break from the mines. Hannah knocked on the door of Adam Sawyer's hospital room, pleased to see him packing his overnight bag.

"Well, hello, young lady."

"Hello, Mr. Sawyer. I'm Hannah Wright, Melvin's daughter. I believe you recently met a distant cousin of mine."

"Ah, yes. I did."

Was it a sin to lie to an old man? She should find out if Lipnicki's Five & Dime made Liar's Bench t-shirts. She could wear it as a subtle disclaimer, kind of like how hanging mistletoe excuses unexpected kisses.

Why on earth did her mind dart to kissing? *Focus, Hannah, on the old man you just lied to.*

"Do sit down, Hannah."

His genuineness put Hannah at ease. She sat on the bed's edge and massaged her aching calves…until she realized she couldn't explain why she was in so much pain. She stopped. "I'm glad to see you're getting released."

"Me, too. There was a day we weren't so sure I was getting out of here on my own two feet. It's been good to be close to my men." He gestured toward the hallway. "Not all of them have been sent home yet, since the accident. They hope to release them before Christmas."

Her mouth went dry. She found it hard to speak.

Compassion filled his eyes. He stopped packing and sat on the edge of the bed beside her. "What can I do for you, Hannah?"

Why was it so hard to ask? "I never met my father because..."

"I know. Another accident. The day you arrived. Your mother, she went right into labor on my mine yard when she got the news he wouldn't be coming home."

"What can you tell me about him?"

"Well, that was darn near thirty years ago. But I remember him. Melvin loved being with people. Could always catch him shooting the breeze at the Liar's Bench."

"I had a feeling." She giggled.

"Maybe I should cook up a few for old time's sake. If only I could remember some of those tales he told..."

She liked Adam immediately.

"Your dad...he'd pass the time telling tales underground. They used to have contests over who could tell the best lies. You might even say your daddy was President of the Liar's Club."

Bryce walked in, keys in hand. "Your coach awaits, Mr. Sawyer." He took a bow.

Hannah's muscles tightened. Would Bryce recognize her?

He looked her up and down. "Well, if this doll is your live-in nurse, I'm moving out of that motel room and right on back home."

If Bryce were living at the motel, she would have to

find a new place to park her car when she was getting ready for work.

"This is Hannah," Adam said. "She just towed in. Her father worked for me years ago."

Adam's son took her hand. "I'm Bryce Sawyer. You work here at the hospital?" His hand lingered on hers.

"No. I teach music to children." She extracted her hand and stood, wanting to get out of there.

"I feel like I teach ankle biters too," Bryce said. "I run Cumberland Coal. Perhaps you've heard of us? Our company is the reason Springhill exists."

Wow. Never mind all the men whose sweat, blood, and tears went into it. No amount of Bryce's solidly handsome good looks could overcome his personality defects.

His father seemed just as put off as he threw Bryce a raised eyebrow. "You giving me a ride home or not?"

"It was nice to meet you, Hannah. I hope to see you again," Bryce said.

She hoped the opposite. Not unless she was hiding under a mustache, bushy eyebrows, and thick glasses.

After Bryce led his father out, Hannah ventured down the hallway, where other miners were too injured to leave. No one ever knew when disaster would strike. What if it happened again? To her? To Josh? And the rest of their team? Where would the Percy family be then?

SHE TURNED HER CAR ON MAPLE to go back to the Percys. As she pulled up, Josh and their team, except Isaak, were rebuilding the front step. That one Ray never had time to finish. The word "tomorrow" often rolled in her mind since then. Ray had no idea he was already living his last day on earth. Last few hours, actually.

She couldn't go home. What if someone recognized her? Hicks put his arm around Lazy Haze, only to mess up his hair. Their rapport made her smile. And so did Lazy's response, taking a swing at Hicks. Of course, Hicks caught it without looking. While she ached to join them, she couldn't encounter them all at once. Not out of her disguise. She caught Josh's eyes before she stepped on the gas and kept going.

She headed over to Main Street. She parked on a side street and walked over to the Capitol Movie Theater. It exhibited a John Wayne movie, *The Conqueror*.

Isaak came out of the theater with a long trail of children. Before she could back up and head the other way, he called out to her. "I'd recognize that face anywhere."

She swallowed. Oh, no. Was it over already?

"I'd heard this delightful rumor you'd stepped into town, Hannah. It sure is 'bout time." He took her in a warm embrace. "I've been long wantin' to meet ya."

"You have?"

"Your daddy and I…we used to write jingles together. Harmonies and all."

Isaak introduced her to six of his children, ranging from age four to sixteen: Denise, Tommy, Heather, Jacob, Jesse, and Christopher. She would never remember them all. And these weren't all. He had five more tucked away at home with his wife. "I gotta pay half a day's salary just to bring them out here for movies and ice cream. But it's worth seeing their faces. You must come over to meet the rest of the tribe. My wife and I, we can share stories about your father."

"Oh, I would be so delighted, Mr. Revere."

"Isaak. Please."

She knew she shouldn't go. The more time she spent with him, the more likely he'd figure her out. But that was a risk she'd have to take. She saw a kindness in Isaak's eyes. Maybe he'd be like a father figure to her. She could use one.

He went on his way.

After the movie, Hannah went home. Her team was gone. She tried out the fixed step. Sturdy. Lasting. Just what Abigail needed.

She wanted to be with the Percys this evening, since she'd missed them all week because of work. She walked into the house. Her path was filled with boxes, bags, and a festive mess. Reds, greens, silvers.

Lindy's tiny body was almost submerged inside one of those boxes. She popped back up, holding a red velvet bow.

"Found it!"

"What is all this?" Hannah asked.

Lindy beamed. "We always decorate the weekend after Thanksgiving in the States. It's tradition." Lindy chattered on about decor, Percy customs, and how Liesel had been in her room all day, avoiding all things traditional.

Hannah tried to detangle garland while Abigail fixed pasta and sauce in the kitchen.

There was a knock at the door. Abigail called from the kitchen. "Hannah, would you tend to the door?"

Hannah braced herself, hoping no one from her team had returned. She opened it. A young man stood there. Hannah recognized him as the boy Liesel sang to during her recital. He wrung his hands together, shifted from one foot to the other.

"Hi, I-I'm Garrett."

"Hi, Garrett. I'm Hannah."

"Liesel won't talk to me at school. Well, not just me. Anyone, really. Could, could you, um, maybe give this to her?" Garrett took a small gift box out of his jacket pocket. "She can open it now, or put it under the tree, or not open it at all. Whatever she wants."

Abigail walked in. "So, Garrett. You're the one who stole Liesel's first kiss?"

The boy's eyes widened. His face turned beet red. "It was only on the cheek."

"Good." Abigail pointed at him. "Because if it were anywhere else, you would have me to answer to."

Ah, what refreshing innocence. She believed him. He didn't seem like he was just trying to impress the mother of the girl he fancied.

After Garrett left, Lucas brought more Christmas decorations down from the attic.

There had to be a way to get through to Liesel. If anyone understood what it felt like to feel personally responsible for a parent's death, it was Hannah.

♫ ♫ ♫

As she lay on her twin bed, staring up at the ceiling, Liesel heard the knock on her door. Why couldn't her mother just leave her alone? Sharing a room with Lindy was bad enough. Couldn't she enjoy the space while Lindy was so preoccupied by all things Christmas downstairs? So what if everyone was already kicking up the Percy annual traditions? Who cared if this were normally her favorite time of year? She wasn't into it this year. What was so wrong with that?

When the rapping persisted, she swung her legs over the edge of her bed and got up, stepping over strips of paper she'd left on the floor. She didn't want her mother to see those, so she pulled the door ajar just a couple inches.

It wasn't her mother. It was Hannah. A flush of embarrassment rose to her cheeks.

"Hi," her cousin said. Hannah held out a little wrapped Christmas gift. "Garrett stopped by and brought you this. I thought you might like to open it. He said you didn't have to wait till Christmas."

Hannah looked slightly pathetic standing out in the hallway, like she felt inadequate or something. Shoulders scrunched up. Was she making her nervous? She had to give her cousin a break. She opened the door a foot so Hannah could slide in and just as quickly shut it. No other visitors were welcome.

Hannah looked around the room. Oh yeah. Those scraps of paper were all over the place. She started to gather them.

Hannah knelt down beside her. "Let me help you."

"It's okay. You don't have—"

Hannah paused on a slice of manuscript paper, musical notes drawn above them. "The song you sang. At the recital?"

"Yeah, so what?"

"That was a great song."

"I hope I never hear it again." She loved the song. She loved being up on that stage, singing and twirling around. A confidence overtook her every time she sang. Being on stage…it was like being home. But now, she regretted the day she ever accepted that stupid solo. The day she asked her family to come see her perform. She bit the inside of her lip to stop its quiver.

Hannah dropped scraps in a wastebasket. Liesel sat at the head of her bed and leaned against the wall. As much as she wanted to be alone, she didn't feel like kicking Hannah out. Her cousin...she was different. She had secrets too. Liesel had a feeling that Hannah could understand her in ways her mother couldn't, but she didn't know exactly how.

"So, you want to open his gift?" Hannah asked.

Liesel took the box. She set it on the nightstand.

"He's cute." Hannah said.

"You think so?" The thought of Garrett made her insides all squishy or tumbling or flip-floppy. He was the single thought that could make her smile these days. So, why had she been pushing him away?

"I know you're not much in the mood to decorate today, Liesel, and that's okay. I wasn't either after my mom died. It's like, for everyone else, the world kept turning while mine...it just stopped."

Tears stung Liesel's eyes. She'd tried so hard not to cry since this all began. If she started, she didn't know if she could stop. "My brothers and sister, my mom...They lost someone too. It's not just me. So why...why are they okay with moving forward, and—" The catch in her throat burned. She couldn't say anymore.

"Everyone grieves in his or her own way, Liesel. I think your mother tries to stay strong for you kids. For some people...they cope trying to bring life back to a place of normalcy."

"Nothing will ever be normal again. Ever. They don't

have this, this weight on them like I do."

"Liesel…"

"No. Forget it. Can we not talk about this?" She swiped away the tear that managed to escape. She had to stop this before it started.

No doubt, Hannah wanted to press into her. Liesel knew it. But at least her cousin didn't try to push her beyond what she could handle.

"Okay. But only if you come sit with me at dinner. I could use a friend myself."

Hannah *needed* her? She wasn't sure if those were just words. For some reason, Liesel didn't feel she could shove Hannah away like everyone else. She obviously had her own hidden pains. Somehow, she would find out what those were.

AGAINST HER BETTER JUDGMENT, Liesel found herself walking into the dining room. For the past few weeks, if she ate at all, she'd mostly eaten in her room. Or with Hannah when she came in the back door after eleven for a late night dinner. That happened on weeknights. Who was she teaching music to, so late at night? Was Amherst that far away?

"I want to sit next to Hannah," Lindy said, as she bounded into the room.

But Liesel snagged that seat anyway. When Lindy didn't protest, she assumed her mother must have gently pulled her back. Her mom had a way of giving any one of them that look…one that commanded a change of path.

She looked over the food spread. Wow, her mother sure didn't skimp on the meal. Every year, the day they'd decorate the tree, Mom would make pork chops, potatoes, and cranberry sauce. She wondered how Mom could still afford to make it this festive. After everything that had happened. Yet, she was afraid the food would sour her stomach. It wasn't as if she had much of an appetite.

Her mother insisted they take hands, and led them in grace. It all felt so wrong. That was Dad's job. Mercifully, it was short. As soon as they said their amens, Lindy dove right into her meaningless drivel.

"We got the tree up, but, Liesel, I wanted to wait for you to help decorate. Can I put the angel on top of the tree this year?"

"It's Liesel's turn," Lucas said.

"Lindy can do it," Liesel said. Why should she care anymore?

"Hannah can help me. So, Garrett gave you a gift. Was it romantic?"

"I don't know."

"A promise ring?"

Ugh. She rolled her eyes. Would that be hinty enough for her prying little sister? Why did everyone have to know one another's business in this household?

Lindy put on a fake man's voice, "Liesel, will you promise to save all your kisses for meeeee?" She even puckered up. She was so immature. What did she know about kissing, anyway?

"Enough, Lindy," her mother said. "Liesel, you can be the first to put a gift under the tree this year."

She couldn't take it anymore. "You guys can have your fun. But I don't care about Christmas. About gifts. Celebrating."

"Liesel, honey." Her mother tried to sound soothing.

Did she think that a calm voice made it easier?

"What difference does it make? Our traditions. Are we supposed to just act like someone isn't missing? That everything isn't completely messed up?"

Forks clanked on plates as people stopped eating. She was spoiling everyone's appetite for her mother's delicious meal. Great. Just what she needed on her conscience. To ruin something else, when she knew they couldn't afford to eat this way.

"Liesel, tell me what we can do." Her mom reached across the dinner table and tried to take her hand.

She recoiled. "Nothing, Mom. There's nothing anyone can do." She stood and started to leave.

"Liesel please. You can't keep running away."

She stopped in the doorway, but didn't turn around. She didn't want to say it. She knew she shouldn't, but she'd held everything in long enough. She had to ask. She spun around, tears blurring her vision. "Mom, you told Josh it wasn't his fault. That he was doing Daddy a favor."

"Liesel, I didn't mean—"

"A favor I asked for."

"No, that's not what I meant. I—"

"It's what you think."

"None of us think that."

"Yes, you do." Tears prevented her from seeing their faces. Mom's. Lindy's. Lucas's. "I see it...every time you look at me. All of you."

Lucas stood up and went to his twin. He reached out his hands and put them on her shoulders. He looked her in the eyes. "It's not your fault, sis." She was so used to Lucas taunting her. Harassing her. His effort to take the blame off her shoulders...it did something inside her.

Lindy stood up, ducked under Lucas's arms and got in front of him, also looking at Liesel with the most confident eyes. She reached up to Liesel's face and pulled her down to eye level. "Liesel, you did not kill Dad."

Mom stood behind her siblings, nodding. "Liesel, we've lost so much. We don't want to lose you too."

Lindy hugged her tightly. Lucas followed, forming a Lindy sandwich. Her mother hugged her from behind. For once, she didn't want to shove them away. She may not believe this wasn't her fault, but they believed it.

And that's what mattered.

Liesel cried. "I wish daddy had never worked in that place."

Her mother said, "At least we don't have anyone else underground. We won't lose anyone else that way."

"Lucas, I'm putting my foot down." Liesel said. "As your older sister…"

"By two minutes."

"And fourteen seconds. You can never work there. Ever. Not even when we turn seventeen."

"He won't have to, 'cause we are opening my candy store," Lindy offered, as if it were a given. She had such faith that everything would work out okay.

Liesel glanced at Hannah, who wouldn't make eye contact with her. Why was she so detached? Was she giving them space to heal? Or was it something else?

♫ ♫ ♫

Hannah opened another box of Christmas decorations, as the Percys decorated the tree together. All of them. Liesel had decided to join them. Warmth filled the room as they adorned the tree with icicle ornaments, glitter stenciled balls, hand-blown baubles.

Liesel had a story to tell about several ornaments, related to memories of her father. Her favorite was a multicolored, mercury glass set shaped like bells. "Dad used to pretend to ring them as we decorated, leading us in a different Christmas carol with each one he placed on the tree."

Hannah couldn't remember the last time she'd had a festive Christmas. Definitely not since her mother died. If anything, Christmases had become a reminder of all that she'd lost. But this year, even with the loss of Ray, it would be different.

Hannah took hold of the green bell and led the Percy clan in a festive rendition of *Joy to the World*. Liesel didn't hold back her beautiful voice as Hannah added accompaniment. It was the first time she'd heard the girl sing since the hours before her father died.

Lindy hung homemade, crocheted stockings by the fireplace mantle, each one embroidered with the kids' names and Abigail. Hannah noticed as Lindy slipped another one back in the box of decorations: it said Ray. The eight-year-old's maturity amazed her.

"Mom, we need to make a new stocking for Hannah," Lindy said.

"Next year, we'll need another one too, for the baby," Lucas said.

"We are going to run out of room. We need a bigger house," Lindy said. "I vote we put the name Lucy on the new stocking."

"Lucy is a terrible name for a boy," said Lucas.

"Just accept the truth. She's going to be a girl!"

As Abigail served everyone hot cider, Hannah noticed Josh outside the window, pouring water on the Percy lawn. There he was, continuing Ray's role, maintaining the skating rink for the winter. How she admired his devotion to this family. Maybe it was regret, working its way out. Or maybe he wanted to be near a family this close to Christmas.

HANNAH SPIED THROUGH THE kitchen window as Abigail opened an envelope of cash she had left for her on the kitchen table. The cash represented another full paycheck from the mines. Abigail's hand rose to her mouth. Hannah knew she couldn't tell her how she was making money and hoped she'd buy the idea that she had enough music students to teach.

It was almost surreal, the way no one knew where she was. If anything happened to her, would anyone know? Or would Abigail think she'd disappeared without a word? Especially if a mine accident left her unrecognizable.

No. She couldn't worry about that right now. For once in her life, she knew where she was going and why. She was helping her family.

The men underground were irresistible. Watching their bonding...no, not just watching, but being a part of it, seeing how they cared about one another. The jokes they played. The silly songs they'd make up. The camaraderie, the family-like atmosphere was infectious. Something that, so far, had been foreign to her. Even though the work was tough, she found herself looking forward to seeing them everyday.

What song would Isaak lead them in that day? What riddles would Plum and Hicks tell? As an outsider, hearing stories about her father and his choice to go underground, she never got it before. Now, she was beginning to understand. Those men would take the shirts off their backs, or give up their last glass of water, or piece of bread, even if they were starving or thirsty or dying. She was sure of it. Given the selfishness of where she had just come from, this was a refreshing change. Despite the hard work, it was not something she wanted to give up. Not anytime soon.

chapter 9

Hannah had never witnessed such a cacophony. Eleven children sure could make some noise. Isaak's wife, Mrs. Virginia Marie Neely Revere—or Mrs. Ginnie, as she preferred—cooked up a feast for the occasion. Hannah imagined Ginnie must spend most of her time at the stove. She didn't appear to mind the chore, or that her children—who were old enough to talk, holler, rattle, and sing—did so, all over one another. And not the same song, either.

While the casseroles heated and bread baked, Hannah headed out to the porch with Isaak and Mrs. Ginnie. They had a few moments while the mother of eleven could step away from the kitchen and sit.

Isaak slid beside his wife on the porch swing. Hannah took a chair nearby, enjoying Herrett Road's view of the mines below. Steam rose above the towering stacks. Most every home on this street had porches. Isaak took Ginnie's hand in his. It seemed that any moment she was nearby, he wanted to express his affection. Hannah knew it was a risk to talk to a miner on her team. But how could she resist Isaak's offer to share stories about her father?

She reminded herself to keep her words few and to speak in a higher register. "How did you meet my dad?"

"I was a twenty-year-old whipper when I got assigned to your father's team. He took me under his wing, showed me the way of a coal mine. Your daddy and I would play together after church. He at the piano, me with my four-string guitar. One I restored myself."

"My father played piano?"

"Your mother didn't tell you that?"

"I knew he sang. I didn't take up playing myself until after her death."

Mrs. Ginnie said, "The day your mother found out she was having you...Mmm. She and your father had tried for years. You were their little miracle. He put on a whole impromptu concert. He liked to sing or whistle when he was happy."

Hannah felt the burn of tears threaten. The words her father wrote about her in his journal came to life. Why did she have to be the miracle he never got to see?

"Did you know he always sang to your mama's belly?" Mrs. Ginnie asked.

Hannah nodded. "She told me."

"He even used to sit there and talk to you about how one day you'd find a love as strong as he and your mama had. It wasn't just his prayer over you; it was his declaration."

Isaak massaged his wife's shoulders. "Have you found that person, Hannah?"

She shook her head. "I guess my daddy would be disappointed." Chalk up one more unanswered prayer.

"Oh, Honey." Mrs. Ginnie wagged her index finger. "Uh, uh. We're not done hoping for you yet. Pretty girl like you. And sweet as strawberry pie."

How could they hold out such high expectations when she hadn't even dared to hope for herself? Not for a long time. Not even when, from outside appearances, she had love, affection, and a man worth marrying before her.

"Mooooooom!" One of the eleven yelled out. Something needed attention at the stove. And now.

When they opened the front door, a waft of smoke hit them in the face. Mrs. Ginnie took it in stride, as though this were normal, an everyday occurrence perhaps.

"No worries." Isaak patted Hannah's shoulder. "When you cook as much as we do in this house, scraps at the bottom of the oven get well done."

Thankfully, it only *smelled* dire. Dinner was preserved. Mrs. Ginnie was one amazing cook. She had lots of practice. The fourteen of them ate at three long tables strung together. These eleven kids didn't need to be remanded to some kind of "kids table." Everyone was an equal member of the family.

Hannah had met Denise, Tommy, Heather, Jacob, Jesse, and Christopher at the movie theater. But now she met the other half of this set: Elizabeth, Rebecca, Jordan, Julie, and Eric.

Every morsel of casserole was devoured, every last slice of homemade bread eaten. Then, the music began at the table. On the table, as if the table were its own instrument, made complete with cups and utensils. The Revere kids knew how to put on a show.

Tap, bang, ding. Tap, bang, ding.

First slow, then fast, until their tableside music making turned into a full-fledged, beat out song. They all kept perfect rhythm with one another, sped up and got louder in sync.

Hannah felt their joy. Joy to be together, joy to make music. What it must be like to grow up in a household this size. This life, it was so different than what she knew. If only circumstances had been different. If only her dad had lived. Maybe she could have had brothers and sisters.

But for now, this would do just fine. They all insisted she was their new sister. She may not look anything like them, as each of them had warm brown complexions, coming from a Mulatto father and mother. But it was an honor to feel a part of them. She hoped she'd be invited again.

♫ ♫ ♫

Bryce didn't have friends to hang out with on Saturday night. Well, he didn't have any friends at all. Normally, he dreaded the idea of walking around Main Street. All he'd get were those looks atypical of the Springhill Welcome. But he couldn't stand the mind-numbing walls of his motel room any longer.

He should have moved back in with his father by now; the invitation was open. But something kept him from taking his dad up on the offer. Moving into his childhood room…there was something so backwards about that. But if he wanted something to eat, he still had to step into civilization. That is, if he didn't want to raid his dad's icebox.

Springhillers had trimmed the lamps that lined Main Street with red satin ribbons and bows, a tradition his own mother started. And was she ever insistent! When one shop owner didn't want them because they'd get wet and dingy over the season, she fought for them with the passion of a cat in pursuit of a mouse. Bryce wasn't sure who'd kept the tradition rolling after Mom's death.

As he passed a few closed shops, he glanced at the Christmas trees. They were lit up for the night, even though most stores were closed. Wasn't that a fire hazard? Though it looked pretty, walking up the otherwise darkened street. Some were colored, some were white, each tree decorated with the personality of its respective shop.

The Barbershop's tree had mini-ornaments on theme: mini shears, fake razors, and barbershop poles. The shoe store had decorated their tree with tiny shoes, boots, and Christmas colored socks.

As he got close to The Avalon, where they still made his favorite hamburger and shake combo, he saw *her*.

Hannah.

She walked up the street, heading away from him. He quickened his step to catch up to her, then touched her shoulder. This caused her to startle. She turned around quickly.

"Sorry, Hannah. Didn't mean to scare you."

She let out a breath.

"We need to talk about work," he said.

Why did that cause fear to cloud her eyes? What did she have to be afraid of?

He gestured to The Avalon. "Come on. I'll buy us a bite to eat."

"I already ate dinner with Isaak Revere and his family, Bryce."

"You drink vanilla cola, don't you? Or a shake? I need to talk to you."

After a beat, he opened the door for her. She stepped inside. Good. She was going along with this.

A brightly lit jukebox took center stage. Teens lined up to put nickels in the slot. While it may not be his scene, she had to like the music, right? Maybe she'd enjoy the sight of teenagers dancing. Several girls in poodle skirts—which fanned out as they danced around—smiled at the duo as Bryce guided her toward an oversized, red-cushioned booth.

"I'll be right back." He walked off, pulling a shiny nickel out of his pocket. He waited for his turn behind an indecisive teen and glanced back at Hannah.

As she spotted a family about to walk by her, she picked up her menu and hid her face. Why on earth would she do that? Bryce traded familiarities with the head of that family, Hicks. After all, he'd worked for his father for years. Hicks walked out with his wife and young son. Why would Hannah feel the need to hide from Hicks? One thing was for sure: Hannah was an enigma he would crack.

He dropped his nickel in the slot and ordered up a love song. *Earth Angel* by the Penguins. Why not? He was out with a pretty girl on a Saturday night. Maybe it would start playing at just the right moment.

As he returned to the booth, he lowered her menu. "Hiding from someone?"

"Of course not."

"Thought you said you already ate."

"A girl can always make room for a milkshake, right?"

"A milkshake it is." He'd let her have her little secret, whatever it was. Milkshakes took time to sip. That would give them time to just be together.

A waitress glided up to their table on roller skates and

took his order. One chocolate shake, two straws.

Until Hannah shot him that glance. He got the point. "Make that two shakes."

The waitress smiled. "And one straw?" She winked, then skated off.

"So, Bryce. You wanted to talk to me about work?"

"Yes. I'd like to hire you to teach me to read music."

Her face relaxed. Maybe she needed work. If that were true, she wouldn't be too mad at him if she found out he didn't really need her services. Not even a little bit. He knew how to read music and write it as well. He just couldn't think of another way to buy her attention.

That's what he was reduced to these days. Buying friendship. Oh, well. At least it had a chance to work for a while. So what, if it took a little white lie to get there?

"You're the only soul in town I know who's lived somewhere else, Hannah. Everyone here...they don't know how to dream beyond these hills. Their idea of escape is the beach, twenty-five miles over. What's your story?"

"If you dislike it so, why did you come back to Springhill?"

"I ask myself that every day, considering it meant breaking the promise I wouldn't follow my father's trail. At least I'll never go underground."

"If your men didn't, you wouldn't have a company."

Interesting. She wasn't afraid to challenge him. That inner strength she had, it certainly was attractive. "Well, there are plenty who can mine around here. Not everyone can run it."

The jukebox switched from *Ain't That a Shame* by Fats Domino to *Rock Around the Clock Tonight* by Bill Haley and the Comets.

Bryce smiled. "Come on, let's dance." He held out his hand.

"No, I can't."

"That's what the parquet floor is here for. Practice. Live a little."

Her curt "No" was clear. This was not happening.

He'd better let it go or he'd risk alienating her. "But you'll tutor me? I'll pay whatever your going rate is with the occasional meal thrown in as a bonus."

"Okay."

"Okay, then."

Now, if only he could convince her to give him a chance outside the professional realm. He could tell, though, she was not one he could rush or push. It could backfire like the railcars that disengaged in the No. 4. But she was the only person in town who didn't hate him or have a history unfairly biasing her against him. He didn't want to lose this chance with her.

Earth Angel began its summoning verse. One day, could he ask her to be his like the song croons? Nothing in her demeanor said she was ready for a slow dance. But just sitting with her, sipping those shakes…it was definitely a step in the right direction.

BRYCE SAT IN HIS WARM OFFICE, watching the snowfall through the glass, glad to be inside instead of out with the bankhead workers. He watched them from his window. Snow blanketing the hills this time of year was as dependable as nightfall. No one ever had to worry if Springhill would have a white Christmas. That used to matter to him, when his mother was around to make it festive. Now, it left him a weird mash of empty and nostalgic.

Cal Weston walked into the office building with Mr. McKay. The round-bellied man with a balding head of stark white hair had worked for his father for as long as he could remember.

Mr. McKay handed Cal his brass check tag. "I'm sorry, Cal. I love workin' for you. But she's too bumpy down there. I know it's little ones, but I got me a wife and two kids to think for."

"We will miss you around here, Mr. McKay. What will you do?"

"I got a job in Boston. This factory that sells eggs and cheese. I gotta tell ya...My Ethel is relieved."

Cal touched the metal object between his fingers. "Well, Springhill's losing a good man, Mr. Charlie McKay."

Mr. McKay stepped out the door, giving one last wave.

Bryce asked, "So, Cal, how are the numbers?"

Cal walked over and handed Bryce a report. A quick glance told him what he needed to know. "These don't meet the winter demand."

"With one mine running, this is all the output you can expect. Bryce, if you have concerns about the work, I'd be glad to take you down—"

"No, it's okay."

"I've got time today." Why did Cal have to persist? Always trying to get him to go underground, like doing so would make any difference to how much coal was dug.

He swung around in his chair and flipped through papers instead. There would be no more conversation about that.

♫ ♫ ♫

The loud crash startled Josh. He turned from the stubborn coal at the 13,000 level and saw No-Longer-a-Newbie Mel flat on his butt. A long piece of timber sat beside the poor guy. Josh stifled a chuckle, wondering how Mel was surviving down here. He didn't seem as strong as the other men.

Lazy Haze cracked up. "You stack like a girl, Rocky."

The small-framed man got up, dusted himself off, and thrust the wood into place. Impressive. At least he didn't let a few bumps keep him down. Josh remembered those first days in the mines well, when he'd started as a laborer.

Without warning, a small rumble rippled through the mine. Josh and his team moved over to the packs that Mel and Lazy Haze had built. Hicks put a hand on Lazy Haze's shoulder. Then, the rumble calmed.

"Was that a bump?" Mel asked.

"Yep," Isaak said. "Just a little one. Your cousin Melvin...he liked to call those bouncers."

While his team schooled Mel on the ways of a bump, Josh mulled over nagging thoughts.

Melvin. Cousin.

Mel had mentioned that before, on his first day. Why did this strike Josh so oddly? He'd forgotten to ask Abigail about the scrawny guy, if she were even aware a distant cousin were working in town. Wouldn't she have said so, if she knew?

But then he took a closer look at Mel's face. His eyes, specifically, by shining his miner's lamp at the man's face. He hadn't gotten a great look at him underground before now. Mel always seemed to disappear after work, without coming into the Wash House. Mel noticed the lamp, glanced his way, then darted his eyes. If Mel wasn't just reeling from the experience of his first minor bump, it was something else entirely. No way. Could it be?

If Josh's suspicions were correct, this was all about to be over. Come next shift, they'd have one less member on their team.

WHEN THE SHIFT ENDED, the team found a blanket of snow had fallen and covered every inch of the ground. It was still at that stunning stage. Its purity made the earth look lit up, like at dusk. It would take a few days for the dark coal dust to settle and rob the snowflakes of their beauty.

Josh hadn't been able to stop thinking about his suspicion since it crept up a few hours ago. Josh knew the pattern. After the team dropped off their lamps, Mel would head away from the mines instead of to the Wash House. He must clean up at home. He. Should he say *she*? He'd know soon enough.

Josh hung back from his buddies. Knowing Mel wouldn't follow them into the Wash House, he followed him away from the mine.

Josh looked back to make sure the others were out of earshot and grabbed Mel's arm. It was time to find out the truth. "How far are you ridin' this?"

"Excuse me?"

"You've managed to pull this charade on the others so far. But they'll catch on. Trust me."

Despite the black coal dust covering her face, he could

see with certainty. He was right. Surrounded by the illuminating snow, he watched her eyes fill.

She waited for the rest of the miners from other teams to pass by. Then she murmured in her regular voice, "Please don't turn me in."

"Women do not belong down there. Come Monday, you won't be back."

Why did he feel so angry with her? Or was it protective? Was he mad she lied to him? Was he just frosted it took him a while to figure that out? Then again, he'd talked about her underground without realizing she was listening. What had she heard?

"It's over, Hannah." He took one last look before heading for the Wash House.

She chased after him. "Josh, don't do this to me. To Abigail. To the kids. With Ray gone, they need the money. I don't have options. I tried."

He stopped to face her, looking squarely in her eyes. Those eyes. How could he not have seen it before? "And what happens if there's another disaster?"

"You'll watch out for me, won't you?" Even disguised as a man, with that ridiculously fake mustache, her soft smile had a way of melting him.

Snow fell again. They both looked up to the sky, its wetness beginning to mix with the coal dust on their faces. His insides thawed a bit.

Josh said, "I want to show you something. Get cleaned up first. I'll meet you outside your house."

After cleaning up in the Wash House, he headed to Five Maple. He waited at the end of the driveway, patiently, for her to emerge from the Percy guest cabin. He had cleaning up down to a science and fifteen minutes to spare.

He wanted to take her to his favorite spot upon a new snowfall. As he aimlessly made boot prints in the snow on the street, he mulled over how he had to admit it. Her commitment to the Percy family was endearing. He might not like what she was doing, but he understood what drove her to such extremes. Wouldn't he make a similar choice if pressed?

Once she emerged, he led her on a short walk. The snow continued to fall. Captivated by her beauty, she was a much different sight than one hour before. She'd sported that wig, mustache, glasses, extra eyebrow hair. Yes, this was much better. This was how she was supposed to be. The true beauty she was.

He kept the conversation light; he'd deal with her job issue in a bit. For now, he was enjoying the chatter about various snowstorms they remembered from childhood. She shared how she had always lived in Canada and enduring snow each year was the norm. How one year they got so much snow she had to crawl out her second story bedroom window to get outside.

"Josh, have you ever dreamed of living somewhere else?"

Josh thought about it for a moment then shook his head.

"Why not?"

How was he going to explain this? Would she think he was corny? "It's gonna sound, well...some towns, they have this way...they find their way into your heart, that's all. Like when you, you hear a song and it sticks with you. This place...it can wrap its arms right around you. Won't let ya go. Lends you a whole dollar when you need just a dime. You just have to be open, ya know, and let it love ya." Josh felt his cheeks blush red. He hoped she wouldn't notice or pass it off as windburn.

He was rewarded with her smile. Was that a glint of interest? "Did you steal that from a travelogue?"

"I know. One-hundred percent sap."

"At least you know where you belong." She looked down at the snow-covered street, kicked a few piles of snow to the side.

Snow-capped trees lined their way. As the wind caused snow to float down on her cheeks, he saw her shoulders droop a bit. Did she not know where she belonged? He'd like to change that.

He led her inside the entrance to Hillside Cemetery. The last time they'd been here, to bury Ray, it wasn't beautiful. But tonight, he knew it would be.

On arriving at the crest, the snow-covered valley below provided a breathtaking view. The mountains across seasoned the beauty. "Prettiest seat in town," he said.

She gazed at the scenery, but he only wanted to watch her. Despite the view he'd led her to, her eyes still looked empty. What held her back? Was she an injured soul? Maybe she'd let him take her hand. It was worth a try. He reached for her fingers.

She recoiled. "What are you doing? I told you."

"Who hurt you?"

"I just...I don't date miners. You, of all people, know what it's like to lose someone."

"Do you think I would trade one minute with those men? One trip to the Pool Hall with Moosey for greasy chips? One Sunday morning in church with Ray? Every day I had them in my life was a gift. I would never have wished them away, just so I wouldn't have had to go through the pain of losing them. That is no way to live, Hannah."

"You don't understand."

"Yes, I do. Who taught you it's okay to push people away because they might leave this world before you do? If your mother had made that choice..."

A shadow crossed her face. He'd pushed too far. "I'm sorry, Hannah. That was..."

"If my mother had made that choice, I wouldn't exist. But she lost."

"I don't think she would see it that way. She got you."

"Without him. All my parents ever wanted...it was me. To have a baby together. In the twisted, messed up way this life works, they got it. But it's like he had to deprive her of my dad to have me. She couldn't have both? Was that best?"

"He who?"

She stared at him, her beautiful eyes glistening. "Never mind."

She didn't need to explain; he got it. She blamed God. He knew, as long as that rift—that mistrust—were there, it would be hard to break through. Hard for her to move forward in life.

What was life without risk? Gains without loss? Joys without sorrow? Even with this, he'd rather live with the potential he'd never win her heart than not try for it.

But how was he going to convince her that love—even in the face of the risk of loss—was worth it? And not just loving him, but also the God who sometimes allows bad things to happen?

chapter 10

"Try these on." Sitting on the fixed front step, Liesel handed a pair of skates to Hannah. She hoped her cousin would fit into that old pair of Mom's skates. Why not enjoy the last gift her father made them? He'd want this. Plus, she hoped this would loosen her cousin up a bit. Skating brought out the kid in everyone, even Mom. And that was as easy as getting Lindy to eat anything green.

Hannah laced up the skates.

"It's like you're Cinderella with the glass slipper," Liesel said. "Now all you need is Prince Charming."

"I don't need a Prince Charming. I'm perfectly content living here with you fine people."

"Oh, come on. Every woman needs a Prince Charming. Including me."

"If Garrett has anything to say about it, you shall have one."

"And for you…Josh maybe?"

"Let's skate."

Ah, avoidance again. Liesel knew there had to be a story. Hannah laced her other skate and stood. She made her way over to the ice-covered lawn.

The rink sparkled in the noonday sunshine. Josh had maintained the rink; it was perfect.

What was not perfect was Hannah's form. She didn't know what she was doing or have a good sense of balance. This could turn disastrous.

"Stand up straight," Liesel said. "You look like you're about to take a nosedive. Trust me. That hurts."

Hannah faltered with a laugh, wobbling the arms that should have balanced her. "Well, it has been about thirteen years since my mother and I went skating."

Liesel glided by. But in fairness, she's had many years of practice. Dad had been making rinks for them since the beginning of Maple Street time. She could skate before she could walk. It was kind of strange, doing this without him.

Hannah flailed, about to fall. Liesel skated over and held her arm out in support, but ended up bumping into her. It sent both of them down on their backsides.

"Ow!"

"Sorry, Hannah. I take full responsibility." Liesel spotted Lucas and Lindy in the living room window, doing a show of hands to rate their falls. Liesel stuck her tongue out at them. They ducked out of the window, leaving her a full view of the lit up Christmas tree.

Life wanted to keep moving forward. But this season was such a harsh reminder of the one who wasn't here. Tears stung. She tried to blink them away, but it was too late.

Hannah reached out and touched her knee with her gloved hand.

Liesel looked over at her. "Do you know what it's like when someone dies because of you?"

"Yes."

"Really?" Liesel looked at Hannah as she nodded. It didn't surprise her one bit that Hannah understood. "What happened?"

"I had left home without permission. In fact, it was because of a boy. But he wasn't anything like Garrett."

"You mean because Garrett is nice?"

"And handsome."

"You think so too?"

"Yes. But he's also a gentleman. And this guy, he wasn't. Mom found out where I was and went out in an ice storm to go pick me up. I never saw her conscious again."

No wonder she understood. Liesel wasn't in the middle of doing something wrong when her father died. Yet she still couldn't stand the guilt. What Hannah had to face...she didn't envy her.

"Hannah, were there others?"

"What do you mean?"

"Others who weren't gentlemen with you?"

Hannah swallowed and bit her lip. "Liesel, all that matters is I'm with you. You guys are the best family I could have hoped for."

"I agree. We're peachy. But Hannah, you still deserve love. The right kind." Liesel felt a grin spread across her face. "Josh is nice. Handsome. A gentleman."

She tagged Hannah and got up off the ground, then glided across the ice. Hannah got up and chased after her, giggling. It was a welcome sound, one Liesel had hardly heard since her cousin moved in.

Hannah eyed the fidgety, nervous boy before her. Garrett stood in the doorway of the Percy home. He was both cute and a little geeky at the same time. She had to admire the boy for not giving up. She stifled a chuckle. No sense in worsening the young man's plight.

"Most people don't know this, Miss Hannah," Garrett said, as his voice cracked a bit. "And don't spread this around, but it's always been my dream to become a concert pianist. Mom says I can take lessons from you. But here. Has to be here. I...I don't, we don't have a piano."

Hannah could see right through him. He had no interest in being a concert pianist; he wanted to get closer to Liesel. But with the need for income, she didn't care about the motive. When he offered to start right away, wagging cash, she welcomed him inside.

On his way to the piano bench, he looked all around the room. To the stairway, the kitchen doorway, the opening to the dining room. Obviously, he hoped to behold the clear, blue-eyed apple of his own eye.

Garrett parked on the bench and started playing on his own. Badly. Maybe she could get these two out on the rink together, now that they had broken in the ice. The rest of the family had suited up and joined them too. But this time, she could keep them away. Give Liesel a twirl on the ice with Garrett alone. Maybe he'd be a more graceful skater than piano player. But she loved his willingness to take a risk. To sit there, make a fool of himself. All for the hope of seeing Liesel.

Her mind traced across the heart of what Josh said...that those who weren't willing to risk loss didn't gain either. Look at Abigail. She lost big. But Ray also gave her four children, a fifth on the way. Would her aunt have made the same choice in the past, if she'd known in advance she would lose the love of her life?

Garrett's extraordinarily off-key plunk drew her out of her reverie. The boy didn't have an ounce of natural instinct for her precious instrument. This was going to take hefty work, and perhaps good earplugs for the rest of the family.

"How about we start with scales?" Hannah ran through the C-scale for him.

Liesel snuck in from the kitchen, but Garrett couldn't see her. Eyes closed, he feigned seriousness for his craft as he played a bad attempt at the scales.

He flipped his eyes open as the cover for the piano keys started to close gently on his fingers. His eyes found Liesel's adorable smile.

"Ugh. That sound? Painful, Garrett. Painful."

And there, Hannah witnessed the renewed friendship between Liesel and Garrett. Hannah had to admire his successful plot, the boy whose special gift had earned the first place under their lit up tree. The warmth of the bubble lights effervesced their colored liquid to life, much like his kind gestures revived Liesel's tender heart.

THE MUSIC TEACHER SIDE OF HANNAH had to let it go. Lindy seemed to believe, wholeheartedly and loudly, that singing lyrics from *Angels We Have Heard on High* to the tune of *Away in a Manger* made for a smash hit. Let the spunky eight-year-old have her fun. Hannah hadn't savored a Christmas Day since her mother died. Even though there was a gaping hole without Ray, everyone seemed able to keep within the spirit of the season and remember to be grateful for what they had.

Hannah was glad the mines closed long enough for her to enjoy Christmas without having to explain her absence. For whatever reason, Josh hadn't blown her cover. How long that would last, she didn't know. But she continued to go to work each time their team had a shift. Josh seemed to pay a lot more attention to her, though, including feeling protective. Thankfully, their team hadn't seemed to notice.

So far, Abigail bought the fib that she was teaching lessons in Amherst after kids got out of school for the day — going house to house. This explained her long, evening absences, including the drive back. Abigail always left her a delectable dinner for her arrival, even though she was never awake to greet her.

Abigail sat by the tree, passing out gifts to each young member of the family. Hannah noticed her adorable, though small, protruding belly. Death may come to this town in unexpected ways, but new life was crashing this scene. Life would go on.

The kids were playing outside with the best Christmas surprise: Ray had handmade each kiddo his or her own sled and carved their names on them. Receiving them was almost like getting a special visit from Ray himself. Plus, as tight as funds had been, it did Abigail's heart good to be able to give each child such a nice Christmas present.

Hannah helped Abigail clean up the lunch dishes. The kids had scarfed that meal down so fast. Who could blame them? They couldn't wait to get outside to try their new sleds.

"Abigail, where did my parents live?" Hannah asked.

"How about I show you?"

THE KIDS SLEDDED DOWN Wosley Street. Abigail waved at them, promising to be back soon with Hannah. Lucas and Liesel raced each other. Lindy taught Lenny how to use his sled. Hannah knew she'd make such a good mother someday.

Hannah and Abigail headed the opposite direction, where Wosley crossed Main, while Abigail shared a bit of history with her. Hannah had no idea the family still owned the place her parents lived. They never sold it. They just boarded it up to keep it in the family. It had been her great grandparents' home on Dad's side until they had passed on. Hannah's mom and dad moved in after the wedding, as it had been sitting for a couple of years at the time. They had fixed it up, something Abigail mentioned would have to be done again, if anyone were to move in.

Grit covered the doorknob. Abigail pried the door open to the two-story house.

The room held covered furniture, a thick layer of dust resting on the sheets.

It was so surreal, like stepping into a time capsule. How strange and how wonderful to walk into this home that hadn't been occupied in decades.

All this time, it just sat here on Chapel Street. Preserved. Waiting. She'd even walked by before, not realizing her mother and father lived here until his mining accident. As her hand traced the back of an old, yellow sofa with mahogany wood accents, dust transferred to her fingers. "Why didn't Mom ever come back here and sell it? Or get rid of their stuff? We were always hurting for money."

"When your mother took you and left, she had a job lined up in Toronto to help support you. And plus, she could stay with her sister. I think she wanted to get away from reminders. That's why she never came back. She could focus on you instead of her grief."

Hannah gently pushed a rocking chair back and forth. "I asked her so many times if we could come here. Meet you. She never wanted to, even though she talked so fondly of you. Really. It always baffled me. But I was too young to push her to do what I wanted."

"That doesn't surprise me." Abigail folded her hands across her growing belly. "I was only ten when my brother died, but we, we shared this special bond. She and your father, they loved each other and got along better than I had ever seen out of two married people. Even Ray and I had our squabbles. Honestly, if it hadn't been for you and your birth, I don't know if she would have survived his death. For a while, we were afraid…"

Hannah knew exactly what Abigail was reluctant to voice. Many times, Hannah suspected she was the only reason her mother was alive. Her only reason to live. She was a good mother, but a nervous one. Always fearful something bad would happen anytime Hannah left the house. Her overprotectiveness was smothering. Her mama's sister continued that quelling after Mama died. So much, she had to just break out on her own. Or thought she did.

She couldn't blame her rebellious mistakes on them. If she hadn't gotten into some of those messes, she probably would have shown up in Springhill a lot sooner.

Hannah walked through the place with wonder, her gaze falling on old chairs with wooden backs and patterned fabrics, a roll-top desk, a Silvertone radio atop a table. Oh, how she would love to add that to her music memorabilia.

She pictured her parents decorating a tree, listening to Christmas songs on that radio. Snuggled up on the sofa. No television. Not in sight, at least. Maybe they didn't have one back then.

Dusty books occupied a built-in bookshelf. How well read had her parents been? Had they dug into *Robinson Caruso, Secret Garden, Pygmalion, Age of Innocence, The Anne of Green Gables* series? "When my mom didn't come back, why didn't you sell this place?"

"Well, it's paid for. By my grandparents. Ray and I figured we'd keep it in the family. I don't know if we'll be able to hold onto it. If finances get tighter, we could sell it. I'm sure the furniture isn't worth much."

Hannah shook her head. "Oh, I think it's so valuable. It's beautiful. And knowing they sat here, talked here..."

Abigail smiled back at Hannah. "Well, then sometime, when we're all back on our feet, maybe you can take over the place. Though it will need a tender touch."

Despite its old, unkempt appearance, Hannah felt the warmth of home. Peacefulness, even. Why couldn't she have grown up here with both her parents? Her mind should be filled with memory after unforgettable memory of her father chasing her around this living room, tickling her until she was gasping for breath. Or her mother teaching her how to bake cookies or make a cake for Daddy's birthday.

Instead, her first memory was from the big city of Toronto, where she and her mother lived with her aunt. Sharing one room, one bed. How awkward that had been, once she'd grown into her teens.

"Hannah, did you leave anyone behind in Toronto?"

"Nobody that matters anymore."

"Oh?"

"Trust me. Some things are better left behind."

Hannah ran her hand across a dusty, olive green armchair near a window.

"I remember your father writing in that journal from this chair."

As soon as Hannah could, she would get his journal and reread it from this very spot.

Could she build a future here? Could she eventually settle and have a real home? For now, Abigail needed her. She had no problem staying right where she was, putting all her resources into her aunt and the kids. But someday, there might just be a way she could reside where her parents intended to live out their "happily ever after."

One day, she'd even decorate a Christmas tree of her own in front of that window. The one where her father sat, with bubble lights and tinsel. Maybe she'd even be pregnant one day.

Whoa. Did she really just let her mind go there? Dare she hope to have her own "happily ever after"? Seeds of desire began to sprout. The inclination to cast them away taunted her. Yet, seeing this home — dusty as it was — birthed a yearning. Long forgotten dreams of love, family, a real home, security — they all needed a good dusting off.

An image of Josh flashed across her mind. What would it be like to share this dream with him? No. She couldn't do that. Anytime she'd dared to hope, something got in the way. There was always some rude awakening. She wouldn't fall for that. Not again.

♫ ♫ ♫

January 1957

Was Josh making too big of a deal of this? He was disproportionately excited, just to be invited. As the calendar turned to 1957, the Percy family headed to Main Street for the New Year's Day Parade. He loved seeing Hannah get a kick out of Oreo the Dalmatian, still habitually guarding that corner of Maple and Junction on their way by.

They made it in time for the first float, squeezing in between the crowd. Townsfolk road a variety of decorated floats.

Abigail and the kids surveyed from the sidelines. But the one whose face lit up the most was Hannah. Watching that light come to her…it did something to his insides. She was peeking out of her shell.

When she first arrived, there seemed to be such hollowness, maybe even lifelessness in her eyes. But now, there was a spark growing in them he hadn't seen before. An ember that could be fanned into a flame.

Liesel sidled up to Josh as she watched the floats. "Don't love her too tightly." She said this so matter-of-factly.

Josh looked over at her, but Liesel continued to watch the parade. He pondered how right she likely was. How perceptive she was to pick up on his feelings.

"Joshua Theodore Winslow." He knew the shrill pitch of that voice and Mary Lou's tendency to over enunciate Theo in Theodore. A most unwelcome interruption.

Josh turned. There stood Mary Lou. Could he ever be so lucky that she'd give up her obsession with him? Even better if she'd just marry someone else. That would end this question she'd kept open in her heart, despite the many times he'd already answered it.

"Mary Lou."

"It's been too, too long."

Not long enough.

"Has it?" She planted a wet kiss on his cheek with her candy apple red, Max Factor lips. He only knew that because it was one of those sundry details she loved to share with him about beautification products she carried in her store.

He quickly stepped back as Hannah glanced over at them. "Mary Lou, this is Hannah."

Mary Lou didn't look at Hannah. Instead, she focused on his cheek. "Oh, dear." She licked her thumb, then used it to remove whatever traces of Max she'd left behind. "So sorry."

Obviously, she wasn't. Mary Lou's jealousy was as transparent as Bryce's incompetence at the mines. She flicked her hair then crossed her arms. She even pushed her bosom up a bit. No one had taught her the art of being subtle. Subtle was attractive. Hannah was subtle.

"I 'member you. Hannah came into the store askin' for a job. Josh and I go way back, don't we, baby?"

Her baby? *That,* he certainly was *not.* Abruptly, Josh pointed. "Isn't that a spectacular float?" At that moment, any float would have been spectacular. Anything to break free of Mary Lou's clutches. "There's Isaak. Hey, Isaak." Josh hooted and hollered at his dearest teammate underground, well, other than Hannah, of course. Six of Isaak's kids rode the float with him, singing in perfect harmony: a New Year's song.

After the parade, Josh was invited — thankfully, without Mary Lou — to have dinner with the Percys. He didn't know why, but later into the evening, Hannah slipped out. She'd said she had somewhere she needed to go. He couldn't accompany her. Yes, he'd asked. He didn't want her going out by herself, as a snowstorm had just begun to hit. She was insistent on going alone.

The more time he spent around her, the more he didn't want her out of his sight. That was one reason he hadn't turned her in yet to the Company. He hated that she was underground, putting her life at risk, but he got forty extra hours a week with her out of the deal. Could he give that up? And knowing her identity, he enjoyed watching her interact with their comrades, pretending to be Mel. Sometimes, he enjoyed trapping her into conversations she'd likely rather not have with them. It was like harvesting a private joke, day in and out. It fostered a new rapport in their friendship. Yet he feared for her life. There had to be some other way to take care of the Percys, so she wouldn't feel obligated to go underground.

After he'd gone home, he went to climb into his warm, welcoming bed.

Suddenly, he heard pounding on his front door. What on earth?

He added a housecoat over his flannels and raced for the door. He opened it. Hannah stood there.

"Hannah!"

She was wet and shivering. He led her inside the doorway and closed it, trying to preserve the heat.

"What's wrong?"

"Why didn't you tell me?" Hannah's eyes flashed.

"Tell you what?"

"March 15, 1929. Ring any memory bells?"

Oh. That. "I wanted to."

"But you didn't."

"You didn't come clean with me about going underground either."

"So, we're even now? In some secret-telling department? Was this a contest?"

"Why are you so mad?"

He watched her breathe, in and out, nostrils flaring a bit. She tried to contain whatever frustration she'd bottled inside. This had to be about more than a kept secret.

"How about I make us hot cider?" he suggested. "You need to thaw out." *Literally.*

After a few stubborn moments, she relented.

By the time Josh joined Hannah with steaming cider, she'd warmed up by the fire in one of his plush robes. She seemed as mesmerized by the fire as he was with her.

"Why didn't you tell me our fathers died together?" she asked.

"I don't know."

"Is there something you don't want me to know about it?"

Josh's mouth went dry. How would she take the news? "Seven men were working on the 11,800 wall in the number two. And she bumped. Five of those men died."

"Are the other two still alive?"

"There's this one guy, Yates. He's not a miner anymore. Doesn't even remember who he used to be, actually. And the other one...it's Isaak."

"Why didn't you tell me? Why didn't he?"

"I...I don't know."

"What are you not saying about that night?"

"Nothing. It's just, a tragedy that I wish hadn't happened. For you or for me." He took a sip of his cider and cleared this throat. "Hannah, I don't want you underground anymore."

"Why?"

"It's dangerous."

"Then, why is it okay for you?"

She had a point. Weren't they all guilty of putting their lives at risk every day? Wasn't it the family members who suffered the most? He should know. Hannah, too. The Percys and everyone else in this town who'd lost someone, which was mostly everyone in Springhill.

No one was untouched by the tragedies those mines caused. So why did something that caused so much pain, also bring so much joy to the men who bonded? It wasn't just about provision. Yet, how could he convince her to stop, when he enjoyed having her around so much?

chapter 11

Hannah breathed in and out, fighting nausea. Just the idea of what they were about to do made her sick to her stomach. Josh, Isaak, and Cal tackled the unenviable task of breaking down the cement seal on the No. 4, while the rest of the team waited to go inside.

Her legs shook badly. Lazy Haze looked over at her. She dug her heels into the winter ground, held her arms close. Maybe he'd just think she was cold. The only reason she looked forward to getting inside that mineshaft was to get out of the sunlight, where her team couldn't get a close look at her face.

Had Bryce assigned their team to this task because he disliked Josh? Sure, it had to be done by someone. But still. When they arrived at work that day and Bryce stopped them from going down on the rake, his narrowing eyes on Josh had revenge behind them. For what?

Cal, Josh, and Isaak broke through the last of the barricade into the No. 4. The unintentional grave was now opened.

Immediately, their noses filled with a stench. Rotted

corpses. She covered her nose with her arm. Maybe the fabric of her jacket would filter out some of that horrific odor. The idea of going inside…How could she do it? How could any of them?

Josh looked at her, an unspoken concern in his deep brown eyes. He nodded to the team. One by one, they silently followed him into the pit. Cal, Isaak, Hicks, Plum, Lazy Haze and herself.

As they got into the darkened cave, the smells grew exponentially. It was like unsealing a coffin that had baked in the sun for months.

There was no fighting it. She stepped over to the side of the slope and heaved. No one blamed her. No one looked at her oddly. They got it. She felt tempted to scream, "I'm a woman! Let me out of here." But no. She had to press on. It was the right thing to do. Too many widows and orphans hadn't been able to find peace or closure without having funerals.

Working through exploded passageways created barriers. Parts of the mine were not where they used to be. They used their lamps to sweep across the floor, to see if they spotted any signs of a life cut short.

After they stumbled upon their first victim, she saw Josh wipe away tears.

Why was Bryce nowhere to be found? Shouldn't he have been here to help the victims' families finally lay their men to rest?

Tears flooded Hannah's eyes. Someone did this for her father. Someone collected his body after the accident. And Josh's father. Would this madness ever stop? What if she, or Josh, or Isaak, or anyone else on the team were next?

Spring 1957

THEN SINGS MY SOUL, my Savior God to Thee. How great Thou art. How great Thou art.

Hannah peeked at the congregation through a small slit in the double doors. Her pale yellow and white dress hung below her knees.

Hannah hated the look on Abigail's face earlier when she once again declined to attend church. Abigail was good to not push, but she saw her aunt's shoulders droop.

After they left without her, conscience won out. She dressed and came over. But how could she go inside? It wasn't just that she was afraid she'd run into her team members. She may look different, especially today in a spring dress. Yet, if their distant cousin Mel became a part of the conversation, it would jeopardize everything.

But still. That wasn't it. Wouldn't stepping inside this place be yet another lie to add to the list she'd had to keep straight these days? Wasn't sitting on those pews, on the other side of these double doors, an unspoken admission that one believed? She could lie to people, but could she lie to God? He could see right through her, if he were there to see at all.

Her father used to think so. Her mother, too. The congregation sang a verse.

O Lord my God,
When I in awesome wonder,
Consider all,
The world Thy Hand hath made.

Every voice in harmony from the choir sounded over fifty years old. Was that a Gulbransen they were playing? Or a Steinway? How she'd love to get her fingers on a Steinway.

I see the stars.
I hear the rolling thunder.
Thy pow'r throughout,
The universe displayed.

She always struggled with the lyrics of this song. Were they true? Did he hold such power? If so, why didn't he choose to exercise it more often in times he could? Was she missing out on how great he actually was? Maybe not. To believe someone was *not* up there ignoring her and everybody else…it was easier that way.

She cracked the door a bit, getting a better look at the congregants. Isaak sat with his wife and eleven kids on two full rows near the front. Isaak's voice resonated above all of them, even though he wasn't in the choir. Abigail and the kids were on the third row, right behind the Reveres. Did the Percy kids enjoy being here? Did they believe the lyrics, despite the way their lives had been permanently altered over the past few months?

It was one of her mama's favorite hymns. She'd often hear her humming the tune while she made dinner. They never had much money, but Mama seemed to turn meals into events. Her favorite was on the rare occasion they could have fish, which her mother baked in a lemon cream sauce with parsley flakes.

How great Thou art,
How great Thou art.

Someone approached behind her. Hannah spun around to leave, so she wouldn't be ushered inside. She almost slammed right into Josh.

"Not staying?" he asked.

"I, I just need to get going."

"You have somewhere else to be?"

She paused. She'd done enough lying in this town so far. This was not a time that called for it. "No. Plus, you know it would be bad if I ran into any of our team."

"Tell you what. How about we go somewhere else? Maybe Mel can give this place a try next week."

She laughed. "Right. Because running into Abigail is a great idea."

He didn't push her to go in. He always seemed gentle-handed, something she wasn't used to from past relationships.

But this wasn't a relationship. Nope. Not at all. A friendship, maybe. Yeah, that's what this was. That's all it could be, as long as he spent forty-hours a week underground. So, why did she just say yes to going off somewhere with him?

LIKE A LOT OF PLACES ON Main Street, Cumberland's Ice Cream Shop was closed on Sundays. Josh produced a key that unlocked the door.

When they slipped inside, he locked it back up and flipped on a light switch. The inside was full of color. It was almost like every pastel floor tile represented a different flavor of sherbet, that new type of ice cream that blazed on the scene not too long ago. Mounted metal stools with light blue and white cushions lined the counter. Black and white checkered tables rested against the walls with blue, straight-back chairs. The bright pink counters reminded her of bubble gum.

Josh walked behind the counter and opened a freezer that housed twelve flavors.

"You sure the owner doesn't mind?"

He grabbed two dishes. "Ben gave me a key a while back. He was one of my dad's best friends. The strongest memories I have of my dad were coming here. When he worked day shift, he used to take me here most every night. We didn't have an icebox at home, so we could only eat ice cream while out." Josh scooped out various flavors. "Rule was, we had to try four different flavors each visit. He had this sayin'..."

Josh handed her a variety of flavors in a bowl.

"'No matter how bad life gets, there's always ice cream. And the tastes of life make it worth living.' I think that's why I like cooking so much."

"You like to cook?"

"One of my favorite things to do."

"My mother would have liked you." Truthfully, out of all the men she'd ever laid eyes on, Josh was the only one.

"I could make you dinner sometime, Hannah."

"If you enjoy cooking, why don't you turn it into a profession somehow?"

"Because I'm a miner."

"Don't have to be."

"You trying to get me to change so you can accept that dinner invitation? Which hasn't expired, by the sweet way. Dessert included."

She buried her mouth in a delectable bite. "Mmmm." It was the creamiest concoction. "That is...Mmmm."

"Nice try. I still want an answer," he said.

"No, really, this is..." She covered her tongue in another mouthful.

He hoisted himself up over the counter with his strong arms, like jumping out of a convertible. He joined her at the counter, taking the seat beside her.

He took a spoonful of his ice cream. "So, what beef you got with church?"

"I told you. I can't be seen by our team. And they go to the same one."

"Don't gimme that smaze."

"I just… I'm not ready, okay?"

"For God or for me?"

She licked her lip, tasting remnants of strawberry.

"Well, see, I consider that good news," he said. "Not ready implies a day of readiness will come. And I will wait for you, Hannah Wright."

He took a bite of chocolate and seemed to delight in smacking it around. "But I will say, making your peace with God, that's much more important than sayin' yes to me."

Honestly, she didn't know if that day would ever come. For Josh or for God. How could she trust that either of them would not abandon her when she needed them most?

♫ ♫ ♫

When Bryce arrived at Hector's Pool Hall, Hannah was already at the piano in the back. No one seemed to mind the melodic interruption. In fact, some patrons had stopped their games to enjoy her playing. She didn't seem to notice. Her back was to them, facing the wall the upright was pushed against.

What was that song she was playing? He draped his guitar over his neck and strolled to her. She didn't even seem to notice his complementary chords. Her eyes were still closed.

The key changed and he followed her. She opened her eyes and kept playing, but glanced over. It didn't stop her effortless flow. At least she made it look effortless. What Bryce wouldn't give to have that kind of raw talent. He had to work for every ounce of skill he'd mustered. If only he hadn't started so late in life. His father never listened when he'd asked for lessons, like it was a waste of time or money. But he was one of those kids whose parents could have easily afforded it. Dad didn't want to help foster something in him that wasn't grooming him for coal. So he taught himself, mostly.

As she concluded her song, the clapping began. And it grew. Hannah looked behind her, perplexed, like she had no idea anyone had been listening.

She nodded and smiled, but she looked embarrassed. Almost like she didn't like attention. Most people in this town craved attention.

But Hannah was unlike anyone in this town.

And that's what he liked about her.

HANNAH AND BRYCE SAT IN A BOOTH, one of her music teaching books open before them, just like she had the other few times they'd met for lessons. Bryce had a hard time concentrating on her description of the differences between notes on the base and treble clefs. By the time she switched to staffs and bar lines, she must have noticed. She closed the textbook.

"Bryce, how's your dad?"

He wasn't used to anyone caring about him or his family. "Still requiring a push to get him to his doctor's appointments. Which he never would've needed if he weren't running such a volatile company."

"At least he's still here for you to cart to the doctors."

What was her story? Beyond what everyone knew…that his father's mines had taken away her dad. He didn't want to ask her about that. No sense in reminding her, his family's role in the tragedy of her life.

She got right back to business. "The second part of this book will help you transpose notes from one key to another. That happens a lot, especially when playing in groups."

He tried to listen, really. But all he wanted to do was get to know her in a deeper way. "Hannah, I know you left Springhill after you were born. What was life like, away from here?"

"What does that have to do with teaching you how to read music, Bryce?"

"Nothing, really. I just…you never talk about your life before coming here."

"Maybe I like my life better here."

Well, at least she wouldn't be taking off anytime soon. He said, "Growing up here, I wanted nothing more than to get out of here."

"Why did you come back?"

"That's a good question, Hannah." Why had he come back? Was it because he'd heard about the explosion and knew his father would need him? Or because he had failed, miserably, trying to make a living outside of this place? Of course, he had no idea he'd arrive in time for his father to have a heart attack. But still. He never intended to stay this long. The truth was, he had nowhere else to go.

THE SUN BEAT DOWN AS ONLOOKERS took seats on the bleachers in Lion's Park. They sipped on colas or coffee, ate hot dogs or doughnuts. The greenery was vibrant, a welcome change after a long, cold winter.

As Bryce walked up to Lion's Park with his dad, he saw the Fencebusters readying to batter up for a heated game of baseball against the miners. It may have been a practice game, for fun. To the miners, fun meant cutthroat. When Bryce was a kid, he'd go to the regular games with his mother when the Fencebusters would play against teams from Halifax, Stellerton, and various New Brunswick towns. His dad was too busy working to show up. But he and Mom would sit in the stands with a thousand others from all over. But today's practice game was small...just locals.

A woman pinched up her face at Bryce and his father on her way by. Yet another one did the same behind her. Then a child. Maybe the two women were wives of men recently lost. Clearly, they blamed him. However it could be translated, it was completely misplaced. Unfair. But did the people of Springhill care?

His mother always told him it was in his head. He was reading too much into it. But no. He knew what people thought of them.

When everyone hated him, even as far back as elementary school, how was he not supposed to resent it? As if it were his fault people's fathers died. He didn't force them to go underground. Neither did his father. At least Dad gave them a way to make a living wage, right? But the other kids didn't see it that way. After all, his own father was safe above ground.

One of the miners from the No. 2—Bryce could never

remember his name — glared at just him. Not his dad. Bryce leaned into his dad. "Nothing keeps them happy. Except thoughts of the day you come back."

"Well, they'll be scowling a long time, if that's what they're waiting for, Son. I had another incident this week."

"Incident? You mean heart attack?"

Before he could answer, a very pregnant woman with a little boy at her feet caught Dad's attention. She stood at a vendor to buy ice cream.

Dad went over to her and put cash down to pay for the treat. "Hi, Lenny."

How did his father manage to know everyone's name, let alone their kids' names?

"You having chocolate today?" his dad asked.

The boy hugged his mom's leg, but peeked out with a tiny smile. Bryce had to admit the boy was cute.

The woman turned to face his dad. "Thank you, Mr. Sawyer."

"You're welcome, Mrs. Percy. I, ah, I am sorry."

So, that's who she was…Ray Percy's widow. Hannah's aunt. She was expecting another child?

"You're sorry? Do you ever get tired of saying those words, Mr. Sawyer?"

Bryce felt something familiar in his heart…a piercing for his father who he knew would wear the weight of guilt over this one. Why did people have to be so hard on Dad? He may not have always gotten along with him, but his dad was a good person.

Hannah walked over to Abigail. His pulse sped up a bit.

"Can I help carry anything, Aunt Abby?" Hannah asked.

Abigail gave Hannah a tray of ice cream cups and took Lenny's hand.

Hannah looked over at Bryce, blinked, like she didn't realize he was there. "Hello, Bryce. Good to see you."

Was it really? She seemed to want to get away as fast as she'd breezed up. She and Abigail headed into the stands where several other kids were already waiting on them.

♩ ♩ ♩

The scoreboard announced Fencebusters 5, Miners 3. Lucas stood by the board, as it was his job to keep up with the score. Hannah knew she was taking a big chance being out in public. But how could she miss this? Her whole family was here. Josh, Lazy Haze, and Plum were playing. She was glad Isaak and Hicks were seated a few rows ahead of her and not behind. Hicks sat with his wife and son, who looked to be about four years old.

Josh, who was up at bat, took a few practice swings. He looked up at her in the stands, gave her a little wink.

"Josh! Smack that ball." Everyone in the entire stands could hear Hicks.

Isaak and his family, all in the row in front of Hicks, made such a racket. "Go, Josh! Go. Hit it!"

The stakes were high. The miners had almost never won against the Fencebusters. Yet here they were, in the last inning, just two behind. Josh was up at bat with Lazy Haze and Plum on base.

They were actually *in* this game. They could tie it. Even win.

The Fencebusters' pitcher threw the ball. Josh eyed it, timed his swing just right and whacked it hard. It seemed to shock even him. It took him a moment to drop the bat and run. It traveled all the way to the fence, with the outfielder huffing to get there. Now, who's the Fencebuster!

Lazy Haze and Plum raced for home plate, which tied it up, 5 to 5.

"Whoa ho, Winnie! Run, run!" Isaak yelled.

Everyone flew to their feet, even Abigail. Cheers erupted as Josh made his way toward home plate.

"Whoa ho, Josh! You can do it," Hannah shouted, forgetting to keep a low profile. Liesel glanced over at her and giggled, adding her own cheers.

As Josh slid into home plate, it brought their score up to six. Hannah jumped up and down. "Yah, Miners!"

She watched Lazy Haze and Plum help Josh to his feet, then smack each other on the butt. It almost made her wish Mel could have joined them today and been part of this victory. They bought "his" excuse he was going out of town this weekend.

Lucas changed the scoreboard to reflect three runs. Fencebusters 5, Miners 6.

Even though the Fencebusters also belonged to the town, it was a sweet win for Springhill.

"Soooo…" Liesel said to Hannah in that sing-songy way.

"Soooo what?"

"You are Josh's cheerleader now, huh?"

"He helped the team score three for the win. This entire town is his cheerleader."

"If you say so. But I think you're the only one whose cheers he'd bottle and replay if he could. Come on. Let's go congratulate the team."

Hannah watched Liesel bound down the risers. Could she join her? Here she was, already at risk, being out in the open. But she was beginning to love this town and the people in it. She wanted to be part of it, not hide out. But her need to keep her identity at work a secret kept those desires in check. Better judgment forced her to hang back with Abigail, while Liesel skipped onto the field, high-fiving all the men.

chapter 12

Liesel hated when her mother made her wear a dress to church. So what if every other woman and girl in Springhill wore one for services? She wasn't the blending in type, like creamer with coffee. She was more like oil on water, rising to the top.

And stockings? Whose idea were these most uncomfortable atrocities that slid down her legs, looking like doughnuts around her ankles?

Her mom shot her a look, from the end of the pew. She couldn't help fidgeting. The reverend was preaching about freedom in Christ. How ironic.

Freedom was not something she'd experienced in her household. When Josh came by earlier to ask if he could walk to church with them, Hannah chose to stay at the piano and work on a song. Liesel was tempted to plop down with her and refuse to go to church too. Not because she had anything against church, of course. Her mother was getting on her nerves. What would be so wrong with letting her and Garrett go to the drive-in? It wasn't that far out of town.

Okay, so maybe bringing the argument back up in front of Josh wasn't the smartest idea. "Mom, please." Liesel had begged, even though she knew begging had little affect on her mother.

"You don't have a chaperone," her mother said, then yelled up the stairs. "Lindy, Lucas!" Then she directed her attention toward the piano playing virtuoso. "Hannah, I do wish you would join us for the service."

Liesel huffed. "Mom, none of my other friends, none, need a chaperone to go to the drive-in. It's just a movie."

Josh had to go and pipe in. "They should have chaperones at that passion pit. And for those submarine races."

"Not helping, Josh."

"Oh, yes he is." Her mother winked at Josh. Winked! Was this some kind of conspiracy? "Garrett's dad is letting us borrow his ragtop wheels. So, he obviously thinks this is appropriate."

"Oh, that'll convince her." Josh raised a brow.

He was not her friend right now. "It's the re-release of *Gone With the Most Romantic Wind Ever*," said Liesel. She threw her folded hands up to her chin, in true begging fashion. "Can we go if Hannah comes with us?"

"And Josh." Josh volunteered chaperone services with a raised hand. Okay, so he redeemed himself a little there. So what, if it was all about his desire to get closer to Hannah, not help her? If it worked, it worked.

They were out the door to church, without arriving at an acceptable resolution.

Her mother smacked her arm from across the pew, jarring her back to reality. Apparently, she forgot to stand up with the rest of them as the closing song began.

A Mighty Fortress is Our God.

Yeah, Mighty Fortress was right. Only its barred walls stretched across Five Maple Street.

As they headed out of church after the Freedom vs. Fortress divide, Mary Lou Lipnicki sidled up to Josh in the walkway leading out of church. She even tried that flirty, batty eyes technique. Flipped her hair back and forth. She must not have realized when she'd turn away from Josh her hair would hit him in the face. Clearly wasn't working on him. Clear to everyone except Mary Lou. Josh extracted himself to catch up with them.

At the bottom of the church steps, her mom shook Reverend Bacon's hand. As they headed into the churchyard, Hicks, his wife and son came up to them.

"Abigail. Josh and I here have mighty enjoyed working with that cousin of yours." Hicks hacked.

"What cousin?" Abigail asked.

Liesel shot a glance at Josh, whose complexion paled. *He knows too?* Hannah didn't even know she'd figured it out, seeing a man duck into the guest cabin several times, yet coming out as her female cousin for those late night dinners. It didn't take long to realize what Hannah was actually doing to earn sixty dollars a week. A miner's paycheck.

Hicks hacked more. "Sorry, just a little tickle."

His wife added, "Just a little black lung."

"Your cousin Mel."

"Who?"

Uh-oh. Liesel didn't have time to hear what Josh was going to say about that one. "Meet ya at home, Mom." She took off. She had to warn Hannah. Lucas didn't follow her, thank God.

When she flew in the front door, Hannah was still at the ivory keys. "We gotta go." She didn't want to scare her, but she had to get Hannah out of there, before her mother came home and started grilling.

"What is going on, Liesel?"

"Trust me. Go grab a sweater and meet me out front. No less than two minutes."

Thank God, Hannah complied. There was no time to answer more questions. Liesel quickly scribbled a note to her mom and flew out the door.

Moments later, she led Hannah toward Grey Street to avoid the path she knew Mom would take home from church.

"Liesel, what are we doing?"

"I left Mom a note, saying you graciously offered to chaperone. We'll hot rod to the beach early. Score some valuable stall time."

"Stall time for what?"

"Because you don't want to talk to my mother right now. She's gonna dig out the truth."

Hannah grabbed her arm, forced her to stop her fast pace.

"What truth are you referring to?"

"Yours. I know what you're doing. If anyone in town rats you to the company..."

Hannah's complexion literally paled in two seconds flat. "How did you..."

"I've seen you coming home. Took me a while to figure you weren't hiding a dreamboat in the guest cabin. But you'd go in a man and come out a lady. Honestly, I didn't think you were that kind of girl, to stow away a secret love. But at church today, Hicks spilled it to Mom, all about working with Cousin Mel. Now, Mom is bound to start asking questions. And she's soooooo maddeningly perceptive. If she wanted a job, she could be a private eye."

"Oh, no. Why didn't you say something earlier? All those nights we sat up and had a late dinner?"

"Those have actually been some of my favorite moments since Dad died. Having you to myself, while everyone else is asleep. Girl talk. I get why no one can know. This town is not known for keeping secrets."

"How long have you been keeping this?"

"Since right after Christmas. Hannah, I need to know. What's it like? Is it scary?"

"I thought it would be. But the men, they make it okay. They all have these goofy names for each other. They even gave me one. Rocky."

"Rocky?" Liesel cracked up.

"They have ways to pass the time. Playing tricks. Making up songs. Telling lies. Liesel, it's...there's nothing like it."

Liesel reached forward and hugged her cousin tightly. "I don't want to lose you next."

"You won't." Hannah's weak smile was not reassuring.

"How do you know that?"

"I thought you said we needed to floor it on out of here."

She was right. They made it over to Garrett's house, home of the ragtop they'd use to get to the drive-in. It took a full thirty minutes before they could reach Josh by phone to ask him to meet them at Garrett's. He'd be driving that ragtop. Liesel knew he'd have no hesitation about spending more time with Hannah.

Finally, they were on their way. Josh drove the convertible Chevy down Monument Hill toward Collingwood and Oxford, which led to the beach. Something about seeing Hannah sit next to him in the front seat felt right to Liesel. Also right was Garrett sitting by her side. Man, what a dreamboat he was. But Josh was driving too slowly. She did not need her mother stopping them from leaving town.

"Agitate gravel, Josh."

Josh sped up, leaving Springhill in the rearview.

♪ ♪ ♪

Hannah had never been to a drive-in before. It was one of those luxuries she and her mother couldn't afford. What a sight. All those cars parked on sand, up against speakers. The movie screens draped between two poles. According to Josh, some of the most popular cars on the market were here. Mercury Montclairs, Monarchs, Meteors, Ford Crown Vic, Pontiac Star Chiefs, other Chevys. They'd fit right in, as there were many convertibles.

The beach was a distance away, so cars were in no danger of getting swept away. Some set up lounge chairs on the sand in prep to watch the flick.

Josh pulled the ragtop into a spot not too far from the canteen.

When the projector started the animated preshow, Josh asked if she would like to head to the canteen for snacks.

Could she leave Liesel and Garrett alone in the car?

Liesel had a fearlessness she wished she had for herself. All the more reason not to leave the kid alone.

Josh read her mind. "They'll be fine. I had a little pre-chat with Garrett." He glanced at the young guy. "Right?"

"Right." Garrett nodded. Garrett had been nothing but sweet since she'd met him.

Hannah traipsed off with Josh. "So, what on earth happened at church after Liesel left? How much does Abigail know?"

"That she's got a distant cousin in town. One she's never heard about nor met."

"Uh-oh."

"Hicks didn't think much of it, but she sure did. And she wondered why on earth I hadn't mentioned Mel all this time. Of course, you and I know why."

They arrived at the canteen, a wooden shack well equipped to serve nachos, hotdogs, shakes, vanilla colas, and other delights. A girl in a cream sweater, pink poodle skirt and loosely curled hair pulled up in a ponytail held the arm of her handsome date. Her beau's dark hair was slicked back. He wore pressed slacks and a long sweater.

How had she missed those days of her adolescence? She never had a carefree date such as this. She hugged her arms around her waist.

The guy lifted the tray of food. The young woman kept her hand snug against his elbow as they both, all smiles, headed away from the canteen.

Josh stepped up to the pink-gum-smacking cashier. "Two vanilla colas, one chocolate shake, one strawberry, please."

When the girl moved off to gather their order, Hannah asked, "If Abby finds out...What if she can't keep my secret?"

"They've never let women work in the mines, and I hardly think Bryce will change that. Especially not for you. One of the few beautiful women in town who treats him well."

She searched his eyes. What was he implying?

"People have seen you together."

"We are most certainly not together, Josh. But I don't think he's as bad as people have made out either. He knows what it's like to be caught between a rock and a coalface."

"No, actually, he doesn't. And you don't want Abby going around town asking about her missing cousin Mel. Why was that your cover story?"

"I needed to use my real name for the paperwork. And if anyone met me and saw a resemblance, maybe they'd buy the family connection. I've been surprised this hasn't come up before."

As they carried drinks back to the convertible, Hannah saw Garrett gently slip his arm around Liesel. She tapped Josh's elbow, stopping him. Why not give them a moment?

Liesel smiled at Garrett, innocently. He kissed her forehead, then directed his eyes back to the screen as *Gone with the Wind* started. *Good boy, Garrett.* Hannah envied Liesel's flair for enjoying simple things like this. Would Hannah ever be that comfortable? Could she get there too?

They resumed their walk to the car, delivering milkshakes to the backseat.

Josh and Hannah sat down in the front seat and sipped vanilla colas. The four watched the movie in silence, captivated by the love story on screen.

As the music swelled in the end, Hannah and Liesel brushed tears off their cheeks. Josh looked over at Hannah in that way that told her he found her sentimentalism adorable.

He said, "Come on. Let's go home."

Home. Normally, the thought would excite her. How would she maneuver questions about Mel, should Aunt Abby inquire if she's heard of such a person?

On arrival back to Springhill, Josh stopped outside Abigail's place to drop them off.

Before Josh could get out, Garrett hopped out of the car with the grace of a leopard to open the passenger side door for the ladies.

He leaned into a gallant bow, offering his hand to Hannah first to help her out, then Liesel.

"Tonight was my pleasure, Ladies."

"Thank you, Garrett," Hannah said. "Tell your dad thanks for the wheels."

Liesel's hand got a sweet kiss.

Josh winked at Hannah.

Garrett took off his high school letter sweater and draped it over Liesel's shoulders. Now, this was getting serious. The young lady had a reason to smile again.

Hannah found herself thanking God for this special grace he had for the girl. She'd been through so much.

But wait. Did God have anything to do with this? Could he? Did he show up with blessings to make up for the pain? Truthfully, nothing could replace a father. But other blessings could make the pain easier to live with.

Hannah looked away so Garrett could kiss Liesel's cheek in peace, catching eyes with Josh who was watching her. He saluted her, his smile dimpling his own cheek.

Garrett got back in the car, and the girls watched the wheels kick dust as the boys drove away.

Liesel hugged the sweater with her arms and squealed.

"Somebody's been bitten," Hannah said.

"I have it on good authority that one Joshua Theodore Winslow the sixth, seventh, eighth or whatever would hang the moon for a chance to get jacketed with you."

"Aren't we a little old for that? I don't even think they had those when we were in high school."

Liesel fanned her arms out and spun around. "You're never too old for love." She landed right in front of Hannah and looked her in the eyes. "Or to get over the fear of it."

Ouch. How did the fifteen-year-old gain such perception? It seemed this child knew her better than anyone in town.

Liesel giggled. "Can we stay up all night and gab about boys?" They walked to the guest cabin instead of heading into the house.

As they stepped inside, they found Abigail sitting on the cot. Various pieces of Ray's clothing were in her lap. Other pieces of Hannah's disguise, her mustache, wig, littered the cot.

She was cooked.

"Liesel, go into the house." Abigail's nostrils flared as she breathed.

"Mom?"

"Now."

Liesel's eyebrows creased downward at Hannah, then she slipped out.

"I have been trying to figure out what you've been hiding since you got here," Abigail said.

"Aunt Abby, I'm just trying to help."

"Then, tell me the truth. Is that too much to ask?"

"No."

"Explain."

Liesel barged back in the door. "Mom, trust her."

"Liesel, I told you to go—"

"—No. Mom."

"Liesel, it's okay." Hannah nodded to the door.

Abigail asked, "What do you know about this, Liesel?"

"I know Hannah has done more to help this family than anyone. Especially me. You want to know why she runs the other way any time a miner walks her direction? Including why she can't go to church with us? It's because she is a miner, Mom." Liesel's face burned red. "When we had nothing, she went out and got the only job she could...in the mines. She is why there is still food on our table."

Hannah had never been defended like that before. This kid had become one of her favorite people on this planet. But would she be forced to leave her and the rest of the family, because of these lies?

Abigail covered her mouth. "I was afraid. After what Hicks said at church, about this distant cousin Mel. The amount of money you've been bringing in, so close to sixty a week. Then I found all of this. I wanted to be wrong."

"You can't tell anyone, Aunt Abigail."

"Hannah, I do not want you down there. I don't care if we have to scrape every penny..."

"Mom, there are no pennies to scrape," Liesel said. "She didn't have a choice."

"Hasn't this family lost enough? Hannah, if something happens to you..."

"I have to stay. It's the only way."

Abigail unexpectedly crouched over. "Ah!"

"What?" Hannah asked.

Abigail gasped, yet managed to smile. "I think Little One is fighting to come out."

HANNAH SECRETLY WORKED with the kids—while Abigail was recovering in the hospital—to get a new room ready for the baby. *Room* may be a little generous, as it was anything but roomy. More like a nine-by-five storage space on the second floor. It would do. They handmade decorations, sewed fabric into blankets, and restored an old crib last used by Lenny, with the help of Mr. Yeardly at the furniture store. When Hannah tried to pay him, he insisted it was a gift for Abigail. And no, the old bachelor wasn't trying to buy a date with her, even though he joked about it.

To Lindy's complete delight and Lucas's chagrin, the newest Percy kid was a girl. By the time Abigail left All Saints Hospital, Little One had a name: Laurel.

"No sense breaking the L train," Abigail had said.

Lindy may not have gotten her Lucy and Lucas didn't get his Larry, but Laurel was perfect in every way, named after Ray's grandmother.

Neighbors made sure they were stocked with newborn clothes and supplies. Hannah could not fit one more casserole in the icebox. There was always someone to stay with the kids if Hannah needed to go to the hospital to see Abigail and Laurel, or to work—which any helper assumed was in Amherst.

Life was different here; life was good. It seemed like Springhill had been blessed with a reprieve. Nothing could go wrong.

chapter 13

Winter 1957

The next five months whirred by. Before Hannah knew it, shop owners on Main Street were putting up their Christmas trees again. The town's decorating crew had draped colored lights—in crisscross fashion from one lamppost to the next—over Main Street. The chill had returned to the air. Time had offered the warmth of healing. People seemed ready to celebrate again. Especially after they'd bonded together in November for a one-year memorial service, honoring the fallen men of the No. 4.

One particular Saturday afternoon, Hannah was put on Christmas shopping duty. Aunt Abigail sent young Lindy with her, the now nine-years-and-two-quarters live wire. Lindy peeked in the window of a clothing store. "For Christmas, I'm buying you a new 'stache, Hannah Bana."

"Oh, really. You're not supposed to tell me, ya know. Presents are secrets."

"Yeah, but that one Mel's been sporting...it's getting scraggly. I could give it to you early."

"Mary Lou sells them at the Five & Dime."

The young girl dragged Hannah by the arm. "Come here. I want to show you something."

They landed outside of an empty shop, nestled between Harroun's Clothing and Mr. Yeardley's Furniture Store. Lindy put armloads of goodies and gifts for her siblings down on the sidewalk. Then, she plastered her face against the glass. It sat empty, awaiting a new shop owner. "This is it, Hannah. The place I want."

"Really? Right here?"

"I can see the sign. Miss Lindy's Penny Candy, right over the doorframe. Is that too many words?" Breathlessly, she pointed to one of the two windows on either side of the door. "There, I'd put ribbon candies, all different colors of course. Many shades of pinks, yellows, greens, oranges. It would be a big draw."

"I believe it would, Lindy."

"And I'd make fudge and taffy in that other window. Not just Maple Taffy. All flavors."

Hannah loved the way the young girl already knew how to dream, how to envision her future. "Maybe you could give me a job, kiddo."

"I'd be delighted to make you my personal helper. Let's do it now. Get you out of that mine—"

Hannah whipped her finger to her lips. "Shh." One listening ear was all it would take to blow this whole thing up. "What used to be here?"

"A dairy store. They brought in milk and cheese from a dairy in Parrsboro."

If only they had the resources to start their own family store, maybe things could change. Maybe she could even convince Josh to come help them. He could bake. Get him up from underground too. Wait a minute. She wasn't planning to be with him. Why should it matter what he did for a living?

"Hannah! Lindy! Yoo hoo!" Miss Mary Lou Lipnicki flailed her arms, waving from the Five & Dime a few doors down. "Hello, Little Lindy." Mary Lou trotted over to them.

"I'm kinda not little anymore, Mary Lou. Keep up." Lindy snapped her fingers twice.

Mary Lou pinched the kid's cheek. "Lindy, you must tell your mother, I've been selling some of them dresses she made with those matching dolly clothes. Can she get me more in time for Christmas sales? I'll throw in an extra twenty percent."

"I'll ask her," Lindy said.

"And while you're at it," Mary Lou's eyes narrowed on Hannah, "tell your cousin not to steal my Joshua."

A polite smile was the best way out of this. "Come on, Lindy." Hannah tapped the kid's shoulder. "We need to finish up."

Lindy gladly picked up her packages and turned the opposite direction of the lovelorn lady.

Once they were out of earshot, Lindy giggled. "She's hopeless, isn't she?"

"Now, Lindy, we can't say that we blame her, can we? Everyone just wants to be loved."

"Ah! So, you admit Josh is a dreamy ship?"

"You mean dreamboat?"

"Yeah, that. When are you gonna let him take you on a real date?"

That was one excellent question.

"SO, HANNAH," LIESEL CHUCKLED. "Am I your date?"

Hannah began to question her judgment. Was this a good idea? Inviting this loose cannon of a teenager to the Miners' Christmas party?

"Liesel, remember. I am Mel, not Hannah."

"Right. Little hard to forget, when you've got fuzzy brown fur growing from your upper lip, Hannah. I mean Mel." Liesel covered her mouth to suppress another laugh. The girl was enjoying this entirely too much.

They arrived outside the Armory, the hall most often used in town to throw parties. This was all about strategy. Let a family member finally be seen with "Mel." Added authenticity, didn't it? Only if the young, blonde-haired beauty didn't blow her cover.

Noise bled into the parking lot from the festivities going on inside. The Miners' Christmas party crawled with every miner in town and their spouses. They'd skipped throwing this event last year. No one felt like celebrating then.

Bryce had asked her to come as his date. Naturally, she declined. It wasn't like she could go as Josh's date, either. Though his pronounced hints were adorable. But how could she risk seeing her entire team while Mel was noticeably absent? This was far too *Twelfth Night* for her comfort. She'd leave dancing dual identities to Shakespeare. It was enough to pull off playing Mel for the evening.

Just Mel. No Hannah.

Yes, going as Mel was the best choice. They'd arrive late, make their appearance, then duck out as early as possible.

As they stepped inside the crowded hall, Bryce and his father raised their glasses to the crowd in a toast. Adam

Sawyer said, "We are thankful for all the work you men have done this year. This has been a good year for us, a welcome reprieve after the difficult ending of 1956. We've had an accident-free year, and we're thankful each one of you is with us. We would be nothing without you."

A fellow miner in the crowd grumbled to a friend, "This is the first year someone hasn't died in the last ten."

The other miner said, "But who's counting?"

"It's been a good year for Springhill," Adam said, as he raised his glass. "Thank you for your service."

"Here, here," Bryce seconded with a raise of his drink. Everyone took a sip.

"Now, there's plenty of food, so dig in," Adam said. They didn't have to tell anyone twice. The buffet of hors d'oeuvres would go quickly.

"Rocky!" Lazy Haze used her pet name. She turned around to see him heading toward her through the crowd. "Good to see you out. Me and the boys, we were just saying how we never see you off work hours."

Hicks stepped in behind Lazy Haze. "Hi there, Rocky."

"Don't mind my cousin," Liesel threw in. "He likes to spend his free time with us, is all. Once he decided to show up. We had to hear about him being in town from you, Hicks. Can you believe that?"

Got to appreciate the girl's knack for a cover up. Abigail had better hope this one stays on the narrow road, as comfortable as she was with lying. Guilt tugged at Hannah. After all, Liesel's lies were for her sake.

"And I wouldn't miss this," Hannah said, in a deeper voice than normal.

Isaak walked up. "Hello, Mel. Good to see ya."

The way Isaak looked into her eyes made her squirm.

If anyone had a chance of figuring her out, it was him, especially since she'd spent time with Isaak as herself. "Where are the kids?"

"Ah, we didn't want Adam to run out of food too early." Isaak winked at her, and headed over to build a plate of delectables.

What was with that wink? Was he on to her too?

She felt an arm slide over her shoulders. Josh, his face sporting a wide grin. "Good evening, Mel." He emphasized the L in Mel. "I was beginning to wonder if you were gonna make it." He seemed to enjoy draping that arm around her. Securely.

Bryce snaked the crowd their direction. She quickly ducked out from Josh's arm and went the other way. If Bryce found out who Mel was, this would all be over.

♫ ♫ ♫

Josh's assignment for the day after Christmas, Boxing Day, was to teach Lindy how to make homemade candies. Hannah had surprised the girl with a special candy-making kit for Christmas.

Josh and Lindy's first attempt at making taffy didn't work out so well. They were missing one key ingredient for the finished product: waxed paper. Hannah was profusely apologetic. Yet, she did nothing to help clean up the mess. Lucas and Lenny enjoyed the unsightly castoffs. Lindy tried to charge them pennies, just for practice. That fell as flat as Josh's hair after a night wearing his miner's lamp. Liesel passed on the candies; she wanted to save her girlish figure to impress Garrett.

Abigail seemed content to nurse baby Laurel, and watch Lenny play with his new erector set.

After standing all day at the stove, Josh collapsed on the couch between Hannah and Liesel, to watch a holiday special they'd tuned into on the TV. He'd surprised them with a new set for Christmas.

Just as he'd started to massage his aching calves, an ominous whistle sounded.

"What is that?" Hannah asked.

Lindy leapt up off the couch and headed for the front door.

"Fire whistle," said Lucas.

That whistle blasted three times fast, then three times slow. He knew the code. That meant the fire was close. "Sounds like it's on Main Street," Josh said.

Everyone jumped out of their comfy chairs or up off the floor to join Lindy at the door. They ran around to the side of the house. Smoke rose above the trees. "Definitely Main Street. I'll go check it out," Josh said.

"I'm coming with you," said Hannah.

"Can I go?" Liesel asked.

"Grab your coats," Abigail said. "And be careful."

Lindy and Lucas raced back inside for their woolens.

They hurried toward Main Street. Sweat built up under his coat, despite the cold. Whose store was burning? Whose life was about to change?

Others merged from Spruce, Queen, and Fir Street as they ran toward Main.

They arrived at the corner of Junction and Main, and traced the smoke down to its source:

Mr. Yeardley's Furniture Store.

All ablaze. Embers hopped from its roof onto the adjacent shop. A new blaze erupted.

"Hannah!" Lindy pointed to the new blaze. Hannah put her arm around her. "That's my store. We were going to…" The kid burst into tears.

"You guys should get out of here. It's not safe," Josh said.

Liesel said, "I'm not going anywhere."

Lucas walked over to the post office steps and stood below the clock tower. The rest of them followed. They could get a better look from there.

The Springhill Fire Brigade fought the flame, but the fire hoses didn't seem to make a dent. The flames still roared.

If they didn't get help fast, they could lose the whole street. The center of town. Their lifeblood. One of the only areas people could work outside the mines. Not to mention, it was their supply center.

Josh looked up at the sky. He silently mouthed, "Please help." Would God have mercy on their town?

"Look out!" a firefighter yelled.

The furniture store's roof collapsed. Burning timbers crashed into the inferno. A beam on the outside of the store's frame fell down to the sidewalk below with a loud slam, sending flames skyward.

"Get back, get back!" The firefighters shouted to the crowd.

Light from the flames flickered across Mr. Yeardley's face. He watched from across the street as his life's work went up in smoke.

Murmurs multiplied through the crowd. Where did it start? How did it start? More sirens blared in the distance.

Firefighting teams were coming. Probably from Amherst, Oxford, and Parrsboro. The street continued to fill with Springhillers, some whose very names were burning off signs.

Within the hour, five stores had burned to the ground, with several others just beginning their demise. The wind whipped up. It carried the flames from the pharmacy to the jewelry shop next door.

Just then, a fireman emerged out the front door of the jewelry store. An elderly woman lay splayed across his arms. Flames began their dance in the windows above the store. Must have been her apartment. Thank God, she was breathing.

Why did this town have to fight so hard to survive? Why did it seem *something* was always against it? Wasn't this the first year, in a long time, they'd had a reprieve in the mines?

And now, this. The day after Christmas.

How many more tragedies could this place survive? The people built this town. They may be resilient, but why did they always have to be?

"Is there anything we can do?" Hannah asked. He loved her heart, her willingness to dive in.

"Not unless you have your own fire truck." Suddenly, he wanted nothing more than to make sure she stayed safe.

Just then, the flames arched across the street toward the place where they stood. In a moment, one of the town's most vital stores was ablaze:

Martin's Groceteria.

Josh ran both hands through his hair and clasped them at the back of his head. He'd only felt this helpless one other time in his life: when the mine exploded.

chapter 14

Early 1958

"Bring that one over here," Josh yelled to Hannah.

Hannah picked up a timber from a supply stack that Josh needed for the grocery store site. Those around her may have wondered why she was strong enough to do such a thing. That's what over a year of practice underground does for you.

Only this effort…this was about rebuilding.

It may have been tempting to let Main Street go after the Boxing Day Fire. Just for a day, when they stood in the midst of the devastation. Even the post office and its prominent clock tower were gone. But watching Springhill's progress at their own hands was rewarding.

Three of the iconic places in town that were not harmed were Hector's Pool Hall, Lipnicki's Five & Dime, and the Liar's Bench. The bench being preserved might have had something to do with Hector and Hicks literally picking up the renowned seat, carrying it down Main Street, and storing it in the pool hall for safe keeping till the danger was over.

With fourteen businesses wiped out, an action plan for rebuilding was set into motion. Everyone in town agreed. The grocery store would be the first to reopen. It wasn't just about convenience of necessities.

This was for Martin.

When the miners' families had come up short, Martin had left accounts revolving. It was no question that everyone would band together and return the favor.

When Hannah decided to leave behind the world she'd known and come to Springhill, she had no idea of the tragedies that would strike this town. Yet, she didn't regret her decision. No. This was her home now.

"Oops." Her timber smacked Mr. Yeardly in the shin. "Sorry, Mr. Yeardly."

"No problem, Hannah."

"You know we're rebuilding your store next."

The old man had one tooth that was shinier than the others. "Hannah, I think this fire, it showed me this may be a good time to retire."

"What? You loved running that store."

"I love having more time for dancing with the ladies at the Lodge too. This summer, I'm thinking of throwing a few dance parties myself."

She laughed. He sure seemed a lot younger than he was. Late eighties, maybe? She put the end of her plank down on the ground, held it in place where it stood taller than her. "Mr. Yeardly, why didn't you ever get married?"

"I guess I had too much fun filling my dance card when I was a young one. By the time I thought about picking somebody, they was already committed."

Her face must have betrayed her.

His eyes twinkled when he smiled. "Now, don't go

feeling bad for me, young lady. I like flirtin' too much. I did just fine. But you, what'cha waitin' for?"

She glanced over Josh's way as he wiped a layer of sweat off his forehead. Even though it was the dead of winter, the physical labor kept them warm.

"How about you fill out Josh's name on your dance card? Just tell him I want you to save one slot for me."

"Of course, Mr. Yeardly."

"Everyone in town knows he doesn't fancy that Mary Lou girl. He wants you."

He wanted her? Someone else had wanted her, but as one to control, not cherish.

She carried the plank over to Josh. That white T-shirt he wore under his coveralls sure showed off his sculpted muscles. "Sorry, Josh. Mr. Yeardly wanted to get in his daily flirting quota."

"I saw that. I'm sure you made his day."

And somehow, she knew. If she'd ever choose to make Josh's day, he'd choose to cherish her. Not control.

"Come and get it!" Lindy called out to the workers from her sidewalk table. The Lindy Comfort Station included free sugary treats. The kid was already building her reputation.

Hannah walked over and grabbed a chocolatey truffley treat. Martin was already at the table, tasting one. "Mmm, mmm. Lindy, you got something here."

Lindy didn't miss a beat. "And when we finish the rebuild, I want a counter in your store to sell my delicious goods. I'd like to test the market before I open my store."

"You got it."

"And we split the profits, 50-50."

"You drive a hard bargain, little lady." They shook on

it. In this town, people's word was golden. When they said they'd show up, they showed up. When they promised to do something for you, they did it. When they said, "We will rebuild," they meant it.

With chocolate still melting on her tongue, thoughts of not letting Josh get away nagged her. She'd taken chances in the past, and they'd backfired. She'd watched Abigail at home cradle little Baby Laurel, who Uncle Ray never got to meet. Yet, Aunt Abigail seemed to have no regrets. Could Hannah continue to let fear drive her life? Or was it scarier to move into a relationship, only to risk losing that love?

She wished they could make a career of something on Main Street. Especially since, lately, the men of the deeps had started to complain again

Unsafe. Pressure build-up.

Those were just a few of the words she'd heard either on the way down on the rake or from men on her team.

♫ ♫ ♫

Spring 1958

"The engineers came back with these for us to consider." Bryce posted two drawings on a board in front of Cal in the office. Finally, he had something to show for all those long, yawn-inducing meetings with the engineers all winter. Even into spring, now. They'd been suggesting a different way of mining in the No. 2. They weren't sure if the method would help with production speed, like he'd hoped. But at least they claimed their new plans were safer for the miners. Reduce some of that pressure.

Bryce traced his finger along one drawing. "This one depicts how the walls are forty to fifty feet apart."

As Cal stepped closer to get a good look, Bryce pointed to the other. "This shows how the walls will be lined up if we go down to five feet."

"They're confident this is the best method on that level? I'm not sure about this, Bryce."

Why did Cal have to question everything, including expert opinion? Let him do his job. Let the engineers do theirs. "It's all in black and white, Cal."

"I still think the two of us should go down, take a look, and especially talk to the miners. See how they feel about this potential switch."

"I trust the engineers." Bryce glanced at his watch. "Plus, I have a meeting today, off property. Feel free to go down and do the survey."

Bryce headed out. It was the easiest way to avoid Cal's relentless requests for him to go underground. That was not going to happen.

Plus, he had somewhere to be.

IT HAD BEEN A LONG TIME since he'd set foot on the high school grounds. How he loathed high school and everything about it. His classmates. His teachers. The looks he got because of who he was, as if any of it was his fault.

Today, he needed to talk to one particular young student. Better to seek her out here, than to run into her on Maple Street.

At three o'clock, the end-of-school-day bell signaled. It had always been his favorite sound of the day. Not much had changed around this place.

There she was.

A smitten boy was holding her hand. The boy pulled her into an embrace, then gave her a peck on the cheek. Bryce exhaled. *Go home, already.* He didn't have all day.

Mercifully, they parted. Finally, Bryce could get a private word with her. "Lisa," he called.

She didn't stop walking. He jogged to catch up to her and tapped her shoulder. "Hey, Lisa."

She turned around. "Lisa? Try Liesel."

"Liesel. Sorry. Liesel Percy, right? Now that we're acquainted, I'm —"

"What do you want, Bryce Sawyer?"

She already knew him? This couldn't be good. Not the way she just said that. "It's about your cousin."

She stared at him, as if waiting for him to continue. Her pupils seemed to narrow. Why did she suddenly look nervous as she shifted her weight from one foot to the other?

"If you don't mind, I have a couple of questions for you about your cousin who works for me."

"Ah, about Mel?"

"Her name is Hannah."

Her sassy tone evaporated. "How...how did you find out?" She kicked rocks out from under her shoe.

"Huh? She told me." Not everyone completely ignores him in this town, right?

The girl just cocked her head to one side. "Are you going to fire her?"

"No. Why would I? She knows her music."

The girl let out a breath and stopped shifting her weight. "Oh. Hannah...she teaches you music?"

"Yes. Guitar. What did you think she taught me?"

Now he understood why he never spent much time with teenagers. They didn't make much sense.

"What…what's your question?" She asked.

"I want to reward her for all of her hard work with me, teaching me to read music. But I'd like to do something personal. I was wondering if you could tell me more about her. What she likes…"

"You mean what she fancies? Besides Joshua Winslow? You know, Josh, right?" She lifted an eyebrow.

Why did she have to knock the wind right out of him? She didn't notice. Or maybe, she just didn't care.

"We had this spectacular double date at the drive-in. We, as in Garrett and me. Josh and Hannah. When you find someone, we can make it a triple. You can even pay. Maybe that's what Hannah would *l-like*." Her tongue flicked out of her mouth as she emphasized that L.

She smiled, pivoted the other direction, and walked off. At a deliberate clip too. Even the younger generation didn't care for him. He couldn't win.

He was not about to wrap up Josh Winslow as a thank you gift and give him to Hannah. No. He wanted her all to himself.

♫ ♫ ♫

Josh never got tired of playing jokes on his buddies underground. When Lazy Haze chose to live up to his name, he deserved whatever he got.

Plum gave two thumbs up as Josh tied Lazy's shoelaces together. Lazy snored, leaning against the coalface wall. Hannah looked at Josh with that parental disapproval, but he could see the smile behind her eyes. Or Mel's eyes, in this setting.

Isaak struck the flat of his pick against the shaft's wall with an infectious rhythm. Morale always soared when Isaak did that. It helped pass the time. In over a year and a half of working this shift together, they'd made up at least two hundred songs. One of these days, they should sell them. They should call themselves the Musical Miners or something like that.

"There was an old man..." Isaak's smooth voice crooned to his beat.

Plum added, "Whose name was bland..."

"He lived in the sand..." Hicks sang.

"Instead of on farmland," Josh threw in and tossed a look Hannah's way, signaling it was her turn.

She seemed to choke for a moment. "His waistband expanded because he ate food that was canned."

Okay, so, maybe the Musical Miners wouldn't sell a single copy. But at least it was entertaining.

"You're not playing right, Mel." Josh winked at her. "That's too many syllables."

Hannah smiled, threw a little wink back.

"Speakin' of waistband, this shift here over yet?" Plum lifted his pants a bit.

Oh, no. Don't go there, Plum.

"I's getting' that itch in my rocks. And it's my anniversary, boys. Yes, it is."

Yep. He went there. Plum moved his pants up and down several times, a bawdy hint of his evening rendezvous plans with his wife. If only he knew there was a lady present.

"Keep it to yourself, man." *Please, please keep it to*

yourself.

"You're green-eyed, Winnie. Wantin' your own backseat bingo," Plum said.

"Speakin' of...any bingo with that Hannah girl?" Hicks asked.

Oh, Lord. Not a question he wanted to answer with Hannah in the room. "Cut the gas, guys."

"I hear Bryce is trying to get dibs on her," Hicks said.

Josh picked up his tool and slammed it into the coalface, loosening a big piece.

"Ooh. Somebody's gettin' frosted," Plum said.

"Lay off, boys." Isaak borrowed Hannah's parental look and threw it at Hicks and Plum. He commanded such respect. They shut up about Bryce. Mercifully.

"You know what, Josh?" Hicks said. "I's startin' to believe she don't exist. Never run into her. Odd, this bein' a small town."

"I've seen her," Isaak said.

"She's my cousin," Hannah added, with that deep voice of Mel's. "I run into her all the time."

"Come on, Josh," said Hicks. "Tell us 'bout her."

"Yeah, Josh. Tell us," Hannah said.

Even *she* was getting in on this game. Despite how dark it was underground, her teasing eyes met his.

He kept his look direct. "Hannah...she's the finest woman I've ever eyeballed. But she's buttoned up 'bout herself, her past. And stubborn as a burro."

"I don't find her that way at all," Hannah said with a silly grin.

"Mel, you ever been married?" Hicks asked.

Josh watched her.

She hesitated, then said, "No."

"Ever come a hair close?"

"Once."

Hmm. Was that true?

Plum asked, "Tell us, Rocky. Her knockers knock ya?"

Hannah let out a gasp, almost blowing her cover by the sound of her voice.

Josh quickly said, "That's enough of that talk, Plum. Every woman deserves respect. Don't talk about them that way." He shifted his glance Hannah's direction. She offered the slightest smile, seeming to appreciate his defense. "Now, everyone, back to work."

♫ ♫ ♫

They'd be mortified if they knew a woman were present. At the same time Hannah sure enjoyed being "one of the guys."

Her stomach growled long before the dinner break arrived. She worked alone, since Lazy Haze hadn't done one blessed thing except snore.

When break time came, everyone sat against the walls digging into their lunch pails. Hicks, Plum, and Josh sang a ridiculous song at the top of their lungs.

Welcome to the ole Number 2.

Where the rocks are hard and the coals are few.

Till a bump shakes her up, scrambled sunny side up.

Lazy Haze didn't even stir at their ditty.

Isaak slid down the wall beside Hannah and leaned over to her while the others entertained themselves with their off-kilter rhyme schemes.

He quietly asked, "How are things going for you down here?"

"Good. Really. I thought I would hate it."

Could she ask him? The question had been burning on her heart for a while now about the day her dad died. "Isaak, Josh told me that you were there the day my cousin, Melvin, died."

He nodded. "Worst day I'd ever had in these mines. I was new at it. Hadn't dealt with many bumps. Three of our team, well, they died just like that." He snapped his fingers. "Josh's father, he was pinned under all this coal. Melvin rushed back. Tried to dig him out. Each piece, one by one. But another rumble hit a short time after. It sent coal and timber piling on both of 'em."

Hannah glanced over at Josh, who was still engrossed in silly crooning.

"Me and Yates. Nothing we could do." Isaak cleared his throat as his eyes watered. "Died a hero, your Daddy did."

Daddy? Wait a minute. Isaak knew her real identity?

Isaak placed a reassuring hand on hers. "Don't worry," he said, as he raised a brow. "*Mel*, I won't tell."

Tears sprung to her eyes. She released a breath and glanced at Josh.

Lazy Haze snorted loudly as he woke up. "Hey! Why didn't no one wake me? Dinner time already?" As he took a step forward, he tripped over his tied shoelaces. "Ah!"

Everyone cracked up, at Lazy Haze's expense. He had it coming; he did sleep through half a shift.

Josh doubled over, clutching his stomach. Seeing him so light, so carefree...if Hannah was certain about one thing, she couldn't lose this. She couldn't lose any of them.

chapter 15

Summer 1958

Hannah left the front door open, to allow warm afternoon air inside the musty place. It was her first time back to her parents old home since Abigail revealed the house. Would seeing the rest of her parents' private home make her feel better or worse?

She slipped into their old master bedroom. The bed still here, stripped of its coverings. Her cheeks burned as she let herself wonder. Was this where she was conceived? She shouldn't linger over such thoughts.

Maybe one day, when she didn't need to live at the Percys anymore, she could make this her home. She'd never had one. Especially not that yellow cottage.

A vision lit her imagination. What a wonderful Bed & Breakfast this could make, welcoming visitors to town. Maybe Josh could cook…

Wait. She couldn't plan her future with him. No sense letting that roll around.

She, as the caretaker, would stay in this room. The upstairs could house guests. Yes, possibilities abounded.

Arriving at the top of the steps, she noticed three doors. Two remained opened and one was closed.

The first room was a sewing room with fabric, various threads and needles, a rocking chair, and a Singer sewing machine. Huh. So, her mother enjoyed sewing here too. She'd never had a machine, just a needle and thread. She often made Hannah's clothes. Once she hit her teens, that was embarrassing.

The next was a guestroom with just a full bed, a dresser, and a nightstand.

Her hand turned the knob of the third room. With a click, the door opened. She gasped. Whatever air she had left dissipated.

A crib.

A changing table.

A dresser.

A rocking chair with a lamp beside it.

A stuffed bear sitting on that chair.

A dusty blanket left behind in the crib.

All uncovered, unprotected for almost three decades.

There was no fighting the tears. Sobs overtook her. Before she knew it, she found herself on her knees, wrapping her waist in her own arms. Never before had she felt the sense of being an orphan this deeply. Not even when her mother passed away. The reality of her father had been so remote to her back then, but being here. Being where he intended to raise her with her mother, it was too much.

The stories that should have been read to her from that rocking chair. The songs that should have been sung.

Life was so unfair.

If she had grown up in this home — with both parents

together — would she have made the mistakes she'd made? Would she have been a different person? She'd never know. Life didn't give repeats.

What was that noise, outside the front door? Footsteps. Had he found her? Followed her to Springhill? He'd love nothing more than to rip her away from any life she'd tried to build, wouldn't he?

She peeked out a window from the second story as she saw *him* ascend the front steps. She let out a breath.

Josh. *Whew.*

The railing moved loosely in her hand as she descended the stairs. That was her life. Everything she should be able to depend on was in utter disrepair.

She stepped into the doorway. "You scared me."

"Sorry. I was on my way to Hector's and saw the front door open. I wondered if someone broke in."

Before she knew it, she had wrapped her arms around him. It was as if her very life and safety depended upon him.

He placed a hand on the back of her head.

His nearness, it felt so good. And somehow, she knew she had to let go. It wouldn't be right to raise false hopes. "Want to see the inside?" She moved away from him as quickly as she could, heading back into the house.

Josh stepped inside and strolled to the living area. He gazed at a photo of her parents on the mantle. His finger removed the dust that covered their faces.

"You know, Hannah, this place being on the corner of Main, it would be a fine spot for a music store. Maybe even a music school."

"Trying to kick me off our team?"

He cracked a smile.

"And what is your dream, Josh? If you never had to go back down..."

"There's only one dream I'm missing." His fingers traced the photo of two people in love.

A pang stabbed her heart. She walked over to him and joined him at the mantle. Yet, his eyes remained focused on the photo.

"Josh, Isaak told me the story."

When he didn't look up at her, she gently touched his face so he would. His eyes sparkled in the sunlight that peeked through the window.

"Josh, did you think I would hold it against you, that my father died trying to save yours?"

He hesitated before he finally answered. "You blame yourself for your mother's death."

"How...who told you that?"

"Liesel. She wasn't trying to break your confidence or anything. I pressed her a little hard."

"If you want to know something, why don't you just ask me?"

"You're not the easiest person to get an answer out of. Do you have any idea how hard it's been, to get to know you?"

"Why are we getting off point? I wanted you to know, I don't blame my dad for going back. Or yours for needing him. At least, I don't think I do." She took the photo of her parents. "I...it's not like your dad did anything to make it happen. It's so arbitrary, isn't it? Who gets caught down there? Who doesn't?"

She touched her father's face in the photograph. "Maybe the awful, selfish side of me, which I hate, wishes my dad had kept going. That he could have been here, to see his prayers get answered. But, no. That's not who he was. It's not who I'd want him to be. I just hope I'd do the same, you know, if any of our guys needed me."

"Any of us would." With the back of his hand, he brushed away the tear that slid down her cheek. "Come on. How about we enjoy a stroll down Main Street? It's nice out there today. It'll be a non-date."

That sounded fun. They'd have to stop by Lindy's Candy Booth at Martin's Groceteria. They could check on whichever Springhillers were working on rebuild efforts that day. It was heartening to see all the progress they'd made, seeing wood she'd helped nail or panels she'd helped paint.

The furniture store was having its grand reopening next weekend, as a partnership between Mr. Yeardly and his retired neighbor, Mr. Megeney, a man who'd probably be dancing into his nineties as well.

From across the street, they spotted several volunteers building the new clock tower for the Post Office. Josh pulled Hannah toward the Liar's Bench.

"Come on." He took a seat and gestured for her to sit beside him. "Tell me all the lies you've told since you moved here."

"Do I lie about the lies? Or does telling the truth violate some code of the Liar's Bench?"

"Surprise me."

"What do you want to know?"

"About what you told Isaak down below. Was it your alias, Mel, who was almost married or you?"

"Ah, lemme go ask Mel." She tried to stand, but he yanked her back down. She chuckled.

"Clever. Neither lie nor truth. Well?" he asked.

"Neither of us."

"Is that the truth?"

"This is the Liar's Bench. You decide."

"Okay. Next question. Would you like to have that dinner I'm going to cook tonight?"

She hesitated. Really, what could it hurt? Josh was her good friend. "Just dinner?"

"Just dinner," he reassured.

That's when she spotted them. "Uh-oh."

When Josh started to turn around to see what she saw, she grabbed his hand and pulled him into the small alley beside Lipnicki's Five & Dime. They hovered near the brick wall, out of site. Temporarily.

"What is it?" Josh peeked out from their hiding place.

Why did Lazy, Hicks, and Plum have to choose this moment to be-bop around town? They were headed their way.

"Ah, ha," Josh said. "So, Mel doesn't want to be social today?"

"Shh!"

He was peeking out way too far. She pulled him right back, trying to keep them both out of sight.

It didn't work. They'd been spotted. One by one, each face peered at them. The three men were in full-on spy mode.

She grabbed Josh's face. "Kiss me."

"Huh?"

"Now!" They couldn't see her face if Josh covered it, right?

If she'd had a camera, she would've captured his perplexed face. Priceless.

Before planting one on her, he glanced back at his not-so-subtle friends, waved them away.

Then, he did exactly what she asked.

He kissed her. Gently. His hands cupped her face. His eyes were closed.

Maybe I should close mine too.

She did, then took a moment to drink in each sensation. His lips. Their warmth. His breath. His scent. Tingles skittered through her entire frame. It felt so sweet, so affectionate, so real.

And it didn't scare her.

She almost forgot they had an audience until Hicks said, "There really is a Hannah," followed by his trademark hiccup and hacking cough. The three nosy miners whistled one of their silly songs. They didn't even try to hide the fact they were spying. Then, they continued on their way down the sidewalk, hooting and hollering.

Once they were out of sight, Hannah retreated from the embrace. She looked up at Josh. "Sorry about that."

"Thank you, 'cause you know I needed that apology." His dimples signaled he didn't really need it.

He squeezed her shoulder. "Anything to keep up your charade, right?"

That love stuff kept shoving its way to the surface, clamoring for her attention. She'd have to shovel it away, like rocks tossed in a stone pack.

She couldn't fall in love with this man, could she?

♫ ♫ ♫

There was no denying it for Bryce. He was losing his father. Maybe not in the traditional way others in this town had lost theirs. Yet it was still because of mining.

In many ways, he wished their family had never moved to this Godforsaken town. His grandparents were from Prince Edward Island. His grandfather had been the owner of one of PEI's biggest fisheries when Cumberland Coal came calling. They needed a bail out and better management. His grandfather had the capital to buy into the company and to reshape it from an arm's length. Instead, he took over. He relocated his family, and they never left. In a way, this was his grandfather's fault. He was the one who forced his dad to work in the mines as a day laborer, then a miner. Dad even worked in the Lamp Cabin for a while. Grandpa wanted him to earn his way toward future ownership.

Well, when his dad tried that with him...it didn't work. Bryce couldn't figure out why anyone would choose to settle here, in Springhill, instead of among the panoramic, rolling hills mingled with rivers and seaports of Prince Edward Island. It was a place he'd much rather live. He wondered if he could talk Hannah into taking the ferry over with him for a day and get a taste of first-class seafood.

He didn't know how long he'd been standing there, dreaming of another land. But his father's abrupt voice interrupted. "Can't you hold the door?"

"Sorry."

He widened the front door of his dad's home. The old man hobbled inside. It was hard to see his dad needing a walker to get around, even if the doctor said it should be temporary. He just needed strength after this latest, small heart attack. At least they released him from the hospital. Whether that was safe or only because he had gotten insufferable with the nurses, Bryce didn't know.

Bryce stepped across the threshold he once shared with his parents. His mother was the one who crafted it into a home. It had gone seriously downhill in the years since her death.

Bryce turned on the living room lamp. That highlighted the coat of dust that had been accumulating.

"You could take your old room back," his dad said.

"I'm comfortable at the motel."

He led his father over to his favorite chair. Its light green cushions looked almost brown now, the foam beneath the fabric starting to show through.

His dad plopped down. "Get me some tea."

This wasn't the time for the child to parent the adult about etiquette. His disease—and probably some of those medications—were taking their toll.

As he stepped into the kitchen to put water in the kettle, his father yelled from the living room. "You have one bonus going for you. Hannah didn't grow up here, so she doesn't know you." Why was his father talking about her now? Hadn't he grilled him enough at the hospital? "Because if she did…she'd know how little regard you have for the men who work for you. Their names. Their stories."

He fought the urge to forget making the tea and storm out. Dad was getting old. That was all this was.

"What does Hannah like for breakfast?"

Why on earth was Dad asking that? Of course, he had no idea. He was tempted to mouth off that she loved poached eggs, lightly salted with a side of cornmeal Batty Cakes topped with raspberries and cream. Bryce peeked his head into the living room. "I don't know. Why?"

"What's her fondest memory? What games did she play as a child? What do you know about who she is? And what have you done to find out?"

Oh, so that's what this was about. Another laundry list of his inadequacies. Not only had he distanced himself from getting to know the miners who worked for him, he was failing in the love department as well. He grabbed a mug out of the cabinet and blew the dust out of it. No sense in arguing this out with Dad.

But he had to admit it: his dad was right. Not that he'd tell him that. As many music lessons as he'd taken from Hannah over the past year and a half or so, she'd always avoided any personal talk. Their time together was strictly professional.

If she wouldn't share details with him willingly, there had to be some other way to uncover who she really was.

♫ ♫ ♫

Josh covered Hannah's eyes while she blindly balanced the picnic basket. A blanket rested over his shoulder. "No peeking, now," he said. He led her toward his favorite place on Heather's Beach.

"I got it. No peeking." Her mouth stretched into a wide grin. She must genuinely be enjoying herself. She was starting to loosen up around him. What a breath of fresh air she was, in a coal-dusted world, often blanketed in sadness and tragedy.

"Almost there," he said. As they arrived at the small

cliffs that overlooked the beach, he lowered his hands. "Okay."

"Now?"

"Yes."

"Like really, now?"

He laughed, "Yes." He took the basket from her hands and set it down. She opened her eyes to behold the water below the cliffs, and their orangey-reddish clay soil.

Her jaw slacked as she took in the panoramic of the Northumberland Straight, the red sand, the little cottages that lined the shore. The trees.

"You like?"

She nodded vigorously, then pointed across the water to an island. "What's that over there?"

"Prince Edward Island."

"I had no idea you could see it from here."

"You can get there by ferry. You drive on up and they take you and your car across the water."

"Wow. It's, it's...beautiful."

"I know. We spent a lot of time here when I was kid. We'd rent a cottage over in Pugwash down the beach that way." He pointed to their right.

The sun began to set, bringing a small chill into the end of summer night air. He said, "We should come back here sometime for the sunrise, when you can see it coming up over the water."

He liked the idea of making future plans with her. He led her down to the water where they could share a picnic on the sand. He said, "Now, I want to establish. This is not a date. It's just dinner."

She laughed and dug through his picnic basket of finger foods. "Mmm... Elegant."

"Do I detect sarcasm, Miss Hannah?"

"Not even a slice."

"Had this been a date, would'a been elegant. Dignified, even." Josh cracked a teasing smile.

"Like if this spread were for Mary Lou?"

"I never said I'd marry her. She proposed to me. Can we not talk about her?"

Hannah foraged deeper into the basket and found his secret stash: four pints of ice cream on a block of ice. They settled in to eat the less-than-fancy but oh-so-perfect picnic dinner. He could sense her relaxing.

"Josh, did you ever come close to marrying someone?"

"Ah. The good ole Liar's Bench question revisited."

"But this isn't the Liar's Bench. You have to tell the truth."

He released a breath. "No."

"How come?"

"I am a patient man. I never wanted to rush into the wrong thing."

Somehow, he knew he'd better not return the question, one he'd tried to ask on that iconic bench. He didn't want her tension to return.

After their picnic dinner, Josh led her up the coastline, where they heard festivities and music.

"Where are we going?" she asked.

"One of my favorite places when I was a teenager. It's only open during the summer. They board it up for the winter so it won't get ruined by the weather."

They passed a small canteen. The Hop served up vanilla colas and malts. Teenagers congregated out front. Then they approached a barnyard-like structure, with wide open doors and open shutters all down the sides. It let the cool summer air inside. A record played loudly.

Hannah stepped into the open doorway with Josh. They eyed fifty, maybe sixty teenagers dancing with one another in large groups.

They were doing that dance number, the Jitterbug. Almost all the ladies wore poodle skirts.

"Aren't we vintage for this place?" Hannah asked.

"Only if we act like it." Josh led her inside the dance pavilion.

Josh glanced down at his slacks. They were nothing like the slick black pants all the other guys wore. Hannah, at least, had a skirt on, even if it wasn't adorned with poodles.

Over in the corner, they spotted a separate group of teens laughing it up. They tried to keep a round ring going in circles, as they swiveled their hips.

"What are those?" Josh asked.

"I heard someone call them hula hoops," she said.

"Ooh, we gotta try the hula hoop."

The teens made it look easy, but apparently, these things took practice. The hoops landed right around their ankles. Hannah got the hang of it first. Of course, she had the right kind of hips to sustain it. Josh didn't mind stepping back, watching her swivel. Loop-ty-loop.

She challenged another girl to a contest on the floor, to see who could last the longest. The two ladies hoops clunked, causing them to fall to the ground in unison. Laughing and breathing heavily, Hannah gave her hoop to the next girl in line.

"Let's dance." Josh grinned. She didn't say no. They faced each other, moving to *Yakety Yak* then *Great Balls of Fire*.

When the DJ decided to slow it down and started Elvis's *Love Me Tender*, Josh lightly took Hannah's hand. He kept her at a respectful distance as he led a slow dance.

She seemed fine at first, even receptive. But a short way into the second verse, she pulled away. Without looking back, she hurried for the barnyard's front double doors.

He'd scared her. But how?

THE SUN HAD GONE DOWN, but the stars and moon offered a moody glow over the water. They silently retraced their steps. This was no time to push. He would let her lead.

After a few minutes, she finally spoke. "I'm sorry, Josh."

"It's okay. You don't have to be." When it seemed like she wasn't going to elaborate, he looked up at the sky. "I sure love looking at God's handiwork."

She glanced up at the stars. "Shouldn't you try to find someone more aligned with how you see the world, how you believe?"

"You know, Hannah, I don't think your problem is about belief. I think it's about anger. With God." When she opened her mouth to protest, he held up a finger. "Let me finish. I get it. Being angry with God...I was there. Believe it or not, God gets it too. He can take it. I would be a lot more concerned about you, if you were indifferent to him. But to be angry? That implies you care."

"I don't know."

"If you want to label this a belief problem, it's the struggle to believe he is still good...even when he allows bad things to happen to us or those we love. Like our fathers." He was tempted to say more but tamped down the impulse. He was just grateful she didn't storm away from him, or even contradict his suspicions of the matters of her heart.

Finally, she spoke. "Did your mother...did she try to stop you from working at the mines?"

"We always knew I'd have to, as soon as I turned seventeen. As you know with Abigail, compensation, when someone passes, it never pays enough."

"But you stayed there. Even after your mother died."

"It's the only life I know."

"Did your mom ever remarry?"

"No, she and my dad...they were like one person. Once he was gone, she was only a half."

"I never want to be half a person. Because what if—" She stopped, couldn't seem to finish.

"My mother would've never looked at it that way. Is that why it had to be 'just dinner'?"

"It happened to my mother too. She did her best with me, really. But she never got over losing my dad. She wouldn't even bring me here, to Springhill, to see anyone else. Like she couldn't face the reminders of what she'd lost. And I begged her. I always wanted to come meet Aunt Abby. I wanted to have stronger roots. To get to know everyone. But no. She had to keep us away. It was like she stopped living when he died and only existed because she had to take care of me. That's what love does. Causes pain no one can live with."

Josh ached to convince her otherwise. Love was worth the risk, even in the face of the loss that may come. Will come. It was inevitable. How could someone live always protecting themselves? That wasn't living.

"Josh, you can't promise me you won't hurt me."

"No, I can't. Not the way you mean. But I wouldn't hurt you the way someone else clearly has."

She broke her eye contact with him, but he lifted her chin to face him. He leaned down and kissed her gently. On the lips.

She let him, but just for a few moments. "Please, don't do that again." She did not have much conviction in her voice, but he had to respect her wishes.

Maybe he'd taken it too far, voicing his suspicions that someone had hurt her. He knew this had to be about more than her mother, or him being a miner.

What was Hannah hiding?

chapter 16

Fall 1958

Hannah knew something was up by the look on Josh's face. Was it fear? Cal had talked to him and the men on the coalface about some new method. Even Isaak seemed concerned, and he was usually the most fearless among them. They had already started talking about switching to this method earlier in the year. Something about lining up the walls. It sounded like they were finally going to implement that change, even though it had been hotly debated the past few months.

"Are you sure that's wise?" Josh seemed to already know the answer to his own question. He clearly did not like whatever Cal suggested.

"We have to move you guys to the 13,800 to pull that wall up."

Hannah remembered that number from the diagram. It was the deepest level in this mine. Two miles down. As if they weren't already deep enough.

Plum shook his head. "They're gonna kill us, Cal."

"The engineers feel strongly this is the best way to

reduce bumps."

Plum yelled, "We'll increase the pressure right above our own heads."

Josh threw a glance her way, his brow furrowed. The tension in the cave could cause its own underground earthquake.

Hicks was the only one who didn't speak up in protest. Despite their collective disagreement, they moved down the slope toward the 13,800.

Hicks said, "It's unsafe down here either way, guys, so what difference does it really make which level we's on?"

Josh touched Hannah's arm, encouraging her to walk with him at the back of the group, while the rest pressed forward. He quietly said, "Take the rake up, now. We can be done with this. I'll figure out how to help take care of Abigail and the kids."

"Josh, no."

"I'll sell my house, I'll —"

"I want to be here with you. With all of you."

"I don't want you here." He said it a little too loudly. The team turned around.

"Josh, what's going on?" Isaak asked.

"Nothing."

"I'm not leaving, Josh."

Once set up at the new location, Lazy Haze and Hannah, as Mel, needed to build new packs. Hannah noticed Lazy Haze hadn't said a word since Cal's visit. He was passing more gas than usual though, so she didn't have to guess how he felt about it.

Isaak kept trying to soothe them all with his hope the engineers were correct. More than once she saw him pray.

The labor was harder at this level. Hannah had trouble

keeping enough air in her lungs. Was it really that much thinner just 800 feet further down? Maybe it was her nerves. If Josh were afraid for her life, it meant they were all in danger.

Her breath quickened, almost leading her to panic. She had to slow it down. In and out. Did she want to give herself away? Get out of all this? No. She wasn't afraid of losing her own life.

She was afraid of losing *him*.

AFTER THEIR DINNER BREAK, Cal brought over a team from another level so they'd have more working the wall.

They all seemed to work in silence. So unusual for miners. Hicks finally broke that silence. "Man, she's hard today, isn't she? A good widow maker would shake her."

"Don't be jokin', Hicks," Plum said. "They got no idea what they's doin' to us."

"Have a little faith, Plum," said Isaak.

"Ain'tcha worried? You've got eleven kids out there, Isaak," Plum said.

"Almost twelve. Any day now, our new little one will arrive."

Plum threw down his pick and leaned against the wall. "I'm not doing this. I don't wanna kill us all."

"Come on, Plum. We need you," Josh said. "With less walls working, our production will be low."

"And so will our paychecks," Hicks added.

"They say it's safer. Maybe this can help." There was no conviction in Josh's voice. "We gotta stick together on this, guys. Remember that town out there? She needs us. We'll be fine."

Hannah so admired his resolve, his team leadership. And it was all an act, a performance worthy of the Liar's Bench.

"Josh is right," Hicks said.

Isaak put on his best, singsongy voice, "We are all one Springhill miner." He added a slap to his knee to supply a beat.

"Nothin' could ever be finer," Josh added, offering a counter beat with his chipper pick against the wall.

"Except eatin' in a juicy diner," sang Hicks. He plunked fake drum noises with his tongue, as they looked to her for the next lyric.

"Or sailing on an ocean liner."

The men and Hannah looked to Plum, willing him to play along. Plum gave them half a grin. "I'll try nots to be such a whiner."

Fear and danger couldn't match the bond of this group. They laughed. Lazy Haze farted.

"Aw, Haze!" Plum whined.

"That didn't rhyme," she threw in, then had to stifle her girlish laughter when they all chuckled.

All in a day's work. Though today was anything but typical.

THIS WAS ONE MEETING Hannah didn't want to miss. But she couldn't go as herself. She had to go as Mel. She had to hear what the Miner's Union rep had to say. He'd called an emergency meeting at Miner's Hall about the new methods they'd been using in the No. 2 for the past month.

She didn't know Mark Steinberg well, but he was passionate about his job. He tried to protect the miners at all costs. Some miners felt like he drew too hard a line, that he made it "them against the company." They feared they'd lose their jobs if he tried too hard. Mark's t-shirt reminded everyone who he stood for:

United Mine Workers.

A table was up front with places for Cal, Bryce, a man she recognized as one of the engineers, and another man flanking Bryce. Hannah had heard him called Douglas, but she wasn't sure what he did. They all faced Mark, who gripped a podium.

It was standing room only, as miners had already filled the seats in all rows. Hannah stood at the back beside Josh, hoping to keep her distance from Bryce and anyone else in town that knew her as Hannah. She picked at the corner of her mustache.

Within the first few minutes of the hearing, Mark was already boiling. "They cannot move the wall up that quickly. You know the history of the number two. If you want to line her up, it should be slow."

A miner that Hannah had run into a few times, Gerald, rose from his seat in the audience. "We get blamed 'cause we's scared to go to work. We gets told if we don't, Springhill will done close."

"Who's claiming that?" Bryce asked. "Not the Company."

"You's read the newspaper lately?" O'Malley threw in, another miner who worked the same shift as Hannah. She'd sat with him once on the way down on the rake.

O'Malley was right. Public opinion seemed to be negative lately. With all the grumbling about the new methods, some people in town seemed concerned the Company would pull out and leave this town to fend for itself. They desperately needed this industry.

Plum stood up. "We're criticized for worryin' we won't see our wives again after we kiss 'em goodbye."

Mark tried to put on a more reasonable tone. "All we're asking at the Union is that you keep 40 to 50 feet between each wall and slow the process down."

Cal said, "Look. The engineers say we have to line up the 13,800 as quickly as possible to reduce pressure."

Mark shook his head. "Think about it. What if you rolled a bowling ball down there? If the walls aren't lined up, the ball will stop at the first level. If you line them up, it'll keep rolling. It could wipe them all out."

Hannah had no idea what that actually meant. But Mark sure sounded like he knew what he was talking about. And clearly, he was afraid. For all of them.

"You wouldn't be reducing the pressure, you'd be tripling it!" Mark let that hang. Silence rested over the room like a thick cloud of coal dust.

♫ ♫ ♫

One of Bryce's favorite ways to spend a Saturday off work was at the Capitol Movie Theater. Movies allowed him to pretend he lived somewhere else, even was someone else. Especially on these autumn days when the weather was turning cooler. Plus, Hannah was meeting him.

No one knew when he took a few days off work this week it was to hop the train from Springhill Junction to Southampton, then work his way over to Toronto. When he got nowhere trying to take his father's advice—to try to get to know Hannah better when he was around her—he decided to take matters into his own hands. There was no mistaking it. She was hiding something, something that seemed to be holding her back. What he uncovered left him feeling even more perplexed about her.

"Hi Bryce."

He turned around to see Hannah in line at the ticket booth behind him. "Thank you for meeting me, Hannah."

"Explain to me how seeing a movie is one of your music lessons?"

"The man who did the music for my all-time favorite film, *It's a Wonderful Life,* also did this flick."

Her brow furrowed a bit.

"Don't worry. This counts as one of my paid lessons." No, it wasn't a real date. It was as close as he could get. At least he could pretend, even just for a couple of hours, a woman had chosen to be with him.

"Two please." He put a couple quarters down on the ticket booth counter to pay for them.

He handed tickets to the doorman on their way in. "Would you like popcorn, Hannah? A soda?"

"No, thank you."

They made their way into the theater in search of seats. Today's feature was James Dean's, *Giant.* It had won an Oscar after its release and their tiny Canadian town was just now getting a run. Maybe watching a western romance with Hannah would do some good. Put ideas in her mind.

Concentrating on the movie was a challenge. Throughout the whole flick, she kept her hands folded in her lap. But given what he knew, it wasn't so surprising she'd keep to herself.

When it faded to black and the lights came up, they

stayed in their seats. She asked, "So, you hoping to switch from the mining profession someday and write music for films?"

"Maybe."

She smiled. Did that impress her?

"I think everyone needs to have a dream," he said. "And it shouldn't be confined to the four walls and thirty-eight streets of this town."

As they strolled away from the theater and headed up Main Street, Bryce mused over James Dean's character. "So, it would appear confidence and a stubborn streak appeal to a woman."

"Only in a picture show when that woman is paid to say lines."

As a miner, Gerald, crossed their path, he seemed to glare at Bryce.

Bryce waited for him to pass. "It gets tiresome, the men of this town. So thankless for all we do for them."

She stopped walking down Main Street and faced him. "Have you ever labored one day down there? Worked at a breakneck speed so your company, this industry, can stay afloat?"

"Hey. I've been in this industry my whole life. And what would you know about it anyway?"

"You have no idea who these incredible men are. They put their lives on the line every day. For you. For Springhill. For their families."

Oh, boy. This was not going the way he'd hoped. "Look. Forget about them for the moment. What's important is, I know you, Hannah. Better than anyone else here. We're a lot alike. In more ways than you realize."

"What do you mean?"

"I know what it's like to run away. Even when you're not sure what you're running to or if it will be better. I'm sure you had a good reason to run. To come here. I assume not long after your wedding?"

Hannah's face betrayed something, horror maybe? Shock?

"It's okay, Hannah. Really. You're safe with me."

"What are you talking about?"

"I'm not here to judge you. I wanted to understand where you were coming from. So I took the time, Hannah. To find out." She had to be impressed by how much he cared, right? "I went to Toronto. I came across the place where you used to teach lessons. They said you'd quit and lost touch with the school after you'd gotten engaged."

He pulled out a newspaper clipping that displayed a photo of her with a man, Will Felten, next to their engagement announcement. "That led me to find this."

She grabbed it out of his hands. Well, he certainly wouldn't get that back.

"How could you do this? You had no business digging up anything about me."

"Well, you wouldn't talk—"

"That was my choice, Bryce. Mine. If I wanted you to know, I would have told you. Did you tell anyone there where I am?"

"No. They thought I was looking to take music lessons from you. I do have some degree of discretion."

"Not enough." She turned and headed off quickly. It was like she couldn't get far enough away from him. Was this it? The end of their professional relationship and their friendship? She was the only friend he had.

There was one person in town who, even though he

wasn't a friend, should know about this. Josh. He had a right to know the person he'd been trying to woo for two years was already married.

♪ ♪ ♪

Josh couldn't believe it. Could it be true? No. This was just one of Bryce's ways of getting under his skin. It had to be. There was that knock at the door. He'd called to ask Hannah to come over. Might as well know the truth.

When Josh opened his front door, Hannah grinned ear to ear, a tray of candies in front of her. Round chocolate drops with colored sprinkles. Homemade nonpareils. "Lindy wanted me to bring these to you. She says they were her best batch yet. Not even ugly."

He stood there frozen. How could he confront her? Would their friendship be over?

She shifted her weight from one side to the other, still standing outside his doorway. "Are you okay?"

"Your friend Bryce came by."

"I wouldn't call him a friend. I just teach him how to read and play music, is all."

"He's playing you. He's known how to play music since high school." If Bryce's lies bothered her, she didn't show it. She eyed the hand he kept gripped on the door. "Is it true, Hannah?"

"Is what true?"

"Are you already married?"

Her lower jaw opened, but words didn't come out.

"Just say it, Hannah. I need to know."

"Can I come in?"

After all they'd been through, he at least owed her a chance to explain. He stepped out of her way.

They passed by the kitchen, where he'd left a half-eaten dinner for one. Bryce's visit caused him to lose his appetite for lamb chops and stewed vegetables. He ached for the day he could cook elaborately for more than one. He thought he was finally getting closer to that day. What a joke.

She sat on the couch. Instead of sitting by her, he plopped down on his chair.

"I am not married."

Oh, thank the good Lord above. A breath escaped his lips. "Then what was Bryce talking about?"

"Bryce found my engagement announcement. What he didn't know, I was here on my supposed wedding date, November 3, 1956."

"The explosion was November 1st."

"Obviously, I was not in Toronto getting married. I was with you, and the Percys, waiting for news about Uncle Ray. Bryce didn't deserve an explanation, but you do."

Even without knowing what she had to say, compassion bubbled inside for her. He wanted to promise her the one thing he couldn't: that life from now on would bring her joy and happiness. "What happened, Hannah?"

"I left just a few days before the wedding. I was living with my fiancé's parents. But I couldn't go through with it. I had to get out. I got in my car and landed here."

Josh took a moment to gather his thoughts. He was relieved, but also confused about what drove her to abandon another man. Right before they were to meet at the altar, of all places. It would kill him if she ever did that to him. "So, you were here—with us—when you were supposed to be walking down the aisle?"

She nodded, her eyes brimming. He'd seen bouts of fear show up in her. He had a sense she did this for her own protection. He took a chance. "What did he do to you?"

"Said he loved me so much, he couldn't help it. He wanted to shape me into a better person. It was for my own good." She let the tears streak her face.

He found her so vulnerable. He wanted to scoop her up and protect her for the rest of her life.

"I just wanted a family. His parents, they were just as controlling as he was. It's like they came to my rescue when I had nowhere to go, only to hold it over my head. They made me quit a teaching job where I had friends. Like they were afraid I was going to talk about what their son was doing. They would only let me teach a few students from home, where they could watch my every move. They made me feel so obligated to them. I didn't know how to get out. It was like being in a mine, where all this pressure was building up. I knew if I didn't leave, it would cave right in on top of me. So that October, I got out. Just a few days before the wedding. It's like I woke up and realized, if I didn't get out then, I would die there."

He moved over to her on the couch and touched her face, wiping away a tear. "Not everyone who says 'I love you' is like him, Hannah."

She shrunk back a bit. "We haven't known each other that long, Josh."

"Almost two years."

"I knew him for three before we courted. And it turned

out I didn't know him at all. Or his parents, really."

"I know what matters about you." He placed his hand on her knee. "I know you twirl your hair in your fingers when you get nervous. You tell lies, every bit as good as I heard your father did. But not without good reason. You are the most unselfish person I know, willing to risk your own life for your family." He swallowed, bracing himself. "I know I want to marry you."

She got up from her seat, paced away from him. She wrung her hands, then turned around. "You can't promise me that every day you'll come home."

He stood. "Neither can you. How long are you gonna protect yourself, Hannah? Yes, it's a risk. But take it with me."

"You talk about risks? You're the one who's too afraid to act on a dream. One you're good enough to realize. You don't believe in yourself enough to leave what you know, to do what you love. Instead, you cling to this work that could take you away. And I can't live with that, Josh. I'm sorry."

She kissed his cheek. It was the sweetest yet saddest kiss he'd ever received. "I have to go." And with that she was gone.

He heard the door close behind her. She'd left a hole he didn't know would ever be filled.

chapter 17

October 23, 1958, 12:00 p.m.

Hannah held Isaak's letter. He'd told her not to open it until she arrived at her father's gravesite. There were still a few hours before her shift, so she started the walk to Hillside Cemetery. Isaak sure was perceptive. He seemed to sense this whole past week that something wasn't right.

Josh hadn't talked to her at work. Wouldn't even look at her. Even sat in silence next to her once, riding down on the rake. A battle waged inside her. The emptiness of missing his smile, his winks, their little moments of connection. It showed her what life might be like if he were truly ripped away from her.

If she didn't do something—if she couldn't stop fear from getting in her way—she would lose.

She was already losing.

Since being in Springhill, she'd just begun to taste what it was like to live again. Did she want to let fear get in the way of a potentially wonderful future with a man who was crazy about her?

As fearful as she was about not really knowing a

person, Josh was different. Plus, her family had known him his whole life. That had to count for something, didn't it? Yes. Yes, it did. She had to stop making excuses.

She walked across the cement path of Hillside Cemetery. Its green grass was beginning to turn with the cooling autumn temperatures. The trees were at their pinnacle of color: reds, yellows, oranges, offset with lush evergreens. The maple trees were her favorite. She loved the shape. Plus, the town's hockey team was named the Maple Leafs.

She strolled to her father's marker. He'd died on a Thursday. Since the Main Street fire, people in town had ruminated that Thursdays were bad luck in Springhill. First the explosion, then the fire. Hannah wanted today, this particular Thursday, to be different. To be a turnaround, even if just for her personally.

Despite the damp ground, Hannah knelt by her father's headstone. "Daddy, I think I understand you more now. Those miners. I don't want to miss a joke played on Lazy Haze, or a rhyme started by Plum. A song by Isaak. I want to be there, Dad. Just like you were. I get it. And I don't blame you anymore."

She slid her thumb under the glue that held Isaak's letter closed, pulled it out and unfolded the pages. It was as if she could hear the lilt of Isaak's voice reading the message to her.

"Hannah, last night I stumbled across these lyrics to a song your father had started to write about you, shortly before you were born. We were supposed to get together to finish this. Adding a tune too. But that day never came. I will say he felt like he knew you before you were born. He had faith, not only for you but in you, Hannah. And so do I.

Blessings, Isaak."

Hannah read the lyrics through blurred vision:

"Little One, have a faith so strong.
Let not fear be your song.
Little One, know my great love.
In times of pain, look straight above.
You exist so deep within, my prayer is,
Lord, let her life begin."

A tear spilled on the letter as she continued to read: *"Daughter, if I could have but just one blessing, you'd know my Lord, and your life would sing."*

Hannah looked up from the letter, mulling over the words: *Let not fear be your song.*

It was as if her father's words sent revival into her soul. "Okay, Daddy. I get it." She looked up to the blue sky above. "I…I don't want to run anymore. I'm ready."

Still on her knees, she looked behind her, over the expanse of the hillside. The same direction she beheld with Josh the night it snowed. "I'm ready for you now, Josh."

For the first time in her life, she felt giddiness ripple through her chest. Yeah, Hannah…giddy. Who would have ever thought? "I'm gonna tell him, Daddy. Today. Underground. Not even going to wait until we get off work. Who says Thursdays have to be bad days in Springhill?"

She leapt to her feet, ready to enjoy the world afresh. With a spring in her step, she moved up the path. When she spotted a Springhill mourner heading to a loved one's stone, she toned down her walk. But nothing could wipe that smile off her face. As she looked up at the sky, she wondered. Maybe there was something to her father's faith.

This Lord he wanted her to know. This Lord, who perhaps, had even spoken to her daddy about who she'd become. Maybe this God even inspired Daddy to write down the exact words she'd need to hear nearly thirty years later.

There had to be something divine about that.

October 23, 1958, 2:30 p.m.

"I WANNA WATCH," Lindy said.

"If this is what you consider entertainment." Hannah let Lindy lounge on her cot in the guest cabin while she went through the transformation to Mel.

The kid was home from school with the chicken pox, which didn't seem to bother her one bit. She loved having a day off with the television all to herself. Betty Crocker had been giving her pointers. As Hannah applied her final touch—the mustache—Lindy giggled. "No wonder no one ever recognizes you. You make an unsightly boy."

"Thank you. I'll take that as a compliment."

"That was one of my favorite shirts Daddy used to wear."

Hannah buttoned up the pale blue shirt she'd taken out of Abigail's donation box.

"Will you come see me when you get in tonight from work?"

"You'll be asleep, Lindy."

"Come see me anyway."

Hannah saw something flash in the young girl's eyes. Fear, maybe? "Are you okay?"

"I don't know. I have a weird feeling."

"Chicken pox are weird."

"Do you have to go to work today? Can you stay home

with me?"

"I have to go, Lindy." If ever there was a day she belonged down there, it was today. She couldn't wait to see Josh, couldn't wait to tell him she was finally ready for him.

So what, if she were sporting a mustache when she said it? He could see right through to the real her.

And apparently, he liked what he saw.

WALKING TO THE MINES THIS DAY was different from the others. She was tempted to run *to* them. Oreo the Dalmatian wagged his tail as she jogged down Maple, past Junction. He never bothered to get up.

Josh wasn't in the crowd nearby that headed through the archways that announced Cumberland Coal.

Just as she was about to cross under them, a hand grabbed her arm. Hard. Bryce.

He started pulling her away, toward Lion's Park. He was holding her arm so hard that she wasn't quite sure what was wrong. Was he mad at her or Mel?

"Well?" he asked. "Explanation?"

She took her chances and stuck to her usual, lowered voice of Mel. "For what? What did I do?"

"Cut the gas, Hannah."

Oh, boy.

"I came by the Percys' to talk to you and saw you leaving the guesthouse."

No use trying to hide it now.

He put his hands on his waist. "You're done."

"Bryce, please."

"You have taken advantage of me and my company. Your list of lies keeps growing, doesn't it?"

She cupped her face in her hands. Then she looked up at him. "I lied to help the Percys. The compensation provided by your company wouldn't feed two of those kids." When she heard other miners passing by on Main Street, she had to lower her voice. "But my aunt has five kids, Bryce. Five. With no husband here to help."

"That doesn't excuse you going into the mines. Women are never allowed down there."

"There were no jobs."

"It is not safe for you, Hannah. Don't you get that by now?"

"Then, why is it okay for every one of those men to go down there? Why is my life more precious than theirs?"

♫ ♫ ♫

October 23, 1958, 3:00 p.m.
Josh climbed on the rake. Isaak, Lazy Haze, Hicks, and Plum had already boarded. Despite his frustration with Hannah, he still scanned the area. Where was she? Why wouldn't she be here yet? She was always on time.

Guilt crept up for avoiding her all week. But what else was he supposed to do? He loved her, and her ongoing rejection hurt.

Lazy Haze whined, "Isaak, sing me a song. Remind me why I come back everyday."

Hicks asked, "Anyone seen Mel?"

The rake lurched forward to pull them down below. He had to admit. A hole gaped with her absence.

October 23, 1958, 6:53 p.m.

GRUMBLING STOMACHS SIGNALED dinnertime at the 13,000 level. With the 13,800 now pulled up long-wall style, their team was back to their normal place.

Josh moved away from the rest of the team. It wasn't like he was in the mood to talk.

Plum called out to him, "How's that girl you was sweet on?"

"It's over." Josh caught Isaak's eye.

Suddenly, the strata rumbled above them. Chunks of ceiling shook loose. Not a big deal. They'd grown accustomed to these little bumps.

"Haze's been eatin' beans again!" Plum said. "Wish a bump would bounce that possum knick-knack my mother-in-law given us. Oust it right off the table."

Hicks laughed. "I know what'cha mean, Plum. We got us a chartreuse lamp, so my wife says. I'd love to find that broked when I get home tonight." Hicks yelled toward the ceiling. "Could'ya shake her up a bit more?"

Josh couldn't get into their jubilance. Thoughts of Hannah preoccupied his mind. Was something wrong? Was she okay?

♫ ♫ ♫

October 23, 1958, 8:05 p.m.

Hannah sat alone in the mine management office at a small worktable, massaging her temples. When would her headache go away? She'd refused to go anywhere since Bryce had busted her. She either had to convince him to let her go down or she'd be here at eleven when Josh came out. Either way, she was not giving up. Her fingers fiddled with pieces of her disguise, now resting on the table. The bushy eyebrows, the mustache, the large glasses.

Bryce came in the door. "Why are you still here?"

"I am not leaving, Bryce."

"The rake operator knows. He won't let you go down, so, you might as well go home. You'll get your final check on Saturday."

"Bryce—"

"Did Josh know about this?"

She remained silent. There was no point in giving him a reason to wreck Josh's life too. "Why did you dig into my life?"

"I wanted to know more about you."

"Why?"

"Did it ever occur to you that maybe I actually like you, Hannah? I was trying to figure out where you came from, so I could get to know you better. It's not like I set out to find dirt or juicy gossip, like others in this town would like. I—"

A loud rumble, a shaking like an earthquake erupted beneath their feet. Hannah gripped the table before her. Clipboards, pictures on the walls, shelves…they rattled and shook to the floor. Lamps and clocks bounced off the desk and end tables.

Bryce grabbed a hold of Hannah, led her down to the floor and used himself as a shield over her.

She stared at the floor's blackness beneath her. What on earth was going on down there? Something was terribly wrong, probably two miles below the surface.

chapter 18

White surrounded him. That was inexplicable when, underground, everything was black. Wasn't he working by his team? Why was it so bright? His eyes sensitive, the light burning. Hadn't Hicks just finished telling him some meaningless, silly joke? Had he added a topper to the punch line? Josh tried to remember. And where was he? It was as if he were lying on his back and standing at the same time, weightless.

Nothing made sense. Was it day or night? And where was gravity? He heard singing. A hymn? Was Isaak at it again? Not just Isaak. Maybe a chorus of people? He couldn't tell.

Josh looked down a long tunnel. A figure stood at the end. One he hadn't seen in nearly thirty years. There was no mistaking that outline of his father's favorite hat.

"Dad?"

The man stepped into view, out of the blurriness the bright light created. His dad was the same age as the last time he saw him. Josh waved at him but, for some reason, he couldn't walk toward him.

His dad didn't say a word. Just wore his signature grin and winked at him, tipped his hat and turned the other way.

"Wait. Dad!"

But he walked away.

The white light snuffed out. And with that, came pain. Pressure. The strong sense of being buried under something. Or somethings.

Chunks were still falling, landing on top of other rocks and pieces of coal. On him. Josh heard the sound of a stone pack's timber crack, followed by crashing. Was the mine collapsing? Even the stone packs were no match for a mineshaft trying to close its upper jaw into the floor.

The sounds were so loud and jumbled together. Who was that yelling? And the moans. The cries of his comrades, both near and far.

Finally, the shaking settled. The ground no longer moved beneath his back. But pieces of coal still fell, like hailstones on pavement.

The weight of coal on his chest caused Josh to breathe shallowly. In, out. In, out. *Stay calm, Josh.* Would the roof cave in further?

He tested his hands and fingers to see if he could move them. Weight and pressure were on the rest of his arm. He brought one hand toward his face, pieces of coal drifting off his forearm. He reached a fist above his head. His knuckles slammed into what felt like the roof. But that's impossible. They could stand up in here a few moments ago. What happened?

Was this "The Big One" everyone predicted? Did that "bowling ball" come rolling down?

A hot flash surged through his whole body. Was

Hannah on her way down when this happened? And how was the rest of his team? Were the men still alive?

There was nothing but pitch-blackness before him. The roof inches above his face.

"Hello," he called out.

Moans echoed in the darkness, but there were no answers.

Suddenly, a whoosh rushed through the mine. Air, maybe? What little space he had to breathe filled with a cloud of dust.

Violent coughs overtook him. A chunk of coal sitting on his stomach fell to the side. He could barely breathe. Any attempt filled his angry lungs with more dust.

Holding his breath was the only option. He waited. Finally, when the air rush stopped, he took the tiniest breaths.

His free hand shoved pieces aside, carefully. He didn't want to add coal on top of one of his men. What if any of them were beside him?

"Hello." Again, there was no response. But he couldn't get any volume from his throat.

Another rock crashed down atop his spleen. He shoved it aside.

The faintest light was on the ceiling above his head. Was his lamp still on? He wiped from side to side, removing the dust that obscured his light source. The lone lamp illuminated the ceiling or whatever it was above his head.

The metallic taste of blood dripped into the corner of his mouth. Probably from his head. It throbbed.

Were any of the men he'd grown to love over the past two years, since the last disaster, alive down here, right now? Or was he alone, the only survivor?

He shifted his head to the side. His light shined on a face.

♫   ♫   ♫

Liesel and Lucas flew through the house from the dining room, toward the front door. They hopped over the shattered glass from the picture frames and the decorative plates that shook right off the wall. Their mother screamed for them to stay inside, but they ignored her.

Lucas stepped out of the house first. "Oh, no."

Liesel quickly reached him and went out on the steps.

The pavement right in front of their home was buckled in the middle, as if some prehistoric animal pushed against it to come out of the earth.

How could this happen? What caused it?

And where was Hannah?

Liesel ran back into the house, where her mother huddled under the dining room table with Laurel, Lenny, and Lindy.

"What happened?" Lindy asked.

"Looks like an earthquake, maybe. It's a mess out there."

"If that were an earthquake…" Her mother didn't need to finish the sentence. Liesel knew what she feared.

Seismic activity was the norm around here, and those underground felt it more than most. But never had they felt such a large jolt at home. Enough to knock things off the walls and out of cabinets.

"Can I please go check?" Liesel asked.

"There could be aftershocks."

"Mom, I can't wait here and wonder if Hannah and Josh are safe."

Lucas arrived in the dining room.

"Lucas, go with her."

"Of course, Mom."

"I want to go," Lindy said.

"Absolutely not!"

"We'll come back and tell you what's going on." Liesel raced for her coat.

Then, she and Lucas jogged down Maple. All they could see were the smokestacks at the mines. The view revealed nothing of what was going on. No mushroom cloud like last time. Maybe that was a good sign.

They turned on Junction Road and neared Main Street. Others raced down, too, toward the increasingly infamous Cumberland arches.

When they arrived at the mine site, it was eerily similar to the day her dad was stuck underground. Such frenzy.

"God, you cannot take someone else from our family, got it?" She pointed her index finger up to the sky.

Lucas took her hand. He never did that, ever. She was his sister, but she accepted it. The two ran with all their might toward the mines.

♫　♫　♫

Hannah didn't care what Cal Weston thought. She was sure he wondered why she was in the office with the rest of them. She wasn't going anywhere, even if he tried to make her. The past couple of years had made her arms as strong as her will.

At the moment, Cal had the phone line into the mine glued to his ear. He kept buzzing. Finally, he reacted with a jolt. "Hello?"

"Hello." She heard a fuzzy voice cracking through the line from the 7,800 level. Cal had tried several attempts to get through. She knew that level well because that was near where they'd get off the first rake. What rake worker could this be?

"This is Cal Weston. What's going on?"

Everyone in the room strained to hear through the receiver — Bryce, Hannah, an engineer whose name she didn't know. Adam leaned on the arm of the couch.

"It's awful down here, Cal. Awful." The man sobbed.

"Peter, what happened down there? Are you okay?"

"I'm fine," Peter said. "But I can't get through on the lines at the 13 and below."

"Does the rake at your level still work?"

"I don't know."

"Did something explode?"

"I don't think so. I think she bumped."

"Try taking the coal cars off, put the rakes on. Let's see if she'll run."

"Yes, Sir."

"We'll be down as soon as we can."

Cal hung up the mineshaft phone and ran to the desk to use the regular line. He dialed. "Mark, it's Cal. It's bad. Call in every available miner from the surrounding towns. We're going to need all the help we can get." He hung up.

"How bad is it, Cal?" Adam asked.

Cal raced for the door. "Won't know till we get down."

Bryce and Hannah followed Cal to the door. Bryce looked back at his father and gestured for him to stay there.

They stepped out to follow Cal. They passed by a growing crowd of family members, spouses, children, and off duty miners. Cal called out to them as he continued his stride toward the mine opening. "We need volunteers, off duty miners, to go down in teams."

Without hesitation, man after man pushed through the crowd. Hannah saw more than one woman fight her instinct to stop her man from going. To be so relieved her husband wasn't underground, only to have to give him up to the rescue mission.

One woman kissed her husband goodbye, with tears pooling in her eyes. But for the first time in Hannah's life, she understood the heart of a miner. She had to get underground. Her life didn't matter as much as theirs.

At the mouth of the mine, Cal addressed the group of men. "Go to the Lamp Cabin. If you don't have your check number with you, write it on a piece of a paper and leave it with Fritz. We need to know who's below."

With her entire team underground, she was not about to stay safely up here. If they didn't survive this, what was the point of her safety?

As she turned for the Lamp Cabin, Bryce grabbed her arm. "Let Cal and his team do their work."

"I'm trained in that mine."

"You should be thanking me that you're not down there right now. I saved your life."

"I am not going to let them die." Passion and determination rose inside her. She turned and stormed toward the Lamp Cabin.

He raced in front of her, blocking her way. "You want to die with them?"

"If I have to. And you would, too, if you knew them. Isaak. He has twelve kids. One of them was just born a week ago. Nothing makes him happier than singing. Hicks, he has little Joey waiting on him. Lazy Haze, he was always afraid of this. He must be so scared. And there's Plum...and Josh. They have to know we're out here. That we're not just walking away."

She swiped away her tears; she had to be strong. "Bryce, I spent almost two years down in that mine. I can do this. It's your choice if you don't go down there. But please, don't stop me."

He eyed her silently, then gently took her arm and led her, not away from the Lamp Cabin, but straight to it.

♫ ♫ ♫

Josh's light shone on Lazy Haze's face, eyes open. Was he alive?

"Hazen!"

Lazy Haze's eyes blinked at the offending light. "Josh? Help!" Lazy Haze's trembling voice pierced the silence.

"Haze?" Plum answered. Josh heard movement.

"Plum, are you walking? This is Josh!"

"Yes."

"Plum, help! I can't do this again. Can't be stuck." Lazy would lose it if they didn't free him shortly. But Josh had to extract himself first.

"I think it knocked me out for a few," said Plum. "I

don't know how long. Where are you, Josh?"

"I'm here." He wagged his light back and forth on Lazy Haze. "Get him up first. I have rocks covering me." Josh tossed another one to the side, working to unbury his body.

"Ah!" Lazy Haze yelped.

"Sorry I stepped on you there," Plum said. "But at least I found ya! Can you stand?"

"I think so."

"Don't' stand up too h—"

"Yee-eeow!"

"...high."

"Now you tell me."

Plum's warning came too late. He let out a little chuckle. Josh was never so glad to hear them spar.

"Can you guys quit horsing around and make your way over to me? I need help moving these rocks."

He heard the shuffles as they followed the sound of his voice and the light source on his head.

"I don't know where my light went," said Plum.

"If your helmet's there, wipe the light. Mine was covered in dust." Just then, a blinding lamp shined in Josh's eyes.

"It's workin'." Plum moved his head to check the expanse of Josh's body. "Looks like you got yourself a nice blankie made'a coal there, Winnie."

"You takin' a nap, Josh?" At least Lazy Haze hadn't lost his sense of humor. That may be key to their survival down here.

Josh smiled up at his friends.

"Are you hurt?" Plum asked Josh.

"Just my head, I think. Get me out of this blanket. It's a

little heavy for the weather." It sure was stuffy down there.

Lazy Haze and Plum moved rock after rock to unbury Josh. There were bruises to be sure, but no mortal wounds. He slid out from under where the roof was lowest so he could sit up.

"Can you wiggle them toes, there?" Plum asked.

"Yep."

"Then, I declare you're gonna make it."

"You don't know that." Lazy looked like he would vomit any second. They did not need that down here. "We don't know if any of us will."

They were still missing two others. Josh called out. "Hicks? Isaak?"

The three waited in silence.

Josh said, "Let's crawl a bit down the shaft, feel around for them."

The three used their lamps to shine on different parts of the 13,000 level, which was almost unrecognizable. It was hard to orient to where they were before the bump happened. Which direction should they look?

"Isaak, Hicks!"

Josh moved his hand across the ground, sweeping to feel for any signs of life. His hand brushed a boot. "I think I found something."

The other two made their way his direction. Josh dug his hand under a mass amount of rock, his hand came out wet, bloody. He had no idea if this were Hicks or Isaak or someone from another team.

They heard a faint voice from under the rubble.

"I can't move."

"Hicks?"

"I can't…"

"Just hold on, we'll dig you out." Josh knew the volume of debris covering Hicks weighed far more than what had crashed on him. It almost looked like the whole roof at this portion of the mine collapsed directly on top of Hicks. This did not look good. He bit the inside of his mouth. "Don't move, Hicks. We're gonna get you out."

"And where'm I gonna go?"

They laughed, letting go of some tension.

Lazy Haze uncovered Hicks's face while Plum and Josh worked on his body and legs.

Oh, Dear God, please tell me that Hannah was not on her way down when this place collapsed. He wasn't sure why she hadn't shown up for work, but he hoped against everything in him that she hadn't tried to come down after her shift started. He hated the idea she could be stuck at a different part of the mine, alone, separated from her team.

From him.

One boulder was too heavy for Josh alone, so he motioned for Plum to help him move it. His arms screamed as he tried to lift it. Finally, holding their breath, they shoved it aside.

Josh's lamp highlighted a mutilated leg, soaked in crimson red. A bone protruded. Hicks had lost a lot of blood already. If he were going to survive, they were going to have to move quickly.

♫ ♫ ♫

"You've got to be kidding me, Bryce. I won't do it," Fritz said, after Bryce told him to give Hannah, her lamp.

Hannah appreciated Bryce standing by her decision. He was the only one with the power to do so. This couldn't be easy for him. He liked her, yet her intentions were clear. She had to save, not only her team, but Josh. Bryce would have to be a fool to not understand why.

Fritz handed over the lamp labeled #364, to match the check tag she'd just slipped onto the board.

They grabbed a couple of extra chipper picks from against the wall by the door, and headed out of the Lamp Cabin toward the mines. She didn't even try to disguise herself. Instead, she let her brown hair fall to the sides beneath her lamp.

Sirens wailed as ambulances arrived on the scene. The Red Cross was setting up a nurse's station for rescued miners. *If* there were any to come. She didn't even know if anyone had come up alive yet.

They rushed past townsfolk who held a prayer vigil. How did it come to this again? Hadn't this town suffered enough? Anger boiled inside her.

"Hannah!" She heard the sound of Liesel's voice coming from the crowd.

"Bryce, hang on." She wanted nothing more than to get underground, but she had to assure the teenager she was okay.

Hannah hustled to the line of waiting family members, dropped her chipper pick on the ground and hugged Liesel. Lucas stood next to her.

The girl squeezed her neck, almost knocking her lamp off. "You're okay. You're okay!"

"I wasn't underground when it happened."

"Oh, thank God. Thank you, God." Liesel tossed a look up to the sky.

Did God really have anything to do with it? She'd rather have been underground.

Lucas asked, "Why are you dressed like that?"

"Because I'm going down."

"What? No!" Liesel cried. "Hannah!"

"I have to. Josh is trapped. And Isaak. Everyone. We have to find them."

"Hannah, please. We can't lose you too."

"I'm sorry." She brushed Liesel's cheek with her hand, then hoisted the chipper pick up on her shoulder. She left Liesel at the sidelines and joined Bryce in the stride toward to the mine opening.

She couldn't look back. No one was going to keep her from going underground.

chapter 19

Josh had to ignore the cries. He was causing Hicks much pain, but he had to tie his jacket around Hicks leg. If he didn't, Hicks would bleed out in a matter of hours. The rescue teams would likely need more than that to reach them. He couldn't imagine the pain of having a bone coming out. And they didn't even have so much as one aspirin.

He sent Haze and Plum off to find Isaak and see if they could find supplies in anyone's bags. Water, pain relievers, food. They'd need to ration off the use of the lamps, to get them to last as long as possible. But they couldn't do that until everyone was accounted for.

They were still missing one man.

"Okay. It's set." The makeshift tourniquet was as tight as Josh could get it.

"I don't know if I can do this."

"We gotta try, Hicks. If anyone can survive this, it's you. Think of Joey."

Hicks swallowed and closed his eyes. He nodded. "When I was leaving this morning, Joey didn't want me to go. He's never like that. He usually just plays with his trains and waves me off. But today, he seemed worried he wouldn't see me again. I didn't think much of it. My wife, Sarah thought maybe he'd had a bad dream or something."

"Well, when you make it out of here, you can tell him it was just a dream."

"We found Isaak." Josh heard the yell from Plum quite a ways off in the distance. "He's okay."

Josh blew out a breath.

Plum and Haze helped Isaak walk into their area. All three of them had to duck since it seemed like they only had about three feet of height.

"How did you get over there?"

"I have no idea," Isaak said. "Thankfully, these boys woke me up from my beauty rest."

"We found some water, a little bit of soup and an aspirin bottle with six tablets left," Lazy said.

"Who did it belong to?"

After a silent beat, "Michael Tooke. Our comrade won't be needing it anymore."

And this would probably happen again and again. They would look for more survivors in the rubble, now that their group was together. Plus, they needed supplies if they were going to survive. If they could stick together, maybe they could last until those on the outside could get to them.

Isaak slid up next to Josh, at Hicks's side. He squeezed Josh's shoulder with his hand. "Good to see you, buddy."

"You too, Sir."

"Look. Guys." Hicks cleared his throat, seeming to have a tough time talking without choking up. "I, I can't move. You, you need to go on without me. You need to see if you can dig your way out of here."

"No," Josh said. "We stick together."

"You'll send help back down for me. I know it."

"You are not staying alone. End of discussion. If we can't carry you out with us, we'll wait down here for them to come to us. That's how it works down here."

♫ ♫ ♫

Bryce and Hannah were in step behind some draegerman outfitted in gasmasks.

The rake wasn't running, so they'd set out on foot. Hannah had paid enough attention on the rides down that maybe she could find their level. If it even looked the same.

As they started down the slope behind the draegerman and other miners, it was clear this mine did not look anything like it had when she'd been here, just yesterday.

Cal Weston and his newly formed team came rushing toward them from below, heading back out rather than going deeper into the mine.

"It's methane. It knocked off our lamps. Everyone out. We need to run the fans first." Several men with Cal guided miners who had clearly been underground during the bump. They were covered in soot.

One of them said, "T'is awful down there. Just awful. We tried to go down to the 13, see if we could find anyone, but it's blocked. Stuff's in globs, like a pile of noodles." Hannah recognized his voice. He was one of the rake operators.

The draegermen kept going deeper into the mine, as they had the protective gear. But everyone else turned around.

Hannah ducked behind Bryce so Cal wouldn't see her on his way by. She hardly looked like a man right now, but she absolutely did not want to turn around and go back out.

Once Cal passed by, Bryce reached out for her arm. "Hannah, we can't. We'll pass out from the gas."

Beads of sweat were all over his forehead, and it wasn't from the heat. This had to be hard for him. All those times he said he'd never go underground. "We have good men waiting for us, Bryce. The best. They deserve this."

The men who had just been rescued turned around and came back down the slope with Cal and approached the draegermen. "We want to go back down too. We have to find them." While they could have been the first men to arrive at safety, they didn't want to go to the surface either.

If they could stay down here, so could she.

Bryce and Hannah continued slowly after the others pressed on. "Bryce, thank you."

"Hannah, I don't know if we're going to make it out of this alive. Is that what you want?"

"The Percys need me. I know. But so does Josh. And Isaak. I don't want his kids to go through what I went through. Or what Josh went through. This mine took our dads. If there's a chance to save them…I know you don't get it because you've never spent time down here with any of them."

"And why should I? Everyone has always hated me because of this place."

"What are you talking about?" She almost tripped on a boulder, pressing forward down the slope.

"I'm talking about Josh and every other kid in town

who lost their fathers."

"Josh would not hold you responsible."

"He did."

"Well, he was a kid then. Wasn't he five years old?"

"I'm talking about later on. High School. It's like there was this whole club of them."

The further down they'd go, the more Bryce would sweat and breathe. A draegerman in front of them noticed. "Hey! There's already a limited supply of that air stuff. Save some up."

He meant it to be light-hearted, but Bryce was obviously struggling. The rescuer then looked at Hannah, eyes widening. He blinked as if he was trying to make sure he was seeing correctly.

"What is she..."

Bryce held up his hand, with authority. The man knew to let it go.

The jumbled slope before them felt as long as the Great Wall of China. Suddenly, they came to a wall of debris from top to bottom. It looked non-penetrable.

The workers in front bent over to slide rocks to the sides, but their slope was narrow.

Hannah touched Bryce's arm. "Are you okay? You don't have to stay. I can do this alone."

"I'm...f-fine." He was clearly not fine.

"Really. You don't have to do this for me. I can go on my own."

"I'm not doing this for you." He seemed determined to continue.

A rescuer up front asked, "Isn't this the slope that goes to the thirteen?"

"Supposed to be," another answered.

Hannah couldn't believe it. No matter how much debris they tried to set to the side, the wall in front of them remained a solid wall of coal.

She shoved her way to the front of them, and with her chipper pick, started hacking away at the wall.

"Hey! What's a woman doing down there? Get out."

"She stays." The man couldn't protest against Bryce.

Hannah picked and picked, but wasn't able to make much of a dent in the wall. Sobs threatened to escape. "Josh. Josh! Can you hear me?"

One of the men behind her grabbed her arm. She turned around, her chipper pick poised as she faced him.

"I am not going anywhere. Don't even try to stop me!"

♫ ♫ ♫

Liesel went into the Salvation Army tent. She grabbed a doughnut and water. She needed energy; it was going to be a long night. Lucas had run back to give their mother the good news that Hannah was alive. The not-so-good news she was going underground, and that Josh was unaccounted for.

As she stepped out of the tent, she saw the headlights from hundreds of cars heading into town. Many Springhillers had family from other areas. All of them would try to get here to find out if their family members were alive or dead. Most cars idled in line with nowhere to go. Teens from high school directed traffic. They didn't let any cars through those arches that weren't emergency vehicles.

This was not something Liesel ever wanted to live through once, let alone twice. If she thought she would get away with it, she'd grab a lamp and go down with Hannah.

She saw Isaak's daughter, Heather, come out of the tent with her little brother, Jordan. The child had gotten a powdered doughnut all over his face. What would Isaak's family do if he didn't make it? She couldn't imagine.

"Liesel!" Garrett was here? She turned. Just seeing him here caused her to crumble. All control of her emotions was lost in his arms. He hugged her tightly as she cried.

"Any news?" he asked.

"Not yet."

"Can I do anything?"

"Josh is down there. And Hannah."

"Why would Hannah be there?"

"She went in to try to rescue them."

"What?"

"It's a long story."

Suddenly, they heard a commotion up on the hill by the mine opening. They raced to the top, right up to the barricade. A couple of miners had just come out. The first ones rescued.

Liesel scanned their faces, didn't recognize any. A woman jumped the barricade, raced over to one man. She squeezed him tightly.

Energy surged through the crowd. People clapped and cheered, happy to see confirmation of the first signs of life.

Now if only that trend could continue for the rest of them.

chapter 20

Josh propped Hicks up against the wall. He could sit up with his legs straight in front of him, but could do nothing to move for himself. The waist-down paralysis could be permanent.

They pooled together what little they found of food and water. The thirst was excruciating.

"Now, just a capful," Isaak said, as they were about to pass a round of water. "We gotta make this last. Except Hicks. You take enough to swallow that aspirin."

The wetness on Josh's tongue brought relief but also made him ache for more.

Isaak said, "Well, men, it seems we'll be here a while. Let's take a short break. But then we should move this gob out of our way and build packs to hold up the roof."

"You think she'll bump again?" Lazy Haze asked.

"We can never be too careful."

Lazy cried, "Not again, not again."

"Hold it together, Haze." Hicks said, in a soothing voice. Josh was amazed by Hicks's fortitude. He was worse off than all of them. "We's all gonna be fine."

"You weren't here during the explosion. You have no idea."

"Sure is lucky for Mel he decided not to come to work today," Isaak said.

"Isaak, what if she was just late and on her way down?"

Lazy Haze snapped his head over to Josh. "She?"

Isaak raised an eyebrow at Josh.

"I don't care if I blow her cover, Isaak. I love her. She is never coming down here again."

"Uh, she? Mel is a she?" Lazy asked again.

"Mel is Hannah," Isaak raised his eyebrows at them, even cracked a little smile.

"That girl you's sweet on, Josh?" Hicks asked.

"Yes."

"You mean I done passed my gas 'round a lady?" Lazy Haze's eyes widened.

"Your gas done christened every corner of Springhill." Plum smacked Lazy Haze's arm.

"You knew, Isaak?" Hicks asked.

Isaak nodded.

Hicks pushed up a bit with his hands, to try to sit up a little straighter. "Why did she do it?"

"For the Percys. That's why I let her," Josh said. "But if we get out of here..."

"When." Isaak was right. He had to speak positively. Isaak said, "Survive this, Josh, so I can sing at your wedding."

"Hannah doesn't want to marry me because I chose this instead...here. The mines." Josh never wanted to cry around his comrades, but he couldn't help himself. Could they get out of this alive? Did they even have a chance?

Could he build the life with her that he ached for so badly?

Isaak touched his shoulder and started one of his favorite old hymns:

Great is Thy Faithfulness.

Maybe it was the lyrics or the familiarity, but listening to Isaak sing felt like a soothing balm on an open sore. He hoped, despite the lack of water, that Isaak would never stop singing. They needed the fuel of hope, no matter how long it took for someone to rescue them.

♫ ♫ ♫

Liesel couldn't bring herself to leave. It didn't matter that it was after two a.m. Garrett stood by her side the entire time. Somehow, he just knew what she needed.

The next morning, Lucas and Lindy came back with breakfast sandwiches that Lindy and her mother had made for them and others in the crowd. The four of them walked through the crowd with a tray, passing them out. Some were too nervous to eat, but others needed the boost. No doubt, different Springhillers would do the same gesture for days to come. At least they could feel like they were doing something. Disasters like this made everyone feel so helpless.

One hundred and seventy four men. That's how many Fritz had reported were underground when the mine bumped. If it bumped. No one knew yet if this was a bump or an earthquake. What did it matter? What really mattered were all those lives, hanging in the balance.

She hadn't seen Hannah since she'd gone

underground. But she had spotted some rescue workers coming up with men, not all of them alive.

Just as she passed out another sandwich, a new widow wailed at the sight of her husband.

The mine owner walked through the crowd, doing his best to console family members. As if anyone could say anything that would help. The man looked frail, much older than the last time she'd seen him.

When Hicks's wife railed at him, Liesel almost felt bad for him. "This is your doing, Sawyer. You send good men down there. My Hicks. Joey's daddy. But at what cost?"

Come on. It wasn't his fault. The owner didn't force people to work for him. Not even her own father. He chose to be there. So did everyone else. And now, even Hannah chose to go into that deathtrap.

Shortly after that incident, she caught a glimpse of Adam Sawyer going underground himself to join the rescue efforts. She wondered, in his state of health, if he'd come out alive. She imagined by this point, he didn't care.

Being out here, everyone put someone else above himself. Or herself. That's the way it was in Springhill.

♪ ♪ ♪

Bryce had sworn decades ago he'd never come down again. There was a reason for that. But he knew this time, he just couldn't stay away. He couldn't let Hannah go down there alone. What kind of man would he be?

But it was so hard to breathe. For all of them. It was clear there were gasses in the air. The fans they had set up at the mouth of mine were helping, but not enough. And the heat. It was so stuffy in there. Having so many sweaty bodies sardined didn't help, but he knew everyone wanted to help save the men.

In a way, despite the discomfort, it was the first time in Bryce's life he'd felt a part of this town. He didn't know that was possible here. Down in these depths, he was one of them. Not the owner. Not the boss. They weren't even giving him those looks he was so used to. If anything, they seemed glad he was here. Maybe even respected him a little.

They took turns chipping at the wall of coal before them, continuing to progress down into the mine. They had to chip it away with either a chipper pick or a sawed off shovel, then try to get the coal out of the way. They formed an assembly line, filling buckets with debris, then passed the buckets off to people behind them. Each person moved the debris further up the mineshaft.

Bryce worked next to Hannah, taking whatever buckets she'd pass off and moving it down the line. For a woman, she showed remarkable strength.

"Thank you for doing this, Bryce," Hannah said. "For coming down. I know this is a first."

"No. It's not."

"When were you down here before?"

Should he tell her? Could she take it? Finally, he spoke. "I was here. That day."

The thought of it almost made him hyperventilate. If he didn't step out of the assembly line, he might collapse. Instead, he dropped to his knees. He lowered his head and focused on his breathing. He could not have a panic attack. Right here, now, in front of all these people? No way.

"Bryce? What are you talking about?"

"I came down here with my father. I was five years old. He broke the rules to bring me down, but he was the owner. I'd begged him to show me the mines. And this rumble, it ripped through the mine. Josh's father, I heard him yelling first. It was so awful, the sound. And then I heard others with him."

"My father?"

"Yes." Just thinking about that day made it harder to control his breathing. Sweat dripped down his nose.

"You don't have to stay here, Bryce."

No, he had to do this. He had to fight. He made himself stand up, so he could continue to be a link in the chain, helping get these men out. If they were still alive. He grabbed the next bucket and passed it along. "Let's give some kids their fathers back."

Hannah smiled at him with…was that admiration? Something he had never seen. It may not be love or the kind of female adoration he had hoped for out of Hannah. But it mattered.

♫ ♫ ♫

Josh couldn't just sit here anymore. He had to do something or they all would die. "Isaak, how about we go check around, see if we can find anyone else?" He looked at Plum and Lazy Haze. "You guys stay here with Hicks."

"And turn off your lamps," Isaak said. "We need to save the power."

As they crawled their way around another part of

what he assumed was still the 13,000 level, his hand landed on a leg. He felt around for an arm, a wrist. He checked for a pulse.

There was none.

He made his way to the man's face and shone his lamp on it. Recognition struck. They'd ridden down the rake together so many times. Didn't know him very well, but still. He knew of him to have a family.

"Hugh Levi," said Isaak.

Josh felt around for his lunch pail, a half eaten bag of chips left inside. It was something.

Suddenly, a man called out to them. "Hey! Is anyone out there?"

"Yes. Where are you?" Josh answered.

"Over here." It sounded like the man was tapping a piece of coal against the wall to signal where he was.

They found a small opening in the debris that led downward into a small side cave. What did this used to be? He shone his lamp inside the hole. It lit up the man's face. "Gerald?"

"Yep! It's me."

Josh and Isaak crawled through the opening.

"Are you hurt?" Isaak asked.

"Not too bad. But I couldn't move around much and wasn't sure where to go. Down that hole there…" Gerald pointed to his left. "Two others, Rex and Stewie. They both have busted hips."

Josh peeked through the opening. The men were asleep or unconscious. But at least they appeared to be breathing. "They aren't going anywhere."

Isaak said, "Maybe we can find more food to bring to them. We're up the slope there a bit. Hicks can't move either."

Gerald looked at the pail in Isaak's hand.

"Isn't that Hugh Levi's?"

"He, ah, he's gone." Isaak bowed his head.

Gerald nodded. "I promised my wife this was my last month in here. That on my birthday, come November first, I'd get my retirement. Just one more week was all it would have taken."

There were going to be a lot of promises broken if no one ever found them.

♫ ♫ ♫

It was against her better judgment, but Bryce insisted that Hannah take a break. She needed to refuel, or she wouldn't be useful to anyone. How could she sleep? She needed to let Liesel know she was okay.

So far.

As she and Bryce emerged from the mine opening, the early morning sun made them squint. Cal was in front of the crowd, addressing them with news. The union head, Mark Steinberg, stood beside him. News cameras recorded their words. If this were anything like last time, Hannah knew the entire world was focused on this little town.

"Sixteen men have been rescued," Cal said. "Five men have been confirmed dead. The gasses are bad down there, despite our efforts to keep it ventilated. Most of the 174 men were at the 13,000, the 13,400, and the 13,800 levels. The collapse is so severe, we regret there is little hope any man who worked on the 13,000 level or below is alive."

Anguished cries peppered the hillside. Hicks's wife got in Cal's face, holding Joey close to her body. "My Hicks is not dead till you bring me his body. You do not give up!"

"We will not stop searching until every man is found. Alive or dead. All we can do is hope for a miracle. It's happened before in Springhill. Maybe, maybe it will again."

Hannah couldn't help it. She vomited right there on the grass.

HANNAH SIPPED LEMON TEA with honey at the kitchen table. "Aunt Abby, how do you keep your faith? Time and again God hasn't shown up for you. Or me." The tea soothed her souring stomach.

Abigail put her teacup down. "Oh, that's where you're wrong, Hannah. God may not show up the way we'd like sometimes. But his mercy…it extends far beyond whether he chooses to save a life or allow it to be taken."

How could she even think like that? Hannah didn't want to argue with her, so she kept her mouth shut.

Abigail continued. "Let me share something with you. When I lost my brother, your dad, I was just old enough to start forming my own belief system. I was ten. And let me tell you, I was tempted to not believe. It's like I'd hinged everything on whether or not God acted according to my wishes and desires. Like he wasn't God if he didn't save my brother. But there's so much more to it than that, Hannah. This life here, it's just a blink. There are so many other mercies we enjoy every day, with every single breath we're given."

Hannah swallowed the lump in her throat as Abigail continued. "You know, Ray and I were blessed with twins, right out of that gate. But Liesel, she didn't make it easy from moment one. She almost died. When she recovered, the doctors told us it was a miracle because no reasonable excuse existed for her recovery. God gave me that mercy. I can't get mad at him for not extending the same mercy to my husband."

"I don't know how you can say that, Aunt Abby."

"Am I only grateful to him when he does things my way? I could focus on him allowing Ray to be taken before Laurel arrived, or on the fact that he allowed Laurel to be conceived before Ray left this earth. I have five wonderful children, each one a blessing from him. And they all need me."

Hannah brushed away a tear. Could she ever find this kind of faith? This kind of trust that, no matter what, she could still love and trust God? For the first time, she loved a man who actually treated her well. He seemed to love her unconditionally, no matter if she received him well or not. Perhaps that's not unlike how God wanted to be loved.

"Hannah, I know you feel like you're only looking at losses. Your dad, your mother. But you have gained a lot. I think you should take time to think about what those are. Not the least of which…he didn't let you go underground for this disaster. He spared your life." Abigail tapped on the table. "And for this family here, we are grateful for that mercy. Plus, you arrived when I didn't even know I was going to need you most." Abigail covered her mouth, as she choked up. "That's God's mercy. On me. You were able to tend to Liesel and her grief in a way that I couldn't. You helped her when I felt like I had nothing to give her. You may feel like God keeps taking away, but he gave us you. That's his mercy. You were sent to us from him."

"Are you saying you think Josh is going to die? Or that he's already gone?"

"Absolutely not. I am saying you must be at peace with your Maker either way. This life is so short. It's not worth holding a grudge for eternity."

Yet, it seemed like an eternity since she'd seen Josh's face. But she hoped, and even prayed, God would allow her to see him again. She wanted to look Josh in the eyes, face-to-face, and tell him how much she loved him. How worth the risk he indeed was. How perfect he was for her, and how safe he made her feel.

If only she'd get that chance.

chapter 21

Whenever he'd close his eyes, Hannah's image would pop before him. Her chestnut hair, deep brown eyes. Those feathery lashes. This happened a lot. Josh could barely keep his eyes open. They'd all agreed to take a break, get some rest before continuing to search around for supplies or men. They were in total darkness, saving what little battery power they had left. Three lamps had already burned out.

Isaak crooned a sweet sounding lullaby, well, he would call it a hymn but with Josh so tired it was lulling him to sleep.

"Farther along we'll know all about it. Farther along we'll understand why."

Hicks, Lazy Haze, and Plum joined in on the lyrics. "Cheer up my brothers, live in the sunshine; we'll understand it all by and by."

Isaak passed around the aspirin bottle, filled with water, signaling it was time for the next sip. It didn't help. It made the desire for water even stronger. And it wasn't going to be enough to keep them alive much longer.

How much time had gone by now, anyway? They had

no way of keeping track. Josh appreciated the way Isaak stepped up as a leader down here. He wasn't in this alone.

Hicks wasn't going to last much longer. Where were the rescuers? They'd heard no one so far. Hadn't it been long enough for them to break through? If they were still looking for them. What if they thought they were dead?

"That's it. I'm putting my foot down," Plum said. "No more overtime for me."

Hicks played along with Plum's humor. "I'd put mine down too if it didn't hurt so blasted much."

Josh scooted over to Hicks. Time to see how his dressings were doing. He flipped on a lamp. The jacket was so blood soaked, it was a wonder Hicks was still conscious. It was time for fresher dressing. Josh tore his own shirt off.

"Josh, you need that."

"Not as much as you do."

Hicks howled in pain as Josh removed the jacket. Isaak came over to put pressure on the wound. He also murmured a prayer.

Hicks's inhalations quickened as he tried to breathe through the pain, but he was struggling. That man was a fighter. He let them attend to the wounds with Josh's sweaty shirt.

Then, Josh leaned back against the wall. Would this ever end?

Lazy Haze broke their silence. "I told you when I was stuck here for four days during the explosion, they paid me for one lousy hour of work. Nothin' for the days I was stuck."

Hicks closed his eyes and added in a singsongy tone, "Stuck in the mud and the muck."

Isaak played along, "Because he ran out of luck."

Josh said, "When he forgot to duck."

Lazy Haze harrumphed, not enjoying their joke. "How long have we been down here? We're like trapped rats, I tell ya."

"Come on, Haze," Isaak said. "Don't lose it on us."

"We're close to the bottom, ya know?" Haze breathed loudly.

"We can't keep your mind for you." Plum hit the coalface next to where he was sitting.

"You think they'll make it in time? Before Hicks's loses his blood?"

"Hazen!" Josh yelled. Why couldn't he just shut up?

Lazy Haze bordered on hyperventilation. "And he's the one who swore it was so safe. Always tried to tell me. What if they turn the air off?"

"They won't."

"They will if they think we're dead." It was the fear no one wanted to voice. And there it was. "We were all here during the explosion. They did stop looking."

He had to admit Haze was right. It wasn't only the gasses, but they'd given up hope anyone else was still alive. What if that's what was going on now? What if they'd stopped, either because the mine had filled with methane or because they thought no one who wasn't already outside had survived? What if they were the only group still stuck and no one knew to search for them after the gasses subsided? History had told them they didn't necessarily keep searching until all the bodies were recovered. Not at the risk of losing more men. Was that what was going on now? Had they given up on them?

Isaak crawled around the space. "Let's tap on the pipes again. Someone might hear us this time."

"We've already tried!" Lazy Haze whined.

Isaak crawled over to the pipes where he'd left a shovel. He banged on the pipe, letting the rhythmic sound echo.

Tap. Tap. Tap.

Then he waited for a response, the return of a tap, signaling someone had heard.

There was none.

Nothing but silence.

♫ ♫ ♫

"Be careful down there." Liesel walked Hannah to the end of the driveway, the sun peeking out for the morning.

"I will. I promise." Hannah knew sometime later that day, the teenager would be outside of the mines waiting for a chance to see her face emerge. Waiting for some kind of good news. But for the moment, Liesel stood in the middle of the street in her pajamas.

Hannah had lost count of how many days had gone by since the bump. Three? Four? She'd spent so much time trying to help with the rescue efforts, sometimes she never saw the sun.

Just as she got to the neighbor's house, Liesel called out. "No matter what happens, Hannah, we'll be here."

Hannah looked back at her and nodded before making the trek to the mines. Last night, Bryce insisted she go home and sleep or he would stop her from going underground. He'd found her lying on a bench in the Wash House, stationed under Josh's bucket. She couldn't stop staring at the last piece of clothing he'd changed out of before going underground.

"Time to go," Bryce had said.

"I keep thinking if I lie here long enough, the pulleys will come down, and my guys will change their clothes."

Bryce seemed to understand, but still insisted she go home before they could head back down. On their way out, she couldn't help but look at the check tag board. So many numbers were still hanging from them. So many men unaccounted for.

Josh's tag was there: #212.

She was so tempted to slip it into her pocket.

As she turned on Junction, Oreo the dog perked up. Instead of lazily sitting in his usual spot, he padded over to her. Memories of her first day in town flooded back, when Josh first told her about the black and white landmark.

Oreo sat at her feet and licked her hand. "I know, Oreo. I miss him too." She petted his crown. "I'll find him. I promise." And she went on toward the mines.

Main Street was eerily quiet. On a normal day, people would be out, continuing the rebuild efforts. Only two structures seemed to buzz with life: All Saints Church and the Springhill Record. The Record was probably making sure the world stayed current on what was going on. News crews from all over the world set up camp outside the mines 24-7. They wanted to be there for any change. She'd heard the Queen of England had sent a telegram from Buckingham Palace, asking to be kept informed. That's how far-reaching people were who cared about this town.

As she passed the church, she heard singing from inside. Must be an early morning, prayer service for the victims and those still missing.

For the first time, she felt a pull. Something drawing her to go inside. Maybe some version of peace lived there, the same one that drew Josh and Abigail. Maybe later. For now, she needed to get back to the mines.

As she walked through the arches of Cumberland Coal, her heart brimmed with pride. This was her town, her people. She was going back down to see if she could save them.

As she was about to head to the Lamp Cabin, Isaak's wife, Mrs. Ginnie, called to her. She was in the crowd, there with all twelve of their kids, cradling the newborn. Hannah swept her up in a gentle embrace, careful not to squish the baby. "Mrs. Ginnie, how are you holding up?"

The elegant woman let go and got a faraway look, a peaceful smile growing on her face. She didn't look like one who'd spent the past few days living with the angst that the husband of her twelve children wouldn't come home.

"I was sitting in my living room, watching the TV last night. And this quartet came on, started singin'. They sung, *'Farther along we'll know all about it. Farther along we'll understand why.'* I think my Lord's telling me my Isaak may not be up for a while, but he's comin'. And he's coming up alive."

Hannah wanted to believe her. Badly. She couldn't bear to think of Josh not coming up from underground. "I hope you're right."

By the time she reached the Lamp Cabin, Bryce was already suited up. He waited as she turned in her check number. Reluctantly, Fritz handed her a lamp.

As she and Bryce were about to head underground, his father, Adam, caught up to them.

"Bryce?" Adam looked like a mixture of impressed

and confused. Especially about Hannah.

"We're doing what we can, Dad."

"Why is Hannah..."

"It's okay, Dad. She needs to be here. And so do I." Pride seemed to swell in the aging gentleman's eyes, as if this were the moment he'd been waiting for his whole life. Likely, he was too thankful to see his son getting involved to care about what she was doing.

"Wait for me. I'll head down with ya."

"No, Dad. You don't have to, let us..."

"I'm coming with you."

Bryce nodded, relenting.

Once Adam was equipped, the three joined the team that continued to cut at the virgin coal. The only way down the slope was to dig a new path.

They took their places in the assembly line. Each took turns chipping away at the front of the pack. That was the hardest job of them all. But everyone did it. No one complained. Most of the men took off their shirts, they were sweating so badly.

Hannah, naturally, couldn't do that. But she took her turn, chipping away at the stubborn coal.

♫ ♫ ♫

Who knew a chocolate bar could bring such joy? Josh let it melt across his tongue instead of biting it. Made it last longer. Lindy would be so proud. What he wouldn't give for one of her treats. He couldn't dwell on that right now. The past while — who knows how many days — they'd taken to gnawing on the bark from the timber that Lazy Haze and Hannah used to build the stone packs. During one of their escape attempts, they happened upon an abandoned lunch pail that had that chocolate bar inside. They divided it out into eight equal pieces, for themselves and the comrades stuck below them. By now, they had been able to move Gerald up to their holding space.

"This is the last of our food," Gerald said.

"Can't we do somethin'?" Lazy Haze asked.

"We can pray." Isaak tried to hand a piece of chocolate to Hicks, but he waved it off.

Gerald said, "I gotta make water. Shame to waste, isn't it?"

"I hear tell it's safe to drink," Plum offered.

"But, can we really do that?" Lazy Haze asked.

Isaak said, "There's no pride down here." No one would have ever thought to drink his own urine. But was it a way of survival? Maybe.

After Gerald stepped away from them for privacy, Hicks spoke up. "Guys? I think my time's comin'."

"No," Plum said. "You don't get to leave before we do. And that little boy of yours, Joey is waitin' on you."

Hicks labored to breathe. "Was I wrong all this time? Was it selfish of me to be here? I love you guys, I do, but what's my family gonna do? How is my wife gonna take care of Joey alone?"

A lump lodged in Josh's throat. He tried to swallow it away. It was no use. What Hicks was asking about…it was exactly what Hannah feared all along. How could he have chosen this over her?

After everyone drifted off to sleep, Josh slid up next to Isaak. How hard it was to talk, his throat so dry. His tongue was so thick, like having a mouth full of dry cotton.

"Isaak, do you think we're gonna die?"

"No."

"Do you honestly believe that or are you trying to have faith?"

"A little of both. Our men out there won't quit till they find us."

"They stopped last time."

"They had to. The fires wouldn't go out. It could have exploded again."

"If you died today, would you have any regrets?"

"I promised my Ginnie a thirteenth child. What about you, Josh?"

"Hannah believes everyone who loves her will hurt her or leave."

"Then survive. Prove her wrong."

"Liesel even told me. Shouldn't have pushed so hard. Should've been safer. For her."

Abruptly, Hicks woke, gasping for air, but it wouldn't come. It jarred everyone awake. They crawled over to him, as he struggled to breathe.

"Oh, no. No, no, no. Hicks!" Lazy Haze cried out. "You can't do this, buddy. We need ya." But it didn't matter. Within moments, Hicks slumped over.

Desperately, Josh felt for a pulse. There was none.

Perhaps in God's mercy, he took Hicks away.

chapter 22

October 29, 1958, 1 p.m.

"No one has come out of that mine alive in almost a week. Do we continue to risk the lives of all these volunteers?" Bryce hated to say it, but someone had to. His dad, Cal, and the engineers in the office stared at him across the table.

His dad raised a steely-eyed gaze. "We won't stop until every single body is recovered. Even though it's unlikely anyone is alive."

Bryce had to force his dad to stay behind, promising to go look for the men with Cal. His last trip down had almost done his father in.

As he was about to go beneath the earth, he saw no sign of Hannah. This would be the first time he'd go down without her.

Maybe he was protecting her this way too. No one else would let her descend into the deeps without him, for sure.

He was doing this for himself. And for the men. Since the beginning of time, he'd been accused of not caring, of not putting his life on the line. Well, now it was time to risk. And as much as he liked Hannah, he knew. She didn't see him in a way that something could grow between them. He knew her heart was set on one particular man. One who was underground right now. Whether he was still alive was unknown. But if he were, somehow, Bryce would find him.

1:45 p.m.

INSIDE THE MINESHAFT, one draegerman had the nerve to say, "This is tough when you know you're just contributing to a proper burial."

"Don't talk like that," Cal said. "Don't even think it. Not with 100 men waiting to be brought home."

Bryce respected Cal. He was glad he could finally be down here without hyperventilating.

Suddenly, they heard something.

Cal's hand flew up. "Shh!"

Tapping.

A chill ran up Bryce's spine. He'd heard of this, the signal that miners would give from below to let them know they were trapped. Is that what this was?

Tap. Tap. Tap.

Cal took the sawed off shovel and tapped the metal against the pipe he heard the tapping come from. Three rhythmic taps.

He waited. Silence.

His face fell in the silence that followed. Was it just water dripping on the pipe? Or something else?

And then, they heard it again.

Tap. Tap. Tap.

Cal dove to his knees, putting his mouth against the pipe at a seam.

"Hello. Hello!"

It echoed through the metal, then settled down.

They waited.

Then, they heard it from far below. "Hello! Come and get us."

Cal let out the biggest whoop. Infectious cheers grew from every single person down the assembly line.

Cal shushed everyone.

"Who is this?"

"O'Malley."

"O'Malley. Is anyone with you?"

"Try twelve of us, Weston! You wanna chat all day or get us out?"

"We got a little bit of coal between you guys and us, blocking our way. But you can count on it...we'll get you out."

A little bit? That's one way to describe it.

"We need water down here," O'Malley yelled hoarsely.

"We'll get some to pour down the pipe. Just sit tight."

"Ya think we're goin' anywhere?"

The rescuers laughed and dug with a lot more energy than they'd had in days.

Finally, they'd encountered survivors. Bryce wished Hannah were beside him to witness this.

October 30, 1958, 5 a.m.

IT TOOK SIXTEEN HOURS to dig O'Malley's team out. Bryce helped the last two of the twelve.

The jubilant crowd erupted into cheers. The sun was just coming up for the day. They'd blindfolded the men, so the brightness wouldn't hurt their eyes after six and a half days underground.

His father's face was a welcome one, as he took him in a hearty embrace outside the mine. Bryce couldn't remember the last time his dad hugged him like that.

A reporter captured the group on camera as he updated the world on the miracle rescue. "It's unbelievable. Just when the mine officials were telling us there was no hope, twelve miners have been found alive in the deepest coal mine in Canada. In all of North Amer—" The reporter couldn't finish speaking over the lump in his throat.

Bryce knew from the names O'Malley called out that Josh was not among this group, or anyone else from Hannah's team. They sent up that list of names to be read to the crowd earlier, so family members could wait for them.

When he spotted Hannah among the crowd, he knew she was aware Josh was not on that list. She still managed to smile at him, happy for those rescued.

Emergency medical workers helped guide the men onto stretchers to lead them to immediate care. Family members enjoyed tearful reunions.

The reporter continued, tears streaming down his face. "They all just came out. These men everyone believed were dead. We hear Prince Philip is on his way to meet the miracle survivors at the hospital. He's coming in, all the way from England"

Bryce knew, without a doubt, that Hannah loved Josh more than anyone on this earth. As much as he cared for her, he had to do what he could to give her what she wanted. If there were any hope Josh was alive, he was going to find him.

For her.

♫ ♫ ♫

November 1, 1958, 4 a.m.

It had been two long days since the miracle twelve emerged. And now, Hannah hated every word coming out of Adam Sawyer's mouth to the reporters and the family members that still waited, still hoped for another miracle rescue. Bryce stood beside her.

"It's been two days since we stumbled upon the miracle of twelve men waiting on us. We believe it's not possible that anyone else is alive." Adam cleared his throat. "It's been eight days. Perhaps, it would be best, if you would go home, get some rest. Truth is, as hard as it is to face, we're just looking for bodies now."

People absorbed his words, even listened to him. They started turning away, ending their eight-day vigil. But something in Hannah refused to give up. If those twelve could survive, others could too. And if any group were capable, she knew it would be hers. She'd have to see Josh's body before she'd give up.

Bryce looked over at her. "You want to go back down?"

"I need to do something. But I'll be back. Will you still go down?"

Bryce nodded.

"Thank you, Bryce."

She marched away from the yard. She couldn't give up. There was no doubt this miracle was God's mercy on this town. If God could save those twelve men, he could save her team too.

NO SERVICE WAS GOING ON, but the front door of All Saints' Church was unlocked. Hannah stepped inside. It felt so strange coming here, wanting help, when she'd done so much to avoid it since she'd arrived in town.

Her mother believed, even though the mines took her father. Her father believed, even in the midst of the years his prayers for a child had gone unanswered.

And down deep, Hannah had to admit, so did she. Josh was right. She was angry, not indifferent. *An angry believer.*

Could she speak to God? Would he even listen to her after all these years? She stepped to the foot of the altar. No one else seemed to be around. She should say something, she supposed. But where were the words? Nothing at all would come out.

She couldn't bring herself to pray, so she moved to the piano, sat down and played. That same tune she'd heard from the steps nearly two years ago. The tune of one of her mother's favorite hymns poured out of her.

Amazing Grace.

Was blind but now I see.

The words echoed in her mind as she stopped playing.

Had she been blind? Was Abigail right that she had spent too much of her life focusing on what God wasn't doing rather than what he was? Or where he was? Had she missed all of his little graces? Those are no less amazing than the big ones.

That God would show up for any of them was astounding. She'd failed to pay attention, failed to give him credit for all he'd done. Instead, all these years, she'd focused on what he hadn't done.

Sorrow pierced her heart. Sobs overtook her as she

moved to the altar, regret for all the anger. Why had she let it rule her life?

Like a flood, images moved across her mind, memories from the past where God had shown up.

A bad situation drove her to this precious town, a place that had embedded itself so deeply into her heart. A place she would have missed out on, had she gone through with the wedding. A union that she knew—without a doubt—would have eventually killed her. That was God's mercy.

He gave her the courage to leave. Her choices got her into that situation, but he protected her as she left. The way she had tried to form a family with the wrong people, only to be led away to the right one. That, too, was grace.

The fact Will Felten hadn't come to find her when she left right before their wedding—that had to be God's mercy and protection. The stifling grip he'd had on her was proof he didn't normally let go easily.

Like Abigail said, the fact that she was led here in time to be there for the Percys, that was God's mercy, not only on her, but on them. No matter what the outcome with Josh, she had to stay strong for them. She had to live through this.

God gave her fifteen years with her mother. Her mother could have given up when her dad died. What followed her mom's death until October 30, 1956, when she first stepped into Springhill, was obviously difficult. But not all of that was his lack of mercy. She'd made bad choices in her need to survive. She didn't always listen to that still, small voice her mama always said she should pay attention to—the one that warned her the man she'd set her sights on was not good for her.

And Josh—even though she'd spent most of her time resisting him—he was a sweet balm on a soul that had all but given up hope in the idea that love could come to her. God's mercy.

She buried her face in her hands. "Lord, I'm sorry to have ignored you for so many years, to have blamed you for so much. You did so much to protect me and I kept refusing to see. I ask you to protect Josh now too. But even if you don't, you are still God. My merciful God."

The idea of Josh not returning to her sent racks of sobs shaking through her body. And yet she had more peace than she'd had in a long time. Her wearied frame seemed lighter, as the anger lifted. It had trapped her in a cell all this time.

"God, I want to tell him. I want to tell him that no matter how bad life gets, there's always ice cream. I want to tell him that I love him. Because I do. No matter how much I don't want to, I love Josh Winslow. Lord, if he's still alive, tell him. And even if he's not, could you still tell him? I want him to know that Hannah Melody Wright loved him. Lord, I'm sorry I've doubted. I'm sorry I ran away."

Somehow, she just knew Daddy and Mama were smiling down on her from heaven. Maybe dancing. Singing a song, even. As serenity overtook her, she drifted off to sleep at the foot of the altar.

♫ ♫ ♫

Liesel stepped inside her mother's bedroom. That sounded strange...her mother's room. She'd always thought of it as her parents' bedroom, even after two years. Some things take a long time to get used to. Her mom sat up in bed, reading her Bible, while Laurel slept in the crib beside her.

"Mom, Hannah never came home last night. I think I should go back."

"It's wet out there, Liesel."

She stared at her mother, not about to take no for an answer.

"Take my coat." Thankfully, her mother relented.

As she started the walk down Main Street, she was surprised to see Hannah emerge from All Saints' Church. Her heart skipped a little at the idea Hannah had finally gone into that place. There was something different about her face. A peacefulness, maybe.

Hannah joined her. "You shouldn't be out here. It's cold."

"Don't go all mother on me. When you go back down, can I go with you?"

"Absolutely not, Liesel. It's too risky."

"It is for you too."

"I know. But your mother, she'd never forgive me. Let's go see what's going on."

WHEN THEY ARRIVED AT THE MINE YARD, the crowd had thinned considerably. Liesel wasn't sure if it was the freezing rain or if everyone else had, indeed, given up hope.

She followed Hannah to the hillside. It was as good a place as any to wait for Bryce. She had to admit, she was glad Hannah couldn't go down right now. When Hannah dropped down to the ground, Liesel kneeled beside her.

There were no words, but then again, no words were needed. She stayed by her cousin's side for hours, sometimes praying silently on Hannah's behalf. She needed her to make it through this, no matter what the outcome. She took her hand and squeezed it.

♫ ♫ ♫

November 1, 1958, 9:15 a.m.
Hannah must have fallen asleep, leaning against Liesel on a set of chairs inside the Salvation Army tent. She awoke to the sound of activity outside.

She roused Liesel and they ducked out of the tent, as the crowd cheered and chattered loudly.

"What's going on?" Hannah asked one of the onlookers.

"They're bringing up another group!"

"How many?"

"They didn't say."

Could it be? Would Isaak's wife be right, that it would take a long time but Isaak would come up? Would he bring Josh with him? And Hicks? Lazy Haze? Plum?

Hannah watched as Adam emerged from the mouth of the mine, helping a miner step out.

Plum!

Hannah squealed at the site of him. She sprinted for the front of the mine, with Liesel on her heels.

Behind Plum, two other miners were carried out on stretchers. Blindfolded and covered in coal dust, it was hard to tell who was who.

Hannah rushed up to Plum. "Plum!" He yanked his blindfold off.

"Where's them bushy eyebrows, Mel?"

"You're alive!"

"Thank you for not stickin' around to watch me shower."

Hannah laughed and hugged him, though he grunted in pain. "Sorry."

"I forgive you, ya liar."

"Josh? Is he..."

Plum turned around and pointed to the opening. Lazy Haze and Isaak were carried out on stretchers. But they looked good, drinking from water canisters. Lazy Haze spotted her.

"Haze! Isaak!" She rushed over to them.

Another set of rescuers carried a stretcher with a covered body. Her heart just about stopped. Who was that?

"We lost Hicks down there, Rocky," Lazy Haze said. "He tried his best to make it. He just..."

She squeezed his hand, then looked to the crowd where Hicks's wife, Sarah, waited with little Joey. She hated knowing the body beneath was that woman's beloved husband.

Mrs. Revere and her children rushed toward the opening to greet Isaak. That she was even still here holding vigil was a sign of her faith in what God had told her. Mrs. Ginnie wrapped her arms around her husband. "Thank you, Sweet Jesus. I knew it. I knew you'd come back to us."

Isaak craned his head up to kiss her. "I told you I'd give you that thirteenth child, and I am a man of my word. It may take me a few weeks."

Ginnie howled in delight and kissed his forehead, as

she balanced their newborn with one arm. The kids surrounded their daddy.

Gerald was brought up next on a stretcher. He spotted Isaak and Ginnie's reunion. "Mrs. Ginnie, that husband of yours, he hasn't stopped singing since we got trapped. Kept us going down there, he did."

"Why am I not the least bit surprised?"

Isaak kissed her hand. "You give me another cup of water, and I'll sing you a song too, pretty lady."

"Isaak, did Josh—" Hannah stopped short as she saw *him*. Josh, the man she was so completely, hopelessly in love with. A draegerman held Josh on one side, helping him to the surface.

Supporting Josh's other side...it was Bryce. Josh wasn't on a stretcher, but he was blindfolded. And *shirtless*.

"Josh!" She ran over to him so fast, she almost knocked him over. But somehow he found the strength to catch her.

"Hannah!" He whipped off his blindfold to look her in the eyes. "I'm so thankful you're alive!"

"I wasn't underground when it happened. But you...Joshua Theodore Winslow the Sixth. The one and only love of my life."

He hugged her tightly, clinging as if his life depended on it. "Hannah, I have to tell you—"

"—No, no. I have been waiting to tell you. Eight and a half days now, to be exact. I do know you. You have shown me over and over who you are. And I love who you are. Josh, I love you." Happy tears spilled down her cheeks.

"You realize you're giving me full on permission to pursue you."

"Yes, Josh. As a matter of fact, I do."

chapter 23

January 1959

For Bryce, the hearing was over. The Royal Commission had adjourned. There'd been weeks of testimonies. He and his dad sat through every last one of them. Miners, witnesses, experts, engineers, union officials. Everyone had an opinion, but now, the report was done. They'd investigated the nagging question: was this disaster that claimed 75 innocent lives man-made? Was the company responsible? Or was it a natural disaster?

The Commission's conclusion: *inconclusive.*

There was no way to prove the long-wall mining methods caused the disaster, nor was there a way to say it didn't. They had to live with not knowing. Listening to many speak, both for and against, was tough.

It would always remain a mystery, but at least it was over.

Bryce left the reading of their findings with his dad, glad for the outcome, thankful that even Hannah spoke up on their behalf.

They walked down the steps of Legion Hall. His dad

said, "We won in there."

"Did we?"

"They've been using this method throughout mines all over since the twenties. There's no way to prove if it was the cause."

"What if some of the miners were right? I was the one in charge when the engineers suggested it."

"We'll never know. Son, that is the burden of my life. Never knowing if there was something else that could have been done. I don't think we'll ever reopen here."

"I have a feeling Springhill will survive without us. They always come back."

Bryce took one last look at Hannah, who was buoyantly talking with her team. She clung to Josh's arm, with the hand he'd wanted to hold himself. He knew in many ways, he didn't deserve her.

Josh did.

He'd be moving on out of here anyway. This place...it wasn't where he belonged. After the mines lost another 75 men, he couldn't bear to take the looks, the blame. It didn't matter what the Commission said. People would fault them anyway. He'd lived under that his whole life. It was time to start afresh. Somewhere new.

"Bryce, I was thinking. It's time I retire. Maybe we can get on out of here. Get a place on Prince Edward Island. I'd like you to live with me, if you'll have me."

His favorite place on earth with the only family he had left. That sounded good to him.

"Sure, Dad."

"Really? You'll go with me?"

Bryce nodded. Maybe he could even find love there.

"You can even play me a song or two, Son."

♫ ♫ ♫

It may have been a bitter cold, January night, but everyone in town wanted to be there to honor the fallen men. Hannah felt such comfort with Josh's hand in hers, as they walked over to Main Street. Even though she wore mittens, she knew beneath was her mother's engagement ring, there to symbolize that soon they would marry.

There had been talk of holding this vigil on the grounds of the mines. But instead, they decided to hold this special ceremony on the newly finished Main Street, a place where the town would find new growth. Looking ahead, not behind. Just like Mama used to say.

The Percy kids and Abigail passed out candles to the seventy-five people appointed to represent the fallen men of the Bump. Their widows or children, parents or siblings. Each miner had one representative to hold a candle in his honor. The seventy-five stood in the middle of the street while onlookers lined the sidewalks.

Reverend Bacon opened the night with a prayer of thanksgiving, a prayer of hope.

At the pastor's signal, the Mayor of Springhill turned off the street lamps. They all stood in darkness, other than the moon and the stars. They lit the first set of candles, held by several sons of fallen men. From there, each family member used the fire of the candle next to them to light their own. And down the line it went, until the street was illuminated. The crowd bowed their head in respect for those they'd lost.

"And now, I'd like to ask the miracle nineteen to come forward," Reverend Bacon said.

One by one, the nineteen miracle survivors of the

Bump moved toward the front. They could walk now, all released from the hospital. The group of twelve and the group of seven. Josh released Hannah's hand to join his team. She spotted Hicks's wife in the crowd, holding that candle, in the middle of the street. Joey stood beside her. Hannah stepped up to them in quiet support.

When the men got to the pastor, the Percy kids were waiting with miners' lamps. They handed one to each of them and had them stand in a straight line at the top of Main Street, looking down to where all the candleholders and onlookers were.

"Please blow out your candles."

And with that, the street was once again in darkness. The crowd silently waited.

Then, one by one, each miracle survivor turned on his lamp.

Lamp on. Lamp on. Lamp on.

Including O'Malley, Gerald, Lazy Haze, Plum, Isaak, and Josh. All nineteen were shining brightly before them.

It was silent for a moment, then the whole place exploded in applause for the nineteen survivors. The spirit of the town revived, basking in the miracle of God that had saved the lives of these nineteen men.

Camaraderie didn't just exist underground; it flourished in the hearts of everyone who had the privilege of calling himself or herself a Springhiller. In steadfast, Springhill fashion, a hummed melody permeated Main Street. It was started by Isaak, then grew with the aid of the harmonic voices of his children. When Isaak added the lyrics, they captured the song that was birthed in the hearts all: *We Will Rise Again.*

♫ ♫ ♫

"Ah!" Hannah yelped as Josh accidentally splattered her with fresh paint. "That goes on the door frame, Mister Joshua Theodore Winslow the Sixth. Even though there's no three, two, and one."

Her soon-to-be new home was filled with people. Her team. Her family. Everyone lent a hand to the new venture that would keep two families afloat in Springhill. Well, if "lent a hand" could be defined as Liesel chasing Lucas through the living room with a can of shellac. Some things never changed.

Soon, her parents' old home would be a Bed & Breakfast with a nook that served breakfast and lunch to guests and townsfolk. Even Lindy would have her own portion of the enterprise, running her candy store. But more importantly, Josh would have an outlet for his masterful chef skills and a way to support them without going underground.

"I love you, Hannah Melody Wright, for believing in me, for showing me I can leave what I know to do what I love." He put the paintbrush in a cup, picked her up and swung her around.

A giggle erupted from her overflowing heart.

Then, Isaak, Lazy Haze, and Plum walked in carrying the dining room table they had refinished outside. The gagging noises began.

Lazy Haze said, "You guys are sappy."

Isaak patted Lazy Haze's shoulder. "Oh leave 'em alone, Haze. Great to see you happy, Josh."

"Thank you, Isaak. So, you made that thirteenth child

yet?"

"We're working on it," he said with a wink. "You two will get to be thinking about that soon." He wagged an authoritative finger. "But not till that walk down the aisle, now. When's the wedding?"

Hannah smiled, eyeing Mama's petite diamond ring on her left ring finger. She couldn't wait to add the wedding band to it. "Next month."

Plum pointed his index finger at them. "I better be getting an engraved invitation. What'cha gonna name this restaurant, Josh?"

"I was thinking *Tastes of Life*."

"That's corny. Isn't that corny?" Lazy Haze teased.

Hannah didn't care if it was corny or not. They were starting their new lives together. Josh would sell his home, to help with funds while they started their business. And they'd live at the Bed & Breakfast, in her parents' old bedroom.

They'd supply a haven for travelers and get to work from the safety of home. Lucas and Liesel would work for them. It would be a family-run business, to continue to help supplement the compensation paid to Abigail for Ray. Hannah would even be able to take on private music students.

Lazy Haze said, "I liked what you said to the Commission, Hannah. About getting Springhill to love ya. Where'dja cook that up?"

Lazy Haze was referring to her testimony, when she got up on the stand and spoke on the Company's behalf and the miners who chose to go underground. She'd had a rare understanding that no other woman possessed. She didn't even get it that first day she'd driven the Champ into town. But now she did, understanding what drove them to go underground every day. It was their families and the people they were with. She knew Josh would recognize what she'd said. She'd caught his eyes from the witness stand.

"Some towns find their way into your heart, ya know, kind of like a song. When you open your heart to this place, it will wrap its arms around you. It will lend you a dollar when you need a dime. You just have to let it love you."

Yes, it may have been sappy. But that didn't make it less true.

She beamed at the love of her life. "I was just sharing something I'd heard from this sap I know, who convinced me, risks and all, it's worth it to love."

Plum put on a sing-songy voice. "They fit like a hand in a glove."

Haze added, "With love pure as a turtledove."

"Sent from heaven above," Isaak added.

"Ain't that the truth," Josh declared.

"That didn't rhyme," Lazy Haze said. "Isaak, he ain't playin' right."

"I don't have to play right," he said as he wrapped his arms around Hannah and looked her in the eyes. "I'm home." His dimpled smile melted her a little.

Springhill had made it through so much; this town could survive anything.

And so would they.

Here. At home. That's what Springhill and Josh had become to her too. A place to build something beautiful. A place where there would always be ice cream.

And a song.

♩ ♩ ♩

After the Bump, the No. 2 mine was sealed and the
Company moved out of Springhill.

It was never proven that lining up the coalface walls was
the cause of The Bump. It was, however, the suspicion of
the men of the deeps.

The Singing Miner, Maurice Ruddick (fictionalized as Isaak),
went on to father his thirteenth child.

Author's Connection to the Mines:

Charles Hugh McKay
(the author's grandfather)
Survived the No. 2 Bump in 1958

Thomas McKay
(the author's great grandfather)
Worked as a coal miner

John Dickson Weatherbee
(the author's great-great grandfather)
Survived the Feb. 1891 Springhill disaster in No. 2 mines
that killed 125 men

Melvin Weatherbee
(the author's great-great uncle)
Melvin was the brother of the author's great grandmother,
Edna Weatherbee McKay.
Melvin was decapitated in the
mines in 1908.
He was born in 1887, got married in 1907, and died on Dec.
21, 1908, No. 3 main slope.

Acknowledgments

Special Thanks To:
All of those who helped me research this story or allowed
me to interview them, including:

Dad — Tom "Tommy" McKay
Joyce & Gerald Harroun
Caleb & Pat Rushton
Bill Booth
Jerry Gillis
Ken Melanson
Herb Pepperdine
Jack & Keith Bourgeois
Dr. Arnold Burden
Lloyd Moss
Ken Warren
Norma Ruddick
Cumberland Museum
Gary Copeland
Peter Harroun
Roberta McMasters
Debbie Betty-Brazie
Don Tabor
Springhill Heritage Group
Springhill Mine Museum
Halifax Chronicle-Herald
Springhill Record

The Giver of Miracles and Amazing Grace

Special thanks to Valarie Tabor Alderson whose tribute ceremony to the miners at the 50th Anniversary of the Bump was the inspiration for the tribute at the end of this novel.

Special thanks to the family of Maurice Ruddick, who allowed me to fictionalize his story for this novel. As the hero who became known as "The Singing Miner," he served as the inspiration for the character of Isaak Revere. An extra thanks to Valerie Ruddick MacDonald and her husband Barry for being so supportive of my creative efforts in sharing Valerie's father's story. She shared so generously of her life and herself in keeping her father's memory alive.

Thanks to Ethel Fisher Gilbert for being willing to talk to me about her father, Lester Fisher, the man who died in my grandfather's place. Lester had asked my grandfather to trade shifts with him on the day of the Explosion. This backstory was the inspiration for the story between Josh and Uncle Ray.

And finally, special thanks to my family, especially my dad and Aunt Joyce, who let me ask them tons of questions about my grandfather's life so I could retell it here. My grandfather survived The Bump after being stuck underground when the earth quaked. His devotion to his family and getting out of those mines inspired many pieces of this story.

A Note from the Author

I hope you enjoyed reading this story as much as I enjoyed immersing myself in the world of Springhill and getting to know its beloved people and town.

There is no doubt in my mind that God showed up and performed some amazing miracles in that place. Yet, that doesn't wipe away the sorrows of those family members who did lose their loved ones. I encourage you this day to take the time to look for God in the little things, those graces we sometimes forget, rather than just focusing on the challenges we're facing or what we don't have.

I hope this book serves to honor those men who lost their lives, the heroes who worked so hard to rescue them, the underground heroes who did all they could to survive, and the women and children who stood in support of them.

Here's a little fun fact. My husband and I are the couple on the cover. It was taken on our wedding day. I took a lot of our personality traits and put them in the love story characters of Josh and Hannah. With this being a family project, I figured using us was appropriate.

If you enjoyed this book, I would appreciate you recommending it to your family and friends. Please share your thoughts by leaving a review online.

And remember, no matter how bad life gets:

There's always ice cream.

Book Two:

Spirit of
Springhill

Miners, Wives, Widows, Rescuers & Their Children Tell
True Stories of Springhill's Coal Mining Disasters

By
Cheryl McKay

SPIRIT OF SPRINGHILL

Front Cover Mining Grounds photo supplied by and used by
permission of the Springhill Heritage Museum.
Front Cover Miner's Hand photo by Christopher Price
Back Cover Miner's Pick & Tags photos by Cheryl McKay
Cover Design by Christopher Price (Roads & Rivers Media)

Interview segments & material used by permission of the interview
subjects.

To inquire about the rights to the screenplay, *Song of Springhill*,
contact the author: Cheryl@purplepenworks.com

2018 — Commemorative Edition

For those who
keep hope alive
in the midst of great adversity

TABLE OF CONTENTS

The Interviews

Springhill's Story in the 1950s

Spirit of Springhill is more than just a book of interviews; it's a record of a legacy. It's a tribute to the people of a small town in Nova Scotia, Canada: those who died, those who survived, those left behind, and the heroes who worked tirelessly to save people's lives. Springhill has been a town that has endured many tragedies, yet it's also a place to find inspiration in the ways it has bounced back from adversity.

Ironically, as I was nearing publication of this book (in 2014), Springhill received news that it was losing its township status after 125 years of being an independent town. Every person I spoke to about this was clear:

You can't take Springhill out of the Springhiller.

The people of this town are proud of their heritage, which for most goes back many generations. Springhillers know their parents' stories, their grandparents' stories, and the stories of many of their ancestors.

My journey to tell the story of Springhill started in 2001. As a screenwriter, I believe there should be a movie that shows the disasters, followed by the astounding miracle rescues that happened in this town. My dad had often told me he thought the story would be worth telling in a movie; he was right. I found a town plagued with great tragedy, but also, astounding miracles. The resulting screenplay is what was used to develop the novel version, *Song of Springhill: a love story.*

The miracles blew me away. If I made this story up in a screenplay, you would find it tough to believe. But it happened!

During such tragic events — long after loved ones thought their men had died underground — large pockets of men would be found alive. This didn't just happen once. It happened during the 1956 Explosion (where a pocket of 50 men were found days after the disaster), and in 1958 when two groups of men were found. Twelve men were found six days after the Bump, and yet another set of miners was found eight and a half days after the Bump. Seven men came out of the No. 2 mine alive that day — to the cheers and delight of the town that had feared they were gone forever.

What captured my heart the most in digging into the stories of this mining town was the close-knit camaraderie that existed among the men, and their loyalty to one another. True friendship forever tied them together. Then there were the women of Springhill — ones who displayed an unwavering strength in the midst of the unknown, sometimes displaying an inexplicable faith.

To research for writing the script in 2001, I started interviewing survivors, widows, kids of the victims, children of survivors, rescuers, other mine workers, doctors, engineers — anyone who would talk to me about what happened in this town in the 1950s. I ended up with this collection of interviews that tells the behind-the-scenes stories of what went into the fictional version, as told through the screenplay and novel, *Song of Springhill: a love story*.

These pages hold stories narrated directly by the people themselves, some of which have passed away since I interviewed them. I'm honored to have preserved this little piece of history in their words and in their honor. There are so many heroes among the good people of Springhill.

My grandfather, Charles Hugh McKay — also known as "Dado" to his grandchildren — died when I was fifteen years old. I wish when I were younger, I had been more interested in asking him questions about his life as a miner, and the miracles that spared his life. It wasn't something he voluntarily talked about when not asked. Years after he passed away, I embarked on a quest to get to know more about what his life was like. His check tag number was #712 just like the one my father's hand holds on the cover of this book.

It was several key pieces from my grandfather's life that served as the inspiration for the story, regarding his involvement in both the 1956 Explosion and the 1958 Bump.

My aunt, Joyce Harroun, was the first to share with me his story relating to the 1956 Explosion. She said my grandfather switched shifts that day with another man and got off work just a couple hours before the mine blew up.

This meant that my grandfather's life was spared, but the man who switched shifts with him died. If my grandfather had gone to work at his normal time that day, he would have died for sure. I never would have met him. It also meant that the team of men my grandfather was used to working with died that day too; he lost a lot of his friends. It was the only time my aunt ever saw my grandfather cry up until that point in his life.

I went on a quest to discover who this person was who died in my grandfather's place. You will get to read about him later in this collection of interviews, as I was able to find that answer.

In 1958, my grandfather was trapped underground

when The Bump hit, which was one of the biggest disasters in coal mining history. It was also the deepest coal mine in North America at the time.

In this book, you will hear about the three tragedies that struck Springhill in the 1950s: the 1956 Explosion, the 1957 Main Street Fire, and the 1958 Bump.

I am forever grateful to all of those who allowed me to talk to them about these events, and for their permission to use their stories. I hope you enjoy reading about what these beloved people shared with me.

I do hope through this book of interviews and the fictional novel, I've captured the heart of this beloved town and its refusal to give up on its own, its refusal to surrender hope in the midst of the direst of circumstances.

Springhill, you inspire me. Current town or not, I hope your unquenchable spirit continues to inspire others by letting your story live on.

You show us that miracles do happen.

Cheryl McKay (Book Author)

The Interviews

The majority of the interviews are written in a Q&A format, in the interview subjects' own words. If they handwrote or typed these surveys, I preserved the Canadian spellings they used. The interviews that are not Q&A style were most likely conducted in person. It's an honor, after over a decade, to finally share these stories. (Please Note: most of the photos are decades old so the resolution will be low.)

Disaster

Survivors

Caleb Rushton
Survivor of the 1958 Bump
(Interviewed July 2001)

1. What was the daily routine, working in the mines, from start to finish? Describe a normal day at work.
Normally, men went to the Wash House from their homes. They would change from street clothes into their mining clothes. Then they went to the Lamp Cabin, handing in a check number for which they received a battery-operated lamp. Then they waited for the trolleys to take them down in the mines. When they got off the trolleys, they walked into the actual work places. Miners dug the coal. Labourers did various jobs. As a miner, you had to have papers to dig coal. Papers weren't required by the ones who did the labour work. At the end of the shift, all would walk out to the trolleys and return to the surface. They turned in their lamps and retrieved their check numbers then went to the Wash House where they would shower, put street clothes on, and go to their homes.

2. What was the work itself like? Did your job responsibilities rotate?
The work itself was quite hard, digging coal, lifting heavy timbers, shoveling stone. Job responsibilities didn't change or rotate unless a person got to do a different job. He might

request a different job or his boss could get him another job. Ordinarily, you were stuck with the job you were given upon being hired.

3. What was the procedure for the shifts and shift changes? How often did you change the shift you'd be working?

When you started in the mines, you were put in jobs that required help or extra help. Mostly these jobs were kept for various periods, depending on whether men were off on compensation or had decided the work wasn't for them. This gave someone else a chance to get a particular job. There were three shifts a day. 11pm to 7am, 7am to 3pm, and 3pm to 11pm. The work week was Monday to Friday so you changed weekly, on Mondays. The 11pm-7am shift was a maintenance shift. The 11pm shift was worked by men who preferred this type of work or that shift.

4. What would you have done for work if you weren't a coal miner? What were the options back then?

The types of work available at that time were a store clerk, truck driver, logging work in the sawmill, janitor work. The turnover in these jobs was very little, and the mines paid the highest wages for the area.

5. What was the pay scale for a miner? What kind of lifestyle could a miner afford?

Miners were paid on a contract basis, so much for a ton of coal dug. At the time, miners could get as much as $15.00 plus or minus for a shift, whereas labourers only received $10 a shift. A miner of that day could have a moderate lifestyle. They weren't rich but comfortable.

6. Did you rotate which team of men you worked with? Or did you usually work with the same men?
I worked with the same men.

7. Where were you during the 1956 Explosion?
At the time of the Explosion, I had been working in the Lamp Cabin as a repairman. I was on a steady 7am-3pm shift. I had gone home, and we had just sat down to eat when we heard the bang.

8. Before the Bump, what was the attitude of the miners about working in the No. 2 mine? Did they feel like they were in danger?
Before the Bump, a lot of older miners said that there would be a serious bump if they brought the walls out together. They felt they were in great danger. The mine manager was only taking orders from the people above him. None of it was his fault. The mining union and board members told the company not to line up the walls. But they kept using that method anyway. The new method did not increase production. Most of us just wanted to keep our jobs, so we kept quiet.

9. You are considered one of the "Miracle Survivors" of the Bump. When they thought everyone had perished underground, you were found with a group of men six days later. Talk about those days you spent underground. What was it like, and what did you do to survive?
During the six days underground, we slept and talked. Our lights only lasted a couple of days, if that, so we could not move around that much. During the night of the Bump and the next day, we looked for ways of escape, but there were

none. We didn't have the tools or the energy to dig our way out. Interaction was normal under the circumstances. We talked about our families, friends, told stories, had a few laughs. I really think sleep took a lot of our time, and we didn't realize we were sleeping. I know this was true in my own case. I had a wristwatch with a luminous dial so I could keep track of time.

10. What was the biggest struggle for each man stuck underground?

The biggest struggle for the men in our group was not being able to get out and not knowing when we would.

11. How was your relationship with your fellow twelve miners before the Bump vs. after the Bump?

My relationship with the men of our group was always friendly, as we had known each other for years. That friendly feeling prevailed after the Bump also.

12. Describe how you were rescued? How did the rescue workers get to you, and what happened as soon as they got you out?

We were rescued because barefaced miners toiled selflessly to dig through about 200 feet of coal to get to us. They had to put the coal in buckets and pass it back between their legs to the next fellow in line. Their workspace was only three feet wide and three feet high. Then they lugged us out on stretchers to the trolleys. No easy task! We were taken directly to All Saint's Hospital and given tests for a couple of days.

13. What was your recovery like?

I recovered quite quickly, but was unable to work for a couple months.

14. Did you ever go back into a mine after the Bump?

I never returned to the mines after that. They actually stopped paying us the moment the mine bumped and didn't pay us for all the time we were stuck underground.

15. Explain what it was like living in Springhill: town life, church life, the people, entertainment.

At the time of the Bump, Springhill was a quiet little town of 7000. Now it's roughly 4000 (in 2001). People were friendly. Mining brings out a closeness you don't see in other places. Church life was good and we attended weekly. As I said, people were friendly and always willing to help one another. We had a bowling alley, a movie theater, Fraternal Lodge, and Service Clubs. Many variety concerts took place in the theater.

16. What do you know about my grandfather's rescue (Charles McKay)?

After the Bump, your grandfather walked most of the way out, up the west side of the back slope. It was an auxiliary slope where the haulage equipment was, where miners got in the cars to ride up and down the mine, the same one they'd used to move the coal out by swapping the cars. It was not in the heat of the Bump. It still had damage, and they would have felt it. But it wasn't nearly the same damage where my group was trapped.

Author's Note: I had a chance to talk to Caleb's wife, Pat, about what this time was like for her. Pat said, "I had been working at the church that day, met my mother in the street, and went to the mines. I went to the mines until the first people came out. It was like a dream, crazy with people coming and going. People were everywhere, like reporters. I waited at the first aid station outside the mines." Pat said the whole time they were waiting for word on whether Caleb was alive or not, she never felt like she could say he was gone. She didn't want to think one way or the other until she had confirmation.

In Loving Memory
Caleb Rushton
(January 16, 1923-June 10, 2008)

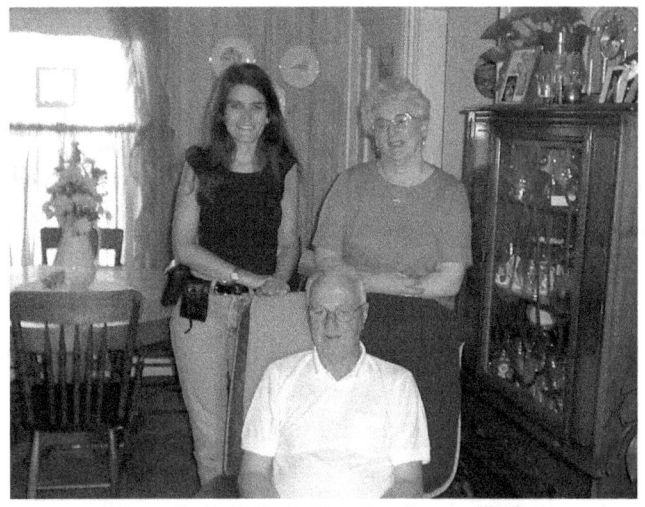

Cheryl, Caleb & Pat Rushton (2001)

1. What was your job in the mines?

You could get miner's papers by working a couple of years first in the mines. Then you could take an oral exam, about what to do and not to do. Labourers would build supports for the roof, run trips, build stone packs. As labourers, we worked with miners, not separate. We would fill 24 coal boxes on one trip up. Twenty-two men would work together and all get the same pay. For example, when 22 miners were on the wall, the labourers, two sets of two men would be on the bottom and top building stone packs.

2. Were you working the day of the Explosion?

I was not involved in the Explosion, since that was in the No. 4. I was working in the No. 2 during the Explosion but on day shift, building supports for the roof. So, I wasn't around.

3. Tell us about working in the No. 2 during the Bump:

We had an early bump that day and shut everything down. It was really quiet down there. The problem was in lining walls up. The miners knew there'd be trouble. [The company] in Cape Breton decided to do this method, to try to stop bumps. It didn't work. The union was concerned too. It wasn't about greed. They didn't get more production out of it.

The No. 2 used the retreat wall system—drove the levels on the way in and extract the coal on the way out. The No. 4 was advance wall. If walls had been staggered in the No. 2, the Bump would have happened at the 13,400 level and no others. It wouldn't have affected the other walls. But it did because they had lined them up. That made it worse.

It ended up being a big mess underground. People, good people, my best friends, we were stuck down there together. We celebrated Garnie Clarke's twenty-ninth birthday underground and sang to him. We ate a chocolate bar that I found in someone else's lunch. We also tried to eat an egg sandwich, but it had gone bad.

After a while, I really thought it was over. And then, they found us.

4. What was your rescue like?
I was put on stretcher to be rescued and carried out. At the time of the rescue, I was lying in there and saw lights. Then I was in All Saints Hospital for one week. Once I got out, I saw they had paid me for six hours the day of the Bump. The company didn't take responsibility. They packed up and walked out of town.

5. Did you work as a coal miner after the rescue?
I worked in a syndicate mine for ten more years.

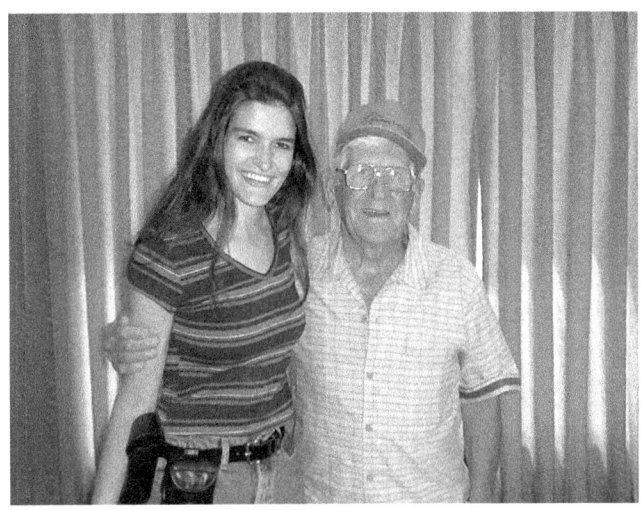

Cheryl, Herb Pepperdine (2001)

Ken Melanson
Survivor of the 1956 Explosion
(Interviewed July 2001, while he was the Underground
Supervisor at the Springhill Miner's Museum)

1. Were you worried about safety as a miner?
I wasn't afraid of the mines. I wanted to work there because of the better pay. It was $10 a day instead of $4-6 in other jobs. I felt like Harold Gordon (Mine Manager) was a smart man. The engineers plus other board people and Gordon had to make decisions on mining practices. He couldn't have decided that alone. He was a man doing his job.

Before the Bump, there were complaints about safety. Many said, "The big one is coming." There was too much stress down there. They thought it would happen. The coal face was tight, hard to dig. Sometimes that indicates a bump is coming. Staggering the walls was the norm, but they lined up the walls.

Harry Terris (the board member and head of the union) was on the side of the miners who felt it was unsafe. Before the blow up in the No. 4, we had been having problems all that week. We may have even had a small fire. The first shift had to work with gas that week.

2. Talk about the day of the 1956 Explosion:
I was 19 years old. I was with two friends at the Miner's Hall right before the Explosion. We hung out, then went to

work. Neither of my friends came out alive.

When I arrived at the mines, I went to the Wash House, then the Lamp Cabin, then inside the mine to the 5400 level. At 5:07 p.m., a coal car jumped the track and cut the electric cable. I was inside mine from Thursday to Monday morn. It felt like the other side of Hell. I didn't think we'd get out. We had no food or water.

I was with Con Embree's group of fifty men. We created a barricade for the gas, to block it. We cut notches in the pipe to breathe through. We were very scared, especially once we saw cement in the water that flowed into mine. That meant they used cement to seal the mine. We felt like this meant no one thought anyone was alive, so they had sealed the mine to stop the fires. Yet we were alive and trapped.

We found out later Harold Gordon had told everyone that it was unlikely anyone was alive. On Sunday, Con Embree seemed to feel it was over. He asked if anyone wanted to write last entries in the journal that people would find later. We wrote goodbyes.

3. How were you finally rescued?

The rescuers made their way through the auxiliary air slope, barefaced, some of them. Once they found Charlie Burton, the first guy who made it to the surface alive, he told them there were many others alive down there at the 5400 level. Word spread through town with great excitement. We were told not to move—help was on the way. Sadly, Charlie Burton, who survived the Explosion, was killed, two years later, in the Bump. Once rescued, I got paid one hour of pay for all the time I was in the mine.

4. What do you know about my grandfather's story, related to the day of the Explosion? We understand he switched shifts for someone that day and that man was killed instead. We are trying to find out who that may have been.

Lester Fisher and Gerald Dawson are two men who did the same job as your grandfather. Either one may be who took his shift that day. Both of them died.

I liked working with your grandfather, Charlie. Sometimes we'd finish our tasks before our shift was over. He was nice and let us ride up to the top before the shift was done.

Family Members of Survivors

Tom "Tommy" McKay
Son of Charles Hugh McKay — Survivor of the 1958 Bump
(Interviewed February 2013)

1. What was it like growing up in Springhill?

While there were some bad things that happened there, life was simple and fun and you had good friends. You never felt insecure or in danger. Kids today, you can't let them do what we did, like being allowed to leave in the morning and not come home until dinner. We were able to go out and hang with buddies, go exploring in the woods. It wasn't dangerous. Mothers never had to worry about their kids. Whoever's house you were near when out playing at lunchtime, his mother would feed you. I went to church, Boy Scouts, played youth hockey. The simplicity of life in Springhill is what stands out.

As you got to your teen years, you went to dances. Like most boys, we were afraid to ask girls to dance. I went to dances at the Miner's Hall and at the Armory.

The grocery store would trust a miner to pay for food later when he got paid. They'd let you take a bag of food and put it on a tab. I remember going to the store to pick up things and my parents would pay after payday. During mine closures, the grocery store would carry people until the mines were working again.

2. Describe Springhill in terms of a mining town.
It was the industry of the town; the people of the town worked there. You didn't think of it as living in a mining town.

Today, people don't have as much pride about where they live, but I liked living in Springhill. We felt pride about being part of something. We were living in a world before a lot of television and media coverage. So we didn't realize, being there, how the rest of the world lived. We weren't comparing ourselves to other towns. I do remember going to Boston and seeing how big everything was, how much traffic they had, the trolley, a lot of people, and seeing a different way of life.

3. Talk about having a father who was a coal miner. What was that like? Did you worry?
The only time I thought about it is if something, like an accident, happened at the mine. Most times, I didn't really give it a thought. I was young. Around 1954, I started hearing about people dying or getting hurt. I would hear about other people's fathers, and I'd realize my father worked in a place that wasn't always safe. But I didn't think a whole lot about it. When something went wrong in the mines, the first thing I would think was, "Is my father working right now?" It wasn't until later on in life, I reflected back on how he was in danger every day of his life there, just like he was on October 23, 1958, during the Bump. I did sometimes feel envious if a friend had a father who worked above ground because I knew his father was safer. For example, some fathers worked in the hoist house that pulled the cars out of the mine. It seemed safer. Except in the 1956 Explosion, some of the bankhead workers were

killed, and it turned out to not always be safe. My dad never talked about working there and never seemed to express a fear of being there. If he felt it, he didn't say it.

4. Did you ever want to be a coal miner, to follow in your father's footsteps? Did you ever think you would have to out of necessity?

I never thought I was going to be a coal miner. I had no idea what I was going to do, but I knew it wouldn't be that. Later on, out of curiosity, I probably would like to have worked in a coal mine for one week, during normal shifts, just so I'd know what he did. You can never really imagine it; you have to experience it. I believe I would probably have been petrified, but maybe not. In Springhill, they wouldn't let you take your kid to work with you. If I had lived in that town another five years, I would've had to make the choice of whether or not I would work there.

5. How was your mother affected by having a husband who was a coal miner?

She worried about a lot of things in general. So I imagine she was nervous about him being there. When they moved us out of Springhill after The Bump, my mom got a job for the first time in her life and became a nurse. She seemed to be much happier. I wonder if it was partly because she no longer had to worry about Dad.

6. What did your father tell you about the mining accident he had that put him in the hospital before you were born?

He was hit by a coal box, and it crushed his pelvis. It took a long time to recover. It was around the Second World War. He ended up in the hospital for quite a while. I believe that's what kept him from joining the Army. A lot of people went into armed services from Springhill during that war.

7. Where were you when the 1956 Explosion happened, and what did you do?

I had just delivered my last newspaper for the day, the Springhill Record. I was with a friend, Doug Russell. Our mothers were close friends. We were on Lisgar Street, in perfect eyeshot to see the Explosion at the mines below. We were on the sidewalk, on our bikes. We felt the ground shake, turned around and saw a big ball of fire shoot up in the air. It was like watching a bomb go off. Flames shot hundreds of feet into the air. I quickly thought of my father, "Is Dad working right now?" My mental process was that he wasn't there that morning when I went to school, which meant today he was on day shift. Dayshift was now over. I knew based on what time it was, he wouldn't be underground because the shift would have changed. You're selfishly hoping it's not your dad underground. You first think of your own father, but that's human nature. Then your thoughts move to other people's fathers who might be working that day. I knew fathers of my friends worked there.

I went home after the Explosion, but my dad had already left the house to check on what was happening at the mine. I spent a little bit of time out at the mines after the Explosion. Everyone in town migrated over there.

They made us go back to school during the search and rescue operation over the next few days so we wouldn't be in the way. After the Explosion, the only time my father went back in the No. 4 mine was to be a part of the crew that had to recover the bodies of the fallen miners. My dad didn't talk about that at all; we just knew he had to do it.

8. Where were you when the 1957 Main Street Fire broke out? Did you go to the scene?

It was December 26, Boxing Day and the day after Christmas. It was evening. We were still awake, watching TV. In Springhill, we knew there was a fire because they blew whistles. Plus we could tell where the fire was by how many whistles we heard.

My dad and I went to see what was burning. We went over to Main Street and watched the fire from the steps of Saffron's store. The fire spread and that store was gone by the next morning. Later into the evening, we watched the fire from the window of our house on Maple Street. There were a whole bunch of burned out buildings by the next day. It burned out Main Street on both sides and took out some houses on Fir Street, near where we used to live.

9. Where were you when the 1958 Bump happened? Did you go to the mines?

When the Bump happened, I had just left Dawson's Pool Room above Dawson's Groceries, on Junction Road near Main Street. I was on the sidewalk in front of the place, about to go home. The earth shook. I immediately knew this time my dad was working. I went straight to the mine.

I was in the Lamp Cabin waiting for news with many other people. Word came that miners were coming out of the mine, but they didn't say who. And then my dad came through the door of the Lamp Cabin. I was the first person he saw. He wasn't hurt and told me, "Go home and tell your mother that you saw me. She won't believe anybody else." He needed to get cleaned up before he went home.

When I got home, the house was full of people. Relatives were there from Amherst waiting for news. I told them he was out of the mines. They were obviously very happy. My father came home shortly after.

10. How did your father react once he was rescued? Did he want to go back underground?

He was happy he was home but sad many others didn't make it. The mine company's future was uncertain at the time, whether or not they could stay open because they'd sustained so much damage. He'd had a lot of close calls too. His sisters had been trying to get him to move to Boston since after the 1956 Explosion. Every time we visited them down there, they'd talk to him about moving there. After the Bump, they realized there probably wouldn't be much of a coal mine industry. He had a standing job offer in Boston, by someone who knew his sisters, to work for a wholesale egg company. His sister, my Aunt Leona, had already lined this up for him, if he was ever willing to leave Springhill. My dad's other sister, Jen, had come to Springhill as soon as she heard about the Bump, and my father went back to Boston with her to see about the job my other aunt had set up. They left before they found the second group of miners in the second miracle rescue. They heard about that rescue on the radio.

He came back to Springhill a week later and already had the job and announced we were moving. He had wanted to be in Springhill with his mother, but he took the job. He was interviewed in a Boston paper while he was visiting there. The whole world was searching for stories at the time about Springhill, and since he was one of those 174 people stuck underground, they wanted to talk to him about what it was like.

If the Bump hadn't happened, we never would have moved. He felt it was necessary to take care of the family. My parents moved in January 1959. I joined them a bit later. He lived in that little town for over forty years of his life; moving was a tough choice for him. Out of necessity, a lot of people had to move. He had worked in the mines since he was fifteen, for about twenty-seven years.

Cheryl & her Dad (Tom McKay)

Joyce (McKay) Harroun
Daughter of Charles McKay — Survivor of the 1958
Bump
(Interviewed in 2001 & 2014)

Author's Note: Joyce is my aunt (my dad's sister), so her references to Dad or Mom are to my grandfather and grandmother, Charlie & Ethel McKay. In researching to write the script and novel, I wanted a clear picture of what it was like to grow up in this small town back in that time period. My aunt colored in the most detailed picture of this setting, which helped me paint in details for the fictional story. Enjoy the little walk back in time:

1. Share about this town you grew up in and what you did for fun:
Springhill was a great place to be a child and grow up. Summers were long and hot. As children, we always played outdoors.

Behind my grandmother and grandfather's house (Ma and Pa McKay) on Maple Street, there was an old garage full of old wood and mud floors. It was dirty. As a group of kids, Keith Wilson, Juddy Anderson, Jimmie Weatherbee, Jean Megeney (my cousin) and myself and any other brothers or sisters we could drum up made a clubhouse out of the old garage. We met daily. If you had a penny, you brought it and saved for a fund to send to the war. World War II was on at this time. After the meeting, we used some of our collection of pennies at Fox's Store at the bottom of Maple Street for penny candy.

As winter came, we would go coasting behind my Uncle Marvin's house on Maple Street down backfields to North Street.

On Friday nights, Pa McKay, who worked for the liquor store on Main Street, would come home with a large tub of ice cream. We were told that each Friday, we could bring all the kids to Ma & Pa's kitchen and sun porch and Ma would give each of us a large bowl of ice cream. It all had to be eaten, as she only had a small icebox for refrigeration.

During these years, Dad would always take me with him to ballgames in the park on lower Main Street. They'd sometimes close the mines during the playoffs games for the Fencebusters. It was a series with all Nova Scotia teams.

The Hollywood Dare Devils came once a year to perform tricks with the cars on the racetrack surrounding the ball field. They also had racehorses and races on the track.

We also played War with wooden guns, and we'd play Kick the Can.

We skated 2 to 3 times a week at the Arena and went to movies at the Capital Theater. We all had bicycles. We learned to make kites and fly them, and colored Easter eggs. We went to the Hot Dog Stand on Main Street.

Our house was always open to my friends, including for sleepovers. But if the girls got homesick at night, Dad would get dressed and walk them home. (Remember: we had no car!)

Growing up in Springhill was wonderful, as there was a lot to do.

2. What was available in terms of the arts, music, and dancing back then?

I started tap dancing when I was 7 or 8 years old, taught on Saturday mornings in the Capital Theater by Girlie Mason (Brown). For many years she taught about 12 girls. This was free of charge, but you had to be there every Saturday. No excuses! We never missed it, as it was enjoyable.

We danced in several Minstrel Shows that Girlie put on each year with the End men (faces colored black). We'd have a large chorus line of men. The tap dancers usually did one or two numbers at this performance. I stayed with this group of girls until I was 16 years old.

We'd also have school plays at Christmas time.

Around 1948, Jim and Jean Gogan opened the "Avalon" on lower Main Street. It was a dance hall that had a lunch counter and a jukebox. Here, we learned to dance. It was open Friday night, Saturday afternoon and evening. It cost ten cents to get in, five cents to play the jukebox. When we ran out of nickels, Jim would turn the jukebox on automatic so we could still dance. (This is where I met Gerald in 1951, got married in 1953, and we had our 60 year anniversary in 2013.)

On my fourteenth birthday, Mom and Dad paid to take my friends to the Avalon and then we went back to our small house for lunch after. We gathered up more friends than planned! They all wanted to dance, so Dad rolled up my Grandmother Tooke's Persian rug on the living room floor. The piano was played and we danced. The phone was ringing at midnight with parents looking for their kids.

Dad saw to it that they all got home safely. What a party to remember!

Also in Springhill, the different groups or lodges held balls, which were formal dances where women wore long gowns and the men wore suits, shirts, and ties. An orchestra called the "Acadians" played for these. I got my first formal gown at 16, and went with Gerald to the Miner's Hall for one of these dances. Oh, it was elegant! If a ball happened to be at Mason's Ball, Gerald's grandparents, Mame and Roach McKay led the grand march, which they always had at the start of the dances.

I took piano lessons from Gladys McPherson. Everyone took music lessons. All parents thought kids had to take it, but the boys hated it. We'd have a concert at the end of the season.

Prior to taking these lessons, Dad taught me to play the piano when I was a little girl. He played by ear. I could play chords and melody, and he and I would play duets on the piano. Old time music. When I started taking lessons and reading music, I found it very hard. Miss McPherson would get quite upset with me, trying to keep me on track.

Dad's mother, Ma McKay, had a piano in her living room, and that's where we would spend many hours having fun. Jean Megeney, my cousin, was also taking lessons. We would play duets on the piano. Our grandmother, Ma, put up with a lot from us!

3. What kinds of vacations did you take?

Mom and Dad always rented a cottage every year for two weeks for the miner's vacation. We didn't have a car but a friend of Dad's with a truck would arrive and pick us up with bedding, groceries and cart us off to Heathers Beach for two weeks. At the end of vacation, he would come back and pick us up. I can still hear Mom and Dad playing cards out in the kitchen / living room by an oil lamp with neighbors or friends. Their laughter was great. As kids, we'd lie in bed and listen.

Outside of the two-week vacation, we could go to Heathers Beach on Sunday in the back of Herb Boss's truck for fifty cents. He had a large truck with wooden benches on both sides, open to the sky but a gate put across the back so we wouldn't fall out.

Ma and Pa McKay would go on trips to the United States, with Pa's brother Lawrence and Eva McKay. They would always bring back big gifts to Jean and myself. I still have my talking doll they brought to us when we were four years old. We both lived with Ma & Pa on Maple Street until I was five years old, and Jean was twelve. Three generations and two babies born in 1936 all lived in the house on Maple Street.

4. What was school like in Springhill?
Going to school was good. Our school had no gym so we didn't have basketball or gym sports. Our exercise was walking to and from school. (No school busses for town kids!)

High School was always busy. We had male and female teachers. The principal taught geometry. We had history, science, French, English, Geography, Latin, Biology, Music, and Drama.

5. Describe Main Street, as you remember it, before the 1957 Fire:
Main Street was lined with stores: clothing, jewelry, shoes,

hardware, a hat shop. (Everyone wore hats to church on Sunday.) Grocery stores, drugstores, doctor's office, churches. Churches were filled to capacity in those days. You arrived early to get a seat. They had Sunday School, youth groups, and picnics. No one said on Sunday morning, "I'm not going to church." We enjoyed it.

6. Tell me what you remember about your father's experiences during the 1956 Explosion:
The disasters were terrible. Dad was not working for the first one in 1956. So we knew he was safe. He had switched shifts with someone else that day, or he would have been underground.

Young men in their twenties were killed. Neighbor boys and boys we hung around with during our early and teen years died.

In 1956, the people my father (your grandfather) worked with for years were killed. He cried. He was so broken up because his friends were killed.

It was standard to have people killed in the mines, but when it was people you knew or went to school with or your friend's fathers, it got very tough. In 1954, my best friend, Olwyn Hunter's, father, Wesley, was killed in the mines — along with four other men — and I suffered along with her.

7. What do you remember about the 1958 Bump?
When Dad got switched to No. 2, there was a lot of pressure there. He didn't like it. He would have nosebleeds because the mine was so deep.

The day of the Bump, Dad was down at the bottom of the mines, and it destroyed part of the mines was above him. The only way for these men to get out was to walk around and up. Of course on the bank head, no one knew if they were alive or not.

While Tommy (your dad) waited at the mine, I stayed on Maple Street with Mom and Ma McKay. Mom's sisters and their husbands had arrived from Amherst to wait for news. Dad always had white hair, but when he came through the door, his hair was even whiter. His first remarks were that he would never go down in the mines gain. He never did and the mine never reopened.

Joyce (McKay) & Gerald Harroun (2001)

Cheryl, Tom, Denise, Joyce, Gerald, Heather (McKay)
Gebbia & Chris Gebbia (2003)

"Dado" teaching Cheryl to play the organ

Cheryl, Joyce, Charlie "Dado" McKay, Ethel (Tooke)
McKay

Joyce & Tommy

Tommy & their mom (Ethel)

Debbie Betty-Brazie
Step-Daughter of Charles McKay — Survivor of the 1958 Bump
(Interviewed in 2014)

Author's Note: Debbie was my step-aunt, after my grandfather married her mother, years after my grandmother, Ethel (Tooke) McKay, passed away. Debbie used to spend time asking my grandfather a lot of questions about his years as a miner. I interviewed her to see what she remembered about the stories he told her regarding the two disasters. As mentioned, the grandkids all called him "Dado."

1. What did Dado share with you about Springhill?
He shared that Springhill was a very small town with a close-knit community, where everyone knew everyone else. Most men worked in the coal mines.

Dado was extremely proud of Springhill and loved to tell us stories of his mining days, the disasters he had experienced, and how those disasters shaped his life and his family.

2. Did he mention being afraid to go underground?
He said, "I didn't have the good sense to be afraid. I just knew what I had to do, and I did it."

3. What did he share with you about the 1956 disaster?
Dado swapped that day to a day shift so he had just left the mine when the Explosion happened. I do remember him saying he would have been in the mine if he had not swapped shifts.

While Dado was not in the mine when the Explosion happened, many of his friends were. He told the story of how he had finished his shift and had returned home. He was sitting in the living room reading the newspaper when he heard the windows rattle, and then the sound of the Explosion. (He said he could feel it hit first, then heard it.) He put his newspaper down, got up from his chair, grabbed his coat and hat and left the house. He knew what had just happened. No one had to tell him. He and all the other miners who weren't underground went directly to the mine to help.

4. What did he share with you about the 1958 Bump?
He said the longer you worked in the mines, the closer you were to being involved in a mining accident. Dado was in the mine this day working his shift. He said it was the worst bump in the history of North America at the time.

Dado explained that a "bump" is when the ceiling of the mine collapses in and the floor of the mine heaves up. He was working close to some sort of large machinery, and it was that machinery that saved his life and prevented him from getting crushed.

Dado said he and other men working in that area of the mine that were not killed or injured in the Bump began their journey to the surface, walking, assisting or carrying injured miners with them.

The mine was pitch-black. The only light the men had were the lamps on their helmets. They knew they needed to get out as quickly as possible, as poisonous gasses would be filling the mine. Dado said he went by many co-workers who were trapped, injured or already dead. It was so dark they could hardly see. Sometimes, they just knew or sensed they were passing by men who were already dead but couldn't see them.

They could hear other men calling for help. They helped those men that they could get to, but most of the injured were trapped.

They made a map of each location where they believed men were trapped to give to the draegermen who could rescue them.

Dado said it took them many hours to get to the surface on foot. He was not sure how much time had elapsed.

It was the middle of the night when they emerged from the mine, and Dado said there were cheers from the crowds that had gathered when the men appeared. He thought the entire town was there! It was a confusing moment for him.

The group of men Dado walked to the surface with was one of the last groups of survivors to come out of the mine (before the miracle rescues from six and eight days later).

5. What did he share with you about what it was like to see the face of my father once he was out of the mines?

The way he explained it, that moment was one of those "life changing" moments. His eyes found your dad, Tom, waiting for his father to come out of the mine. Dado said it was at that instant he realized, looking into Tom's face and seeing his son's expression, the true gravity of the situation and that he would never go back into the mines again.

The mine closed following the Bump, and the economy of Springhill fell into ruin as the mines had been the main employment in town. With the mines closed, there was no work. Many families were forced to leave Springhill. Dado moved your grandmother (Ethel) and your dad to the United States to the Boston area.

So, if the Bump had never taken place, your dad would not have moved to the States. He would not have met your mother, and you and your sister, Heather, would not have been born.

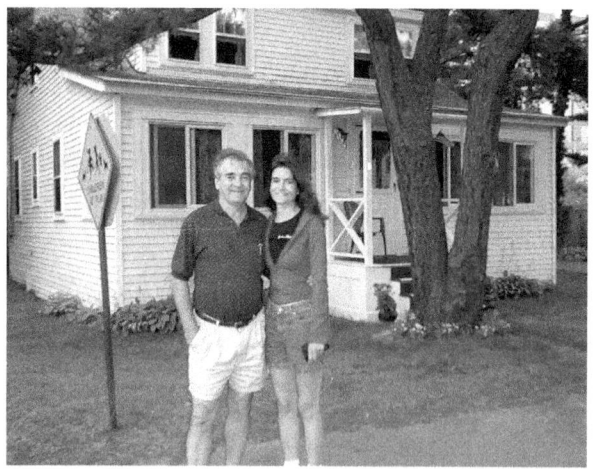

Tom McKay & Cheryl in front of the home where Charles McKay lived in Old Orchard Beach, ME with Debbie Betty-Brazie's mother, Ella

Norma Ruddick
Wife of Maurice Ruddick, "The Singing Miner," — Survivor of the 1958 Bump
(Interviewed in 2001)

Author's Note: The Ruddick family served as the inspiration for the story of "Isaak" as written into the novel and screenplay, *Song of Springhill*. Maurice became known as the "Singing Miner" by singing hymns underground to help keep people's spirits up.

1. Tell us about your family life with your husband, Maurice:
He was a good-natured man and loved to joke around. We had a wonderful life there in Springhill. He was very much a family man. When the day the Bump hit, we had twelve children. Our twelfth was only eight days old. Once he was rescued, we were able to have our thirteenth child.

He was a hard worker. He would work double shifts if people couldn't come into work. Sometimes, the whistle would blow to tell them not to come to work, but Maurice would go down anyway, just to make sure.

He loved to load up the kids and take them out for ice cream. They sang together. Anne Murray was always a good friend to our family and the kids. She sang with them and would come over for hours.

Maurice and his buddies would make up songs going down on the rake. They'd sing everything.

2. Did you worry about your husband in this job?
Being the wife of a miner was an accepted way of life. It was the only work. I didn't worry about him until the whistle would blow to signal there was a problem at the mines. I was able to remain a happy-go-lucky person.

3. What happened the night of the Bump and after, while you were waiting for news about him?
When the Bump hit, *I Love Lucy* was on. It sounded similar to thunder, a loud blast but fifteen times louder. I originally thought it was an antenna. Then I saw people running to the mines. A friend came by and gave me the news of the Bump happening. I was so downhearted, waiting for news.

Then a show came on called *Don Messer's Jubilee*, with Charlie Chamberlain. They always ended the show with a hymn, *Farther Along*. I heard the lyrics, "*Farther along, you'll know all about it. Farther along, you'll understand why.*" These words told me that I would have to wait a while before Maurice would come out, but that he would be okay. This gave me the faith.

As time went on, I couldn't listen to any quartets on screen because they reminded me of him. I'd turn off the TV.

My uncle came over, telling me that it was true what the mine officials said, that no one would be left alive. Yet I kept my faith and never gave up hope. I knew he'd be home. After all, God wouldn't leave me with twelve kids to raise alone. Everyone told me not to get my hopes up. Some visited me, like nurses at the hospital. Others brought us food.

My kids would go to mines for hot chocolate while awaiting news. One fellow brought me coal while Maurice was stuck below. I thought it was a gift, but as soon as Maurice was found alive, the same man came back to collect money.

Four or five of my kids had caught the chicken pox, but there was no room at the hospital for them. The hospitals had been cleared for the miners. The kids had to stay at a doctor's house.

4. Did Maurice feel like the No. 2 was a dangerous place to work before the Bump?

Yes, Maurice felt like No. 2 was dangerous and even made up a song about it before the Bump. He called it: *Curse of the Old No. 2*. It was about dangers and taking a chance with their lives. There had been a lot of accidents in that mine. He always believed there would be a big one. There had been a disaster in the No. 1 in 1891 that claimed 125 lives.

5. What did he tell you about his experience once he was rescued?

Once out, Maurice didn't talk about it much. He mentioned rats were crawling near them. Underneath, they sang and prayed, but it was tough with no water. Their throats were so dry. They sang the *Old Rugged Cross*.

Maurice went in with a man who said he was going down to a lower level. Maurice said to go ahead, saying he had stuff to clean up on the level they were at. That guy who went lower died.

They celebrated Garnie's birthday underneath, dividing a chocolate bar into seven pieces. Barney Martin was in a hole alone. They couldn't get him out. They had to crawl on their hands and knees to get stuff to him.

Once Maurice was rescued (as they broke through

wall), one of the mine employees said to Maurice that the mine company told this man to find Maurice because he had too many kids to take care of!

I told Maurice he couldn't go back into mines, or I'd leave with our 12 kids. Of course I had nowhere to go.

Maurice wasn't hurt. He just had scratches. Some reported that he had a broken leg, but he didn't. He was in the hospital for one week. But he was like a kid once he got home, and he'd sleep like a baby. I thought he'd have nightmares.

One woman told me, "If it wasn't for Maurice Ruddick, our men would be all dead."

In Loving Memory
Norma June Ruddick
(August 19, 1925 – September 17, 2012)

Norma Ruddick, Cheryl (2001)

Norma & Maurice Ruddick (courtesy of Val Ruddick
MacDonald, photo from inside her CD "Yours Truly")

Cheryl, Valerie (Ruddick) MacDonald (2001)

Valerie Ruddick MacDonald
Daughter of Maurice Ruddick — Survivor of the 1958 Bump
(Interviewed in 2001 and 2014)

1. Your dad became known as "The Singing Miner" because he helped keep people's spirits up underground by singing hymns. He even got an award for his heroic behavior, and his story has inspired many. Tell us about your dad:

Dad was given credit for keeping the miners' morale up during their 8.5 days underground with songs and prayers. He was the recipient of "Canada's Citizen of the Year" Award in 1959 — the only black man to receive such an award. It was supposed to go Prime Minister Diefenbaker at the time. Dad was the eldest miner in his group, 46 years old, and he said the other miners asked him to be responsible for sharing the remaining water and little rations they had left, like chocolate bars and whatever else they had. They must have had great trust in him to do this. Dad always said that they were all heroes, and he was accepting that award for everyone, the rest of the miners and the Town of Springhill.

My dad was a very humble man. He used to say, "I am not a hero."

2. What did your dad like about being a miner?

Dad liked being a miner because he enjoyed the physical labor and camaraderie he shared with the other miners, singing their favorite tunes, sharing jokes as they went down deep into the mines to work. He said they were all equal where the light didn't shine and show the color of a man's skin. His father, Ernest Ruddick, was also a miner before him. At that time, that was the main industry, and it provided a living for the family.

Dad liked to hang out with the other miners after their work week at the Miner's Hall at the top of Main Street where they would play cards, crib, and catch up on the town's news. The Miner's Hall is still there. I believe it is a library now.

3. Tell us what it was like during the Bump:

During the Bump, I was 10 years old. It was a sad time, wondering where our father was. We always watched him come home and go to work at the mines, but women or children never went to the mines. We used to make his lunch for him—honey sandwiches on whole wheat bread, hot tea and honey in his thermos and maybe a piece of cake or cookie.

I would go with my three other sisters every day to the mines and hangout at the Red Cross or Salvation Army tents with others that were waiting to hear news of their loved ones. We were hoping we could bring good news back to Mum. It seemed like there was a deep sadness around the town with so many families looking sad and worried. On the other hand, we didn't have school or household chores to do. There were so many relatives around, people coming and going, media reps for newspapers or magazines, so it was a mixed emotional experience at ten years old. There were boxes of food and clothing available, and it was the first time we had ever tasted Cheese Whiz!

When he came out, he told the rescuers, "Give me water, I'll sing you a song."

4. What happened after the disaster? Did your dad tell you much about it or talk about what it was like underground?

Dad talked very little about what happened underground, the private stuff that miners protected their families from and what the conditions were really like. Miners went to work, got their pay, and it seemed like everything else was taken care of. I interviewed Dad once for Fundy Cable TV in New Brunswick. He seemed vague about when they had no food and the things they had to do to survive. They had to drink their own urine, for example. Dad, and miners in general, were very private people.

Percy Rector was the one who got his arm caught in a pack. His widow became a good friend of Mom and Dad's. My dad helped him during the Bump by giving him aspirin underground.

When the miraculously rescued miners were invited to Georgia—all 19 of them and their spouses and families—they told us our family would be segregated. Dad's buddies said they didn't want to go if he couldn't stay in the same place. If he was good enough to be underground with them, they should stick together! But my dad suggested they all go anyway and accept the invitation. This was everyone's only chance at this kind of paid vacation. We came from a poor town. No one had any money. So this was a good opportunity. We all dealt with prejudice back then.

I know it wasn't always easy for him. He didn't have to go to Georgia to find racism; it was right at home. Dad taught us to value ourselves and to keep going no matter what.

5. What did your dad do for work after he was done mining?

He was a good father who always provided for his family after the economic hardships of having the mines close after the Bump. Dad cleaned out houses for a living and any odd job he could get. He picked his own coal and wood to store for winter months ahead. He worked at the carpet factory in Springhill as a Commissionaire.

There was a time in the seventies he visited friends in Ontario, who moved there after the mines closed to seek work. He had just won $800 doing the crossword puzzle in the *Halifax Chronicle-Herald* newspaper. He was so excited. During his trip, he stayed with us (me and my husband Barry) when we were living in St. Catharines, Ontario. You would have thought he'd won a million dollars when he and Mum got off the train to meet us. I guess back then, it probably seemed like it. He brought an extra suitcase of goodies he purchased with some of the winnings, like coffee, tea bags, crabmeat and sardines. Everywhere he went, somebody got a treat. He also gave each of us thirteen kids $10.

6. Talk about how you and your dad and your siblings used to sing together.

He would whistle and sing around the house. He also had a whistling tune he used to call the hens and roosters from the hen house to come for their scratch and feed (made from some concoction he made of left over burnt bread or veggie peelings). Those hens would come running like crazy because they knew his tune. Then he taught it to us. Other times he'd gather us up on a Saturday night and put on a concert in the yard for our neighbors. We'd all be singing and laughing.

Dad always sang and played a 4-string guitar that he improved, and it sounded as good as a fancier one. It was his trademark. He loved to play a reel-to-reel tape recorder and taped most of the early days when he would teach us to sing and practice harmonies. This would have been in the early sixties.

After the Bump, he trained me and two of my sisters, Sylvia and Ellen, to sing harmonies. He would often sing the bass voice and lead. We all took turns learning. When he felt we were ready, he'd spread the news and soon we'd do a lot of performing with him throughout Nova Scotia and New Brunswick. We were known as "Maurice Ruddick the Singing Miner and the Minerettes." We would practice in a side room off the kitchen and Mum would be mending our clothes. It would seem like long hours, especially when we wanted to go to school dances.

Today, we are so grateful for all that Dad taught us of our musical abilities. Because of what he taught us, we were able to sing a variety of songs; harmonies just came naturally to us. We sang Beatles tunes and Mum would style our hair like theirs in those days. Mum used Vaseline to pat our curly hair down.

We sang tunes by Johnny Cash, Bobby Vinton, Irish music, Negro spirituals, hymns, barbershop, jazz, whatever was on the hit parade. He would tackle it all and us girls with him. He even taught us to make musical sounds like a horn with our mouths; he could imitate the sound of a horn like it was real!

Dad started another group with my siblings that consisted of Leah, Iris, Trina, Jesse and Maureen. They were called "The Harmony Babes." They performed throughout Nova Scotia and New Brunswick as well.

It truly was the Spirit that kept his passion for music going. Spiritually, he'd say, "Talk to the man upstairs," meaning our Lord.

7. Tell us more about your father's history:
He was born in Joggins, Nova Scotia, and lived there as a young boy until his Mum died when he was 9. His father worked in Springhill after that. In Dad's time, you only needed a Grade 11 education to be a high school grad; he was proud that he achieved this level. After the mines closed, he attended Vocational School to get his Grade 12.

Dad's kindness was felt throughout our community. For instance, when he went fishing and hunting to provide for our family, he always shared with our neighbors, especially the elders who were bedridden due to illness. When the Salvation Army would get deer meat donated to share in our community, they gave it to Dad to divide and share. They knew he could be trusted to ensure that everyone had some.

At Christmas, the Red Cross and Salvation Army and the Lions Club brought out a turkey and candy and vegetables for us, which made our Christmas for the family.

Sometimes, we would come home from school for lunch at noon and Mum would have a large pot on the stove full of skim milk and peas with bread and molasses — a staple diet — and a dipper full of tea and sugar but mostly milk. Dad always made sure we had something to eat. We never went hungry, and Mum kept the homemade bread plentiful, up to ten loaves a day.

Dad started to suffer from severe arthritis; it eventually crippled him. He was confined to a wheelchair. My dad died when he was 75 years old, in 1988.

He was a good husband to our mother, a good father, and a man of inspiration to the rest of us, and many others who know his story.

* * *

Valerie shared the lyrics from two songs her father wrote about the mines:

Curse of the Old No. 2
Lyrics by Maurice Ruddick
You've heard of Springhill's big producer,
her history's of crimson hue.
But the biggest tale the old miners tell,
is the curse on old number two.

Brought miners from all over the country,
the drillers and all their crew.

A drilling to find the curse and the bumps,
that haunted old number two.

Away Down in the Deeps
Lyrics by Maurice Ruddick
Turn out your lights, boys,
and I will sing you a song.
I will give you a heartache,
as trolleys roll along.

I will sing you a song, boys,
away down here in the deeps.
Where the miners go to make their dough,
and there isn't much time for sleep.

Away down in the deeps, boys,
it is a peaceful life.
A place we know where we can go,
to get clear of a nagging wife.

If we should die in the deeps, boys,
we know where we will go,
Heaven, boys, is away way above,
and hell is right here below.

Author's Note: Val assures me that her mother thought the
lyrics to this second song were quite funny, even with the
nagging wife comment.

To inquire about Val's original music, contact:
macsigns@rogers.com

Rescuers & Family of Rescuers

Bill Booth
Son of Jim Booth, who worked as a barefaced rescuer during both mine disasters
(Interviewed in 2001 and 2013)

1. Where were you when the 1958 Bump happened and what did you do?

When the Bump occurred, I was sitting in the living room in a large chair watching TV. Then I was on the floor, and the house was shaking. My father, Jim, came running down the stairs and he said, "Something happened at the mines." Then he left for the pit head. We didn't see him until 48 hours later.

2. What was your father's role in the rescue operations? And why was he involved?

My father was one of the barefaced draegermen to first go into the mines. They didn't have gas masks on. They crawled on their hands and knees, looking for survivors. He wanted to do whatever he could to help.

When he'd come home, he was stressed out and said it was bad but didn't talk about it very much. He'd rest and then go right back out, and the worrying would start all over again. All you could do was hope for the best. My dad never complained about the danger.

3. What did you do during the rescues?

I would go the pit head and wait for news, but I wouldn't see my father for a long time. I usually waited with another kid waiting for his father who was in the Bump. He wouldn't know if his dad were alive, while I was wondering if my dad, as a rescuer, was going to make it out alive. There was talk about the methane gas below.

Some of the Army Cadets (like your dad) were involved in directing traffic and others were sent to the pit head to help form a human fence to keep the people back. They needed help. So some of the older Boy Scouts, like me, filled in for them when they needed a rest. We weren't old enough to drive and yet we were directing traffic.

4. What was Springhill like after the final rescues?
That Christmas was a very sad one for the town of Springhill, especially those who had loved ones lost in the Bump. But it affected everyone because they were neighbors, classmates, people you grew up with. Sometimes, you'd see a kid get a bike for Christmas, but the ones who lost their dads wouldn't because their mothers couldn't afford it.

5. Share about how your father was honored for his bravery during these rescue operations:
There were four other men who were draegermen that were involved with The Boy Scouts of Canada. My dad was a Scout Master in the Anglican Church for the Boy Scouts of Canada. These five men were awarded the "Silver Cross" for bravery. The "Silver Cross" was presented to them by the Governor General of Canada in the Parliament Buildings in Ottawa, Ontario. All five men stated that all of the barefaced draegermen where just as brave as them, but because they were not involved in the Boy Scouts, they were not recognized.

Ken Warren
Retired Mining Engineer,
Worked in Springhill mines prior to the
1956 disaster, Rescuer
(Interviewed in 2001)

1. What did you do for the mines when you worked there?
In 1953-56, I worked underground for the department of mines and natural resources. I decided to do a thesis on the rocks.

2. There's a lot of controversy about the cause of the Bump. What can you share about this?
There's a theory that the Bump was caused by strong measures in No. 2 seam. The ground below No. 2's seam was at strong risk of bump occurrence. Bumps had occurred there.

My theory about the cause of the Bump is this: the rocks below the seam were layered with coal, then soft, then hard sandstone. When the stress built up, the softer stuff would blow out. They had aligned the walls. The strong layer broke due to stress.

Before they started lining up the walls (using the long wall system), they had used the step system, mining with pillar and room method. Pillars held up the roof. Then they started to have trouble with pillars bursting or deteriorating. Many were killed in the twenties due to this.

A German engineer said mining wouldn't be possible below 4000 feet because coal was too weak any lower to withstand pressure at that vertical depth. So the engineer recommended for Springhill's No. 2 to change to the long wall system and not do room and pillar. The walls in long wall were 400 feet long each, its levels 13,000, 13,400, and 13,800. But in a step system, they are offset by 100 feet or 50 feet. This change made it a 400-foot break first, then the next one, then the next one.

3. Do you think this long wall method caused the Bump?

It was the theory of the miners that had worked there. They felt the walls should never have been lined up because then it would be too long at 1200 ft. And that is what happened. But was it the cause of this deadly disaster? It's hard to tell.

4. What did you do during the rescue operation?

I was not a draegerman. I went down as a barefaced miner during the rescue. It actually wasn't legal because I was no longer an employee. But they forgot and let me help. I had done some odd jobs to help, carrying water bottles for the draeger crew when they'd come back to the fresh air base in between work.

Dr. Arnold Burden
Former Miner,
Doctor / Rescuer during both disasters
(Interviewed in 2001)

What a privilege it was for my father and I to sit down with Dr. Arnold Burden and hear of his adventures. Not only had he worked as a miner, he was involved as a doctor in both rescue missions for the 1956 Explosion and the 1958 Bump. His Army training also prepared him for helping victims or dealing with casualties.

Dr. Burden was a physician in Springhill and on Prince Edward Island. When he worked as a miner, he was still in school studying to become a doctor. He worked in the No. 1 and No. 4 during summers. The other miners were always careful with him, making sure he didn't injure himself or his hands. They'd tell him to put gloves on or to stay between the packs and not come near the coal face because of the bumps. They'd have bumps practically every day. They actually liked those small ones because it loosened the coal. They didn't have to dig or pick, just shovel it into the pan, and go home early.

The whole wall got paid based on production, as a team. Burden described a typical mining shift. "We'd cut the coal, pull it out, put it in the packs, and then move the pans. We had to deal with the gob (waste), too. Once it was time to pull the packs, we'd let it collapse."

When the 1956 Explosion happened, Burden was on

Prince Edward Island. There was no ferry for him to take over that night so he had to wait until morning. "I packed about $800 worth of drugs and dressings and went to Springhill. I knew the hospital there. I stayed at my wife's family home. I helped some of the burn cases. In one case, I had to ask who the person was in order to officially pronounce him dead. It turned out he was someone I had gone to school with." The first victim's name he heard was Pleaman Pyke, who Burden had grown up near.

Burden said, "They were asking for a doctor at the pit head the morning after the Explosion. No one had come out alive yet except for a couple at the surface. So I packed equipment in my pocket. There was not much to do at the hospital since people hadn't been found alive yet. I went to the mines, got dressed up, and went underground. Two draegermen were killed 200 feet from the surface. Some at the surface saw them go down.

"I had worked in that mine in the auxiliary slope (rescue tunnel). One day, the hoist broke, and I had to walk up through the rescue tunnel. It was a sixty-degree angle. Rescuers were collapsing in the tunnel. So I started crawling on my hands and knees to rescue the rescuers and draegermen. I used one of their tanks and used my hands as a tunnel over their noses. I also collapsed once myself in a tunnel, on top of those I was supposed to rescue. It's like they'd send three men down to go get one, then all four would collapse down there because of gas. Eventually, we'd get them up. I had one on my back, then a second one, both unconscious. While helping these two, I passed out. I landed in a hole where I could breathe again."

Dr. Burden had to recover at a fresh air base, an area that didn't have gas. They blew the fans to keep it clear.

Dr. Burden described what caused the disaster: "Three explosions had occurred. Thirteen boxcars came up the slope with coal in them. Twelve boxcars let go and rolled back down. They hit a steep and rolled off and hit a high-tension line. It blew coal, which caused the Explosion.

"I went back down the next day, too. Saturday. It helped that I knew the shaft."

During the rescue efforts after the Explosion, when they started to believe no one who wasn't already above ground had survived, the rescuers realized there was a large group of men alive. Fifty of them! (**Author's Note**: this includes Ken Melanson, who was interviewed for this book.)

"Once they broke through to where the men were, I went down to them. I had to contend with fifty people on my own. The other doctor they sent down got stuck with another guy. Six men of the fifty needed stretchers to get out. I would treat people and then send them up.

"I had a bottle of rum with me. Bob Smith, one of the men who'd been stuck underground, said it was the best rum he'd ever had in his life.

"Some men were face down, unconscious. I thought they were dead. But actually, some were alive. By the point when we found the fifty, the gas was cleared, but there was no oxygen. It took six men to move a stretcher. It was tough to breathe down there.

"To get up the slope, the draeger team had put in a haulage thing. They rigged one with a pulley. I wanted the men who needed a stretcher up first. I sent rescuers with a guy on a stretcher so that rescuer could hold onto the man and keep them from falling and killing those below."

In a tense moment, an engineer showed him a note. It

said: *Evacuate the mine with all possible haste.*

Burden said, "They put a tube through to take air samples. This stuff explodes at 20%. The reading came to 19%. If that had exploded, there were so many doctors up and down the slope. Fifty-two men below it, and the hundreds of people on surface. If it had blown, it could have killed 500 or more people. All the trapped miners, plus all the rescuers could have died, easily. It was so close to exploding again. That's why they said hurry up and evacuate right now."

Yet, when this warning came, Burden still had forty people to contend with. Plus there were two men further down. These men had gone without food and water for five days. He finally got the men moved up except the two. He needed two more stretchers for them. He and Buddy Condy were there with the two men. They wondered if those above forgot them, but when Burden went to check, people were still working.

Once he was sure the rest were dead and there was no one else to rescue, Burden went back to his practice on Prince Edward Island. Yet he was always ready to return whenever Springhill ran into trouble, like during the 1957 Fire and the 1958 Bump.

When the Bump happened, he actually felt the rattle in his building. "It felt like a low flying plane dropped three bombs."

When he got to the mines, they gave him coveralls and a lamp. They had heard it was pretty bad down there. He and three others went down after 9 p.m., most of which had no gas masks on. They went down the back slope, helping some men along the way. They weren't terribly hurt, like walking wounded. (**Author's Note**: my grandfather was likely one of those men he crossed paths with on the way down.)

Their safety lamps kept going out, and they couldn't relight. The gas wasn't too bad; they kept on going down and got beyond the gas.

"We got to Leon Melanson. Only part of his face and shoulder could be seen. The rest was under coal. I gave him a shot of Demerol and kept going down. Four hours later, I knew it would wear off, so I went back to help him. I saw a foot under his armpit. The other guys thought there was a dead man under him and that foot belonged to the other guy. They wanted to take the leg off the dead man. But I suspected that wasn't another person's foot. I told them to keep on digging. There actually was someone else under him, but the foot belonged to Leon himself. It had broken off. He did lose his leg once he was in the hospital.

"As I went to other levels, like the 13,400, I couldn't recognize them because they were so damaged. We couldn't get near 13,000.

"Two men were trapped where draegermen couldn't get to because of the packs on their backs. They tried to get over and couldn't. After he'd been underground for fourteen hours, they had to send another lamp down.

"One new rescuer had a chocolate bar in his pocket. So I asked him, 'When did you eat last?' The guy said he'd eaten a little while ago. So I asked him if I could have it since I hadn't had a bite to eat."

As bodies were taken out, each one had to be identified by the doctor, a mine official, and a union official. They all had to sign how the identification was made and how they died. They used tags to identify the body and put another tag on the casket. Caskets were sealed because of the smell.

It was over 70 degrees down there. They'd call the minister of a fallen miner and have that minister go break the official news to the family. They tried to arrange for that to happen first, so the name wouldn't be released to the press until the family knew.

"I filled out a book of death certificates as they identified them and gave them check numbers. I kept a list of what they died of. But then I got a call that men were found alive. A mine worker heard men talking through the pipes. I was in the mine manager's office when names of the twelve were called. When I heard they wanted to put Vitamin B in the water they were sending through the pipes, I overruled them. I knew if they did that, the men would throw it back up.

"So I went back down and got them water. We tried to feed them first through a plastic hose, but it bent. Then I asked for 100 feet of copper tubing and pushed it through. Gorley Kempt asked for more water. So, we sent more. Gorley yelled that he didn't have anything to put the water in and was afraid they were wasting it. But we assured him: there was more water available. We had to pressurize it with a tree sprayer to get it to go downward, since it was more like straight across. The wall between us and the miners was parallel.

"It took eighty-two feet of digging to get to those men. It was all virgin coal, never been cut before. It wasn't just debris we had to break through to get to the twelve trapped men. The men had no idea how far away we were. We just kept saying, 'We're coming. Rest. Take it easy.' We didn't want to tell them how far we were. It took fourteen hours to cut that tunnel. It was a very small space for all these people. We couldn't stand. Any debris had to be removed in an assembly line. Everyone sitting in the tunnel had to pass back buckets. We used sawed off picks and shovels. Whoever was in front had the hardest job, so we'd take turns.

"The rescue group got longer throughout the tunnel, as it was a longer way to pass back coal. Once we broke through, it filled with coal dust. Ten were in one place and two were off in another area. One had a bone out through his skin. The other had a broken shoulder. The ten had been able to bring water to the other two. They just couldn't move the men up to the rest of the group because of a lack of tools and equipment. They shared everything they had left and used an aspirin bottle cap to divide up water, before the rescue." (**Author's Note**: Caleb Rushton, who was interviewed for this book, was one of the men in this first big group of twelve rescued.)

After the first miracle rescue of the twelve, Burden got word that more men were alive underground, that Springhill was experiencing another miraculous rescue. By this point, it had been eight days since the Bump.

"We got Barney Martin out through the hole first; he had been stuck alone, away from the other six. We got a stretcher for him and shipped him out. Then two others had started up. It was a domed ceiling with no support. The rescuers made it to the last six people. They got right to these guys. We didn't need to send them any food.

"Maurice Ruddick said, 'My God, I'm glad to see you fellas. Give me a glass of water, I'll sing you a song.' Then Bobby Calder said, 'Maurice, I was sent down specifically to get you out.' Maurice asked, 'What do you mean?' Bobby joked, 'The compensation board told me with your wife and twelve kids, there'd be no money for anybody else.'"

(**Author's Note**: Herb Pepperdine, also interviewed for this book, was with Maurice's group during this final rescue.)

Eighty-one men were rescued the first night. (One of those would die later in the hospital.) Taking into account the two miracle rescues of twelve and seven men, of the 174 men trapped underground, 99 of them lived and 75 of them died. No doubt it's due to the rescue efforts of Dr. Burden and many others that they were able to save as many people as they did.

Dr. Arnold Burden, Cheryl (2001)

Children of

Victims

Jerry Gillis
Son of Angus Gillis — Victim of the 1958 Bump
(Interviewed in 2001)

Angus "Gus" Gillis was one of the miracle survivors of the 1956 Explosion; he was stuck with a group of 50 men underground, long after they thought everyone was dead. The men waited with their leader, Con Embree, and were eventually rescued. However, when the 1958 Bump hit, Gus was not one of the survivors.

Jerry Gillis, son of Gus Gillis, was in the military at the time of the Bump. He had made arrangements to come home when he first heard about it. However, by the time he got there, his father was already declared dead, a victim of the poisonous gasses that filled the mines after the Bump. They knew cause of death because there were no signs of injury when they found him.

Jerry recalls how many in town felt like the way they mined the coal caused the Bump to happen, by trying to line up the walls. However, he believes if people like his father were worried about their safety, they mostly just kept it to themselves. They talked to other miners about it instead of concerning their families.

Like to other kids in the area, mining was considered a way of life. "I never worried about my dad," said Gillis in an interview in 2001. "I was much more into kid stuff before the disasters. People getting hurt just seemed to be a fact of life in Springhill. It seemed like during my teen years, someone was always getting killed. It was an accepted part of life." His mother even seemed to be calm, to not worry about his father's safety underground. If she was concerned, she hid it well. His grandfathers were also miners, so it ran in the family. It was definitely not an easy life.

When Jerry turned 16, there were only a couple of work options for those in Springhill: drive a truck or work in the mines. He never considered following in his father's or grandfathers' footsteps. He joined the Army instead, at 16, with his parents' permission, so he could join a special program. He did this so he wouldn't have to work in the mines.

One of Jerry's memories of Springhill is that when it would snow, it would be a very pretty white for a couple of days. Not long after that fresh blanket of white fell, it would turn dark from the coal dust floating in the air.

He remembers fondly that the town was "very close knit, where everyone knew each other."

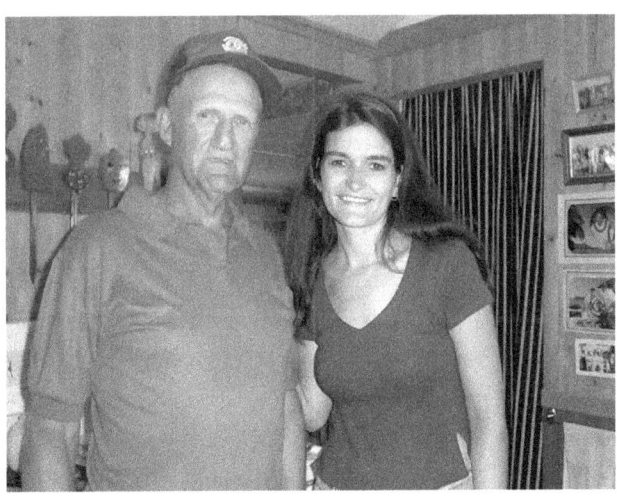

Jerry Gillis, Cheryl (2001)

Jack & Keith Bourgeois
Former Miners,
Sons of Bliss Bourgeois — Victim of the 1958 Bump
Nephews of Herb Pepperdine
(Interviewed in 2001)

Even though Jack and Keith were also rescuers, I decided to put them in this section of the book to honor their father with the other children of lost miners. When I did the interview with Bump survivor, Herb Pepperdine, his nephews were with him. I had the opportunity to sit down with Jack and Keith, two brothers who lost their father in the Bump. Sadly, Keith has since passed away. Jack and Keith were very helpful to me, in supplying research about some of the ins and outs of working in a mine and how the place operated, what the workers did underground if they were a miner vs. a laborer. They were enormously helpful in explaining those differences, and all of that was used when developing the jobs for characters in my screenplay and novel, *Song of Springhill.*

They described the process laborers went through. They'd build the packs that helped the roof not cave in on the miners. They'd also put coal in pans. Jack said, "The pans looked like a coffee table, but they were steel. Miners took coal off the wall from the coal face in front of them, and put them into the pans. They used two big machines, on the end and top of the wall. The coal would shake down into the level, and then we'd fill coal cars. Someone like

Herb, a laborer, would take a trip up once it was full. Then he'd come back with the empties. As the coal face got further away from pans, there was a higher chance that the roof would cave in, so they'd put packs in to hold the roof up behind you. The laborers built those packs. As the wall got further from pans, the overnight shift at 11 p.m. had the job of moving those pans closer to the wall."

This was one of the jobs that Jack had when he worked the overnight shift. "We'd drag the pans for the miners starting the next day. We'd have to reuse the same pack, take a handsaw to it, cut the pack then take a wedge. A short block. We'd knock the block out in a couple of places then the pack could be reused. You'd hope it wouldn't collapse on you while you were doing it!"

When I first started to research this story, I had a hard time understanding the differences between how they mined in the No. 4 — which some felt was less dangerous than the system they adopted in the No. 2. (The old system was room and pillar; the new system was long wall.) Jack described how this worked: "In the old system, a slope would be diagonal. In the new system, walls lined up so at the top you'd look down like you're looking through a straight tunnel. Think of how this would affect something like a bowling ball. If staggered — like in the No. 4 — the bowling ball would have stopped at one of the levels. Instead, it went all the way down to the bottom. It had a ripple effect."

We talked about what it was like for them the day of the Explosion. Jack had gone hunting and missed the Explosion. Keith had just gotten home at 4 p.m. Both of them got involved in the rescue efforts.

Keith mentioned that those he went down with in the

rescue efforts would get overcome by gas. They'd have to be brought out of the mines on stretchers. "When we were at the 4400 level, we didn't dare lift our head more than five to six inches off the ground, crawling, or we'd get taken over by afterdamp, the gasses in the air."

After Con Embree's group was found, Jack was one of the first two miners to reach the men, at the 5400 level. "Doug Beaton was lying in a stone dust box. We thought he was dead, but he wasn't. He was covered with empty stone dust bags and his nostrils were full of dust. After we got the 5400 level men out, they sealed the mines until January to get the fire to go out. There was a great fear it would blow up again. There were more miners in the mine doing rescue work than trapped miners."

Keith shared, "Once rescued, most of the miners ended up in the unemployment line. They got physically checked out to make sure they were okay, but no other help."

Jack recalled, "When I worked underground, I worked near my dad but not with him. I used to go down and visit his level on days I didn't have much to do."

Keith recalls having lunch underground with his friend, Alfred White, telling him that there had to be a better way to make a living; Keith quit that day after that conversation. Keith recalls, "On March 18, 1958, there was a small bump, right where we were sitting, eating lunch." Alfred died that day as a result of injuries from that bump. (He was the only one who died, that particular day in the mine.) Keith was thankful he didn't feel there was a future in it; he could have been right there with Alfred.

Jack and Keith had both joined the Air Force before the big Bump in October 1958, so neither was there when that happened. But their father, Bliss, was underground.

Jack heard about the Bump on the news, from where he was working in the military. He couldn't get through by phone. "I had to come to town to get any news. My mother had already died by this point. I sat around and waited at the Wash House, under his bucket. Our dad was working at the 13,800 level.

"During the Bump, we had overheard other miners talking about how bad it was underground. They'd said no one else survived. Then, I heard a rumor that my father was with the group of twelve who were being rescued when those names were called. However, I didn't quite believe it and never rejoiced in it. Then my dad wasn't with those men. It took about a week before we officially heard confirmation that he was dead."

On a lighter note, the two shared some fun antics that happened among the miners when they worked there. It gave me some fun material for the scenes in the screenplay and novel underground.

"If a miner fell a sleep, like at lunch, other miners would tie their shoes together so he'd trip when he got up. Or they'd nail his lunch can on the pack by the bottom, so when he'd go to pick up the lunch pail, his arm would stretch two feet because the lunch pail wouldn't go anywhere.

"We always had to tease the newcomers. They'd be told by older miners to get a shovel with the name Jones on it. The newbie would go down below to get one and another miner would say, 'Where are you going with my shovel?' The newbie would say, 'It belongs to a miner up there named Jones.' And they'd be embarrassed to find out all shovels say Jones because it's the manufacturer.

"Another interesting thing we had to do was tie our

pants with boot laces to keep rats from crawling up our pant legs. It was terrible if it went up. You'd have to jump around and shake to get it out."

I also asked them what they did for fun in Springhill, so I'd have some material for the kids in my fictional story. "We loved to hop cars. We'd hang onto cars without drivers seeing us, and it was like we were skating or skiing down a hill by hanging onto the back of the bumper. We'd do this when it had snowed. Our mittens would stay stuck on the bumper once we let go, and of course, we'd get in trouble going home with one mitten. We'd also play a game racing tires. We'd use a steel rim and an old rubber tire and chase it all around town. We'd use the stick to make the tire roll, then steer it."

They also shared they'd go see movies about three days a week, the Saturday matinee, Wednesday matinee, and Friday night, 7 p.m. show. It was fifteen cents to get in. The town also had musical or variety shows since there was a lot of musical talent in town.

"Saturday was payday. The miners would come into town, go shopping, and go talk mining on their days off on Main Street. Downtown was busy on Saturday night. Live, old time bands would play during skating. We could skate all night Friday, all day Saturday and Sunday."

I so enjoyed interviewing these guys to get such a variety of perspectives that helped me build scenes for the fictional story.

In Loving Memory
Keith Ronald Bourgeois
(April 14, 1935-February 7, 2012)

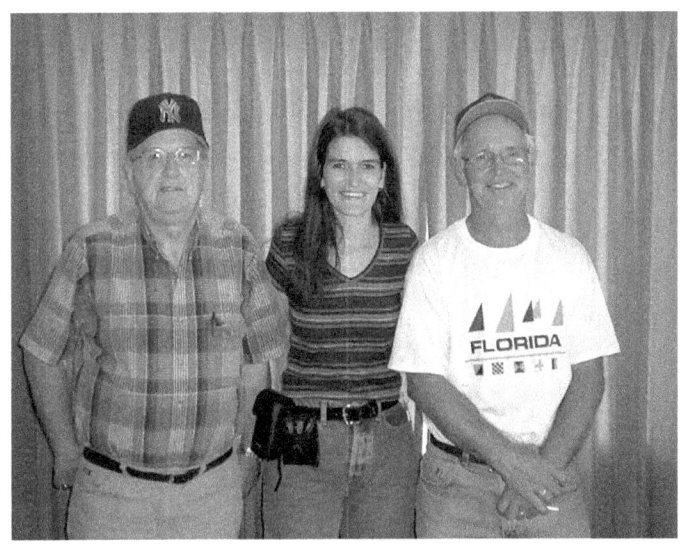

Keith, Cheryl, Jack (2001)

Valarie Tabor Alderson
Daughter of Raymond "Tommy" Tabor — Victim of the 1958 Bump
(Interviewed in 2014)

Author's Note: I would like to personally thank Valarie for the many favors she did for me over the decade of working on this book and *Song of Springhill*.

1. What can you tell me about Springhill in the fifties?

I can remember living on lower Herrett Road when I was a kid. We lived on one side of a double house and my father's parents lived on the other end. It was just up the road from the mine. The house below us had a store in their living room where they sold penny candy. My grandmother would give us a few pennies for doing errands for her and of course, it was all spent on candy! I can remember a little "shack" in the backyard where my grandfather and his friends would gather to play checkers and cards (most likely had the occasional nip). My grandmother was a Baptist who frowned upon playing cards, but she loved to go to Bingo. After my grandfather no longer worked in the mines, he would wait for his sons to stop in and tell him about their day in the pit.

I remember when I was in Grade 1, we moved up to the opposite end of town to help my mother's parents, as they were getting elderly and needed the assistance. My mother's father was a miner and also an avid gardener. He grew a lot of his own vegetables and would spend hours in his garden after his shift in the mine. However, he was retired from mining by the time we moved in with them.

During those years, we all played outside all day long and into the evening. We always walked to school, played ball, tag, etc. with our friends. People would often gather and sing songs in each other's houses. I remember neighbors visiting each other and spending lots of time chatting.

You never missed mass on Sundays and the first Friday each month we had to attend morning mass. We had to go to Sunday School every week and you had to know the answers from the catechism. At Christmas time, you were allowed to take one toy and then we were off to visit family and friends. We made sure we visited all the relatives during the holidays.

I have some fond memories of the vacations in the summer. The mines would shut down for two weeks when everyone went on vacation. My dad always made sure we went somewhere on a little trip. I have a photo of my younger sister, Susan, and I with my dad taken on the PEI ferry the summer of 1958. That was our last family vacation.

I always liked school and was a good student with pretty good marks. I went to university after Grade 11.

My older sister was a teenager, and she and her friends would spend time at "The Stand." It reminded me of Happy Days, where they hung out, talked, and listened to the jukebox. They, too, ate hamburgers, drank milkshakes and had lots of fun with their friends.

The town was bustling then with stores lined up and down Main Street. We had clothing shops, a shoe shop, jewelry stores, a theatre, bakery etc. I guess it was like most other small towns in Nova Scotia. It is so sad to see it today with the modern buildings and empty lots. The majority of the original buildings are gone. It was a one-industry town and never recovered economically after the 1958 Bump.

2. Do you remember anything about the 1956 Explosion? Where were you when it happened? Was your father working?

I remember playing outside about 5 p.m. with my friends on the street. We heard a loud noise and looked up and saw a huge, black mushroom cloud. At first we didn't know what it was. My father was at home, and he quickly jumped into his car and went toward the mine. My grandparents lived on lower Herrett Road, which was very close to the mine. I don't know why, but my brother, my cousin and I ran from our house, way up on Pleasant Street, all the way out to my grandparents' home. I remember people milling around the yard and talking about what happened. Everyone was outside and looking down toward the mine. They talked about an explosion.

It turned out that two of my uncles were working that day. One was rescued and later moved to the Boston area. My Uncle Donald died from gas. He was only 34. It was a very sad day.

I still can't believe that we ran all that way out there; I was only 7 years old. It would be over a mile at least. My uncle who moved away to Boston tried to convince my father to go, but he wouldn't leave Springhill.

3. What were the men like who worked with your father? Were they friends outside of work?

My dad was only 38 years old when he was killed. (He had two other brothers who were killed in the mines. One died in a single rock fall, and the other in the Explosion.) He was a little league baseball coach. He was also a member of the Knights of Columbus and had all the decorations at our house for their annual Harvest Ball. Growing up, many of the guys he had coached would often speak about how much they liked him.

I think most of the men who worked in the mines got along. They were always joking around. I think they worked hard and drank too much. When we lived out in the west end of town, the men gathered around the Liars Bench and would often stay up late into the night talking. It was told to me that my grandfather, Percy Tabor, was the President of the Liars Bench and could tell some great stories.

I will relate one that was told to me. One summer day, a tourist stopped at the Liars Bench and asked to speak to the President of the Liars Club. Apparently, the tourist was a well-known teller of tall tales from the town where he lived in the U.S.A. He challenged my grandfather to a lying contest. My grandfather graciously let him go first since he was the visitor. I don't recall his story, but apparently it was quite an outrageous lie. So, he challenged my grandfather to top that one. My grandfather took his time pondering and then said, "I think I can better that one. I believe you!" We had a pretty good laugh about that one.

My grandfather belonged to the Royal Order of Buffaloes. They would often take turns taking lunch for their meetings. My father went to the store up the street and bought some expensive luncheon meat, sliced cooked ham for his sandwiches. He brought the meat home to my aunt and asked her to make the sandwiches for him to take to the lodge meeting. After he left for the meeting, my aunt noticed that the cooked ham was still sitting on the counter in the pantry. She realized she had buttered and put mustard on the bread and forgot to put the meat in between. She and my grandmother agreed they wouldn't say a word to my dad about it. When he came home that night, they asked how the meeting went. His reply was that it was fine, but he said, "Can you imagine some cheap son-of-a-gun brought mustard sandwiches for lunch?" We often have a great chuckle about that.

4. Where were you when the 1958 Bump happened? And how old were you?

The Bump happened shortly after 8 p.m. on a Thursday night. I was in Grade 4 and nine years old. I remember standing by the kitchen table and finishing my homework when I felt the shaking. I had no idea what it was. We lived with my maternal grandparents at the time. My mother was in the kitchen by the stove, and my grandmother came out to the kitchen from the living room. I remember her starting to cry and she said, "My God, it's the mine." She knew immediately what happened, as she had felt many of them before. The next morning, my mother told us about what happened and said we would have to wait and see. My older sister and brother went out to the mine every day to wait for news and report back to our mother. I was not allowed to go out there, as I was only 9. (Although, there were lots of kids who went out there and hung around waiting for news of their fathers.)

5. Share some other details about the Bump and your father's story:

I remember lots of confusion surrounding that night. My father was working the afternoon shift and so were three of my uncles. My mother's brothers. Both families had men who worked in the mine. I remember the phone ringing and people coming in and out of the house, all talking about the disaster.

It turned out that all three of my mother's brothers got out. One of her brothers was knocked unconscious. When he came to, he was buried in coal up to his chest. He often remarked that if he had been thrown down, he would surely have died. It turned out he was thrown back against what they called a pack stick—a piece of timber they used to secure the wall and roof. One other brother walked out and, yet the third brother was a supervisor at the time. He began to assist with the rescue effort.

My mother told us that my father was late for work that day, as he had a meeting at the Company office. She said when he went to pick up his lamp, it wasn't working and he had to borrow one. Apparently, she was told he had to run to catch the "rake" (trolley) to go to work. She found that odd. Any other time, he would have likely just come home and made the time up later, as it was around the time of the World Series.

Until she passed away, she kept his shoes with a cake of ivory soap in them. They were in the Wash House. My sister still has them now.

6. What did you do while waiting for news?

Within the next couple of days, I was sent across the street to stay with neighbors. I guess they offered to take me so it would make it easier on my mother. I had an older sister who was 16 and a brother who was 12 at the time. I was 9. I also had a younger sister who was 4.

I read the newspaper every day and watched TV. The neighbors were an older couple, and they tried to shield me from the talk of the disaster. I can still remember one day when the man who drove the dry cleaning truck was talking with the lady who was looking after me. He expressed how sad it was across the street (my house) because of my father most likely being killed.

I will never forget reading the newspaper and reading the list of missing men. I got so excited one day when I didn't see my father's name on that list. I can still remember the heartache I felt when I noticed "to be continued" at the bottom of the column and his name was there on the next page. I would cry myself to sleep at night and often imagine that he would come home soon.

Another thing I will never forget is my brother and uncle coming over to where I was staying. My brother took me outside to tell me they found our father. He was only 12 but insisted he be the one to tell me. I was naïve and asked him if dad was alive. He just looked at me and said "no." My brother was the altar boy for my father's funeral. I never attended the funeral, as I was so devastated. I was asked if I wanted to be there and I said "no." To this day, I regret that I didn't go.

During those days, the caskets were brought to the homes because the funeral parlour was so small. His funeral was at the same time as another miner who went to our church. There were so many funerals that they had to double up some of them.

My brother passed away when he was only 43 in 1990. It broke my mother's heart. When she was interviewed for an oral history of the town and disasters, she constantly cried.

My father was Protestant and his father and brothers belonged to the Orange Lodge. My mother was a Catholic. When they married, he turned Catholic and his brother refused to attend his funeral. How times have changed.

7. Is there anything else you can think of to tell about that time?

I remember how sad it was for all the kids at the time of the Bump. I remember there were at least three of us in the same Grade 4 class who lost our dads. At Christmas time, we all received many gifts. You could tell the kids who lost their dads, as we all had yellow hooded sweatshirts. The boys all got Toronto Maple Leaf sweaters and autographed hockey sticks from the team. (During the 50th Anniversary, my son arranged to get another stick autographed from the team and gave it to the Miner's Museum to be on display.) I must say that I have never liked Christmas since that time.

We didn't have the benefit of psychologists or counselors. We were left on our own to deal with our grief. Many other kids (such as my husband) felt the survivor's guilt because their fathers weren't killed in the mines. Many of their friends' fathers died. It seemed like there wasn't a person in Springhill who wasn't affected by the tragedy. Everyone had a brother, uncle, dad, or friend that were victims. I can't really blame the adults for not helping the kids because I think they were just trying to manage to bury our dead. It must have been unbelievably stressful for everyone in town.

Families packed up and left and many of the surviving miners had difficulty finding work. Many of the women went out to work. My mother had little education and four children to care for. The Mayor of Calgary, Alberta, offered to take us out there and start over. However, she felt that she couldn't do that. At least if she stayed in Springhill, she'd have other family members around her. So one of my uncles (my mother's brother) took his family out there instead. He made a living out there and eventually moved to British Columbia where he remained until he died.

One of my proudest accomplishments was when I went to the Town Council and presented them with a plan for the 50th Anniversary. We filled the Community Centre for two evenings with a full house for the Memorial Service and concert featuring the "Men of the Deeps" choir. It was a heart-healing event. Many people came to us – the committee members – afterwards and thanked us for the opportunity to heal some of the wounds. We had national newspaper and TV coverage for the event. I must say it was my son who pushed me to do something. I truly believe I was guided by either the Holy Spirit or something bigger than me. I had no idea what I wanted to do.

As I sat alone one evening, it came to me! I wanted to have a candlelight vigil with 75 people holding a lit candle (each one representing a lost miner from the Bump). As each name was read, the candle was blown out. I didn't want to leave people without hope, so I decided that I would have 19 people on stage with miners' helmets on. They represented those who were found after 6 and 8 days trapped underground. As each rescued miner's name was read, the light was turned on to signify hope. We ended with the song "Rise Again." I wanted everyone to remember how we rose from the tragedy and still survived.

The song says, "We rise again in the faces of our children."

Susan, Raymond "Tommy" Tabor, Valarie (1956)

Ethel Fisher Gilbert
Daughter of Lester Fisher—Victim of the 1956 Explosion
(Interviewed in 2014)

Author's Note: As you know from the stories about my grandfather, he switched shifts with someone the day of the Explosion. It took me a while to research this story and figure out who that person may have been. From Ken Melanson's interview, you heard him give us two potential names, the two men who had the same job as my grandfather: Lester Fisher and Gerald Dawson.

My father felt like my grandfather normally worked with Gerald. That left us leaning toward the idea that he possibly switched with Lester. Then, in my research of newspaper articles, I found one from the fifties that specifically stated Lester Fisher was not originally supposed to be working during the Explosion and that he had traded shifts with a friend.

To follow are clips from the *Halifax Chronicle-Herald*, 1958:

> **Four Bodies Recovered**
> Early rescue operations brougnt the bodies of four men to the surface: Lester Fisher, wno was working an extra shift for a friend; Gerald Dawson, Eph- raim Alderson and Durrell Pep- perdine.

* * *

At the pithead 15 ambulances, scores of private cars, large supplies of medical equipment were in readiness. Some 25 doctors and 40 nurses were also on hand.

Offers of help came from all parts of the continent.

The explosion brought with it a crop of stories of freakish circumstances that put some men among the trapped and others, who ordinarily would have been in the mines, safely above the ground.

That's when I set out to find his family, see if I could learn anything from them about who this man was and get the other side of this story.

I posted my desire to talk to someone in his family on a Springhill Facebook page (Blast from Our Past). I wanted to find out if the stories we'd heard were true and find out a bit about this man who was a victim of the Explosion during a shift when he wasn't supposed to be there. Right away, people got me in contact with his daughter, Ethel.

Ethel, indeed, remembered the same story we had always been told. I had my confirmation that Lester was that person who died in my grandfather's place. I'm very grateful to Lester's daughter, Ethel, for being willing to talk to me (and to Gary Copeland, who connected us. Gary is married to Ethel's cousin, and went to school with my father).

Ironically, it turns out our family is related. Ethel's husband, Bill, was the nephew of my Great Uncle Marvin Megeney. She is also friends with a lot of people in my family. She even has a few items in her home that belonged to my great grandmother, affectionately known throughout Springhill as "Ma McKay."

1. Ethel, tell us about your father. What was he like? What were his interests?

My dad loved to hunt. Hunting season started around October 15th. He liked to hunt anything. Deer. Moose. You could shoot a moose if you found one back then without a permit. He hunted rabbits. He trapped animals like muskrats, beavers, and ducks. He and his friends used to trap them and then go each morning to tend to the traps. They'd skin and stretch them and then sell the fur. That's how they made extra money. Nearly everyone was hunting or fishing for extra money.

Besides hunting and fishing in the winter time, he had a place off the porch of our house, set up to make flies for fishing. People would come from all over to buy those. Back in those days, people didn't have fishing poles like they do today. We had poles all over our house from his projects.

He also built block walls for people around houses and chimneys. Back in those days, you had to do all sorts of jobs. He kept busy all the time to make extra money. He was a good dad. We never went without anything. We always had everything we ever needed.

He and my mother got married in 1935, and they had two children: myself and my older brother, Art.

2. What was your father's job underground in the mines?
He was a chain runner, working with cars as they would come down into the mines. He went in the mines around 1940. My uncle and his brother, Harold Fisher, also worked for the mines. My father worked during the war. So many miners didn't go to war because the coal had to come up for fuel. He didn't talk a whole lot about his work underground.

3. As you know, one of the reasons I wanted to talk to you was to learn more about this man who ended up dying instead of my grandfather because they swapped shifts with each other. What do you remember about the events before the Explosion and what your father was doing?
My dad would often exchange shifts with another miner. He'd switch to working the afternoon shift, so he could hunt in the morning. He exchanged a lot during hunting season. He just wanted to be out in those woods. He was 43 years old at the time of the Explosion.

The night before the Explosion, it was Halloween. Bill (my fiancé at the time) and I got dressed up and went visiting relatives. (We even went to Bill's grandmother's house, Grandma Megeney, to scare her.) When I came home that night, Mom (Janie Fisher) said she was going out to pick up Dad at work. He was working the night shift that night, too. So I decided to keep my costume on and go with Mom to pick up Dad. So he got to see me in my costume. That night was the last time I'd ever see him. He was off hunting early the next morning.

4. What do you remember about the day of the Explosion? Where were you when it exploded?

I was nineteen years old and teaching in Valley Road. Bill came down to Valley Road and told me there was an explosion. My mom was working at the hospital. When Mom came home, we went out to the mines.

My dad was one of the first to come out of those they found dead in the mines. Of course they were sealed caskets, including for the ones at the top of the mines who were burnt by the Explosion. It was a whirlwind around here.

After the Explosion, Mom was accepted into a school to become a certified nursing assistant.

Map of the mine after the Explosion: (courtesy of the Springhill Miners' Museum)

Illustration of No. 4 mine surface and underground showing where the 1956 disaster happened.

Ripple Effect of Life

So, where do you fit into this story?

While my search for this story may have started from the desire to write a screenplay (and novel), what I found was so much bigger.

It's about legacies. It's about what you do with the time you have. It's about how you affect other people.

I think of it like ripples, how when you throw a stone into the water, it tends to ripple out from where it lands, having a far reach.

As small as the town of Springhill is, I want its story to have a far reach and long outlive any of us who had something to do with it — whether we lived through it ourselves or our families lived through it.

As mentioned, I was on a quest to uncover the story behind my grandfather's life being saved from the 1956 Explosion. Yet the sobering part of that story is to know that it also meant the death of someone else. I knew if my grandfather had died that day, I would never have been born. In fact, without death and the multiple tragedies reflected in this story, I wouldn't be here today.

Have you ever pondered the events that brought you to this earth? Have you ever asked yourself the question, "How was I born into my particular family? Why am I here? What was I meant to do?"

The Explosion wasn't the first time my grandfather's life was spared. His first mining accident was in the

Springhill mines in the 1940s, and contributed to him not having to go off to war because he suffered a broken pelvis.

As you know, after the Bump in 1958, my father anxiously awaited news of whether or not his dad was still alive, from the Lamp Cabin, a place where miners turned in their lamps when they finished their shifts. His father's check number, #712, remained on the board, showing that he had not yet surfaced. He had not yet picked up his check tag.

Once the earliest miners were rescued, my grandfather was the third person to walk through that Lamp Cabin door. The first face he saw was my dad's fourteen-year-old face, waiting for him, hoping and praying he was still alive.

When "Dado" vowed to never go underground again and he moved the family to Boston, this move is how my father met my mother. When they met, she was an attractive 16-year-old, a spunky Massachusetts girl that he was set up with on a blind date.

Before meeting her, he tried to gamble this blind date away in a poker game, but he had no takers. When she walked through the door, all of those guys wished they had just won her in the "poker pot." Dad was glad he hadn't given her away, after all, and he's never let go of her since. (My parents are close to celebrating 50 years of marriage.)

This blind date never would have happened if my grandfather had not been spared from the 1956 Explosion or survived the 1958 Bump, the tragedy that made him decide to leave his life of mining. My father has said, unequivocally, he would have had no reason to leave Canada had he not been moved to the United States with his father's career change.

My parents have been married since 1966. It's ironic to think that this disaster (and the fact that "Dado's" life was spared from the Explosion 10 years before my parents got married) is the catalyst that brought me to this earth.

At the same time, it's sobering because so many men lost their lives, including the beloved Lester Fisher who just innocently wanted to go hunting that fateful day, November 1, 1956. He was too young to die.

This story helps me connect specific dots that allowed me to enter the scene. It makes me ponder why I am here and encourages me to want to make the most of the life I am given and do at least a little bit of good with whatever days I am blessed to have.

It reminds me of how we are not promised any particular amount of days. I hope those reading this book will be encouraged to make an impact with their lives, no matter how long they are on this earth.

Any ideas for how you'd like to change the world? Your family? Or even just the life of one person? You never know when that may have a ripple effect on the lives of many others.

I also encourage anyone reading this to take the time to gather the stories of your ancestors. Use this time to record them, while they are alive and able to share their stories or those who left this earth before them. Get them down. You just might uncover stories that are worth sharing with the world.

And remember there are miracles that happen all around us. We need to celebrate them, big and small.

Denise, Cheryl, Tom, Heather (2001)

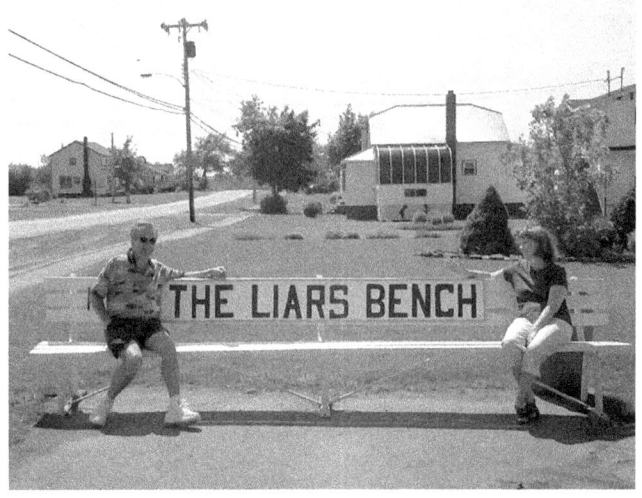

Tom & Denise McKay
Telling "Lies" on the Liar's Bench (2003)

Cheryl & Heather (2001)

The McKays on the site where the
Springhill Mines used to be (2003)

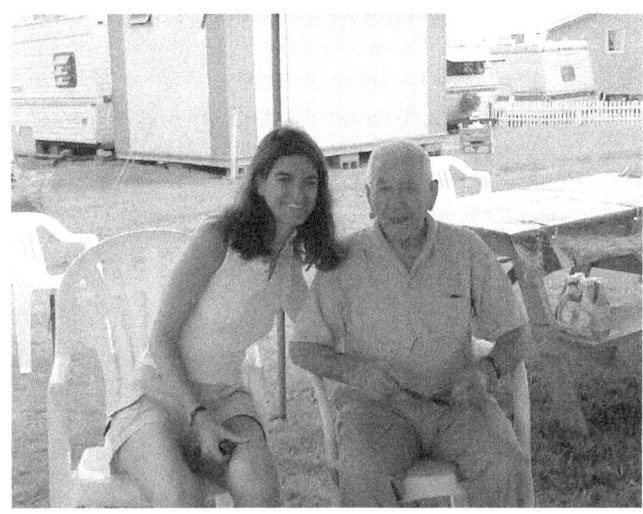

Cheryl with Marvin Megeney (2003)

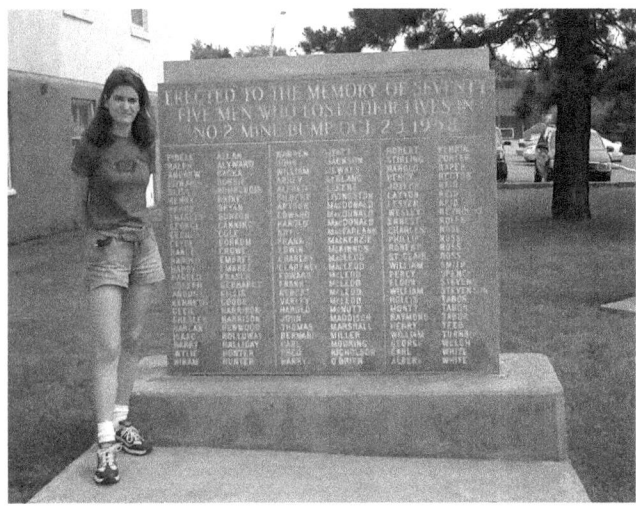

Cheryl at the Memorial honoring
the 1958 Bump Victims (2003)

In Loving Memory of
Charles Hugh McKay
March 3, 1915-January 5, 1986
&
Ethel Mae (Tooke) McKay
June 2, 1913-April 18, 1978

Cheryl, Dado, & Nanny (Ethel

About the Author

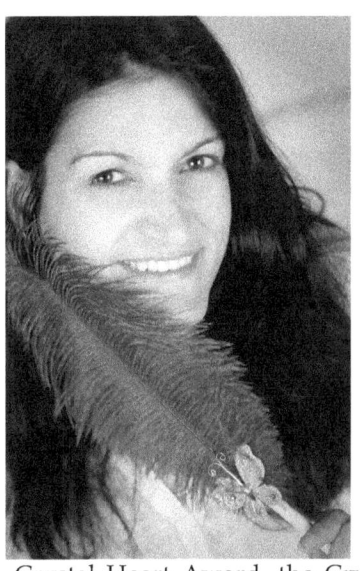

Cheryl McKay has been professionally writing since 1997. Tommy Nelson served as her first publisher, teaming her with Frank Peretti on the *Wild and Wacky, Totally True Bible Stories* series. Cheryl wrote the screenplay adaptation of *The Ultimate Gift*, the feature film starring Academy Award Nominees James Garner and Abigail Breslin. It's based on Jim Stovall's best-selling novel. The film was released by Fox in theaters in Spring 2007 and has won such awards as the Crystal Heart Award, the Crystal Dove, one of the Top Ten Family Movies at MovieGuide Awards, and a CAMIE Award. She also wrote the DVD for *Gigi: God's Little Princess*, another book adaptation based on the book by Sheila Walsh. She wrote a half-hour drama for teenagers about high school violence, called *Taylor's Wall*, produced in Los Angeles by Family Theater Productions. After winning a fellowship, she was commissioned to write a feature script, *Greetings from the Flipside*, for Art Within, which Rene Gutteridge and McKay released as a novel through B&H Publishing in October 2013. Her screenplay, *Never the Bride*, was adapted into a novel by Gutteridge and was released by Waterbrook Press in June 2009. The film version is in development. As one passionate for those who are losing hope in their wait to find love, she released the non-fiction version, *Finally the Bride: Finding Hope While Waiting*. She also penned her autobiography, *Finally Fearless: Journey from Panic to Peace*. She wrote the screen story for *The Ultimate Life*, the sequel to *The Ultimate Gift*. Find her on Facebook, Twitter, Pinterest, or at her website, **www.purplepenworks.com** or **www.finallyone.com**.

Books by Cheryl McKay